Kinds of Love

Kinds of Love

A NOVEL BY

MAY SARTON

W · W · NORTON & COMPANY
New York · London

First published as a Norton paperback 1980

Library of Congress Cataloging in Publication Data

Sarton, May, 1912–
Kinds of love.

I. Title.
[PZ3.S249Ki   1980]   [PS3537.A832]   813'.52
ISBN 0-393-00968-8   79-27520

1 2 3 4 5 6 7 8 9 0

CONTENTS

AUTHOR'S NOTE

The author wishes to thank the National Foundation of the Arts and the Humanities for a generous grant toward the writing of this novel, and Marjory Gane Harkness for permission to use Eliza Bunker's letter, page 242 of *The Tamworth Narrative* (Freeport, Maine: The Bond Wheelright Company, 1958).

CHIEF CHARACTERS

THE LIVING

Ellen Comstock (formerly Lockhart), a widow
    Nick, her unmarried son
Christina Chapman (formerly Holt)
Cornelius Chapman

    John, married to Sybille   } Children of
    Marianne, married to Bruno Spencer } Christina and
    Olivia, unmarried   } Cornelius
        Cathy, youngest daughter of Marianne and Bruno

Eben Fifield, native of Willard, retired businessman and
        diplomat
Jem Grindell, town historian
Jim Heald, his friend, married to Sarie
Jane Tuttle, botanist, long-time resident of Willard
Susie Plummer, librarian and retired missionary
Mary Loveland, matriarch of the Loveland clan
Sally and Timothy Webster, summer people
Mamzelle, the Chapmans' old governess
Ed Taggart, road agent
Dinnock Corey, mailman
Johnny Dole, policeman
Orin Gregg, warden
Mrs. Molly Goodnow, housekeeper for Eb(
Hannah, housekeeper for Jane Tuttle

Old Pete, jack of all trades
Joel Smith, a Dartmouth student

THE DEAD
Rufus Comstock, Ellen's husband, a farmer
Seth Lockhart, Ellen's grandfather, a schoolteacher
Judge Gordon Chapman, Cornelius's father
Olive Fifield, Eben's wife
Sophia Dole, his great-grandmother
Erica Portland, an artist
Miss Morse, General Morse's daughter, a schoolteacher

The untameable, the live, the gentle.
Have you not known them? Whom? They carry
Time looped so river-wise about their house
There's no way in by history's road
To name or number them.
                    —ROBERT GRAVES, "Through Nightmare"

PART ONE

A Walk
Through the Woods

CHAPTER 1

Old Pete, out chopping wood beside his shack, saw the two women go past down the dirt road toward the brook and watched them, as he watched everything within range, with lively curiosity. Ellen must be seventy-five if she's a day, and Christina Chapman can't be much younger, he thought, but they walk like gazelles—"gazelles"—he savored the word. Christina was tall, lean as a bean-pole; beside her Ellen looked like a skinny little kid. But whatever the difference in height, their stride was easy.

"Going to explore the old lumber road, I'll bet. They'll find it changed."

Many were the times in the last forty years that Old Pete had watched those two go off together as if they were kin. He could remember back to when Christina had come up from Boston and spent a winter with Ellen's family, when they were eleven or twelve years old. Christina had married into the Chapman clan, and they went back three generations, among the earliest of the summer people, built a grand place on top of the hill, raised horses and sheep for the fun of it, kept gardeners and stable boys. They came with the swallows and left after Thanksgiving. No one could call them natives. They had a smoother grain. They had not had to struggle just to keep alive, like Ellen and her family, and the difference showed in the two women's faces. Christina stood straight as ever, held her head high, and showed hardly a wrinkle except that deep one between her eyes that made her look curiously intent. But her dark blue eyes could still take a man by surprise with the fire that flashed out when she was pleased or angered.

Ellen showed the strain of the winters, the strain of a hard life. Her thin face was covered with a veil of fine wrinkles now. Her brown eyes had sunk deep into the bone with time. But she had kept her slim figure, and from the back, as Old Pete watched her now, she might have been a girl.

A sight like this would keep him dreaming for the next hour. He had moved about the village from one abandoned sugarhouse or shack to another for the past sixty years, unwilling to work more than now and then, a living encyclopedia of Willard lore, a great talker, hunter, and fisherman. He knew the rich, for he and his dog, Flicker, hunted and fished with them, and he knew the poor as one of them. In the winter he sat by many a stove and gossiped. But he had not been welcome at Ellen's, because he liked to drink as well as Rufus, her husband, and when Rufus got liquor in him he had been a hard man to live with. Ellen had managed by sheer grit, and by her silences that surely had been punishment for that gregarious man.

"Seems like the women around here have been given a grain or two more pluck than the men, and that's an odd thing." Old Pete sat down to cogitate, for he was not a man to let an idea go unchewed over, especially as thinking gave him a chance to light his pipe and lay his ax down.

Christina lifted her head and flashed a smile at her companion. They were walking under a golden and scarlet cloud of maple leaves, and it was irresistible to look up and through to the blue overhead. You could get drunk on the color. It banged like a clash of cymbals.

"I wonder how the old road will be."

"So overgrown you won't recognize it," Ellen answered.

14

Then they were silent, absorbed in the walk itself, content to be together.

"You can still outpace me." Christina stopped to catch her breath. "As you've been doing for the last sixty years. Sixty! Can you believe it, Ellen? Where has it all gone?"

"Seems like yesterday that we set out with a picnic basket and got lost up the minister's hill, lost the trail altogether—do you remember?"

"We were fifteen then. We could still run away!" And Christina laughed her loud boyish laugh, which, Ellen thought, had not changed at all. "The worst thing about old age is that you can't run away. Life has you all right —caught in such a net, it's little short of a miracle to get off for a walk in the morning with an old friend. As it was, Cornelius didn't want me to go. But I needed to see you, Ellen—I needed a breath of fresh air."

"It can't be easy for you, with him so down these days."

"It's harder on him. The stroke made him a cripple in a few seconds. After all, he played tennis when he was past sixty, sailed his own boat when he was seventy. It's hard with all that in you to find it next to impossible to get up out of a chair. Hard to believe it was just six weeks ago."

They had reached what had once been the entrance to the lumber road, but the town graders had torn up the whole bank and left huge boulders and rubble where, a few years before, painted trillium and wake-robin and small ferns had grown. The alders had grown up around old stumps.

"It's horrible!" Christina called out, trying to pick a way in. "How can they do this to the roadside? Does nobody care?"

Ellen smiled a thin smile. Christina's vehemence, her outrage before what could not be changed, had always amused her, for it seemed so innocent. She herself expected the worst and was never surprised when it happened. She followed her tall friend, scratching her face on a sharp twig, but at last they had scrambled their way through and stood in the tangle of brush, close to an old cellar hole where, in the eighteenth century, there had been a clothespin factory.

Now it was possible to discern a faint open path through the bracken and small trees.

"Well," Ellen said, "there's still a road anyway. Look, there's a deer-hoof mark in the mud."

15

"So it is. Think we might see one?"

"I doubt it, with all the dogs loose in the village these days. Why, the deer used to come right out on the green ten years ago, to get the windfalls. It's a rare sight now."

"The wilderness is being taken from us," Christina said, and then laughed, for they were pushing their way now into dense undergrowth along a stand of pine by the brook, "but one can't call this exactly tame."

"It's just a different kind of wilderness, I guess."

But Christina had not heard—she was stooped over to look closely at a perfect round cushion of pale green moss with a brown mushroom beside it. "Dear things," she said. "How long is it since we have made a wild garden to take home? Oh, I do wish I had brought a basket and a trowel. Cornelius would have liked to see these."

A jay screamed overhead. They could hear the brook trickling along somewhere to the right over boulders and under fallen trees. Everything had a wild, damp, sweet smell of moss and pine and fallen leaves. And the two women stood there a moment, just sensing the intricate, rich atmosphere around them, the woodsiness of woods.

"I'm so glad we came," Christina said. Then, gazing around her, she added, "I wish I could have seen it before all the great trees were lumbered off," and led the way on, holding onto the sharp branches for Ellen, handing the end of one to her so it couldn't snap back. "Yes, a raggedy, odds-and-ends kind of wilderness it is now."

Pretty soon the silence all around silenced them, and they were inside the adventure, for it was something of an adventure as they got deeper and deeper in, feeling their way by instinct and keeping to the road by following the sound of the brook. There was no road anymore.

"Isn't this fun?" Christina turned round to enfold her friend in a smile.

"It ought to be close to that big rock where we used to sit. There! See it? Just beyond that pine."

Here they climbed up and sat down, for auld lang syne—Ellen with quick grace, Christina cursing a stiff knee as she slipped and nearly fell and tore a hole in her tweed skirt. Once settled, she leaned her head against the trunk of the pine and closed her eyes.

Ellen watched the water curling round a boulder, making small eddies, and thought she could watch moving water forever and not tire of it.

They were comfortable together. They didn't need to

16

talk, never had. It was the quality of silence between them that had made this friendship last and renew itself over all the years.

Christina lit a cigarette.

"You shouldn't do it, Christy—after pneumonia and all."

"Don't badger me. I'm happy." She inhaled deeply, and was seized by a spasm of coughing.

"See?"

"Oh dear . . ." Her face had become quite pink with the racking cough. "I do hate carrying this decaying carcass around."

Ellen laughed. "I can hear you saying that twenty years ago . . . you've always said it."

"Have I?" Christina was astonished. "I don't remember." —She pushed all this talk aside. "How's Nick?" she asked.

Ellen noticed that she had put out the cigarette.

"He doesn't change much. Lately he's got interested in making bird feeders—invented a new kind that he says will keep jays and squirrels out. You might like to try one, Christina—then he could see if it works."

"Hasn't he tried one himself?"

"Birdseed is expensive."

Just there the perfect harmony between the two women showed a tiny crack or scratch on its surface. Ellen had learned long ago that Christina could never possibly imagine what her life was like, what it meant when a cold spell came early and the heat bill soared, how pennies must be counted. What made it worse was that Christina *thought* she understood.

Christina was dismayed. After all these years, I still do it, she thought to herself. But because her nature flowed outward, because she was an optimist and would not dwell on the darkness, she said at once, "I want to buy one for Cornelius."

Ellen did not say thank you. She was animated at these moments by fierce, bitter pride. She said, "Nick will like that," and got up.

Christina sat there thinking about Nick, the abnormally gentle son of a hard-hitting, hard-drinking man. Either he had been born lacking any masculine drive, or something had been beaten out of him young. He had been drafted into World War II, had come back silent and sick, and had spent five years in the state hospital. When he finally came home to the farm, his father was, perhaps merci-

17

fully, dead, and it was taken for granted that he would not ever again be asked to do a full day's work. He puttered around, adored by his mother, with whom he communicated mostly without words.

While Christina thought about Nick, Ellen had been walking on, and now Christina tried to get up to follow, but found she was absurdly stiff.

"Give me a hand, Ellen, or I'll never get these old bones perpendicular again." Christina felt the strength in the wiry little body as Ellen gave a great tug. "Hurrah! We're in motion. Do you think we could find the old trail and go home over the hill and back?"

"Is that what you had in mind?" Ellen smiled in spite of her crossness. The trail hadn't been used for years. They were sure to get lost. But why not, after all? There was no one else in Willard who could get Ellen out on a crazy adventure like this. "Let's give it a try. But what if we get lost?"

"We won't. Besides, I brought my compass."

"Old Pete saw us go—he'll know if we never come back," Ellen chuckled. "Send that clever hound of his after us."

The mood had lightened. And there was something about a brilliant autumn day like this that called out for adventure, for getting out of the routine. Christina whistled as they pushed their way farther and farther in, then stayed by the brook, watching for a place where they might cross over without getting soaking wet.

"Not many mushrooms this year. It's been too dry," Ellen noted.

"Wasn't there a huge pine just at the start of the trail, along that stone wall?" These were the things one remembered with one's whole system, Christina was thinking. She would never forget that pine and the shape of its trunk, split about ten feet up into two huge branches; but ask her the name of one of her schoolmates in the seventh grade and she would hesitate. Names and dates flew out of her head these days, and she hardly bothered to try to recapture them.

"Yes, and there it is, if we can get over."

"There it is!" They felt it as triumph to have come out just right like this, after fifty years or more. "Topped though," Christina added as she looked up through the great tree and saw its top cracked off, lying caught in the lower branches. "Lightning, I suppose."

They managed to scramble over the brook, although Christina got one leg pretty wet when she slipped on a wet stone.

"All right? You didn't hurt your knee?"

"Nope."

"We follow the stone wall first," Ellen directed.

"I wonder who cleared all this and dragged those stones and built a wall—not more than a hundred and fifty years ago, but it might as well never have been done. I feel for that man. He must have thought he was building a sure foundation for sons and grandsons—but no doubt they went West, or just petered out, until the homestead rotted back into the woods or burned."

This outburst was not answered as Ellen, in the lead now, picked her way upwards. If all went well they would reach the great rock from where, if you managed to scramble up, you got an unexpected view of the village, the pond, and, in the distance, all the way to Vermont on a good day. She was animated now by a strong wish to get there, and she was pushing on.

"Hey, wait for me!" Christina called. It was no longer an idle walk, she realized, but an expedition. "Hold your horses, girl, remember you're with an old lady." And, indeed, she was out of breath and sat down on a convenient rock when she caught up with Ellen.

"I wonder what Jem will do about the bicentennial. It's his baby, from what I hear."

"Oh, he's only interested in cellar holes and gravestones," Ellen said contemptuously. "Especially those of his own family."

"Well, he's asked me to do a chapter of the history on the women of Willard."

"Going to do it?"

"Yes," Christina said seriously. "The subject interests me. Besides, with Cornelius kept indoors, I'll have time on my hands."

"I have to do education."

"Well, if anyone knows about it you do."

Ellen had taught school from the time she was sixteen, until she married Rufus Comstock at twenty-five. Then a Boston girl took over for a while for the sheer fun of the thing, a college graduate, but the old brick schoolhouse had been long abandoned. Willard children joined those of the next village and were driven to the schoolhouse there instead of walking two or three miles as they had done all through the nineteenth century.

"Jem's good at getting slave labor. I don't want to do it," Ellen said, walking on ahead.

"But you'll do a good job. You know you will."

"Seems like I've worked for this town enough for little pay and no thanks. I was Town Clerk all those years."

"I know." They were climbing now, and Christina needed her breath for that. So for a while there was silence. A chipmunk chittered, gave a little squeak, and disappeared like lightning under a stone. Christina's knee bothered her, but her head was a whirl of thoughts, a kind of intersection where the scream of a flicker was noted, and the way the light struck a birch just ahead, or the silent fall of a single golden leaf wavering through the still air; and at the same time she was thinking about Ellen, and Ellen's style, which was to complain about almost everything life asked of her and then do a superlative job; Ellen was a born nay-sayer who lifted herself into action with bitter humor and who, if ever a person could be counted on, could be counted on—this tiny woman battered so consistently and recklessly by life. But underneath both the physical world around them and the person plunging on ahead, this walk had another dimension for Christina: the history of the town that might have been written if Jem had not taken it over—the complex, heartbreaking tale of the slow erosion of any possibility of farming on this rocky, poor land, and what happened to people who had to live with failure, the kinds of ingenuity, courage, and sheer stubborn grit that life here had demanded.

Not only that general a tale was in her thoughts, more alive than usual to the adventure, but something about Christina Holt, now Chapman, herself. How different a person I would be if my father had not come here as a boarder nearly a hundred years ago—if there had been only Boston and no Willard in my life! Who was going to speak of these interchanges? Of what Holts and Chapmans and Bakers and Jameses had brought to this little corner of New England, and what they had been given in exchange? It was not a simple story, and, alas, Jem Grindell was a simple man, a teller of tales, a believer in all the clichés of New England history, a professor of chemistry long retired, grown immensely fat and preposterously

20

absorbed in genealogies. For years Christina had fled at his approach. But now she was cornered.

"There are going to be an awful lot of long-winded meetings, I'm afraid." That is what came out of her meditations, aloud.

They had reached a kind of cliff. There seemed no way around or up it.

"Was this here? Do you think we are lost?"

But Ellen was out of sight.

"Ellen, where are you?" Christina shouted, and was relieved to get an answer from off to the left.

"Over here, bear left. We're lost all right, but I think I know where we are."

Christina glanced at her watch. They had been walking for only three quarters of an hour, she noted, furious to be so exhausted. It really felt as if they had been at it for half a day. Her knee, injured years ago in a fall from a horse, was complaining rather painfully. But if it was Ellen's way to complain and then do the impossible, it was Christina's way never to complain, never to admit that she could be in trouble or pushed beyond her strength— and then pay for her pride, and often do a botched job.

"Where do you think we are?" she asked when she had caught up with Ellen in a gloomy thicket of hemlock.

"I have an idea we have to keep bearing left and we may come out on that road near where the old people used to live."

"You've a better head than I have. I haven't a notion *where* we are."

Christina sat down heavily on a fallen tree trunk as they emerged from hemlock into hardwood again. And Ellen, aware that her friend looked suddenly a bit done in, sat down beside her, although she was eager to find out whether her hunch about a way out onto the road was right. If not, they really were lost, and the compass might come in very handy indeed.

"Crazy old women, we are!" Christina panted, and laughed her bravura laugh.

"Better crazy than dead," Ellen chuckled. "My heart hasn't thumped like this since Micah fell down the well."

"We must have borne left too far—that brook always was a deceiver—remember the time we tried to find watercress and came out, finally, miles from where we thought we were?"

"Bedraggled, all right, and pretty tuckered out."

21

They exchanged a glance, mocking, tender, holding in it hundreds of such memories of escapades and all the tragedies and struggles that a long, rich life brings with it. The watercress walk, as Ellen remembered, had brought them close again after the four years when Christina was at Vassar—and, more often than not, off to Europe in the summer—and seemed to have gone off into the world of the rich forever.

By that time Ellen was married and Nick in rompers, and Rufus had been furious when she got home, late for lunch. He had never understood about Christina. How many times had he stormed at her, "They're rich and we're poor and never the twain shall meet!" At the bottom of his resentment was not envy but contempt. He was a proud man—proud of working as hard as he did, proud of getting up at four to milk. "That man" (as he called Cornelius) "doesn't know the meaning of work." But pride didn't help Rufus in the end when things just got too hard and he began to drink to put fire in his stomach against defeat. Oh, she understood . . . but . . .

Christina saw the shadow on Ellen's taut face as they moved on but said nothing. When two people have known each other this long, the past is near the surface. When they met now, everything opened up, joy, grief. They knew things about each other that no one else in the world knew—the moments of failure of nerve, the secret wounds. It was to Ellen that Christina confided her anguish over her eldest son, John, who had tried to commit suicide before he was forty and still suffered from periodic depression. Cornelius, shamed deeply by this failure so close to the marrow, had never been able to help.

"Now, Ellen, you've got to use that sixth sense of yours and get us out onto a road, my girl!"

"Well, we'll have a try."

Christina was slowed down by her knee and heard the good news from far off. "We're all right, Christy! I'm out on the Mill Road . . . hurry up."

That "Christy" induced a spurt of new energy. It had been her childhood name, but only Ellen ever used it now. It acted like a spur, and within a few minutes of tough scrambling under hemlocks again and over a broken stone wall and a rather perilous dump full of broken bottles, Christina emerged, panting, laughing with relief, onto the familiar road just a few yards from the Preckles' old place.

"Bravo, old girl! I must admit I've had it!"

"It's only ten minutes now down the hill to Old Pete's and home."

They had reached the burned-out remains of the Preckles' house. The small barn had fallen in during the last winter's heavy snows. It was a desolate sight now, the windows all broken, door off its hinges, and the whole thing charred black. Christina, more tired than she cared to admit, shivered as they went past.

"There's something to be said for dying together in a big blaze when you're near ninety," Ellen commented.

"I suppose so. But I'll never forget John's face when he had gone up after the fire truck and came home."

"Guess it would give anyone a turn—we all felt responsible in a way; don't know quite why."

"The loneliness . . ." Christina murmured. And they left it at that. Twenty years ago it had happened, those two old people burned to death and help coming long after they were gone. Sam had tried to drag his wife out, and then they had both succumbed in the doorway only a few feet from safety. That was the irony of it. "But I guess you're right. Ninety is old enough. We won't be climbing around like goats together when we're that old, I can tell you."

"It's funny how one has always thought of dying, but never about old age," Ellen said. "Seems as though I never wake up any more feeling really ready to git up and go. Why, I used to be up for Rufus by four o'clock!"

"Shh . . ." Christina had just time to make them both stand still as a young buck, his small antlers still in velvet, stood on the rise about twenty yards from them. For one long moment the two old women and the deer looked at each other. No one breathed. Then, with a superb bound, he crossed the road, white tail up, and crashed into the woods on the other side. It had been so quick, so silent, so full of magic that they still stood there for a long moment after he was out of sight.

"Oh—oh—" Christina breathed then. "How he looked at us—those liquid eyes! What a look!"

"Worth getting lost for that sight, I'd say."

"I understand so well why the Indians felt the animals were gods. He was like a god, wasn't he?"

"And he'll be shot dead, like as not, come November."

"I'll never get used to it—never!" Christina was vehement.

23

"No, neither will I. But a deer means meat. The way the cost of living has gone up, you can't blame people."

"You know, it's interesting—have you noticed as people get older they lose the wish to kill? Cornelius used to be a great hunter. Remember that time when he and Ned Turner got a bear, a wildcat, and two deer all in one morning?"

"I still have the clipping. They looked pretty proud of themselves."

"That bearskin's in the study still. The grandchildren still lie on it and hug the big head—but Cornelius has changed. Only the other day he told me if he ever got well he wouldn't shoot any more, not even woodcock— 'especially not woodcock' was what he said."

"I wonder why—why he changed."

"I used to hunt myself. Can't imagine it now. Maybe we get less primitive as we get older."

"Though hardly more ethereal." Ellen smiled, for Cornelius had become a heavy man these last years, heavy and solid.

"Maybe not, but maybe we have pity on the living, more pity perhaps, because we feel so frail and in peril ourselves."

"Yes . . ."

They had reached the top of the final rise in the road. Flicker greeted them with loud barks of welcome. There was Old Pete still sitting on the stone wall, smoking his pipe.

"Didn't think to see you come back on this road," he called out.

"We got lost, came out at Preckles'."

Flicker bounded up, leaping in the air.

"Down, boy!" Christina was afraid of being knocked over and spoke sharply. Old Pete called the dog back to his side and watched them walk slowly up toward the farm.

They had been gone about an hour, Pete reckoned, but they did not look like gazelles now. Old Pete, who had his own aches and pains to contend with, looked shrewdly at Christina's limp. But to his admiring eyes the tall woman still held herself like a queen. It's the way she holds her head, he said to himself—as if nothing on earth could get her down. And Old Pete, his feet bound up in rags inside his boots, his old jacket more like the skin of an animal than a piece of clothing, enjoyed the sight of good clothes on a woman. Christina's flame-colored suede jacket and gray skirt, the white chiffon scarf round her throat, looked just right to him.

Beside her, Ellen, all in brown, looked like a frail autumn leaf, but of the two he reckoned Ellen might last the longer. She was nothing but a wiry little engine now, no flesh to wear away—well, the village would be a different place when those two went, they and maybe four or five more. Miss Tuttle—he had not seen her for years out with her basket and trowel, botanizing. She was ninety, and no one saw her often any more. But Ed, the road agent, had told Old Pete not so long ago that he had seen her sitting out on the porch only the other day. When these three women died, the village would lose some quality, some configuration it had had for fifty years. But Pete's long, quiet pause on the stone wall had not led his wandering mind to any great conclusions about why the village had been dominated by womenfolk. Maybe that's just the way things are, he thought. Maybe the Lord made them stronger in spirit and gave men the wits.

"Eh, Flicker?"

Flicker pricked his ears.

"As far as I can see, women don't invent things. They just hold together and keep going what men have invented."

Way off in the distance he could see a little dust blown up by Nick's Ford truck. No doubt Ellen had got him to drive Christina home. It didn't look as if she could easily manage the long hill. And now that this vicarious adventure was over, and Old Pete had watched the two women go off and come back from their walk, he got slowly to his feet. A long sit certainly wasn't the thing for the rheumatism. And slowly he picked up his ax. He had better keep at it if he was to have his winter woodpile ready in time.

CHRISTINA'S JOURNAL—*October 8*

Cornelius is asleep, and I want to think a little about my walk with Ellen this morning. Sometimes I think I'm a loon to go on with this journal. I used to pretend that I was keeping it for the grandchildren—in those days, twenty years ago, I still felt that everything I did must have some justification. Now I guess I'll have to admit that I keep it up for myself. It does for me what prayer must do for the truly religious—sets things in proportion again. It is not important whether it is even read after my death. By then it will have served its purpose.

What is interesting, after all, is the making of a self, an act of creation, like any other, that does imply a certain amount of conscious work. Ellen is very much aware of this, I feel. She would agree with Keats about a "vale of soul-making." Or would she? "Soul" is not a word she uses, I realize. But she does a lot of thinking about herself.

The wonderful thing when one has known a person as long and intimately as she and I have known each other is that words no longer have the same importance. No explorations are needed of the other. No, it is rather that when we are together the past flows through the present, is, in some strange way, opened up—so often painful we tend to push it back when alone, but when we are together it is there, alive and precious. So it is being together that matters, not any longer what we may say or not say.

I was stupid about the bird feeders. Damn it. Money does make one obtuse. I sometimes feel it has been for me like an extra skin, protective against certain currents of life which I have never experienced just because I was insulated. Ellen spends what she has on foolish things often. I count every penny I spend as taken from some good cause. Money is the only area I cannot discuss with Ellen. She has not known either my guilt or my rage about it. It has never worried Cornelius that we spend a million times what Ellen has to spend, on gardeners, horses, the whole enterprise of the wonderful summers here, not to mention the house in town—the servants, entertaining. For Cornelius this is the way things are. Can't be changed. He has no wish to be a saint, bless his heart. But I have felt held back, sometimes prevented from being myself by all that he takes for granted. He thought of my painting as a pleasant exercise, a little as he himself felt about court tennis, I suppose. To take it seriously, to be a professional, would have been not done, would have meant losing one's amateur status. And the same thing about civil liberties— it was all very well to be on the board of the union and to give a certain amount of money (never as much as I wanted to give), but, again, it must not bite into our "real" lives.—Why have I begun to speak of this now?

26

Because that small exchange about the cost of birdseed brought all this old anguish to the surface again. It appears to me that the New England attitude to money (at least in society) is very much like the Victorian attitude to sex. Must tease Cornelius about this!

CHAPTER 2

Jem Grindell had called a meeting for the following Wednesday of all the heads of committees for the bicentennial history, and, to spare Miss Tuttle the long flight of steps to the library, they had agreed to meet in the old brick schoolhouse. Long since abandoned as a schoolhouse, it was used chiefly for the Ladies' Aid sales, for an occasional exhibition of paintings, or for informal meetings. Old Pete had been alerted and had built a wood fire in the stove. The hard benches had been hauled out and set around a big square table.

Jem ponderously laid out a pencil and pad at each place. He had already spent a good deal of town money having special letter paper printed with "Willard Bicentennial, 1769–1969" in bold letters at the top. He was a born organizer when it came to such things, but not perhaps a man of great vision; he was passionate about detail. But no one else in the town cared enough in the special way that he did, and no one else would have taken on the onerous job of getting a town history written and in print. He himself had been working for nearly a year on the genealogies that would be the meat of the book, as far as he was concerned. The essays which he had commandeered on subjects such as local flora and fauna, the part women had played in the Civil War, the missionaries who had gone out from Willard, or the history of the schools he considered to be chiefly window dressing. It was a way, also, of casting a net out for possible buyers,

28

for he himself had undertaken to finance the project, and hoped at least to cover expenses.

Christina, who had gone to fetch Jane Tuttle, was the first to drive up, and Jem hurried out to greet them. Old Pete, of course, was sitting on the fence, smoking his pipe and taking it all in.

"Why, there's Old Pete," said Miss Tuttle. "How are you, Pete?"

"As well as yourself, I hope."

She laughed her whispery laugh.

"I hope much better."

"My dog and I got a wildcat the other day."

"Don't tell me about it, Pete. You know how I hate to hear about the wild animals getting murdered," she said lightly but firmly. "Well, Jem, you got this old creature to come out, and that took some doing, didn't it?"

Beside her, so tiny and exquisite, her ruffled blouse tied with a blue velvet ribbon at the throat, Jem looked like a rather shabby elephant. At ninety, Miss Tuttle still held herself straight, but she seemed to have got smaller and smaller lately. She looked more than ever like a small bird a cold wind might blow away.

"You'd better come in out of the wind," Christina said, taking her arm.

"But it's a fine day," she protested, "and I must just go and see how that pink hawthorn is doing. It looked to me over-pruned." Then she hesitated. "Is everyone there, waiting? Shall I hold up the meeting?"

"All the time in the world," Jem said. "You know how they are. Christina is the only living soul in the town who has a sense of time."

"I felt responsible. After all, I was bringing a very important person."

"Nonsense." Miss Tuttle laughed again. "It's quite absurd to have asked me to participate"—and she was off to examine the hawthorn, a particular friend, as she had planted it in memory of a nephew killed in World War II.

Jem, Old Pete, and Christina watched her go.

"She doesn't miss a trick, does she?"

"It's the old stock," Old Pete said. "Why, her grandpappy climbed Monadnock when he was eighty. You can't get those Tuttles down. They live forever and keep their wits, which is more than can be said for some of us."

Christina was always surprised, when she had a chance

29

to hear Old Pete talk, at how well-spoken he was. In fact, one of the curious things about the town was that the uneducated of Pete's age spoke beautiful English—far better than her own grandchildren ever had. Yet she didn't suppose Pete had had more than six winters' schooling, if that.

"Who was the teacher here, Pete, when you went to school?"

"General Morse's daughter," he said proudly. "It was a fine school in her day—spelling bees, orations; we learned poetry by heart. First thing she did was have us build a bookcase and bring over her books to put in it."

It was a pity, Christina thought, that he was interrupted in these reflections by the arrival of Miss Plummer, the town librarian, for she would have liked to hear more about Miss Morse, who had come to teach for a year or two in the village instead of coming out in Boston, for reasons that remained mysterious.

But Miss Plummer, brisk, domineering, must be greeted now, and Jim Heald; and dear Jane led back from her botanical interests. Only the Websters were still to come.

"Jem"—she heard Miss Plummer's rather loud voice from inside—"when are you going to get this meeting going?"

It made a counterpoint to Old Pete's rendering of a stanza of Whittier's that had floated back into his mind, no doubt at the mention of Miss Morse:

> " 'The rigor of a frozen clime,
> The harshness of an untaught ear,
> The jarring words of one whose rhyme
> Beat often Labor's hurried time,
> Or Duty's rugged march through storm
>   and strife, are here,' "

he intoned, while Jim Heald nodded.

"Good gracious, Pete, what a memory you have!" Christina hurried off to lead the wandering Miss Tuttle back into the fold. And just then the Websters' Land Rover drove up. So at last the committee had all arrived, and Jem shouted from inside, "Come on, friends, we are waiting for you!"

Finally they were settled round the table—all except Ellen, the only one of the group who might be said to have work to do, and who slipped in just as Jem coughed and called the meeting to order. Jane Tuttle leaned over to whisper, "Good to see you, Ellen."

I know more about this town, the real history of it, than any of them in there, Old Pete thought as he sat out in the sun on the fence. Well, might as well find Flicker and go down to the store and leave them to it. Too deef to hear what's going on from here. Jem will be at it for hours, with nothing to say.

And with this comforting thought Old Pete wandered off.

Jem had never been short-winded, and with the years, and now his sense of responsibility, it took him a half hour to get anywhere near his point—which appeared to be, when one could untangle it from the endless digressions, that he wished each of the members of the Bicentennial Committee to lay before the meeting any ideas he or she might have. Christina had not been listening. As always at this sort of meeting, she felt terribly sleepy even before it got well started. She felt cramped and caught, her nature being to act rather than to explore possible avenues of action. Occasionally she and Ellen, sitting at opposite sides of the table, exchanged an amused or impatient glance. The Websters, imperturbably polite, as always, listened judiciously. Jane Tuttle doodled, and several times sighed deeply. Only Jim Heald managed to wear an alert expression. Miss Plummer appeared to have fallen asleep, her chin on her hand, her eyes closed.

Well, we are an odd enough group, Christina considered. Cornelius, with his cheerful, incisive mind, would have been a help, and she missed him sorely. But here we are—a pretty fair sample of what Willard was all about when you came to think of it. Few young people, but a singular range of character in the elderly. Miss Plummer might deal with the world as if it were a horde of natives she must tame and order about, to whom she must set a good example (she had been for years a missionary in Hawaii and, at one time earlier, for a few years in China), but one had to admit that she was a woman of extreme courage and good will—not so much a follower of Christ, one sometimes thought, as a captain in the army of her church. She had taken over the tiny memorial library as her headquarters, cleaned it up, organized it, and commanded all parents of small children to be there at certain hours, or else. Children loved her, recognizing

31

at once a true Girl Scout or den mother in disguise. There was not the slightest doubt where she stood on any subject. Christina swallowed a smile as she remembered that penetrating voice only the other day saying to little Sammy Preckle, "Go out, boy, and spit as hard as you can. That word you just uttered must be gotten rid of *at once!*" The only trouble was that she could have no possible understanding of the extraordinary woman she would be asked to celebrate in her essay on the town library. Miss Erica Portland had been an artist of something like genius, an eccentric, and in almost every way the exact opposite (oh, that subtle charm and that sly humor!) of Miss Plummer. And Miss Portland's symbolic vision of Willard as a phoenix, rendered in a remarkably modern painting which hung over the mantel in the library, was quite beyond Miss Plummer's ken.

"It's a bird, that's all. Apparently being burned on a funeral pyre—but why that crazy old creature thought it resembled the town of Willard I cannot tell you." So she admonished anyone who had the temerity to ask her about it.

Christina was startled out of these ruminations by a question.

"Well, Mrs. Chapman, may we have your ideas?"

"Oh . . . well . . . about the phoenix."

"The phoenix, Mrs. Chapman?" Jem repeated, at a total loss.

"Well, you all know, Erica Portland used it as an image for Willard. I think we should resurrect her vision and perhaps find some appropriate quotations, and use it as the device for the bicentennial."

"An interesting thought."

Miss Tuttle raised her head from what looked like a large ornamental flower she had been drawing, and recited:

" 'Glory, like the phoenix 'midst her fires,
Exhales her odours, blazes, and expires.'—Lord Byron,"

she added with a twinkle.

"Well . . . er . . ." Jem hesitated, sensing a ripple of laughter rising. "Perhaps not quite appropriate. But we may come to something. I propose shelving Mrs. Chapman's thought for a later meeting."

"Except," Mrs. Webster intervened, "that if we build

the bicentennial around a central idea, perhaps we should decide what it is now."

"I never could understand that bird," Miss Plummer said *sotto voce*.

"Yet," Christina came down firmly, "it is, when you think about it, not a bad image for this town, is it? I mean, it has died several times and been reborn, and that's the whole point—Erica's point, I mean, and it might well be ours."

"Could you explain, Mrs. Chapman?" Jem asked cautiously.

"Well, Willard began, like all these towns, as a congregation of small farms. Sheep and the manufacture of woolen garments from the wool brought in the first mills, but all that went before the Civil War, so the town had to find a way of existing. Then the war—and the beginning of the flow west, and the lack of manpower. And finally the summer people, who certainly helped the phoenix rise from his ashes, didn't they?"

"It's a most original proposal." Jem held his pencil balanced horizontally between the palms of his hands. "May I just venture my thought about the theme of the bicentennial?"

Miss Tuttle gave one of her loud, unconscious sighs and began a new doodle, and they all resigned themselves to what would surely be long. It lasted interminably, but Mr. Webster saved the day by summing up the gist succinctly at the end.

"You are saying, Jem, that our emphasis should be on the good citizen."

"Well . . . well . . . yes, I suppose that is what I had in mind."

"What do you think, Jane?" Ellen had not spoken until now, but Christina recognized the edge in her voice. Time was oozing away and they were getting nowhere.

"I?" Jane Tuttle lifted her pale gray eyes in a dreamy look and smiled. "I prefer phoenixes to good citizens."

"Bravo!" Mr. Webster called out.

Jem looked bewildered and sad. It had never entered his mind that there would be any real discussion. He had come prepared to lay down his plans and to have them accepted. It was disturbing to have time wasted by quite unnecessary argument at this point. So he turned now to Jim Heald, old crony and dispenser of balm. Jim's solution was to go round the table, limiting each person to three minutes, and to ask for overall suggestions about the actual celebrations.

"Fireworks," Miss Plummer said loudly. "We must have fireworks on the pond. The children will love that. It brings everyone together."

"Yes, we could even have a phoenix in fireworks," Mr. Webster said happily.

"One at a time, please. Mrs. Comstock is next." Now that Jem was forced to listen, he was anxious to limit the speaker's time.

"Well," Ellen said quietly, "I think we should perhaps stick to the history at this meeting. The bicentennial is a year off, and surely we can decide about the actual celebration later on. You have given us each a subject, Jem. How long do you see these essays as being? And who, by the way, is to work on missionaries?"

"Jim Heald has volunteered for that important task."

"Then I want to know whether we are going to try to tell the true history, or are we just going to flatter ourselves?"

Jem cleared his throat several times. He felt bewildered by the turn things were taking, as if all these old friends around the table and the great work in his care were in some strange way being taken over by a group of conspirators—of antibodies, so to speak.

While he shuffled papers over in his briefcase, trying to find something, Miss Tuttle said, "It would be most unusual if we told the truth. It has never been done on these occasions of celebration and self-congratulation, as far as I know, and that would demand a kind of genius which, I fear, with all due respect to our various talents, none of us can command. By the way, Jem, I must say that I shall be happy to make a general outline and fill in *viva voce* details about the flora and fauna, but to write an essay of even a few pages, worthy of the subject, is really beyond my powers."

"Nonsense, you'll do it splendidly, Jane!" Miss Plummer at seventy-two could not imagine that one might feel different at ninety.

"Here, here it is." Jem looked up over his glasses, not having heard this last exchange, in his agitation. "Here we have it!" he announced triumphantly. "This is what I have chosen as epigraph for the history of Willard."

He adjusted his glasses, waited for their complete attention and read:

" ' "What can you raise on your cold and rocky hill farms?" said a Southerner to the greatest of New England statesmen.

" 'Daniel Webster's answer was a proud one: "We raise men." ' "

"Hear, hear!" assented Jim Heald.

Sally Webster, usually so perfect a lady, unfortunately caught Christina's raised eyebrow and was captured by one of those irrepressible fits of the giggles that are apt to seize on children in church.

"What about the women?" Ellen asked ironically.

"What women?" Jem did not follow her thought.

"Well, didn't the cold and rocky pastures raise women, Jem?"

"Of course," he said, frowning, "naturally. That's understood, that's what is meant, surely."

"Is it?" Christina knew it was dangerous—and time-consuming—to try to argue with Jem, whose mind had been made up before this meeting, and who might listen but would hardly change his plans, whatever anyone might say. But there was an electric current in the room now, and she responded to it.

"If we were to examine the history of this town we might discover that the men have been not only generally outnumbered by the women but dominated by them. That those cold and rocky hill farms raised weak men and strong women is my guess. The strong men left even before the Civil War, and those who stayed either died in the war or came back from it changed."

Jem looked at her with dreary amazement. It was, he considered, typical of women never to be able to stick to the subject in hand.

"Well, since you have been assigned the chapter on the women of Willard, there is nothing to prevent your saying your say, Christina."

"I shall, Jem. I shall." Christina was flushed, cross with herself for nearly losing her temper as she had—saved in the nick of time by Ellen's cautionary glance.

"Now, Sally and Timothy Webster, it is your turn to speak." Jem turned to them hopefully. Newcomers to the town in the last five years, they were rich, handsome, and generous, and still somewhat in awe of the local gentry such as Jem.

"We really don't feel equipped for our task. You did mention on the telephone a possible chapter about the

35

non-residents, but, well . . . What do you think, Tim?"
Sally turned to her husband with relief. Tim was a lawyer
and very good at laying the gist of any matter before a
jury such as this.

"In the first place, I'd call a spade a spade. I think
what you're after is an assessment of what the summer
people have meant to Willard. 'Summer people' has a
ring to it—it contains, as a phrase, a certain amount of
resentment, of course."

Tim Webster looked around the table with a smile.

"Let's face it," Miss Plummer said warmly, "without
the summer people the town would have died seventy or
more years ago. The summer people rescued the town.
Also they brought some men in."

"Though not the kind Daniel Webster had in mind,
perhaps," Ellen added *sotto voce*.

"By 1878 Willard was a dead duck, I'll grant you that."
Jim Heald, interested for the first time, leaned forward.
"The mill had gone. There were fewer and fewer working
farms. Second growth was covering the pastureland. The
town had no money to keep the roads up. The schools
were terrible."

"Well, if so, that's one legend we might explode," Christina said, "the legend of the little red schoolhouse."

Jem had grown red in the face. He felt badgered and
disregarded. "What's the point of a bicentennial if all
you're interested in is tearing the town and all its history
to pieces, I ask you!"

"Oh, come on, Jem," Christina laughed, "we have a
chance to do something really useful."

"I want to give my grandchildren something to hold
onto," Jem said with quiet passion. "I want them to see
what we have back of us—a firm foundation."

Miss Tuttle laid a gentle hand on his sleeve. "Of course,
Jem."

"I'd like to say something, if I may." Tim Webster
looked to Jem for his assent. "It is something to hold
onto, it seems to me, that here in all these towns from
the turn of the century on, a kind of rich exchange took
place between urban and rural people, between the so-
called summer people and the so-called natives. It worked.
It was to everyone's advantage, it seems to me. If I may
speak for us, Sally and me, we feel immeasurably enriched
by what we have learned here since we bought our house.

Our children feel the same way. Willard has become home."

"Well"—and Jem coughed his nervous cough—"all this is very interesting, and I'm sure you will all make a great effort. I need not ask Miss Plummer to speak. We know she will have excellent material in the history of the library and especially a sketch of Erica Portland, one of the eminent women of Willard . . . or," he caught himself up, "would her story really be in Christina Chapman's domain?" But he did not wait for an answer, as he was clearly now very anxious to get back to his own thoughts.

The hour, which had seemed interminable already, stretched into almost two while Jem explained in detail his various projects to do with genealogies, the tracking down of all stones in the cemetery and, if possible, the houses, or cellar holes, or sites of all the houses where the dead had lived.

"I am having signboards made with the names and dates printed clearly on them, and one of these days I'll be around to tack them up."

Everyone present was too exhausted by now to raise questions or objections, although it did occur to Christina that not every person in this secretive place might wish to have his name advertised, or that of the former owners of his house. But this time she held her peace. Miss Tuttle had begun to look withered (there was no other word), and every now and then her head nodded.

"Jem, I'm sorry, but can you excuse us? I promised Hannah to get Jane Tuttle home by five and it's now half past. You know what a tyrant Hannah is."

So at last they were freed from bondage. Ellen ran home to get supper for Nick; the others, too, were eager to be off. And suddenly Jem and Jim Heald were left alone in the dusk to gather the pads and pencils together, just as Old Pete came back to put out the fire and lock up.

"Those women are all so clever, Jim, but I think we're going to stick to my idea and celebrate this town!"

Old Pete grunted as he beat out the fire with a poker —what was left of it.

"Thanks, Pete. I know you'll be sure that's safe before you lock up," Jem said in his authoritative voice.

But Pete had not had his innings, and he had had a couple of beers, and even one beer acted fast. For a drinking man, as he surely was, Pete could not hold his liquor.

"Let me tell you," he said, holding up the poker like a schoolmarm's ruler, "trying to work with women is like putting an ox and a horse in tandem. Those women will run away with you, Jem, before you know it."

"I'm not so sure," Jim Heald said, spreading his arms behind him comfortably along the bench back and stretching his legs out. "Jem has a pretty strong notion of how things will be."

"Giddyap!" Pete yelled in a hoarse whisper about an octave higher than his normal tone. "Giddyap!" and then he sat down too, he was laughing so hard.

"You come home with me, Jim, and we'll talk things over," Jem said, ignoring Pete.

"Wish I could, but Sarie's waiting on me, and I guess I'd better get home," and he slipped away.

Pete caught the guilty look on Jim's face and commented, "Never saw a town or heard of one where people had so little time for getting together. At the very hint of a meeting of any kind they start running for cover like rabbits," and Old Pete gave Jem a gentle slap on the back. "You did well, Jem, to get them to come—very well."

"Thanks," Jem said with a short laugh. "Glad someone appreciates the accomplishment."

"You haven't got a drink on you, Jem, have you? I'm dry as a dry well." Old Pete never asked for a drink when he was sober.

"Now, Pete, you've had enough. You take care of things here and go home and have something to eat. So long, man," and Jem went out into the dusk like some great lonely animal.

Pete sat down, rubbed his hand across his eyes and had a little talk with himself. "Miss Morse," he muttered, "she'd ought to be here—she'd know—standing up there, I can see her now, with her red hair, tall as a bean pole, telling me I had a beautiful voice and to let it out. He staggered to his feet and shouted hoarsely:

'Then out spake brave Horatius,
    The Captain of the Gate:
To every man upon this earth
    Death cometh soon or late.
And how can man die better
    Than facing fearful odds' . . .

38

Oh dear, it's gone, Miss Morse . . . te tum te tum te tum
. . . Forgotten."

CHRISTINA'S JOURNAL—*October 16*

Oh, what a relief it was to come home to Cornelius
after that interminable meeting! It's strange that since his
stroke, especially now that we know he will get almost
entirely well, we have been having a lovely time *together*.
The children will be here for Thanksgiving, and six of the
grandchildren, I hope, but I almost dread the interruption.
We are reading *Swann's Way* aloud. We go for little
drives and have been soaking in this glorious autumn—
the leaves are only just starting to fall and the maples are
stupendous. I am so grateful that we can stay on this
year, maybe even right through Christmas, although
Cornelius begins to talk about going back to the office,
optimist that he is.

The most wonderful thing is that for the first time since
John tried to commit suicide I've been able to talk about
him with Cornelius without one of us getting too angry or
upset for words. Cornelius is beginning to see that, without meaning to, he always managed to make John feel
inferior—he jeered at John's interests—how well I remember the fearful incident over the butterfly-chasing
when John was twelve and was starting his collection.
Cornelius simply would not accept that this could be as
valid an occupation as playing touch football. Oh dear
me, I am so glad I am a woman! At least women don't
have to make such desperate efforts to prove they are
women as men seem to have to do to prove they are
men! Darling John is just as stubborn as his father, and
for so many years they behaved like two stags, horns
locked. I tried so hard to explain them to each other but
always failed. The anger went too deep—it is stupid to
open these wounds. I just have to accept that we made
terrible cruel mistakes with our firstborn, but we loved
him, and some of the love must have been good.

Family life! The United Nations is child's play compared
to the tugs and splits and need to understand and forgive
in any family. That's the truth, I am sure, but, like every
hard truth, we all try to pretend it isn't true.

It was so moving to see John's tenderness when he first
went to see his father in the hospital three months ago.
I'm sure Cornelius felt it and that is why, perhaps, we

39

have been able to talk about the boy—man, I should say. John is fifty, and since he was twenty, for thirty years, he has fought the terrible depression and managed to stay alive. If only Cornelius could admit the courage!

That's what dear Jane said when I drove her home. She laughed about the meeting. "Christina, I did it for Jem. He tries so hard, you know. But my head was swimming off somewhere all by itself most of the time." But she wanted to talk about John and insisted that I come in and have a glass of sherry, Hannah hovering about to be sure I didn't overstay. I have learned so much from Jane over the years, and the last thing is this seraphic way she has of accepting dependence—it can't have been easy for a person of her spirit. How does she do it? She floats— why do I say that? I mean she lets herself be carried by Hannah, yet never becomes a baby, the baby Hannah wants her to be. It takes wisdom to be able to do that with grace.

"We can't measure the courage of that man," she said to me about John. "But has he given up his interest in moths? Tell him to come and see me, Christina—if he comes for Thanksgiving. I do so much want to have a talk with him. He mustn't give up on those things that are in him to do." And she added, when Hannah was out of the room for a moment, "I'm not going to live forever, and I want to see John."

Blessed person. That whole house just breathes with life. Every window is crowded with plants, books everywhere. "You know I'm the luckiest woman in the world still to be able to read—I have to choose, a little at a time —but I still *can*."

I asked her whether she would let me come and make a drawing. I want to do it so much, Jane sitting in the little chair by the window, the plants on the window sill beside her, reading. If I could only get it right! (For once.) She said a curious thing: "It would be interesting to see it. The person inside seems to have so little relation to the person outside these days. Yesterday I got into a fit of giggles when I looked at this wild old creature in the mirror— before Hannah comes to do my hair I do look very odd."

But she really looks like a small moss rose, crinkled and soft and so sweet! And she smells of lavender and sweet peas, always has. I felt when I left that I had literally rested my eyes on her face.

CHAPTER 3

Ellen spent a great part of her day sitting in the kitchen. From her rocking chair in the window she could see the cars go by down the road. The big maple darkened it some in summer but in fall shed a rosy light when the leaves turned. She had a sewing-basket table by her side, and she felt very much like a bird in a nest as she sewed and tucked and made over garments people brought her, some of them that you would hardly have thought worth keeping. It was a long time since anyone had asked her to smock a child's dress as she used to do for Christina when the children were small. That was what she loved— to start fresh with a beautiful piece of fine cloth in her hands; but mostly she mended, turned up hems (would the fashion ever stay one length for a year or two? Now all the ladies had to have skirts turned up to at least mid-knee), patched work clothes.

When Nick was not out in his shop in the barn, he sat in his father's chair by the kitchen table and read by the hour. Sometimes he just sat there, watching his mother's deft hands and the needle going in and out, as if he were listening to a piece of music. They communicated almost entirely by silence, these two, but they were so attuned to each other that Nick knew when his mother had a headache, almost before she knew it herself. And Ellen knew without a word whether he was sitting there watching her quietly because he felt happy and at peace, or whether he was controlling a storm of nerves. If the latter, she sometimes spoke, with an instinct to take Nick's mind off his anxiety: "Christina's leg's bothering her. Never has been right since that horse threw her," or "I'm thinking of digging up the sweet-pea bed—we might have an early winter," or "I do hope Netta brings the pies for Thanksgiving this year."

A great deal more went on in the heads of these two than ever came out of their mouths. It remained a surprise to Ellen the things Christina could talk about, how she ran on about everything. Ellen found herself saying things she never even knew she thought when they were together. But a walk like the one they had before the bicentennial committee meeting had become a rare treat.

Unconsciously Ellen sighed. Nick lifted his head, but when she went on making quick, deft stitches in the hem she was turning, he went back to his *Sports Illustrated*. The kitchen clock ticked loudly. A long streamer of sun picked out the worn places in the linoleum. After another silence, he got up and put the coffeepot onto the warm burner, and Ellen raised her head and smiled. Nick always knew when she needed a cup of coffee.

"Wish I'd never said I'd do that piece on the schools for Jem."

Nick poured out two cups of coffee and added milk to his. Ellen drank hers black. "Makes me nervous," she always said, but she meant that feeling nervous was what she wanted, like a thoroughbred horse.

"Seems like I haven't the energy to go up in the attic and dig around—there must be letters, old spellers. After all, your granddad taught for ten years here in Willard long before I did. And Miss Morse—they were talking about her at the meeting. Don't suppose her niece has anything, but she might."

Nick laughed. "Dad threw the teacher out the window when he was a boy, and the teacher never showed his face again." Like many mild sons of tyrant fathers, Nick enjoyed his father's exploits, especially now that the threatening power had gone.

"He told you that, I suppose. Sometimes there was a grain of truth somewhere—they did have a brute of a man, made the boys stand on the stove to punish them, or whupped them with a strap. It may be your father had enough one day."

Ellen drank down her coffee and picked up her needle, and there was silence again. But Nick, she knew, was not reading; he was thinking about his dad. Queer how he

42

seemed to think well of him when Rufus had been such a hard father to the boy. She smiled, thinking of Rufus throwing a teacher out the window! The truth was that women had been better at keeping order in school than men—although neither "man" nor "woman" was the accurate word, since they were often younger than their oldest pupil. But a girl—Ellen knew from her own experience—could put the fear of God into a sharp, sassy lad, as she had done more than once herself, though her knees were shaking under her skirt. She thought about the schools as her needle flew in and out. It was high time someone talked about how harsh a world it had been: the fearful cold in winter, the way they boasted about the schooling, but she never could get money out of the selectmen for a new blackboard or chalk or new books, and even the firewood had to be extracted stick by stick.

"You're all het up," Nick observed.

"It doesn't do to go that far back," she said quietly, "except maybe to remember how much better things are now. We forget about the chilblains and the soggy mittens and the smell of unwashed children huddled together. It was all awfully poor, Nick. That's what they forget—poor and hard."

She bit off a thread, and Nick, as silent as a wild animal, slipped out to the garden to smoke a cigarette and calm down. He had seen his mother shaken by rage often these past years. There was too much she could do nothing about that tore her apart—little things sometimes, like the way Mrs. Croswell down the road let her dogs rove the village, but more often—and this was what upset Nick —a kind of rage against the world. Seemed as though as she got older she couldn't make her peace. She never lashed out at him, but what upset him was that he sensed she felt like an animal caught in a trap.

Nick drew in on his cigarette and watched the smoke spiral up in the windless air. Two robins were strutting and bobbing up and down in the vegetable patch. Far off, a crow cawed. The big maple towered up like a fountain of light, so gold against the blue, and no leaf fallen yet. It made you stop and think it a wonderful thing to be alive in such a world. Mother should get out more, he was thinking. She gets all locked up inside. And he bent down and tore up the shriveled plants of squash—hard frost had wilted them two nights before. Seemed like she had almost stopped enjoying anything, though she had

43

come back from that walk with Christina kind of lit up inside, the way she used to look. It was strange that all those worst years when his dad had used to go and sit in the barn and weep with the despair of giving up the cows, and get drunk—all those years when his mother, so frail, had kept her head up (those blazing eyes!)—then she had been hard pressed, but she seemed like a flame.

I should help her somehow, Nick thought as he threw an armful of squash stalks on the pile back of the barn. But what he had to bear in himself was seeing and not being able to do. It was as if at the moment of taking hold, of action in any real sense, he was overcome by fatigue, by lethargy, and felt he had to lie down somewhere and sleep. That is the way it had been with Nick since he came back from the hospital after the war, a machine that had lost some vital part. No, he didn't want to think about it. And Nick lay down under the apple tree and looked up through the branches at the sky. He saw a robin's nest he hadn't known was there, and soon he was lost in a long, wordless daydream.

Ellen meanwhile had laid down her sewing with a sudden impatient gesture and gone up to the attic. After all, she thought, it has to be done and I might as well get at it. It must have been years since Ellen had pushed open the low door into the attic, and she never did it without the same queer sensation of interrupting something, for this jumble of the past, stowed away without order, haven of field mice in winter, was at the same time fearfully dead and fearfully alive.

There was just one naked light bulb hanging up there, but she could see enough—at first glance, a wild disorder of abandoned tools, toys, clothes, quilts too worn to be worth mending, but as soon as someone stepped in, strangely alive. It held so much life in it, so much of the past. Now, as always, she hesitated at the threshold, peering around. There was the dear old rocking horse her children had inherited from their grandmother on Rufus's side, the mane and tail nothing but a few black hairs, the leather of the saddle crumbled away into dust. Ellen laid a hand on Blackie's neck, thinking of Nick at about five riding hell-bent for leather. "I'm going to China!" he had called out. "I'll never stop!" He never got to China—only as far as some island in the Pacific, to be shattered inside by gunfire.

But it would never do to stop and think. Every object

in this place could bring back memories of such intensity it hurt. There was Rufus's old hunting jacket that she could never bear to give away with the rest of his clothes, a plug of chewing tobacco dried hard as a stone in one pocket. Ellen stood with the jacket in her arms a moment, then laid it down with a sudden gesture of rejection. Rufus had done things she couldn't forgive, even now. But there was Sarah's old doll. Must remember to give that to little Ellen when they come—might as well take it down now. The doll stared up with her cold china-blue eyes, her faded pink dress dirty and torn, one arm akimbo, but her eyes as cold and clear as when Rufus, in a rare moment of extravagance, had brought her to console Sarah when she had the measles. The way things have of outliving people was scarifying! But Ellen was not in the mood to stop and let herself be assailed—even by Gramp's old birch broom standing in a corner, all worn down on one side. In fact, she never did stop long in the attic. It was too much of a clutter and brought the past rushing in from too many directions all at once. So she laid the doll down on a small chest of drawers that Dr. Foster, who had built the house, had used for keeping bills in. Someone might have a good time looking over what people paid in those days when, often, a doctor was called in the middle of the night to hitch up the buggy and go ten miles or more on country roads to ease the dying or deliver a baby. But Ellen was out for something else just back of the chest, a flat metal box painted black where she had laid away (how many years ago, before she was married?) the schoolbooks she had used as a teacher. She put them on top of her grandfather's reports to the school committee and whatever relics remained from his teaching days.

She picked the box up, stuffed the doll under one arm, and went gingerly down the steep attic stairs, feeling as if she had escaped. Always when she came downstairs into the warm kitchen after a trip to the attic, she felt the same way—as if she had been through a kind of ordeal and escaped alive. Mostly we don't want the past around, she thought. I wonder why, she asked herself as she got a clean rag out and wet it and carefully wiped the dust and grime off the lid of the box so her grandfather's name, painted in dull gold, could be seen—SETH LOCKHART. He had taken the box to Dartmouth with him and brought it back filled with geological specimens. What is it, she wondered, standing there, her hands laid flat on the clean lid, not exactly afraid of opening it but loath to—what is it that makes our own history weigh on us? You have to be past fifty before you can stand to hear all those tales, and then, by the time you might want to know, those who wanted to tell and were not listened to are dead. We don't want to face our own negligence and not-caring, I expect. Even a doll lying there with wide-open eyes accuses.

But before she opened the box, Ellen went to the window to see that Nick was all right. There he was, lying under the apple tree, his arms crossed under his head, looking up at the sky. What things go on in his head! she thought—things I'll never know. He looked happy, Foxy lying there beside him, wagging his tail, and his pink tongue hanging out. There is nothing harder than to get started on a task you don't want to do, she thought, finally lifting the box up and sitting down with it in her lap.

When she opened the lid, she smelled that slightly dank smell of old books and papers, and lifted out a bundle of *School Committee Reports, 1855–65* (that would come in handy) and a very worn *Elementary Speller* that her grandfather must have inherited. "Ebony, editor, effigy, elegy, element, embassy, embryo, emerald . . ." she whispered aloud—and wondered whether the children who learned to spell all those words ever learned to use them. But everyone loved the spelling bees, the next best thing to hopscotch. She lifted out a set of notebooks she had made for herself, by sewing together ruled paper. "Ellen Lockhart, March 1909," it read, in a slanting, careful hand, very unlike her casual way of writing now. It contained lessons in history and faded clippings from newspapers, poems she had copied out for the smaller children to learn by heart, and answers to the problems in an arithmetic book that she had worked out painfully, so as to be prepared.

"Dear me," Ellen said, "I didn't know enough to be a teacher, did I?"

Memories were flooding in, of the whole Ellis family, who came, eleven strong, to school the first year she taught, the oldest boy two years older than she was, and the youngest barely five. But Barney, that oldest boy, was the greatest help and made that first year nothing but pleasure, for he licked his brothers and sisters when they needed it, and every other child in school was in awe of him. There were forty in the schoolhouse, as she well remembered, till ten were out with mumps in the spring term. She could see Barney now, determined to learn, but slow, licking his pencil over and over again before making a tentative answer to a problem in math. For him she had invented a whole series of problems dealing not with abstract numbers but with things he could take in, like shingles and boards and numbers of sheep. Oh, well, he's turned into a good farmer, after all.

She came on four old valentines next, one from Barney after he graduated when he was more than a little in love with her—he was a gawky boy then. But who were the others from? She couldn't for the life of her remember. Rufus never sent her a valentine.

She drew out more textbooks—a worn simple arithmetic, a reader; and there was that Webster she had looked high and low for last year when Nick wanted it for a crossword puzzle! She almost didn't see the crumpled piece of paper in her grandfather's hand, but luckily she unfolded it, the ink so faded she could barely decipher it. What she read set her tingling with excitement.

She looked at her watch—nearly eleven. If she hurried she could get up to Christina's and back before Nick would want his dinner, and anyway it was cold meat and all she had to do was boil some potatoes and a cabbage.

"Nick," she called out, "I've got to go to Christina's. I found something I want to show her. Be back by noon."

Ellen was so excited she did not even think what an unusual thing she was doing, for it was rare indeed that she went to the Ark—Christina came down the hill to visit when she could. But then it was rare to have Christina around so late in the year and to be able to go up there without the risk of running into people from Boston or Europe whom Ellen didn't know. The true residents of Willard, like Ellen, did not "go for walks." This was something the summer people did, and in fact Ellen never walked anywhere except with Christina. Nick drove her to do the errands in town once a week, and otherwise she stayed close to the farm.

But there was adventure in the air as she climbed the hill past the old cemetery, the maples lifting up their bowers of gold. It felt more like September than nearly November, and Ellen soon took off the sweater that she had flung round her shoulders.

The Ark had been well named. It was a brown, shin-

47

gled barn of a house, gabled and porched on every side, two big chimneys high on the roof. It stood on a hill and was approached through monumental gateposts made of granite stones, in the fashion of the nineties, and through a grove of somber hemlocks and cedars that protected it from the passers-by on the dirt road. The stables and a small barn were out of sight over the crest of the hill.

As Ellen hurried through the shadow of hemlock and out into the sun again, she saw Christina absorbed in planting bulbs, a basket for weeds by her side, her head bent, so she was not aware of her visitor till Ellen called out.

"Hi, Christy!"

"Well"—Christina got awkwardly to her feet—"if it isn't Ellen! You darling, to come up and see me!"

"I just had to. I've found something wonderful for the history—but I'm interrupting."

"It's time I stopped. Come on in—or—" Christina hesitated. "It's so warm, let's sit on the porch." She slipped an arm through Ellen's and they walked together. "I've been putting in tulips, a new blue one with crimson and white —hope springs eternal. You know the mice always eat them. But this year I'm trying camphor—maybe it will work. How I love the autumn planting, when all is hope and the garden is just a dream garden without cutworms, mice, or devastating frost in May!

"There," Christina said, pulling off her gloves. "Tell me!" and Ellen caught the glance bright and warm as that of a mother bird. No one could make one feel welcome in the way Christina did.

"Your eyes are so blue," Ellen laughed with the blueness of them. Like a jay's wing, she thought, and she is seventy-five. She turned to look out at the mountain, overwhelmed by the emotion she felt, the commotion of this walk, the sense of life . . .

"Are they? Oh, it's so glorious to be here *now*—not to be in town for once!"

For a moment they sat, looking out at the old spacious mountain, the foreground red and gold with autumn color, the mountain itself dark blue, sharply outlined against the cloudless sky.

"The old thing does look grand," Christina said. "But tell me now—what have you found? What brought you up the hill?"

And Ellen, suddenly shy, carefully unfolded the worn piece of paper from her pocket.

"Shall I read it to you? The handwriting is rather faint."

"Do. I don't have my glasses."

"Well, it's a letter my grandfather must have copied out to preserve—from the school records, it says. It is dated 1838. It says, 'My name is Eliza Bunker. I am 15 and a quarter years old and teach at Willard School. I board at Mrs. Springer's. It is nice and near the schoolhouse. I am paid $1.25 a week . . .' "

"Not really?" Christina asked. "One twenty-five a week!"

"I was only paid forty for the seven weeks when I taught," Ellen answered, "more than seventy years later."

"Go on."

" '. . . and this year taught only one term of seven and a half weeks. I had no trouble except with one older boy who was twenty and had not attended school before.

" 'About the schoolhouse, I wish to say the roof is all gone in one corner. You can see outside. The windows are all broken but we put paper over them. The floor is gone right under the bad roof. The fireplace does not heat except in front of it. The wood was very wet at times as there is no woodshed. There are no conveniences for boys or girls. It is very cold at times. The school was dismissed for three days. Miles Brown brought all the water from his house. It would freeze in the bucket though it was near the fireplace. There is no teacher's desk or chair. No blackboard or erazer. The books were not enough for all and most were tore. The pupils were seventeen with an attendance of twelve. The big boys took my bell so I could not call them in. There were only nine had slates. The boys made a loud noise by scratching on the slates with pencils.

" 'My uncle brought me here in his slay. I do not care to come back. Eliza Bunker.' "

Christina threw back her head and laughed. "Tremendous," she said. "Eliza Bunker at fifteen and a quarter was a girl of spirit. Know anything else about her?"

"I'm not sure, but I think I remember some Bunkers went west. Eighteen thirty-eight—I wouldn't be surprised. If they had sheep—and many farmers had large flocks then—they would have been driven out in forty, when Australian wool began to bring prices down so low they couldn't survive. Yes, I think the Bunkers got up and left.

49

That took gumption too. I've often wished the Lock-harts had. We stayed—and look at us now!"

This was Ellen's characteristic tone, and Christina paid no attention.

"It must have been a different schoolhouse. When was ours built? It only had one room—no conveniences, as she says."

"But the boys still teased by scratching on their slates when I was a girl. Yes, I guess our schoolhouse was built after the Civil War—must have been."

"Good heavens," Christina murmured, "how hard it is to imagine oneself back in time—a little over a hundred years ago and the stark poverty of that school!" She gave a grim smile. "Jem would say that's how they made men, I suppose."

"Learning by rote from ignorant teachers."

"Yet boys did go on to Exeter and Dartmouth—even Harvard. And some girls got to seminaries, I expect. I'm always amazed at how many lawyers came out of this town."

But this did not surprise Ellen. "We're born and raised feuding and squabbling and going to law about fences, dogs, road agents, heaven knows! I sometimes think we keep alive by fighting in this town. There's nothing much else to do in winter."

Christina smiled and listened, for Ellen was looking out at the mountain, and she clearly had more on her mind to say.

"It's different up here," she sighed.

"How?"

"I always have noticed it up here—more space—the mountain—you go to Europe and come back."

"Yes," Christina said, "we can move around, I suppose—" but she was shy of this subject. It made her feel sad and oppressed to think of all that she had. Sad, too, that years ago when they were young girls, before she went off to college, she had imagined taking Ellen to Europe with her. Then life had swept them off on its strong tides, Ellen into marriage with her inferior, Christina into Boston society, into a whole other world. However dear they were to each other—and heaven knows they had shared a lot of grief over the years—there were barriers that even love could not cross.

Ellen had been thinking her own thoughts. "I can see Rufus now, chewing his cud of rage, sitting cramped up in the winter, not enough to do outdoors, building up a grudge against someone until he felt he had to go to law about it."

"I wonder what made him such a punishing man. It was hard on you, Ellen. I know it was." Christina reached over and wanted to take Ellen's hand in hers, but she couldn't do it. Pride held Ellen together, and pride forbade a certain kind of warmth that came easy to Christina.

"No fool like an unyielding woman, and I wouldn't yield." She frowned. "A lot of it was my own fault, Christina. I see that now."

"It sometimes seems to me we learn everything too late, so what the hell's the use of it?" Christina said passionately.

"Nick thinks about his father a lot. Seems as if Rufus had grown in Nick's mind and kind of towers there now. It's strange."

But this was more than Ellen had meant to say and she got up. "Must get back and get that boy's dinner."

And she was off and away, a slight, tense figure, half running down the road and out of sight among the hemlocks, while Christina leaned against one of the pillars of the porch and watched her go, feeling that loneliness of spirit before what has to be accepted, full of suffering and wrong though it might be.

There had been little tenderness in Ellen's marriage, most of the time a cold war between a proud woman and a difficult, passionate man. In the last years Rufus had not been likable even to people outside the family—surly, with a chip on his shoulder. He had done some work for Cornelius on the place, but with an ill grace, skimped on the work and overcharged. Yet Christina remembered the way he handled his horses; the patience came out there, the real caring that he never had been able to show his wife or his children. Ellen must have done a lot of thinking to say what she had just said—remarkable Ellen!

"Cornelius!" she called, with a sudden need to reaffirm what could be reaffirmed here and now. And she walked quickly through the dark hall, past the huge umbrella-stand bear the grandchildren loved, and into the oak-paneled library where Cornelius sat exercising his paralyzed right hand slowly and patiently.

"You're so good, darling," she said, stooping to kiss him.

51

He gave her a quizzical glance.

"You must be starved, but Ellen turned up with a staggering letter she had found about what the school here was like in 1838—and we talked. It will only take a second to heat up the soup."

Before she went out to the kitchen, Christina lifted a heavy log and laid it on the fire.

"Wish I could do that for you," Cornelius said.

"Nonsense, keeps the old woman limber." And off she ran to the kitchen, laid out orange linen napkins on the two trays, and the old Carbone pottery bowls and plates, and slipped English muffins into the toaster. "There," she said to herself, "a little feast for two old lovers."

Happiness welled up in her while she worked. How lucky I have been, she thought, how lucky I am! What was fatigue and the ache in her knee compared to being here together, at this very moment, she and Cornelius, with more than fifty years of companionship behind them. Yet, she thought, buttering the muffins, it's not the past. What is precious is *now*. And she hurried because she could hardly wait to be sitting by his side, there was so much to tell him! She poured two glasses of milk, looked around to be sure she had everything, and went out with the tray.

There was an unspoken agreement between them that it was better to have their meals like this, looking at the fire, than opposite each other at the big table—it made Cornelius less self-conscious, and spared her the anguish of watching his clumsy efforts to get a spoon into his mouth.

"You're so much better, darling—it's like a miracle!" she said when she was settled on the little green-velvet sofa with her tray. "How did you ever learn to be so patient, impatient man?"

"You learn what you have to learn, I guess."

"Some people can't. Just butt their heads against the wall."

There was a pause while Cornelius got down some soup, and Christina, ravenous after the morning's work, ate and drank greedily. Then he said, "Seems as if I've seen more just sitting here than I ever did in my life— that mountain when I wake up. . . ." Their bedroom faced west.

"We've always been so busy. It's good *not* to be. I had

52

a marvelous morning planting those bulbs—just pure heaven!"

She laid her tray down and lit a cigarette and swung her feet up on the sofa to rest her knee.

"You know, Cornelius, I'm glad we never did anything to the Ark."

"Like what?" he grumbled, already on the defensive.

"Well, you know, like painting the walls white or something. It's dark, and some people, I'm sure, think it's gloomy. But it's a lair. It's ourselves. The children would hate to have it changed."

"Children, I have noticed, are conservative when it comes to their parents."

"When I first married you I wanted to change it. I thought when your parents died I'd make it mine. Now I'm glad we didn't," she said, looking into the fire. "Cornelius, let's stay. Let's not go back to town."

"Ever?" He raised his eyebrows and laughed.

"I've always wanted to spend a winter here—a whole year—have all the seasons—not move. Can't we?"

"Dr. Paine—we'll ask him."

"Yes, he may want you in the hospital for therapy now and then, but we could take you down easily and come back."

"We'll see," Cornelius murmured.

He was half asleep, and Christina tiptoed out with the trays, covered him with a steamer rug, and stooped down to kiss his hand.

Christina's Journal—*November 1*

Cornelius is sleeping. Somehow I want to go on thinking about him. I feel Cornelius deeply these days. Haven't I always? Yes, but these past years we have each been tired and nervy, devoured by our separate lives—all that work I did for the Civil Liberties Union, and the increased responsibility Cornelius has had at the bank. We met on the wing, and (it seems to me) in Boston went out far too much for our own good, the everlasting dinner parties with their hours of effervescent wit and intelligence that leave one starved in a queer way at the end, and tired the next morning. Of course Cornelius is passionate about his work. Deprived of it for any length of time, he would feel himself half a man. Whereas I would so gladly give up the Civil Liberties Union and everything and spend my old age gardening and reading and seeing real old friends like Ellen. Ellen? Many people, even here in Willard, must think our friendship an oddity. Maybe its very quality lies in the fact that it remains outside social life. It has never become dissipated in *les politesses*. We see each other always at the marrow of our lives— not even the general talk about books read or about politics enters in, or so very little. It is life itself that concerns us as friends. How wise my father was to ship me off to the Lockharts when I was eleven! Probably I might have had a breakdown, but in that wonderful year I was allowed to go my own way, and was enriched beyond words by being part of that family. As I look back over my life, the memory of that year shines with a special light. It seems as if I remembered every single thing that ever happened, from bringing in the pumpkins from the big field to sugaring off. Ellen's mother took me in as one of her own. I miss her still—her quietness and her strength. Ellen has a little of this atmosphere, especially when she is sewing there in the window. I catch a glimpse of her mother in her hands. But Ellen is tart where her mother was sweet—sweet as a good apple. Ellen has been battered by life—bloodied. She has had to grow tough to survive. When I think of my years of college and roving around Europe as a girl, while she was trying to stick it out with her difficult, miserable Rufus, an unhappy man by nature, who "never got a break," as he was fond of saying himself! Why did she marry him? To get away from home, even though home was a good place to be? Or did she get caught after a dance on a night of full moon?—this is one thing I could never ask. But I have wondered. So many marriages in this town take place after the event, to give a child a father. And then the best has to be made of a poor bargain for the next fifty years.

And now it happens every day—in the best families, too. I do worry about Robin and his undisciplined, self-indulgent ways. Those bright, hungry eyes! Probably every granny in the world has said the same about a grandson or granddaughter, and I am not going to indulge myself in the poor old game of deploring the world of the young.

No, I want to think about my darling Cornelius. The sweetness of marriages that last and grow, as ours has. When we first married I was selfish and demanding without even being aware of it. Heavens, how narcissistic young women are! I am ashamed even to think of it now, but I really did look down on Cornelius as such a "square." I was always trying to change him then. Now I wouldn't change him for the world. I love him as he is; his old-fashioned ways seem doubly precious because they are becoming so rare. The intensity of his friendships with his men friends—his loyalty to the Tavern, to Harvard, and the totally unexpected largeness of his political views after the depression, when he became such an ardent supporter of Roosevelt! His feeling about France that really goes too deep for words—this is one thing the children cannot understand.

The other day it came to me as a shock that I had never really *looked* at Cornelius—we have become so much a part of each other, like the two trunks of a tree that branch out from the same root. But since his stroke I have wanted so much to paint his portrait. It is a magnificent head—his eyes set so deep under that open, wide brow, the big, generous mouth—generous and firm, and, above all, the way his head is set on his shoulders. He has grown a little jowly, but it suits him. Heaviness suits him. It becomes his kind of wisdom, never quick or flashy, but grown out of a rocklike belief in the old virtues of honesty, loyalty, scrupulous attention to any responsibility within his ken. —There I go again! As if there were a kind of wisdom within my ken but not within his, arrogant old woman that I am. Or is it only that the wisdom of women has a different source from that of men? I wonder.

Cornelius is much less vulnerable than I. When he looks in the mirror what he sees is that he needs a shave. What I see, with dismay, is the wrinkles around my eyes. I am appalled because I look like my own granny. But inside, the person I really am has no relation to this mask age is slowly attaching to my face. I feel so young, so exposed, under it. I simply cannot seem to learn to behave like the very old party I am. The young girl, arrogant, open, full of feelings she cannot analyze, longing to be told she is beautiful—that young girl lives inside this shell. And, God knows, age is hard on her.

I used to envy the old; I always imagined old age as a kind of heaven. It never occurred to me that my knee would ache all the time, or that I would fight a daily battle against being slowed down, that memory would begin to fail, and all the rest. The young cannot imagine what it is to be fighting a battle that cannot be won. One keeps death at bay, but it is always there, and sometimes it draws very near, as it did for Cornelius. Then we know —we both knew—that we must live every moment to its brim of love and joy, from now on in.

Cornelius has always been a better loser than I. He can lose with grace. I still mind frightfully when he beats me at Scrabble!

CHAPTER 4

The Websters spent the last weekend before they closed up their house for the winter not only putting up storm windows and pine branches over the garden but taking time out to pay a call on Eben Fifield one Saturday afternoon. It had been Cornelius's suggestion that Eben was the man to see. Christina, acting as interpreter for her husband, explained on the telephone why Cornelius felt him to be the best source of information on the subject of summer people.

Eben had been born in Willard. His father had been a farmer, farming inherited land, as his father had done before him. He himself went out into the world, starting as a lawyer and ending up with his finger in a good many pies. He had had something to do with rural electrification, had later invested in electronics, had become an international salesman for a coming firm, and from there had even ventured into diplomacy, when he had been an adviser to Conant in Germany. But he had never lost his love for Willard. And now in his old age he had come here to live with a housekeeper in the old family place. There had been rumors that he was writing a history of the town, but no one had heard much about this for years, and it was presumed that he had felt it beyond his strength, or given it up for one reason or another. "At any rate, you can't fail to enjoy Eben. He's a character," Christina ended her briefing.

The Websters had been so busy reclaiming their own place that, after five summers, they still were discovering new parts of the town hidden away among the hills. The center of Willard looked extraordinarily rural and modest, as if perhaps a dozen families made up the whole population. Actually, there were two or three hundred houses scattered about in the woods, over by the pond lined with summer cottages, and up dirt roads. A stranger would imagine these roads led nowhere, certainly not to the wide variety of large houses, modern cabins, and small farms that helped bring the taxed families to around four hundred, about a third of whom were summer people.

Sally and Tim set off in fine spirits to discover Mr. Fifield, following Christina's directions to climb up past the cemetery and past the Chapman place and then take the third dirt road on the right and be careful of rocks, but keep going up to a high field, and then they would see the Fifield place just over the crest, a white farmhouse with a big white barn attached to it. "Classic," Christina had said, "even to the two huge elms in front planted by Eben's great-grandfather when he built the house in 1800 or so."

Tim was too busy navigating up the road, when they found it, to speak. Once a rock flew up and hit with a terrifying noise.

"No car that takes this road can afford a soft underbelly, I guess."

"Mr. Fifield drives a Land Rover," Sally explained.

The maple leaves had fallen here, and it was sometimes hard to see the rocks under that thick gold and red carpet.

"We could stop and walk the rest of the way," she suggested, but Tim would not accept such a humiliation, and anyway they were up on the field now, driving across cut hay.

"There! There's the mountain! Doesn't it look splendid from here?"

"And there's the house, and Mr. Fifield waving."

"You made it!" Mr. Fifield said, shaking Sally's hand, then Tim's. "The road was not built for these grand low-slung beasts. In winter I'm snowed in here once in a while for forty-eight hours. The road agent would like to see me go to Boston in winter—he tries to persuade me it would be good for my health."

Mr. Fifield, six feet tall, looked down on Sally with a twinkle in his eye. It was the eye of a man who enjoyed a pretty woman and was not ashamed to show his pleasure.

"Come in. Things are not quite as they were when Olive was alive, but Mrs. Goodnow does the best she can, and I'm lucky to have her. I'll lead the way."

The Websters followed the tall figure through a front parlor to a much larger study at the back, paneled in soft brown unpainted pine where it was not lined with books to the ceiling. A wood fire burned in the huge fireplace.

"This was the kitchen in the old days, as you can see —they did the cooking in this fireplace in my great-grandmother's time. Now it's my study. You'll just have to pretend you don't see the mess," he said, turning a lamp out over his desk, piled high with letters, open boxes, magazines, with a small leather elephant raising his trunk at one end, and with other *bibelots*. "Do sit down, Mrs. Webster. First we'll talk and then Mrs. Goodnow will provide drinks. She's not very good at tea, but I presume you will have no objection to bourbon or scotch when the time comes. —Well, now . . ."

Eben Fifield turned to Tim, who was sitting beside his wife on a small sofa. Sally had the impression that Olive must have put her feet up on the sofa while her husband read in the wing chair opposite. The house had the aura still of a feminine presence—the presence, no doubt, that looked down on them from a portrait over the mantel, a pretty woman in a white dress, the eyes in shadow, looking out from under a wide summer hat.

"Yes, that's Olive, my wife. Not a good portrait really —she was as hard to catch as a firefly, and the painter, an Italian, was rather too obvious for his subject. Still, if you half close your eyes you get a glimpse . . . elusive person . . . I'm talking to you like old friends. Grand to be old," he said, rubbing his hands together. "There don't have to be any preliminaries—there isn't time. So let's get down to business. I gather Jem is marshaling his forces and has been lucky enough to get hold of you two. Just what is this plan? He's an old loon, of course. Hasn't the foggiest idea what history is—thinks it's lists and dates."

"He seems to be very busy getting all the bodies in the cemetery listed," Tim said, responding to the sly smile.

"History in depth, eh?" Eben laughed a short boyish laugh. He gave an impression of enjoying life immensely, and the Websters laughed with him. "What is your function then? What place are you to take in this monument to Jem's illusions?"

Sally had often felt in these last years that one of the fascinating things about Willard was that every time you talked to a different person you got a different view. It was like turning a kaleidoscope in your hands.

"He has asked us to do a chapter about summer people. Christina Chapman is doing a chapter on the women of Willard and Ellen Comstock a chapter about schools."

"Well, one thing to be said for Jem, he has got onto the fact that women have always run the town and they might as well write the history—begging your pardon, Mr. Webster."

"Not at all," Tim said, but he was not exactly amused.

"I understand you're a lawyer."

"Yes, sir."

"Mmm . . ." Eben leaned his head back against the back of his chair and looked at the pair before him. "The big thing, of course, is point of view—what you really have in mind to say."

"How can we know till we've found out a great deal more? We've only been here five years, Mr. Fifield."

"Yes, that gives you an enormous advantage. You have not been disillusioned yet. You are still, I presume, in the early stages of a love affair. You will see some things that someone like me will never see, just because I know too much. My guess is that the summer people and Willard have been a fruitful alliance but a prickly one, sort of like a good marriage—we have all known some—that works although always on the point of divorce."

"It's hard to divorce yourself from a piece of property once you own it," Tim said quietly. "I must say I have nothing to complain of—except the taxes," he added with a laugh.

"So as a summer person yourself, Mr. Webster, are you saying that what Willard means to you is a piece of property?"

"Oh no," Sally said quickly. "It's being part of a rural world. That's why we came. We fell in love with the village itself. It feels as if here things are still human somehow. Don't you agree, Tim?"

"I guess so, yes."

"Your husband does not seem to have quite your fervor about the rural world," Eben needled with a twinkle in his eyes.

60

Sally had hardly heard the interruption.

"I wanted the children to have a place where they could be rooted. We've moved six times in our marriage. I wanted somewhere they would know would always be there, and for grandchildren eventually. You do agree with that, Tim?"

"Oh yes. But we really haven't come here to tell Mr. Fifield about ourselves but to ask him to tell us about Willard. I gather that Boston people began to come up here by the early nineties. Am I right?"

"About then—and they came first as boarders, you know. There must have been some idea about fresh air for the children—the summer camp did not exist at that time. So people either went to Europe, which was the usual thing, or they found some farmer to take them in as boarders. The father often came only on weekends, and there were splendid Friday expeditions to meet the Boston train from which the fathers descended coal-black from the soot, in stiff collars and black coats."

"How vivid you make it!" Sally exclaimed. "Do go on."

"I wanted to write the history of Willard myself, you see." And for the first time Eben Fifield put off his genial mask and looked serious.

"Why didn't you?" Sally asked.

"Oh"—Eben shrugged it off—"that's a long story. Indolence, I wouldn't be surprised . . . and Olive's death . . . a lot of things." But now he leaned forward with a new intentness, his hands clasped round one knee. "I'll be honest with you. The more you dig the worse everything becomes. I chickened out."

"You mean you learn things you can't tell?" Timothy ventured.

"Yes, I suppose you might put it that way. In a philosophical sense one might put it that people who live in a climate like this, in a run-down economy like this (it really ceased to function after the Civil War), people who exist on the edge of nowhere, have to live by illusions and dreams. There isn't any present for these towns, so the people in them tend to build up an imagined great past and live in and on that. Jem is a perfect example. His notion of what life was like here in the eighteenth and nineteenth centuries has about as much relation to the realities as a TV Western—the legend of the good craftsman, for instance. Look at the way people handle tools

61

in this town—leave them out to rust, let them break down, throw them away, and then"— Eben Fifield laughed sardonically—"go out and dig in the old rubbish heaps to extract a few old drug bottles, which are sold as priceless antiques!"

"But the bottles are interesting," Sally said. "After all, there were early factories around here. I don't see what's wrong with that."

"If you begin to worship the past, every item has value, especially, perhaps, the items that show your ancestors were a going concern." But this was off the surface of Mr. Fifield's mind obviously, and he laughed it off. "You will think I am being unfair. I just have an idea that the real men around here got out. It's painful to walk these woods and see the old stone walls everywhere, marking what was cleared land a hundred years ago."

"It has a lonely sort of feeling," Sally assented.

"Life has been too hard, you see. It has taken the juice out, generation after generation. Jem *is* right when he talks about self-reliance, I suppose. A hundred years ago a man, a farmer, had hundreds of skills that have gone now—from building a good chimney to breaking in a team of oxen, to making his own tools, shoes, and snowshoes."

"Where did the men go?" Tim asked.

"West, or to the cities." Eben smiled. "Now they go to Florida for the winter and live in trailers. All I am trying to get at in this roundabout way is that the summer people saved the economy, and without them God knows how this area could have survived. When you depend on the rich to keep you afloat—well, it can cause a certain resentment."

"We haven't felt any resentment, have we, Tim?"

"Oh, it doesn't surface. It's there, though. I don't suppose there's ever been a society in which the poor didn't resent the rich, has there?"

"But surely people like the Chapmans have built themselves in," Sally murmured. "Christina is such a warm person."

"Oh, she's a jewel, that woman. But Cornelius's father, old Judge Chapman, who built that enormous place and the stables and rode out in a carriage and pair long after he had two automobiles, just because he enjoyed the dirt roads and said automobiles puked the air (how right he was, by the way)—I think perhaps he was resented at first, and then the town got to be proud of him. He was the town aristo. Yes, they have been absorbed. I think one could say that. And there are others. A lot of professors settled here for the summers—Jameses, people like them. They fitted in right away. They had the Bostonian contempt for ostentation. They were as tight with their money as the natives, and went around in old corduroys and battered duck hats and sneakers." Eben looked amused. "Why, when I was a boy only the locals looked washed—it was rather non-U not to look like a tramp."

He pulled himself to his feet and called, "Mrs. Goodnow, about time we had a drink," and as Mrs. Goodnow, looking very respectable in a flowered print, her gray hair piled up on her head, came to the door, she was introduced, and Eben asked her, "What are your opinions about summer people, Mrs. Goodnow? The Websters here are writing a chapter for Jem about them."

Mrs. Goodnow was not to be drawn. She pursed her mouth. "Same as anybody else. Some are decent. Some aren't. Some drink. Some don't. Some's honest. Some ain't. What shall I bring in, Mr. Fifield?"

"Oh, the usual—ice . . . and glasses . . . peanuts if you find any around. We'll take it from there.

"Mrs. Goodnow thinks I'm going to hell because I drink a half a bottle of scotch during the evening. I tell her an old man has the privilege to do what he damn well pleases as long as the only person hurt is himself."

"It can't be easy to find a housekeeper," Sally said. "Doesn't she get lonely?"

"Her family is over in Marlow—a half hour's drive. And then she was fond of Olive. Olive saw to it that she, then Molly Badger, got through high school. Helped with school clothes, that sort of thing. When her husband got killed at the sawmill, she came here to work. We're bound together by a long past, Mrs. Webster."

"So you see, it does happen."

"Yes, but don't forget I'm the local boy who made good. I'm one of theirs." He sighed.

"You *should* write the history!" Sally said warmly as he took the tray of glasses from Mrs. Goodnow and brought out two bottles from a cupboard by the fireplace, and for a moment the talk was interrupted while glasses were filled.

Eben stood then with his back to the fire, the glass in his hand. He took a long swallow, as if it were medicine—medicine that he needed, and looked out past his guests through the windows opposite to a clump of white birch and the open field.

"The autumn light," he said then, "heartbreaking. The thing is that when you get to be as old as I am you do a lot of thinking. You have splendid long meditations . . . but when it comes to doing"—he smiled down at them without bitterness—"you just ain't got any gimp, as Mrs. Goodnow would say."

"Jem should have asked you to do this chapter," Tim ventured. "We are babes in the wood. It's going to be a mess. Couldn't you be a secret agent?"

"I'd get you into trouble."

"Oh, please do," Sally begged. She felt that at last they were close to getting inside all they had been outside of for five years.

"No, seriously," Eben said, "I couldn't do that to Jem. He's chosen his writers with a definite end in view. This is to be a sunny celebration of ancient virtue and good citizenship as exemplified by the dear little town of Willard. You know that as well as I do."

"But—" Sally hesitated, then decided to venture, "there is a lot to be said about Willard, even if it is a kind of failed town, as you think. I mean, people live here, and it seems to me the life has *quality*. Isn't that partly why the summer people came, back there in the nineties? And now it's more precious, because rarer than it was then."

"Plenty of oddities to laugh about." But Eben sensed that he had gone too far. "No . . . seriously . . . what is this 'quality'? In what does it consist, would you say, Mrs. Webster?"

"I wish you'd call me Sally."

"Very well"—and Eben gave a slight bow—"Sally, my dear."

"Partly that people here have a contact with animals, trees, nature itself. In a city Old Pete would be a derelict sleeping under a bridge. Here—"

"He's a derelict too."

"Maybe, but hunting with Flicker he looks like his own man."

"Oh, he's his own man all right. Only works when he craves a six-pack . . . lives off the dump . . . there's quality!"

Eben sat down again, nursing his drink.

"I've been distressing your wife, Mr. Webster, with my cynicism—and she is quite right. I'm critical because I love the old town. When I first came back with Olive, when she knew she had cancer, I decided we would go through that here, together. When a man brings his wife home to die, you know that's really home and no other place in the world would do. I suppose what eats into me is to see so much potential going to waste. Poor education even now—not enough to nourish. I see the young men get caught with some girl and settle for a laborer's job, hunt, fish, do a little inept carpentering, and buy themselves a trailer. The challenge has gone out of life here for the young."

"It's just so much better than a city slum," Sally said.

"And there *are* human relationships that have some depth between people of different sorts. Christina and Ellen Comstock have been friends for fifty years or more by now. And maybe that brings us back to the summer people. There's no doubt that they got a hell of a lot in exchange for their money. *That* I am ready to grant."

There was a subtle change in the atmosphere, partly the dark creeping in, partly a change in the old man's mood, and Tim exchanged a look with his wife, which she caught as meaning it might be time to go. Still, they couldn't get up and leave with a half-finished drink in their hands.

"I haven't really helped you, have I? It takes a while to warm up to the subject—for me, I mean—these days. And then I suppose I stand somewhere in between. I'm with the summer people when they fight against hardtopping these lovely back roads—they want to be able to ride. The natives want to be able to get plowed out in winter. But I'm with the natives when a group of rich men get together and buy up the best beach on the lake for their own purposes—because I used to swim there when I was a boy. The joke is that, on the whole, the summer people want the past and the natives want to put up trailers, shops, God knows what, because it will bring money in. They want speedboats. It's Jem that cares about the past and the natives probably won't even show up for his celebrations. They want motor-cycle scrambles, rock-and-roll instead of folk dances—you know . . ."

"I begin, I think, to get an idea about what our point of view might be—a sort of balance sheet of profits and losses on both sides," Tim Webster said, stroking his chin.

"Yes, and then that balance sheet has to be brought alive through individual stories. That's where your wife comes in. Am I right?"

Tim laughed. "I'm no writer, except of briefs—true."

"Was your father a farmer, Mr. Fifield?" Sally asked shyly. "It looks like you have a lot of land."

"Yes, my dad farmed. He did it well—intelligently, I mean. Made experiments with Scotch Highlander cattle, for instance. But he never made any money, and of his six children only I have come back to live here. None of us boys would have gotten out as we did without the help of old Judge Chapman. He lent me the money to go to Harvard, lent us all money."

"He must have been a wonderful man."

"Yes"—Eben hesitated—"he was. But . . . now here's one of the things wrong with us natives. We resented his help. I have to confess that we did. He smoked these long cigars—let's say he lacked the common touch. He wanted us to do well. And we did (paid him back with interest—that impressed the old boy!), but . . . well . . . he never forgave me because I didn't go all out for Woodrow Wilson. And I guess we never forgave them for posting their land."

"You mean against hunters?" Tim asked. "I've wondered about that. We thought of doing it on our place."

"I wouldn't. The natives take it ill. Somehow or other they feel hunting just about anywhere is their right. Take it away and . . . well . . . you set yourself up somehow against freedom of movement through the woods."

"Didn't Judge Chapman know that?"

"Oh, he knew all right! But he wanted to keep his hunting for himself."

"And I suppose it can be dangerous. I mean if a lot of people are roving around in one's woods with guns."

"Oh yes, he might have been afraid one of his horses would get shot. They come from out of state, crazy people, with expensive cars and expensive guns and shoot at anything that moves—dogs, cats, cows. So, I suppose, one could reason that he posted out of self-protection. Still, it didn't go down well. And the natives have gone out of their way to hunt his woods."

"Heavens, Sally, what a lot we don't know!"

"Yes, well . . ." Eben smiled his secret smile, taking them in, not shutting them out. "It's like a finely woven web of interaction, a town like this. You never can see

66

the whole till you can get hold of all the parts, all the different places where the web is attached, and where it can be broken—has been broken—sometimes for good. People have long memories around here."

"You've been awfully kind, Mr. Fifield, but I'm afraid you've scared us pretty well out of our wits about writing anything down that could be called history," Tim said.

"Oh, you'll sort it all out. Sooner or later a pattern will emerge."

"Anyway," Sally said, getting to her feet, "we'll learn a lot, that's sure. I think it's going to be fun. It's been great fun to meet you, Mr. Fifield. You've given us a memorable afternoon."

"Bent your ears back," Eben said cheerfully, "but I have to try to believe that's what you came for."

He led the way, turning on lights in the hall and at the front door. "The nights are closing in—that's the worst of it. Won't begin to get better till after Christmas."

"I wish we could stay," Sally called back just before getting into the car. "We're leaving tomorrow, till spring."

"And then the hibernating bears will come out to welcome you. So long!"

Eben watched the tail lights disappear over the crest of the hill, then turned the lights off and went back to his study.

"Made a fool of myself," he thought. "Old men should listen, but the fact is they almost never do. Unlicked cubs, those two, but charming—charming. She especially. He's a bit of a stuffed shirt."

He poured himself a drink and sat down again. This was still the hard time of day—the time when dark closed in and he missed Olive.

"Did I talk too much?" he asked the elusive face in the portrait over the mantel. Then, suddenly impatient, he called out, "Where's the old man's supper, Mrs. Goodnow?"

He was not going to let himself go down the long, dangerous, winding path of memory tonight.

CHRISTINA'S JOURNAL—*November 9*

The Websters stopped in on their way back from seeing Eben, Sally all aglow with the good and informative time they had had, Tim a little cautious, I thought. I should go up and see Eben myself—he'll be able to tell me just where to look for that Civil War stuff about the women who got together and lived at the Town Farm. I've always felt that the strength of the women in Willard stemmed from that experience. They found they could do all the men had done and survive. But what happened when the men came back? That's the real story. But I guess it will never be told. It seems to me that Eben's great-grandmother was one of them—could she have been? He might even have a journal. Jem has no idea what a hornet's nest he is parceling out—or a Pandora's box. I must say it's an ideal way for me to spend the winter, if only we can stay here! Cornelius will feel awfully cut off, I'm afraid, but we could get some of the bank people up here surely. He made immense strides in the first two months. Now we have reached a plateau. I don't see much change lately. He can just manage to eat by himself, but it is awfully hard for him to walk even a few steps. I feel he is afraid of falling. He leans on me very hard, one hand on my shoulder, and it's like carrying a ton of bricks. The old knee doesn't like it one bit. Getting him up to bed is a major operation. Sometimes I wonder if I could ask Mamzelle to come back and be with us.—Idiot! She's much too old. It is so hard to imagine, but she must be nearing ninety.

She complains dreadfully of my not being in Boston, and I should somehow get down to see her one of these days. But how? Would Ellen come and hold the fort? I am simply not allowed by life at this point to be old or to give in, in any way, and I suppose that is a very good thing. The time when there was always Mamzelle to lean on, and Papa and Mamma—that's all gone. It seems so strange. Now everyone leans on me, and I'm rather like the leaning tower of Pisa—apparently neither it nor I will ever be allowed to crumble, just stand up in a dangerous crooked way and hope for the best!

It is strange, but I feel some reluctance about going up to Eben. God knows we are old enough to be beyond the point where we can either hurt or move each other in the way we once did. I know he is lonely without Olive. What holds me back? Twenty years ago Cornelius might have minded. But now? No, that is not it. It is that there has always been strain, bitterness I suppose, on his side—long before I entered Cornelius's family, long before Eben ever saw me. His relation to old Judge Chapman was so complex—admiration and contempt, perhaps on both sides. Eben was so ambitious at one time, ruthless. "That boy plays to win, but he doesn't know how to lose," I can remember Judge Chapman saying one day when Cornelius beat Eben at tennis and Eben broke his racket in a rage. But of course Judge Chapman didn't know what was really involved—the burning sense of inferiority because of me, and the will to triumph.

"You have to take it all, don't you?" Eben said, and Cornelius answered, "Yes, if I can. Why not?"

It was cruel, I must admit. Those two could never possibly understand each other. Eben despised Cornelius as a man born with it all easy, and Cornelius despised Eben as a man who (in Cornelius's terms) was not a gentleman.

Lucky for him that he met Olive, and late enough so that he was sure of himself and did not need to torture her as he tortured me. I complain about being old, but God knows I am glad not to be young! The young are not afraid enough of lighting dangerous fires. When I think of the risks I took! The young never foresee what feeling is going to cost. It is there like champagne to drink down—and like champagne, catches up before one is quite aware of what is happening. I came very close to falling in love with Eben—so close that I could never tell Cornelius, even now.

But I married into my own world, and that was right for me.

Now the strange thing time accomplishes is that Eben is (at least most people would think so) of my world. He "made it" as they say. What goes on about all that now in his subtle, conflicted, bitter mind? What did he tell the Websters? I felt suddenly shy when Sally talked about him—his charm, his wisdom. Eben wise? Yet there is no doubt that he was a splendid selectman, one of the best the town has ever had. No wonder he was re-elected, and would have been for a third term but for his own wish to resign. That, I think, was the first time Eben ever resigned power by his own wish. Yes, I would like to talk to him now. What is it that holds me back?

CHAPTER 5

November was the hardest month for Ellen because the shooting made Nick terribly anxious. She could hear him stirring around before daylight, keeping watch for the groups of hunters who occasionally gathered on the village green to go out in a posse. When such a group turned up, he was dressed and out without even a cup of coffee, and disappeared as soon as he got an idea where they might be bound. Ellen was afraid someone might notice how queer her son had become about hunting and hunters, but luckily Nick was not a talker, fled at the approach of a stranger, and kept his mouth shut on the rare occasions when he had to do an errand for her at the village store. And luckily he knew every brook and trail and rock, every hollow and rise, within an area of five square miles. He had hunted it all himself— hunted hedgehogs and rabbits, woodchucks and squirrels, since he was a boy, and when Rufus was alive he and the boy had hunted deer, coons, and bobcats, but that was before the war and before whatever happened to Nick had happened out there in the Pacific islands.

By mid-November Ellen felt some relief—the open season was almost over. In a week or so "they" would be out of the woods. She smiled at her little joke as she bent to her sewing.

On weekends Nick left at dawn and didn't come home till dark—stuffed a sandwich in his pocket and went off, silent, absorbed as an Indian scout. Sometimes he came home flushed and ravenous and said, "Well, I got some men from New York way off the trail of a buck, and they didn't have the sense to know there were does just up the rise in a little hollow of hemlock, and that the buck had been leading them off." At such times Ellen said nothing but gave him an extra helping of stew and held her peace.

Some years back she had tried to reason with him. "After all, Nick, hunting is limited, and people need the meat. We can't be overrun with deer, either."

He had left the table, and his pie half eaten, and gone out. When he came back an hour later, he had thrown his cap down on the table and said quietly, "I know I'm crazy. But I can't stand the blood."

And then to Ellen's dismay he had sat down with his head in his hands and wept. She sat frozen in her chair, and picked up her sewing while he got hold of himself. She knew very well that a man's tears are no relief to him, unlike a woman's. They tear their way out of an open wound.

When Nick had got hold of himself, he said, "Have you ever seen a deer dying? Tears roll out of their eyes."

"It's all right, Nick. I understand," she had said. "But just don't tell anyone—they wouldn't."

"Another thing, Mother. The bucks draw the hunters off to protect their does. They're so much better than people." The very quietness of his tone was devastating.

Always Ellen had recoiled at the idea of what the talk would be down at the store—how Nick had come home from the war a sissy. Probably they thought it anyway. He was too gentle for his own good. And whatever we are told in church (Ellen was not a churchgoer), Nick's kind of gentleness was looked down on in a part of the world that liked to think of itself as still a sort of frontier. Rufus had talked enough about it. A good hunter was skillful, killed quickly and efficiently, never had to follow a trail of blood. To wound, not kill, was a crime. Nick had been brought up to that. They always had a deer hung up in the barn, and Ellen herself was partial to the meat. This attitude of Nick's wasn't quite normal. So this year Ellen was glad to be able to tell Nick how Cornelius felt, that he himself had decided to give up hunting. That was what Christina had told her that day when they got lost in the woods. It was somehow fortifying, for no one could say that Cornelius Chapman was a sissy!

71

"He'd better watch his woods, then," Nick had said.

"Oh, Nick, he can't—he can hardly walk since that stroke."

And she had seen the flicker in Nick's extraordinarily clear blue eyes, and guessed that a thought was slowly making its way down to the springs of action.

"Besides, his woods are posted, always have been."

Nick smiled. "Oh, Mother," he said, and shrugged his shoulders.

"Where are you off to? It's nearly suppertime."

"Just to have a little talk with Old Pete," he said, taking his father's rifle off the rack, and a handful of cartridges.

Ellen's needle flew in and out, in and out—a way of keeping nervous hands busy. She tried to set her mind on the schools and how to begin that essay. The first thing, she supposed, would be a list of all the teachers with dates. That's what Jem was after. But somehow today she couldn't seem to set her mind to anything, kept looking out the window. It was a Saturday just a week after the Websters had closed up, and more than one out-of-state car, filled with hunters in shiny orange or red jackets, went past. She kept an eye out for Nick and Old Pete, but maybe they had gone out the back way, if they did go.

Later on, she told herself, I'll go over to the library and see if Miss Plummer can dig out some school records for me. Might as well use up all this nervous energy doing something besides worrying. I'm a fool. After all, Nick had been rampaging around about hunting for years and nothing bad had ever happened. He kept his counsel, and what he did was his own business. And with Old Pete, anyway, he would be safe. Drunk or sober, Old Pete could be trusted, she had to grant him that. And he liked Nick because Nick was a listener and, God knows, Old Pete was a natural-born talker. In fact, she thought, smiling her thin smile, all Jem really needed to get a history of the town was a tape recorder and an indefinite number of cans of beer and let Old Pete talk for days till he had talked out all he knew.

"No time to be going. Too late," Pete had said first, coming to his door, unshaven, his eyes red. "I haven't even had my supper, man. You come in here and we'll see."

72

"I saw a New York car go up the hill two hours ago. Please, Pete."

Pete gave the tall man at his door a shrewd look.

"What ails you, Nick?"

Nick scratched his head and frowned.

"Nothing. I just don't want to see Cornelius Chapman's deer butchered."

Old Pete chuckled.

"It wouldn't hurt Cornelius."

But then he saw a queer light in Nick's eyes, just a flicker. It came and went. And something told him not to bait Nick. The only anger to fear is the anger of a gentle man.

"I'll go alone," Nick said, and turned away.

"Oh, hang on—don't be in such a rush." And it was agreed that they would go together. Nick refused to come in. Coming in, as he knew from experience, would mean being shown around this cozy palace of Old Pete's and listening to a long, rambling talk. He waited outside, smoking, watching Flicker bark excitedly at a squirrel.

The trouble was that, slow as Nick's own pace was usually, he had been feeling so nervous and tuned up since the hunting season had begun that the half hour he waited was hard to bear. He lit one cigarette from another, and his hands were shaking—no way for a man with a rifle to behave. He called Flicker and rubbed the top of the dog's head, and that contact with an animal, a good animal, did help. When he let Flicker run again, the tension had flowed out.

But before they could get going, the shack still had to be locked, with Flicker inside, and this took a while. Old Pete thought he had the padlock in his pocket. He was always sure that someone would want to steal the treasures he picked up at the dump. He behaved like a miser who has money hidden under his mattress. The padlock was not in his pocket, so he went in and looked, and finally Nick found it, fallen to the ground and hidden under a piece of iron pipe. One thing about Old Pete was that he would not be hurried. "All in good time" was his favorite phrase.

At last they set forth, each with a rifle, Old Pete having borrowed some shot from Nick, and slowly, at Old Pete's pace, they climbed the hill toward the Chapmans', while he kept up a steady stream of talk. He noticed a striped maple.

"Darned if I knew that was there. Best wood for whistles. Know that? Whistlewood we used to call it. I could make one to call Flicker."

And a little farther on, he asked Nick to hold his horses. The fact was that Old Pete was short of breath, so they sat down on a stone wall and watched a chipmunk dart back and forth, chattering.

"We must be sitting on his hole. Mad as a cow in spring. Listen to that!"

All this time Nick said nothing, nor did he seem to be listening exactly. He was simply waiting—waiting for whatever it was that held his imagination, caught and beating its wings like a bird caught in a net. He wiped the sweat from his upper lip. Inwardly he cursed himself for asking Old Pete along—why had he done such a fool thing? Well, if they got into trouble, it would be just as well to have a witness—that was one reason. But maybe the real reason was that Nick was scared—scared of himself and what he might do. It was like patrols in the army—two weren't as trigger-happy as one.

Now they had turned off the fork and were on a ridge, with Chapman land posted on both sides of the road. So far there had been no sign of the car with New York plates. But Nick kept his eyes open and pretty soon he saw the glint of metal down a grassy road that had been used for getting to a lumber lot but was all grown over now. There was no one to be seen around the car. Nick and Old Pete peered in the window.

"Wish I could get hold of that six-pack," Old Pete muttered as he noticed it on the floor.

"We're not thieves."

Luckily there could be no argument. The doors were locked.

"Well, what do we do now, Captain?"

"They'll have kept to the road unless they're crazy. It's nearly dark. You know that hollow just over the hill—hemlock. Stick by the old wall, you can't fail to find it. That's where I saw some does the other day. You go that way, and keep your eyes open for the crazies. And don't forget to load."

Darned if I ever heard Nick say so much in one breath, Old Pete thought as he started to go. He knew where the does were as well as Nick did.

"I'll go up the other way. If the hunters are around,

74

the buck will try to lead them off. There's a half hour to go. And my guess is they may overstay their welcome."

The two men disappeared like Indians into the shadowy trees, as soundless as ghosts. Nick breathed deeply the autumn earth smell, but he had to pay close attention to twigs underfoot and branches that stuck out and had to be lifted and crawled under. The woods were absolutely silent, told him nothing he needed to know. The crazies evidently knew enough to keep quiet, wherever they were. He felt his own breath like a roar in his chest and tried to subdue it, it sounded so loud. A twig snapped under his foot, and he jumped and nearly let his gun drop. Then he looked at his watch—just three minutes to go and whatever happened would be after five and outside the law. He stood absolutely still and listened. A beech leaf made a tiny flittering sound as it swung. It had been a dry fall.

Then, as loud as the silence had been a second before, there was a crackle and crash, the thud of hoofs, and two shots rang out. Nick plunged on into the hollow just over the crest from where he stood, and saw the doe stumble, struggle to her feet again; saw the blood on her right flank, and brought her down with a single shot to the heart.

"Pete!" he shouted. "Pete, where are you?"

"I don't know who Pete is, but that's my deer." A stout man in a flashy red cap and shiny red jacket came panting up to where the doe lay.

"You wounded it, you butcher. And that doe goes to the warden."

"Jack! Trigger! Where are you?" The man put his hands to his mouth and gave a yodel. He paid no attention to Nick, he was too excited.

"Coming!" A skinny young man with very black eyebrows came running, stumbled on a root and almost fell.

"Boy, you got it!" And he slapped the older man on the shoulder.

Just then Pete appeared, slow and silent, and stood beside Nick. "I saw it," he whispered.

"What's this all about? Who are you?" the man called Trigger said as he joined them. "Good work, Al," he said to the older man, and went over to the deer, knelt down to look her over.

"Stay away from that deer," Nick said quietly.

75

"Why should I? We brought it down. It's ours. I flushed her out and my buddy here, he got her."

But he scrambled to his feet and went back to his friends.

"It's ten minutes past five now. It was four minutes past when you shot her. We'll go after the warden."

"Hey, are you crazy?" the young man laughed. "What's five minutes?"

"Worth five bucks to you?" Trigger took out his wallet.

But he took one look at Nick's eyes and put it back. "Let's talk this over," Al said.

"Nothing to talk about," Nick said, very quiet. "You're caught, that's all. Old Pete saw you shoot. I saw the wounded deer. Also you happen to be on posted land. You're trespassing."

"Are we in Nazi Germany or what?" Trigger exchanged a half-amused, half-belligerent look with the two others. They were standing close together now, and Old Pete was standing just behind Nick.

"You're in New Hampshire, in case you don't know," Old Pete said drily. He was enjoying himself. For him it had been a game of cops and robbers, and the cops, he and Nick, had won. Great day! But then, from where he was, he couldn't see Nick's face.

"This your land?" the young man asked.

"None of your business."

"Well, whoever's deer it is, we'd better get her out of here before it gets too dark to see," Al said, trying to change the atmosphere, which was not exactly pleasant.

"The warden will see to that tomorrow," Nick told them. "You're coming with me now, to tell him exactly what happened."

"What's the matter with you anyway?" Trigger asked in bewilderment. "We've been out here all day and you'd cheat us of the only deer we got. What ails you, man?" He gave Nick's stony face a glance. "I'm about pooped, I can tell you."

Nick said nothing, just stood there, his rifle resting in the crook of his arm.

"Well, where's Andy?" the young man, Jack, asked.

"Must have gone back to the car. He said he didn't feel too good. 'Bout a half hour ago. Will he be mad he missed this!"

The four men stood there, no one knowing what to

76

do or say before Nick and his contained fury, which was nonetheless there among them like a dangerous bomb that must be defused somehow.

Old Pete looked shrewdly around, took in the expensive rifles and gear, heavy rope, knives.

"Nick's right," he said. "You haven't a leg to stand on. Why not just call it a day? Bad luck can happen to anyone. Season's young yet. You've got two weeks."

"Listen, we came up from New York. And we're going back there tonight. This was our last chance. Get that through your thick heads," Trigger said, and made as if to go toward the deer.

But Nick managed to get there first, so he was standing in front of the dead doe, facing them.

"Get going," he said.

But while he and Trigger confronted each other, the two other hunters, in a sudden fury of impatience and rage, jumped at Pete, and Jack had him in a lockhold round his neck before Old Pete knew what had happened to him. He gave a throttled exclamation.

"I'll break your windpipe," Jack said. "Now shut up."

"Go ahead," he called out to the other two. "We don't have to stand here and be bamboozled by a couple of loons."

"I'll bash you over the head." Nick had the butt end of his gun ready, and his eyes were blazing. "You dirty thugs!"

"These are dangerous people," Trigger said, trying to laugh it off.

"Never rile the natives," Jack answered with a sneer. He had Old Pete in a firm grip, and Pete was not struggling.

There was a crackling kind of exasperation in the air, but so far only Nick was hard in his anger. The others just couldn't take the thing seriously.

"We can't stay here all night." Al pushed the cap back on his head and scratched his ear. "Can't we settle this thing some way? Tell you what, we'll go back to wherever you guys live and cut the deer up, share it fifty-fifty. How about that?"

"Nobody gets the doe," Nick said between his teeth.

"What good is it to the warden, for Christ's sake?"

"That's his business."

"Are you in cahoots with him or what?"

"I'm not talking. Get going," Nick said.

"All right, if that's the way you choose to have it."
Trigger lunged toward Nick and grabbed him by the arm just as Nick was about to bring the rifle butt down on his head. Jack released Old Pete and ran in to trip Nick up with a side-run, and in a second they were sprawling on the ground. Al, meanwhile, turned to pin Old Pete down again, but just too late. Old Pete shot his gun in the air, with some instinct that a loud noise might bring these damn fools to their senses. No one paid the slightest attention. There was a groan from Jack, kicked in the groin, and a howl from Trigger, bitten in the leg. Nick was taking a beating but wasn't using any energy crying out. He had learned to fight dirty in the war, and he wasn't through yet. His gun had long since been dropped in the struggle. Old Pete turned to Al now for help.

"The gun, man. We'd better get it out of the way. Help me." But before Pete could reach it, he was kicked in the stomach by somebody's boot and fell back, trying to catch his breath.

It was now nearly dark. For the first time Old Pete was scared. Nick was behaving like a man out of his head, all that gentleness turned into violence. His mouth was bloody. But at the moment he appeared to be on top. The three had become grunting, panting, ferocious animals.

It was Al who heard the footsteps and saw a light flashing among the trees.

"Hey," he shouted, "someone's coming!"

"All right, break it up," said Orin Gregg, the warden. He was followed by Andy, who had evidently been woken up to show the way.

"What's going on here?" Andy asked. "Are you guys crazy? It's dark!"

But Nick was beyond hearing or caring, and socked Jack on the chin just as he was getting to his knees. The young man fell over, rolled on his side, shook his head with his eyes closed, tried to get up and fell again. Finally he was helped to his feet by Al. Trigger was sitting on the ground, groaning and retching.

Nick lay back against the dead doe's belly and wiped the blood off his mouth with the back of his hand. Gregg stood there with the flashlight on the three men. Finally Nick caught his breath.

"These men got this doe after five. Old Pete and I are witnesses."

"This man's out of his mind," Al said quickly. "He ought to be in an institution—shot our deer, tried to get it away from us, lied, and finally, as you can see, nearly murdered my two friends here."

"Shit," Old Pete said. "Tell it to the judge."

"Who . . . who . . . told you?" Nick asked. One of his eyes was swelling rapidly, and he could hardly see. Then, "Where's my gun?"

He managed to get to his feet, swaying a little, and held himself up by leaning on Old Pete's shoulder. He put a hand to his forehead as if he were waking out of a bad dream. Meanwhile Trigger was still sitting on the ground trying to pull himself together.

"Mrs. Chapman heard the shots and called me," Gregg answered Nick, after a considerable pause. Everything now seemed to be happening in slow motion, everything that had been happening too fast to take in a moment before.

"You realize, of course, that you are on posted land," he said to Al. "That's one count against you."

"Were you and Nick hunting?" he asked Old Pete severely. "You should know better."

"No, sir," Old Pete said. (The "sir" was ironic. Orin Gregg was a young man and took himself seriously.) "We were not after deer. You might say we were on a wild-goose chase," he said with a sly smile.

"If it was after five—and I doubt it," Trigger said, "that man shot too."

"The deer was wounded. Someone had to put her out of her misery," Old Pete answered. Nick seemed too bewildered to say anything now.

"Well, this will take some going into. It's dark and we'd better get going. I'll see to the doe tomorrow. At present it is state property."

Gregg led the way and, slowly and painfully, the small procession followed after. The atmosphere had changed. Everyone was too exhausted to feel anything but his own bruises. Nick had wrenched his shoulder. Jack limped. The men were relieved, if anything, to have to spend the night in a motel and be taken to court in the morning. They signed papers and gave addresses, standing by their car. Then Orin took Old Pete and Nick down the hill in his.

Nick was silent. Old Pete did all the talking, and it was a rather odd story.

"Well," Orin said, "sounds crazy to me, all of it. It's not good that you were caught on Chapman land with guns. Mrs. Chapman said her husband was cross about the whole thing. Who's going to believe this story about chasing the deer away from the hunters? And if they do, what will people think? Any way you look at it, you two come out as pretty strange critters. Well," he ended as he drew up at Nick's mother's door, "we'll all see better by daylight. Expect you in my office tomorrow at ten—and you be there!"

Nick stood in the doorway, one eye closed, his mouth still bloody, his hands covered with dirt, and gave his mother a painful smile.

"It's all right, Mother. I did what I wanted to do. Now I'll just wash and we can sit down."

In spite of the way he looked, Ellen sensed that all was well with Nick. And that was all that mattered, though he was a pretty horrifying sight for her to take in without being warned. He's got into a fight, she thought, but somehow it has made him feel better. It was Ellen's way to make mountains out of molehills about the small misadventures of daily life, and to complain a great deal. When it came to a real crisis, she was in her element. When Nick came down he had on a clean shirt and had washed his face. He would feel a great deal worse by tomorrow, she thought. But she contained herself and they ate in silence, Nick trying hard not to show that his mouth was pretty sore, she trying hard not to notice the swelling round his left eye.

"Lucky thing that Orin showed up when he did. Christina called him."

"When you're ready maybe you'll tell me what happened," Ellen said quietly.

"I'm going to bed. Tell you in the morning."

CHRISTINA'S JOURNAL—*November 18*

It is hard to know exactly what happened the day before yesterday at five or a little after. We heard shots. Cornelius wouldn't let me go out alone, so I called Orin. It is the first time I have found how terribly frustrating it is for Cornelius to be helpless. I am sure his anger was really caused by that, not by what happened—the realization that strangers could trespass on his land and he couldn't go out himself and drive them off. Now he talks about trying to find a couple to live over the garage, relieve me of the cooking and do odd jobs. If we are to stay here all winter, as I so hope we may, this is a good idea. The man could plow and shovel, and we wouldn't be so dependent on whomever we can get, by hook or by crook. Old Pete is hardly capable now of climbing the hill in a snowstorm. But what Cornelius doesn't know is how hard it is to get anyone who will be willing to live so deep in the country—and they must be reliable. Well, I shall have to put my mind on it. Right now I am troubled, too troubled to think about that.

Naturally I haven't had a word from Ellen. She never has been willing to come to me when there is trouble. Then pride takes over. She keeps herself to herself, and it's a foolhardy friend who tries to penetrate the barrier and offer help. Orin says that Nick seems to have gone berserk and got himself into a bad fight with three men from New York. According to Nick, they wounded a doe, an awkward shot on the flank, and he, Nick, killed her with a clean shot to the heart. But it was after five and Nick is standing on that, and that the strangers were not only trespassers but disobeyed the law and must be held to it and pay the penalty. Orin says they got plenty beaten up (Nick must have been beside himself with rage to handle two men alone) and have had their punishment. Cornelius says that Old Pete and Nick had no business being on our land with guns, whatever the reason, and he only half believes Nick's story. The New Yorkers talk about suing for assault. So it's rather a mess. I simply cannot bear the thought of a real rift between Ellen and me—and by now you can trust someone to have informed her that Cornelius is "after" Nick.

Nick, that gentlest of men! But Ellen did say that day we had our walk that he gets nervous in the hunting season, and that she is always anxious about him. He hates the "furriners" who come up for our deer. Who doesn't, for that matter? But this time he seems to have behaved like a madman, a man possessed. There is talk of having him examined. Orin believes that until the deer season is over he would be safer in a hospital. He got a bloody nose, a banged-up eye, and strained his shoulder, but none of that could make an excuse to send him to a medical hospital, and Ellen will certainly bar the door to anyone who tries to take him off to Concord to the state hospital.

I thought of calling John, but he gets on his father's nerves, and Cornelius is in no mood to be patient with anyone. I came up here to my upstairs desk to be alone because he was so cross with me. I just had to get away. —It was such a peaceful time. Why did this have to happen? My first loyalty must be to Cornelius. He is the one who needs me. I must do what he wants, but deep down I am on Nick's side. I too hate the killing. I understand so well. And I suspect those New York men of lying, or at least of putting as bad a light as possible on Nick's behavior. Whom are we to trust? Old Pete came up and waited till I was out in the garden to have a word with me. He says it was just a game like cops and robbers—hunting the hunters, he called it—just a little fun. He said the men from New York started the fight. One of them got him in an armlock and he nearly choked, and Nick didn't move till they jumped him.

"You know Nick," he said. "He got excited—we all did."

Poor Old Pete, he was so upset, trying to make light of it all, but I could see he was worried. And when he asked to see Cornelius I had to say no. He just isn't in any state to face an argument with anyone. And he looks on Old Pete as riff-raff, a good-for-nothing, lazy old man who lives off the dump and gets drunk whenever he can get hold of a six-pack. "Can't hold his liquor, pees in his pants, and would bend back the ear of an elephant with his everlasting imaginary adventures"—that's what Cornelius thinks. But John loved him when he was a boy. I can't forget that. Old Pete was his Paul Bunyan and Johnny Appleseed and Davy Crockett all rolled into one. He has a good heart, that man. And he has what I sometimes think of as the true wisdom of the failure. He stands outside and looks us all over—we who have everything he hasn't got—and he feels no envy because he likes his life. He has chosen it. He is, in a strange way, the freest spirit in Willard, because, I suppose, he has nothing to lose. Oh dear, what am I to do now? Go to see Jane? She's so frail one hesitates to lay a burden there. Eben? Why not? I'll tell Cornelius I have to go to the store. I feel so bottled up. I must talk to someone.

What makes me anxious is that I have seen other

incidents in this village that could tear the whole web of our society. Rumor does it—people being at the same time so close-mouthed about their own troubles and so ready to gossip about other people's. I've seen how it can happen too often, roll up like a snowball into a solid mass of rage and hatred when really the start was nothing at all. This time a lot is involved. Orin's father once had a knockdown fight with Rufus Comstock when Orin's father was road agent one winter, and Rufus got into one of his towering rages because one plow broke down and he couldn't get out to the barn. So Orin is hard on Nick and Ellen. There is no love lost between the tribes. And everybody's a little more keyed up than usual with so many guns and out-of-towners around in hunting season. Two dogs have been shot already. Cornelius has to have some outlet for his frustration, but would it were not this one.

What amazes me is how tightly woven we all are together at the roots, how strong the roots are, and how deep they go into the past.

CHAPTER 6

It was one of those days when there seem to be more leaves whirling about in the air than on the ground— a windy, dusty day. Eben had been out chopping kindling for Mrs. Goodnow. But the wind, the restless sky, made him restless. It was always like this in late autumn when skeins of geese went over, and every year Eben felt a pull in his chest. "Why not go to Japan?" he would ask himself, surveying the black mass of frost-killed squash in the vegetable garden.

"I never cut down the peonies," he told himself. "Time I covered the garden." The flowers had been Olive's province, and now that she was gone he almost heard her telling him these things, or saw her in his mind with a little cart and the clippers, bending down, so absorbed in her work that she did not hear him coming. He knew what he ought to do now, but he felt childishly cross about it. "I just won't," he said to himself, and went deliberately past the peonies and up onto the porch, where he stood a moment looking out over the pasture at the mountain.

Then he became aware that a tall figure was making its way across the field. For a second it looked so like Christina that he half raised his arm to wave. But no, this woman, whoever it was, limped a little. Christina, tall and straight as an arrow, would not limp, and she had not come up here for years. So Eben turned to go in, impatient with himself and these shadowy figures from the past that never left him free these days.

"Eben!"

There was no mistaking that imperative voice. By Jove, it must be Christina after all. And Eben went quickly out to meet her.

"Not you!" he said, laughing at her. "Not you limping like an old lady!"

"It's this darned knee . . ."

"Well, come in, come in. You didn't walk all the way, I hope?"

No, she had left the car on hardtop and walked up, and seen a fox; and now her brilliance, the flash of blue in her eyes swept over and erased his first vision of an old lady.

"I'll take you down in the jeep. That's no road for a lame knee—but it keeps the world from my door."

He led her into his study, apologizing for disorder, explaining about Mrs. Goodnow, kneeling down to set a match to the fire in spite of Christina's protesting that it was hardly worth lighting a fire, as she could only stay a few minutes.

"I must just say a word to Molly," she said, and Eben could hear their two voices, warm with laughter, in the kitchen, and the whole house felt to him lit up, alive again. Life had been ebbing out of him lately in a queer way. Now here it was, flooding back. What had brought her here at last? What in all the world?

Only when she was settled on the little sofa did she really look at him—a quick, searching look.

"It's not fair, Eben, that you look so young. I thought it so brave of you to stay on here after Olive died, and I've been meaning to come and pay a call all these years. Four? Five?"

"Five," Eben said shortly. "Exactly five in December."

Christina caught the dart and stumbled on. It was a rather awkward moment after all.

"It's life, Eben—what with Cornelius (you know about his stroke), the children, the grandchildren—the summer simply flies away. We don't have a cook any more."

"Well, what brought you finally—after five years?" he asked more kindly. "Whatever it is, I am grateful."

"I need your advice. There's been trouble—a hunting incident on the place. Because Cornelius is so helpless now, he feels it more deeply than he should. In fact, he is in a terrible rage. I'm so worried about Nick and Ellen" —and the whole story poured out.

Eben sat in the wing chair smoking his pipe, his eyes

half closed. At one point Christina thought he might have fallen asleep.

"Jim Heald's the man," he said when she had finished. "He'll get them to talk it over. He's awfully good at this sort of thing. Those New Yorkers will be only too glad to come to an arrangement. They don't want to be hung up with a court case."

"Of course." Christina rubbed her forehead with one hand, a gesture so like the young Christina that Eben smiled.

"Now say 'Carruthers, how can I be so dumb?' "

And they roared with laughter, for that was what Christina had used to say—had even said when she had a bad fall from her horse and was half stunned.

"Why didn't I think of Jim?"

"Maybe because you really wanted to see me," Eben teased.

"Maybe," Christina said gravely. "I've been shy," she admitted. "But, Eben, the real problem is Cornelius. He wants to have Old Pete and Nick penalized for trespass as well as the New Yorkers."

"They were trespassing, of course. Too bad, really, that they had guns with them."

"Yes, but you know how people feel around here— they might just as well be Indians whose land was taken from them. Posted land just does not apply to the village —that's what I mean."

"Do Jim and Cornelius hit it off? They used to, as I remember."

"Oh, all right, but Cornelius doesn't take to advice gladly."

"Like his father. The old man was as stubborn as a mule when you came right down to it, especially when he was in the wrong. The Chapmans have always felt that whatever you did or said, you stood by it. One does not admit a mistake, especially a mistake in judgment."

"You seem very sure." Christina bristled just slightly.

"I knew the Chapmans before you did."

"True." It was an absent-minded answer because Christina was thinking that the amazing thing about life is how little people change. Except for the white crest of hair, except for the stooping shoulders, this might be the old Eben. "The Websters came back from their call just radiant, and talked about what a wise man you are." She lifted a mocking eyebrow.

"And you came up here really just to make sure they were fooled?"

"*Are* you wise, Eben?"

"About some things maybe," he answered. "I have thought a lot about this town since Olive died—oh, a sort of game of solitaire. I haven't thought much about myself though. So it depends what this wisdom is."

"I'm afraid," Christina said in a low voice, "afraid of a rift between Ellen and me. She'll never forgive Cornelius if Nick is held for trespass. And, frankly, I wouldn't blame her."

"Cornelius knows the man's war record, I presume, and that he came home more or less a cripple."

"Oh, yes, but you know Cornelius—he expects so much of himself and of everyone else."

"How is he?" Eben asked.

"He's wonderful, Eben—so patient and good. We live from day to day."

"Hard on you," Eben murmured. He felt awkward. There was too much pain and antagonism just under the surface.

"Oh, no," Christina said, "for me it's been wonderful. I know that sounds heartless. It is just that we have got to know each other again. It's like a reprieve—this quiet time. Why am I telling you this?" She got up and stood looking down at the fire.

"God knows," Eben answered.

Christina was, no doubt, questioning her impulse to come here. She was intensely loyal. Yet she *had* come, and Eben was not sure why, even now. The pause had become rather long.

"Talk about Ellen," he said.

"Oh, Ellen's Ellen. Just as ornery as ever, but we have been through so much together. Life here would be too strange for words without Ellen. Only the other day we went for a long walk in the woods and got lost."

"I have always been interested in this friendship, outside the cadres."

"What do you mean?"

"Well, after all, you don't invite her when you have guests. I bet you've never eaten a meal in her house."

"We go for picnics," Christina said, surprised to realize that what Eben said was true. There were certain barriers, and over all the years they had not been crossed. Yet she had talked with Ellen about things—John, for instance—that she would have exposed to the eyes of no

87

other intimate—things she could hardly even discuss with Cornelius.

"Yes"—Eben looked up at her with sudden animation, leaned forward hugging one knee in his clasped hands— "it is all that, the web of relationships that we take for granted and do not examine, that has interested me lately. It is not really a very democratic town, you know —not *really*," he repeated.

Christina sat down again. She had the feeling that she should not have come. She had forgotten why it seemed so imperative. But Eben was thinking aloud now, and she couldn't simply go away without even knowing why she had come in the first place.

"What are you smiling at?"

"Myself."

"You find yourself amusing?"

"Absurd, Eben. It's absurd at my age to act on impulse, not think things through. Of course I should have made a beeline for Jim Heald. Instead I came up here because—" She turned on him her brilliant smile, a teasing smile. "Heavens knows why! Maybe because you, Eben, have cut through the web. You know us all from top to bottom, don't you? I guess I came to you because you would see all sides of this silly business."

"Most people in the town would agree with Cornelius about Nick and Old Pete. Has that fact occurred to you? There's nothing they'd like better than a good old-fashioned feud—something to chew over on the long winter nights. I sometimes think people here live on rage. It's at the root of everything—the grudge—the grudge that may go back a generation or two."

"Yes, I suppose so," Christina sighed.

"Orin remembers that Rufus once slapped his father's face when the old man was road agent. Do you remember that? It was finally settled out of court, but not before the whole town had taken sides one way or another. Orin would probably like to see Nick in trouble."

"Oh, Eben, I can't believe that. People aren't mean."

"They are and they aren't." He looked across at her quizzically and cracked his knuckles. "I'm mean, I guess, because I have never quite forgiven old Judge Chapman. He helped me get into Harvard but I was blackballed for Porcellian."

"Absurd man, to want to get into that stuffy nook of old Bostonians. Why did you?"

"Just because I couldn't. A young man's humiliations haunt."

"But, good heavens, Eben, you're wildly successful compared to any one of us."

"I've made money, if that's what you mean."

"You're a person in the world. Who cares about stuffy old Boston?" She felt dismayed at this Eben—the Eben she knew very well from the old days. And here he was, flaming with imagined slights. Instinctively she looked for a change of subject. "John simply sneered at the clubs. It's quite absurd of you, Eben," she said almost crossly.

"Yes, that's the way it goes. I wanted what I couldn't have, and John rebelled against what he could have. You're right, Christina—alone here I brood too much."

"Tell me something—when you were searching around for that history you were supposed to be writing (and why didn't you do it?)"—but she didn't wait for an answer—"did you find out anything about the Webber place?"

"What about it?"

"I understand most of the women, children, old men, and boys spent the Civil War up there, a kind of community."

"Yes, that's a fact. That is what happened." He became animated again, pulled himself out of the dismal bog of his reflections of a moment before. "What a story if one were a novelist, eh?"

"It's hard to imagine all they must have had to learn, from driving a team of oxen to sowing and reaping, and all the woman's work as well—weaving blankets and socks for the men at the front. Wasn't your great-grandmother one of those women?"

"Yes, Sophia Dole must have been a moving spirit. I found accounts all written out in her spidery hand. It looked as if she had been the leader. My guess is that it was her idea. She was headstrong—my grandmother used to talk about her. She had a hard hand with the boys and a fierce temper, but she was brave. Shot more than one wildcat herself in those years—or so the legend goes. Never wore a corset . . ." He stopped to look over at Christina. "Jem has got you into this fandango of his, has he?"

"Yes," Christina laughed. "I have been handed 'The Women of Willard.' "

Eben's eyebrows shot up ironically. "So you're going to be a writer after all?"

"Don't tease me." Ease had come back to them now, but Christina looked at her watch anxiously. "Oh, dear, I must go. Cornelius doesn't know where I am." She caught Eben's amused glance and blushed. "I didn't tell him."

"You'll have to come back. 'The Women of Willard' is a rather rich theme for further conversations. I'll look around and see what I have in my notes. Come back," he said, "won't you?" For Christina was standing, and he rose to go with her. "I'm going to take you down in the jeep."

"Well, that would be a help."

"Maybe I'll have the strength now to cut down the peonies. Olive would scold me to have left them looking so dismal."

"Oh, how you must miss her, Eben!" Christina stood in the road beside him as they looked out over the field and at the mountain. Perhaps he had not heard. He strode off to the barn to get the jeep and she waited for him with memories and images whirling through her mind—the excitement of Eben again, that electric current that had always been there between them, suddenly turned on. And Cornelius—she was impatient to be home, to tell him about Eben, to suggest that they invite him for Thanksgiving. Would that be wise? But she had not liked herself for admitting to Eben she had come secretly. That must be set right with Cornelius. And somehow—somehow she must persuade him to let Nick and Old Pete off.

"You know, one thing about getting old," Eben said when she was sitting beside him in the jeep, "is that the past and the present flow together. The past doesn't even begin to interest people until they are in their fifties. Then it begins to, at least about their own families, but when you get to be over seventy it's not a matter of looking things up—they are just there all the time." He shot Christina a quizzical look. "I've had long thoughts about my great-grandmother, Sophia, lately."

Christina's answer was cut off by a bounce as the jeep went over what felt like a boulder.

"We don't know where we're going but we know—or want to know—more and more about where we came from. Around here, it looks as though we had come from a strong breed of women."

He drew the jeep up behind Christina's car and for a moment they sat there.

"I don't want to go, but I must," Christina said.

"Well, if you must, you must. You've made the day glorious for me. You know that, of course."

He gave her a hand-down from the awkward height of the jeep and stood in the road and watched her go. He was bursting with ideas, memories—a rich confusion that made him decide, after she was out of sight, not to go home after all, just drive around a bit and watch the blowing leaves, the dusty, golden day, as if it had become a new-found treasure—this sense of being fully alive.

CHRISTINA'S JOURNAL—*November 20*

Things do blow over. But I have been absurdly anxious. Angry, I suppose, because after so many real anxieties—John, and Cornelius's stroke, that I have faced without panic—this comparatively unimportant incident about Nick makes me feel as if I were walking on quicksand. I shan't rest easy until I have seen Ellen, who maintains her absolute silence, as if we didn't exist.

Cornelius says that if the New Yorkers are prosecuted for trespass as well as shooting after five, he cannot, in all justice, let Nick and Old Pete off. And I suppose he has reason as well as the law on his side. The trouble is that people just aren't reasonable. If we are to stay on this winter, I can't bear the idea that we shall be looked on as enemies by at least half the town, and as friends by people who are glad to humiliate Ellen and Nick. It appears that she is resented—she has always held apart from the town and gone her own way. For years it was because of the trouble Rufus got into. She was fiercely loyal and simply closed the door rather than admit Rufus was often in the wrong. Her rage has taken the form of adamant withdrawal and silence, and people who felt compassion for her in the hard days, and had the door closed in their faces, haven't forgotten that.

I have tried to explain all this to Cornelius, to show how it is all a network of relationships, all of which will be troubled in some way if he insists on prosecuting Nick and Old Pete. He just says, "That is their business. Let them mind it as best they can. I am still able to mind ours."

He put up the "No Trespassing" signs himself. I still

remember how tired he was at the end of that long day. I sense that he is involved somewhere below the conscious level—and that is why talking about it does little or no good. Maybe, *au fond*, he wonders whether he was right to post our land and is on the defensive. He doesn't even try to explain to himself why he decided five years ago not to hunt any more.

Meanwhile the beautiful peace we shared a few days ago seems to have gone up in smoke. The subject we do not talk about has built a wall between us, just as it was after John's bad times. I long for Thanksgiving and to have the children around, and especially the grand-children, the dogs, something to break into this enclosed, breathless place, to let a little wind in. Of course Cornelius dreads their seeing him like this. But he and Robin can play checkers. We can read aloud. And I am seriously thinking of getting them to bring Mamzelle up with them.

I told him I had been up to see Eben. He didn't like it—that was clear. And Cornelius is right in a way. I did go without telling him, and I did enjoy myself tremendously. Eben has this wildfire quality still. We catch fire from each other, even now after all these years—over fifty! I told Cornelius that I would have to go at least once more, to find out about the women in the Civil War. "Do as you please," he said.

Anyway Jim Heald has been a great help. Eben was so right there. The New Yorkers have gone home, to come back if it ends by becoming a court case—their case against Nick. Jim is convinced that they did attack first, but in court a great deal might depend on other evidence of Nick's instability. There is nothing to do for the present but wait and hope.

It is winter suddenly, the end of autumn. The few remaining leaves went in a rainstorm the other day. I have been out raking madly. It is true that we must look for some help. My knee bothers me a good deal. I feel depressed and I miss Ellen. All this has made me realize how much I depend on her, if only for her sour humor. She never tries to look on the best of anything, and that is rather a relief. To each other we can say quite frankly that life is hell a good deal of the time, and take that fact as the Almighty's joke on us. It is a tonic.

"A strong breed of women," Eben said—and how right he was!

CHAPTER 7

Christina woke to a crystalline morning after rain. The mountain looked dark blue, very sharp and clear in outline against a rosy sky, and when she slipped out of bed and went to the window the whole lawn was silver with hoarfrost. Cornelius sighed in his sleep and tried to turn over with a small groan; then she could hear his loud breathing as he slipped back into that underworld of unconsciousness, the world of sleep, the healing world.

She stood for some moments in her nightgown, shivering, breathing the silence in, the ancient peace of the mountain, the sense of earth turning gently and inexorably toward winter. Standing as witness to such simple grandeur as plain daylight, she found it absurd to be anxious—and decided there and then to go down after breakfast and see Ellen. Sooner or later they had to talk things over. The old mountain in the dawn made human affairs look less complex than perhaps they really were, but at least it dragged one out of the mire to contemplate the large and the inexorable—the slow natural growth and change, the light coming later and staying less long each day (it was now seven and the sun just rising), and ourselves as part of some things that did not change, that took us along with them, war or peace, and would be there whether we were or not. It was restful just to think mountain. For us who have no religion in the old-fashioned sense, who can say no prayers to a listening God, nature itself—nature and human love—polarize, and we pray by being fully aware of them both. So Christina thought as she bent over Cornelius's flushed face and kissed his forehead, remembering their old cat, Mitten, who used to wake Cornelius by licking his forehead.

His sleep was deep these mornings, and he did not move. When she came back an hour later with his breakfast on a tray, Cornelius was smiling. "I dreamt that Mitten woke me by licking my face—such a sweet dream . . . How are you, darling?" he murmured, and she knew that in some mysterious way the barrier between them had melted in the night. It was truly a new dawn.

"I was Mitten," she said. "I woke to the mountain— so beautiful in the dawn, and I came and kissed you, but you were fast asleep."

"Mmm . . . kiss me again. I'm awake now."

And so she did, feeling as if his warm hand clasping hers held so much life in it that it was like getting a transfusion. In spite of the stroke and rather like a baby, Cornelius could grasp her hand now with terrific power. That had been the first sign of change—the first sign that the circulation was beginning to be normal again. Giving her so much love in this way, he pulled himself up into the day.

While he had his breakfast she sat on the end of the bed, and what he saw was Christina against the mountain.

"I'm going down to see Ellen," she said. "I feel I must."

"Yes, you must."

"It's going to be all right, isn't it?"

Cornelius managed a crooked smile as he swallowed his oatmeal.

"Maybe. You'll know how to do it, Christina— whether Nick needs help . . ."

And that was how it was left—an admission, on Cornelius's part at least, that what was really important was not anything about trespassing, but Nick himself. Though if he expected her to be able to tackle that with Ellen, he was a good deal more optimistic than she was.

While Christina washed the dishes and later helped Cornelius get up and shave and dress, a time each day when they had evolved a sort of nursery-jokey talk that worked very well to support them both through Cornelius's dependence and his hating it—all the time, underneath, Christina was conscious of the way it is, when two people have shared a life for many years, that the most important things never get said in *words*. They are communicated through some sort of current, sensed rather than explicit. We *are* rather than saying, she thought, and this morning we *are* loving, and without even saying the words Cornelius has made it clear that he is over his anger. This was the root of marriage, really—just the opposite of the excitement of discovering another person through words, of sparring and getting a rise, as she had the other day with Eben. We *are together,* she thought, as finally, about ten, she got into the car and drove down the hill.

Ellen had seen her stop in the drive and was at the door as Christina got out.

"Just stopped by a second," Christina said, "on my way to the store."

"Come in," Ellen said. "I'm busy, though. You'll have to forgive me if I stick to my last." And she went back to her chair by the window and picked up a half-finished curtain. Her manner was unyielding, and she had not even offered Christina a chair.

"Who are those for?"

"Mrs. Croswell."

Christina sat down in Nick's chair at the table. She felt the pause growing between them. Anything she thought of saying seemed dangerous.

It was Ellen who filled it, with a polite question.

"Are your children all coming for Thanksgiving?"

"I think so. I had such a dear letter from Olivia—there's the usual problem about her cat and John's children's schnauzer, not to mention Marianne's dachshunds, but she can put them in a kennel, I suppose. What about your Thanksgiving?"

"Oh, they'll be here—the whole pack of them. I just wish they would think of helping out a little—it always falls on me."

"The rock of ages." Christina attempted a light tone, but there was no response. Ellen sewed on for dear life, her face closed.

After a moment she bit off her thread and said, "They might bring the pies. Of course Sarah works hard, but Micah's wife never thinks of helping."

"Why don't you ask her?"

"I don't ask for things," Ellen said.

No, Christina thought, that's the trouble; you don't

ask for anything, even my love that is yours, and you know it well."

"You're angry with us, and I can't bear it."

"Angry?" Ellen laid down her sewing at last. "No, I'm not angry. You mind your business and I'll mind mine."

"That's just what Cornelius said. It never occurred to me before that you two could be alike—but I guess you are."

"Stubborn as mules, both of us," and the ghost of a smile passed across Ellen's somber face.

"This whole thing will blow over, Ellen. I'm terribly sorry about Cornelius. I think he got cross because he feels so helpless."

"Maybe." Now Christina saw the flush rising in Ellen's throat, and that her hands shook as she picked up her sewing again. "But he had no right to take it out on Nick. Nick was only trying to keep trespassers off."

"How is he?"

"Nick? Nick's fine."

"I heard he'd got rather bunged up in the fight."

"Expect you've heard plenty. Orin's a big mouth."

"Still, there was a fight?"

"Those foreigners attacked and Nick beat them up— two of them. First time I was ever glad of what he learned in the war."

"He's all right, then?"

Christina could see that Ellen was torn between a longing to talk and the need to punish them for meddling— she wanted to give a little, but it was a struggle.

"Nick came home that night with a black eye and· a bloody mouth, with a sprained shoulder, but he was happy. He did what he wanted to do—just like Rufus after one of those rages." Ellen was surprised herself at the comparison. She had never seen any resemblance between Nick and Rufus before. "Yes," she added, bending to her work, "it did him good to break out for once."

"Oh, dear, I suppose so, but . . ."

"But what?" Ellen was on the defensive at once, and Christina didn't finish her sentence. It would do no good to refer to the fact that Rufus "broke out" when he had been drinking.

"Nick is such a gentle person; it doesn't seem like him a bit."

"Nobody's going to call him chicken after this—and

96

I'm glad myself to know he can defend himself. I shan't worry so much."

"You told me you were anxious because the hunting upset him. I'm glad if you can be less so now," Christina said.

Just as if she were a wild bird, you could get only so close to Ellen, and then she would fly up out of reach.

"If you came here to give me advice, I can do without it."

"Oh, Ellen, we've been friends since we were kids and went blueberrying and slid in your father's hayloft. If I can't say what's in my mind to you, it's just too bad."

"I don't know what brought you here but I've had enough of people suggesting that Nick should be sent up to the state hospital, I can tell you."

So that was the trouble.

"Whoever said that?"

"I don't know. Things like that get around in the air. Some people I know mind everyone's business except their own."

"Well, Nick is loved. Some people may be anxious lest he do himself harm, for all you know."

"Some people really care. Know where he is now?"

"I can't imagine."

"He's up at Jane Tuttle's, that's where! She telephoned over and said she wanted to see the man who was out to protect the wildlife instead of letting it be butchered. That's what Jane Tuttle said."

"She's felt it keenly that New Hampshire permits the shooting of does."

"She's a great lady," Ellen said fiercely.

"She certainly is," Christina assented with a smile. "I guess none of us really know how hard it must be for someone as independent as she still is to be so dependent." Christina was glad to grasp at a change of subject. This was something they could discuss without every quill of the porcupine Ellen standing up in menace— at least she hoped so. "Hannah has to be an intimate friend —it's the only way to make life possible. But she's not Jane's equal in any way—intellect or sensibility—so she must sometimes seem like a crude jailer. Oh, how I admire Jane for managing it as she does, with so much love."

"Hannah would die for her, that's sure."

"But isn't it wonderful, Ellen, the way all the boys

97

Jane used to take out on expeditions to bird-watch or look for ferns and mushrooms make a beeline for her whenever they come home, grown men now? John will be up there within an hour of his getting up here for Thanksgiving."

"She's grown old mighty well, that woman. Kept her head on her shoulders."

"And a twinkle in her eye. She was so funny about Jem and the history. Remember?"

Ellen was standing in the window with her back to Christina, and her mind was clearly elsewhere.

"You think I should send Nick up to the doctors for an examination?"

"I don't know, Ellen. We've seen some pretty hot fights in this town. It seems as if men go wild sometimes. I just don't know. Maybe Jane will help about this. I would trust her judgment. I think she's truly wise about people—a strange thing to say about an old maid like her, who never brought up a child of her own."

"Well, she brought up a good many who were not!"

Christina badly wanted to go and put an arm around Ellen's stooped shoulders, hug her hard. But such a physical expression of affection would have been momentous, and so, out of place. That was not the way they had ever behaved. Tenderness—it didn't show itself often here. Instead she went on thinking aloud about Jane and what made her what she was.

"Sometimes I think old maids know more than we do. We get so absorbed in our families."

"They either dry up or they ripen, like good apples."

"Oh, Ellen, it's so good to talk to you!"

"Whatever brought that on?" At last Ellen smiled.

"Just the way you say things like that. Do you know why I came down this morning?"

"I have some idea."

"No, it wasn't really about Nick. It wasn't about Cornelius. It was just because I couldn't bear not to be straight with you—in the clear. I couldn't bear the barriers going up between us, you and me, Ellen."

"I was angry, I don't mind telling you."

"But you're not angry now?"

Ellen drew herself up and looked straight at Christina for the first time. "We're friends, Christina, I'll grant you that. But we're not family. I'll always put family first."

"Oh, dear, I suppose we all do—and that may be what's wrong with the world." Christina looked around the kitchen, so warm and livable, all things here worn and used and loved—the geraniums on the window sills, a little peaky still from the change to indoors; Nick's magazines in a pile on the table, and the dog's bed, an old quilt, under it—and sighed. She felt that, dear as it was— homely and dear—it was in some way an inviolable world. She might be allowed just inside the threshold but never really at its hearth.

Ellen was off on another tack. Speaking at all had been hard because it released something she had never said before.

"We'll never understand each other, not really. You don't have your back against the wall."

"In some ways, no . . ."

"You Chapmans don't even realize what it is to be you."

"I was going to say that in some way every human being has his back against the wall. Cornelius—it's a terrible struggle, Ellen, for him to walk a few steps, lift a spoon to his mouth."

"Maybe, but he thought he could master us here in the town, keep us off his land by putting up some signs. Nick went in to help Cornelius—to drive the hunters off. I don't get over it that we have been blamed."

There it was again, the thorn all this talk had not removed, the sore angry place. Christina felt helpless.

"Ellen, you know how I feel. I can't say more."

"Talking won't get us anywhere anyway."

No, Christina thought. But listening might.

"What do you want, Ellen?"

"To be left alone with Nick. We understand each other."

"Very well," and Christina got up to go. Somehow things had got out of hand. Let out a little bitterness and the whole ocean of it bottled up in Ellen began to pour out.

"You can't have to fight as hard as I've fought to be full of sweetness and light. I'm sorry, Christy."

"Oh, good heavens, Ellen, don't apologize. We're *friends!*" This time the impulse to put an arm round the fierce little person at bay before her won over caution. The end was wordless. It was the two women held close in spite of themselves. Nothing had been solved, but they *were* friends.

Ellen watched at the window as Christina started the car. She didn't wave. But she felt like doing it. And then she thought, it's easy for Christina to be generous. It's hard for me. She felt all beaten up inside with not yielding.

CHRISTINA'S JOURNAL—*November 23*

I guess there will always be a rift in the lute, but I'm glad I went. The thing is that Ellen thrives on struggle and lives on pride. Every now and then she has to have a reason to get angry. She gets all fiery and up in the air, and maybe it's good for her. Feeling of some sort keeps the machine functioning. But what dangerous stuff it is, even at our age—especially at our age, I think I mean. In some ways we grow more vulnerable as we get old. It all costs more—anger, passionate love. People imagine that the old no longer feel intensely. What rot! It seems to me I feel everything more, or that the range of what can make me feel grows all the time rather than diminishing. The young are so self-reliant. They go rushing about colliding with reality at every turn. Minor explosions take place. They think no one has ever felt what they feel. The trouble is that when one is old, one recognizes the same old feelings taking over. One is too aware of the dangers, the exhaustion, the cost of tension—and one is pulled this way and that, as I have been lately between Cornelius and Ellen, trying to see both sides.

I wonder whether she will get Nick to a doctor. She is more frightened than she admits by this capacity for violence in him. No one knows better than she what a dangerous man Rufus became before he died. Nick is not like that, but he appears to be developing a kind of obsession about wild animals. Jane will help. Jane will know what to say.

Two weeks ago I felt becalmed. I felt that Cornelius and I had been given a holiday, everything cleared away that harassed us—so queer when the reason for this was that terrible stroke. When I lay down beside him with my hand in his, I felt we were floated on our love. Only two weeks ago! Now life has charged in, as it always will, I suppose. Not only this business about Nick, but Thanksgiving looms. But oh, how wonderful it will be to see them all—fourteen at table, fifteen if I can persuade Cornelius to invite Eben. I'm afraid he won't, because he doesn't want to be humiliated by his own clumsiness. And it might be dangerous. Eben tends to show off, I fear, and might talk too much.

What I must do right away is to go up to the Love-lands' and see if one of the children would be willing to help in the kitchen. None of my grandchildren, alas, is able to take over and really help. But of course Olivia and Marianne will. Could we manage alone? The trouble is I want so much to be free to enjoy them, free to talk, and especially free to help Cornelius, for he will need help. I am rambling on with too many little things on my mind for this journal to be of much use. Can I ask John to bring Mamzelle?

If we could only really imagine each other's lives. I am thinking of Ellen, and so many others in the village, no doubt. They brush us off as "the rich." They never imagine that everything we have costs in responsibility, in time, and devours us. Just the houses! When I think of the time Cornelius and I spend getting things taken care of—trying to find help. I wish we could get rid of the house in Cotuit. Of course the children love it, and it has been useful as a place to give John and Sybille for their holidays. I long to get rid of possessions. Sometimes I think Old Pete is the one wise one. But when Ellen throws at me that I have never had to struggle I feel like saying, "Maybe. But I have had to learn to be capable in a hundred ways that were no pleasure or nourishment really. If I had not been rich, I might have become a good painter." Instead, right now I had better get the silver out and see what needs polishing.

I would like to say to Ellen, "The things that bind us together are stronger than the things that divide us"—especially, between her and me, all our childhood memories. But here in the town we are bound together in a million ways we never think about in normal times. A forest fire is needed to make us see it—to make us know again how we depend on each other, all of us. In the hurricane of '38 there were no rich or poor. We suffered together and helped each other survive, as a family. Ellen thinks of family as a small, tight entity—really it has become herself and Nick alone—just as I have felt lately that it is Cornelius and me. There's the center. There's what cannot be touched by anyone, for good or ill. By Eben? Fifty years ago perhaps. Now he would get lost in

101

the labyrinth of all my days and nights with Cornelius long before he came anywhere near the central being. Yet, it was fun to see him, to feel that sparring edge again, to be teased and admired. We need now and then to redefine ourselves in the eyes of a beholder with Eben's verve, and I must presume that I did something of the same sort for him. He has always been vain, and in that respect he is rather feminine.

Cornelius is calling, "Where are you?" and I had better go down and make him a cup of tea.

CHAPTER 8

It had been rather a hard morning for Jane by the time John turned up. Hannah was in one of her jealous and put-upon moods, banging away in the kitchen. She had pretended that the pale pink blouse Jane wanted to wear needed washing, really, Jane suspected, because she knew how becoming it was, with a black velvet bow at the throat. Then, in a fit of remorse, she had insisted on washing it there and then, so it had been quite damp when it was finally ready to put on.

"You spoil me, Hannah."

"I'm not fit for human consumption," was Hannah's answer, a formula she had devised when she was especially low in her mind.

"Well, I should really prefer a lamb chop, if it comes to that," Jane said. She had discovered that the only way to tame Hannah in these black moods was to tease her. Hannah smiled her crooked smile, and at last there was peace.

It had long ago ceased to seem strange to Jane that she should end her days with this jealous, difficult, devoted, and passionate creature at her side. But whenever Jane looked at the lined, haggard face and the worn, rough hands, she knew that this was an angel in disguise, and we must be sure to recognize and welcome the angels when they are sent, as Hannah had been, as a literal answer to prayer. It would be quite impossible to live here at all without this small, stout dragon to protect her. Jane sighed and folded her hands together as if she clasped

103

her intimate self between them, and saw she had a half hour in which to gather the splintered pieces together and meet John with the balance and openness to his need which he had every right to expect from her, ninety or not. She sighed and rocked, and felt the tensions slowly flow out. After a while she picked a sweet geranium leaf off the pot on the window sill beside her and rubbed it before inhaling its pungence. How little people knew about very old age! It would be quite absurd to mention to anyone—least of all to Hannah—that this scent of rose geranium filled her with what might be called bliss. As far as the senses go, she was thinking, we still live in large part in and through them. Very small things—apparently small, such as a mushroom, or a cup of tea, or a half-remembered line of poetry that suddenly came into focus and brought back the whole poem, or the delicious luxury of clean sheets—these little things now made the difference between hell and heaven. Sometimes Hannah's rough hand smoothing her pillow, or one of her awkward gestures of affection, became angelic. The hard thing was to be someone else's possession, and not yield up that central small entity, the self, that must go on to the end, if possible, intact.

Of course she heard the car long before John himself came running in and gave her a prickly kiss, reeking of tobacco.

"John . . . darling boy . . . you've grown a beard!"

"Yes, doesn't it suit me? I feel I have become an authority on almost any subject now that I have a beard."

"Sit down, sit down. I have to get used to it."

"Oh, how good it is to be here. You're just the same—marvelous, beautiful as ever." John sat on a low chair, pulling it close so he could hold both her hands in his.

At this moment Hannah came in with a tray holding a decanter with sherry, two glasses, and a plate of thin ginger cookies on it, saw the beard, and let out a cry, while John leapt up to relieve her of the tray.

"A holy terror," she said, half laughing. "You nearly made me drop my tray!"

"We shall have to get used to him, Hannah. He seems to have become suddenly a very old boy, a stately and judicious boy."

Jane was flushed with the happiness of seeing him, the happiness of the occasion, for John always made his visits an occasion. Jane thought he was the most human and lovable creature she had ever known. And since he had been about four years old and gone for walks with her, observing everything, they had shared one of those special relationships possible between an old maid and a child, a relationship full of delight for each of them. Now he was taking a little box out of his pocket with that shy, eager look in his eyes she knew well, and was handing it to her.

"You've brought me a present!"

"Of course. It's Thanksgiving, isn't it? This is a little thanksgiving, Jane. I do hope you will like it."

Whatever it was, was wrapped in tissue paper, and it took a moment to unwrap.

"Oh," she said, "it's a turtle!"

"Indeed it is. It's a *netsuke* from Japan, made by a master. Isn't it great?"

He watched her turn it over, feel the soft boxwood, observe the delicate carving of the paws.

"It's just what I need, John. I need something to hold in my hand sometimes. How did you guess?—I'm afraid it was frightfully extravagant," she said.

"Oh, yes, but after all, unlike my revered father, I think money is for spending, not for keeping. You know that, Jane."

"How is your father? Dear Cornelius, I think of him often—what it must be for that powerful physical person to be limited as he has been."

"I'll tell you something—he's never been better. It's marvelous to see how he has taken this." John clasped his hands on his knee and rocked as he did when he was thinking, always had done. "Somehow or other I can talk to him. I never could, you know. Even Mother feels it—except for this damned business about Nick."

"Yes." Jane turned the turtle in her hands. "That was a pity. But surely it's on the way out as a problem." She gave him a keen look, half closed her eyes and announced: "The beard is all right, John, now I'm used to it."

"It makes me into a father figure at last." And he laughed. "The children think it's a huge joke, but I am sure they are impressed. I might be president of an obscure college, or have just written the definitive work on mushrooms."

"And Sybille?"

"She doesn't complain about a prickly kiss now and then."

Jane laid the turtle gently down on the window sill and for a second leaned her head on the chair back. "They want me to write a chapter of the history—it's Jem's idea—about the natural history of Willard. You know, darling, I can't stay awake and concentrate really for more than a half hour, so you will have to help me, maybe write it. Will you?"

"Oh . . ." John stroked his beard for a moment. "Well, why not?"

"You know it could be a book in itself. I have always wanted you to do it—like White's *Natural History of Selbourne*."

"A mere masterpiece—that's all you expect, eh?"

"You might pour me a glass of sherry, and one for yourself. And do taste these ineffable creations of Hannah's."

So they sipped and munched for a reflective moment. It was one of Jane Tuttle's great charms that she could induce and carry on intimate silence with those she loved.

"We have to remember, John, that the newcomers often have no idea what the region has to offer—the configuration of brook and lake, the wildness of these woods, even the second growth and the brush which keep the woodcock here. Birds, wildflowers, bushes and trees, mushrooms, butterflies and moths—the wild mixture of it all! And what it does to a pond when the exhaust from those motor boats begins to pollute! Last year I managed to get down to the pond and couldn't find a single tadpole!"

"Last year when they widened the road down by the old mill they tore out that whole bank where the painted trillium used to be."

"Oh, it's a terrible thing!" Jane said. "I lie awake at night and worry. It happens little by little, but then quite suddenly a whole landscape has lost its quality, its character. I think Nick's concern, and his rage, stem from this —he senses it."

"You know, the bad thing is that the natives, the real people around here, still look on the land as something to be exploited, not to be treasured."

"Some do. The Lovelands up the road, poor farmers, living hard, they have more sense about animals—wild animals and all."

106

"What you really have in mind then is a glorious paean of praise to the region."

"Well, in a way, I saw it in my mind's eye as a *secret* natural history—what does not yield itself up at first glance. I always remember how dismayed poor old Henry James was the last time he came home. He felt it was a dismal, Raggedy-Andy kind of wildness. He felt at a total loss before a wild piece of woods." Jane savored this memory, obviously. "And I teased him about all that was hidden away among the underbrush."

"What did he say then?"

"Oh, you can imagine. He said it was a curiously uncivilized landscape—unshaped, I think he said. It does take some getting used to if your image of woods is a kind of park where every dead branch is picked up."

"And every beer can too. You know, Jane, I think someone should organize the Boy Scouts or something to clear the roadsides of just plain junk. Last year I found arbutus in flower just about buried under rusty old cans and broken bottles."

"Couldn't you make a start now? There'll be so many of you there at Thanksgiving."

A smile was just visible through the beard, and John shrugged.

"You know the family. They are dead set against anything organized. Every one of the children has some project he is bound to get at. Besides," he admitted, "no one pays the slightest attention to me. My children treat me like a curious old piece of junk myself." He sat with his head bent now, his hands held loosely between his knees. The mood had quite suddenly changed. "And why not? I am not exactly a success, Jane."

"Nonsense!" she said firmly. "John, put your mind on this natural history, or whatever it is to be. It could take so many forms, couldn't it? Seasons, for instance . . . or, of course, simply divided into flora and fauna in a straightforward old-fashioned way."

Jane went off into a long thought about this, and John swallowed down his glass of sherry and poured another, an act she read as a sign of quiet desperation.

"What I really had in mind, if we could manage it was a walk through the woods along a brook and coming out at a lake and a view of the mountain, and just to say what was there in the four seasons."

"How long is this thing to be?"

107

"Well, it's only one chapter. I suppose at most twenty pages. Jem has no idea what he is getting into, really."

"Who's paying?"

"I think he expects to cover expenses with sales."

John laughed. "Who'll buy it? the summer people?"

"Everyone who has a relative in the cemetery," Jane said demurely. "You know Jem and those genealogies of his. As a matter of fact, John, people are keen on this. The search for ancestors . . . Come back and sit down. You make me nervous."

John in the last few minutes had begun to walk up and down in a compulsive yet absent-minded way. He had done this as a child—and then the answer was to go out for a walk, keep his mind occupied, keep him from closing into depression and what Jane called "negative thoughts." Now there was nothing to do but talk.

So he sat down like a patient child, pretending to pay attention.

"I'd like about a thimbleful of sherry in my glass," she commanded. "Could you rough something out this weekend, talk it over once more before you go back?"

"Good heavens, no," John said crossly. "In all that hullabaloo up at the house?—Comfort playing records, Christy practicing the flute, Robin and Cathy arguing?"

"Yes," Jane sighed, "I suppose it's too much to ask. But, John, I'm getting to be a very old lady. I won't last forever."

"You have to," John said, half serious, half laughing. "I can't possibly live without you."

But Jane did not rise to this. She felt rather exhausted. For a moment her head nodded. She had closed her eyes. Perhaps she slept for a few seconds, and John observed her with some anxiety.

Meanwhile Hannah, who had been watching the clock, came to the door and made signals. It was clearly time to go, and John got up, prepared to tiptoe out. But they had reckoned without Jane, who now opened her eyes and said, quite sharply, "Hannah, you are not to look at the clock. I need to talk with John. I'll rest all afternoon."

"And I'm the one who'll pick up the pieces," Hannah said, shaking her head.

"I won't stay long. I promise," John told her, as she closed the door with a bang, rather like a jack-in-the-box.

"Thump, bang!" Jane sighed. "She's a dragon. I pretend that she is a real dragon. It's the only way to stand it."

"But she does take good care of you?"

"Of the old baby I have become, yes; of the real person I am, well . . ." She smiled. "We'll not talk of that. Old age is a great trial, John. One has to be so damned *good!*"

They exchanged a look full of amusement and tenderness. And John sat down again, took one of the small, dry hands, and held it hard in his.

"Tell me now about yourself, John. I've badgered you with town history—I just had to get it off my mind—but of course it's you I care about, dear." She waited. "I know you've had a hard time lately."

He let her hand go and lit a cigarette.

"It's so good here." Then he gave a deep sigh. "If you really want to know, Jane, I wake up every morning about five and wonder how I can get through the day."

"I suspect that more people than we can imagine do the same thing. What do you do then? I say poems to myself. Sometimes I play a game of solitaire."

"You are full of health, Jane. I am full of sickness—sickness of soul, I suppose. When I see my father now, having such a struggle to lift a spoon to his mouth, I feel so much pity for him. You see, I am like that *inside.* I am a sort of paralytic person *inside.*"

"Sybille doesn't help? She seems such a life-giver."

"Yes, but I feel I am a constant drain. She has lived with my depressions, my moods, my calamitous attempt to be done with it all. How can one have a real relationship with a man like me? She treats me like a dangerous animal who must be treated very carefully or it will turn and rend."

"No," Jane said quietly. It was not clear what she meant. Perhaps she didn't know herself. "No . . . you were meant to be a serious naturalist. I wish you would go back to the moths, John. There's work to be done!"

"I have to earn—try to anyway. The business is a big joke, but we do just eke a living out of it. And the routine, going to the office—well, at least it gets me out of the house. Listen, Jane, I'm fifty. I feel the important thing is to last it out for the children. They're what really matters now. That's what I try to say to myself, how I keep the demons down."

"It's absurd to be making envelopes, or whatever it is

109

you do, when you have the curiosity and mind you have. I've always felt it absurd. Your father was very wrong to set you up in that way."

"Father was terrified—wanted to push me into some slot where he would still have control, where he could keep an eye on things. Father did his best—I have come to see that lately. Poor man, I was an ugly duckling."

"Of all the boys who have come and gone out of this house you were the most interesting. I have always considered that you had a touch of genius, John."

"Oh, well,"—he pounded his knee with a closed fist, but it was not a gesture of defiance, or will, simply a nervous tic—"I just don't have the brute power, the ambition, drive. Nothing drives me hard from inside. Isn't it interesting, Jane, that Nick has suddenly turned so wild? He always seemed so mild—mild as milk. I do wish I could have seen him knock down those men!" John laughed with the pleasure of the thought.

They were startled and dismayed then to hear a gentle knock at the door.

"Oh, dear," Jane whispered. "How awful! Who can it be?"

John got up and went to see, and there, of all people, was Nick, holding a huge dead owl in his hands.

"Good heavens, Nick!"

"Found it in the road up by the Websters' early this morning. Thought Miss Tuttle might like to see him."

Jane was already on her feet.

"Put it on the table, Nick. Oh, isn't that beautiful!" She lifted one wing to show the great span and the overlaid pattern of feathers, soft brown and white. "Hit by a car, do you suppose—flying low?"

"There isn't a mark on him anywhere."

"And the strength in those legs and claws," John said. They drooped now, long and bright yellow.

Jane was handling the bird intently, all her powers suddenly awake and alive. "It must be a Great Gray Owl, Nick. Yes, I'm pretty sure that's it, but we'll have a look," and she went to a small bookcase and drew out a field guide. Together the two men and the tiny old lady pored over the page of owls. "Not a Barred Owl—see, he doesn't have the barred breast. Yes, here it is—a Great Gray. Well, Nick, that was quite a find."

For a moment they all three stood looking down.

"Athene's bird," Jane murmured. "You can see why the

owl has haunted men. Oh, if we could only see his eyes, so round and gold!" She laid a hand gently on the incredible softness of the head, as if to bless it. "Thank you, Nick—thank you for sharing this marvel with us."

"I'll bury him now," Nick said, lifting the bird in his two hands and holding it close to his chest.

Jane and John went to the door with him, and just as he was about to go, she asked, "All quiet on the hunting front, I hope?"

"I guess so," and he walked off toward his car, a tall figure wrapped in loneliness.

"Sharing his inner person with no one," Jane said. "I am touched that he came."

Then they turned back into the intimacy of the little low room.

"It was rather wonderful, wasn't it?" John said, standing by the table, for it was clearly time to go now. "You know, Jane, I was thinking as we stood here together, sharing the beauty and the sadness of the thing, that somehow this is what Willard is all about—this is what makes it precious, even to my independent children. They come back here and it's always a place where Nick, sensitive, uneducated, and wild, and you, with all that you are, and I, so worldly and confused—such a dud, really—can all communicate about the things that really matter. That's the magic. It's where all kinds of lives can meet. I wish the history could somehow say it."

"Well, it won't." Jane smiled and sat down. "But we, at least, can try to do something distinguished. I would like that, John. For me a sort of final message. You'll help me, won't you?"

"I will." The cloud had lifted. He spoke firmly.

Hannah once more appeared in the doorway.

"Yes, Hannah, this time I'm really on my way."

"We were interrupted by a dead owl," Jane said.

"Crazy people!" Hannah sniffed and vanished.

Alone again, Jane sat for some time turning the turtle over in her hands. She had a great deal to think about.

CHRISTINA'S JOURNAL—*November 27*

This is my last moment for several days to write something. John came last night, dear man, to help make beds and get things started. Little Mary Loveland did a wonderful job of cleaning, and even washed the kitchen floor for me. The pies are ordered (I do wonder whether Ellen's daughter will have thought to bring theirs) and will be delivered. I still have to boil the onions, make cream sauce, stuffing for the turkey. But I am full of joy and energy. It is so exciting to think of seeing the children and the darling grandchildren. How silent the house has been! Wish I had thought to get the piano tuned, but someone will bring a guitar, and there's Christy's flute. Surely we can make some music.

Cornelius has planned to have Thanksgiving dinner on a tray by the fire. It will be more comfortable and less of a strain for him that way. But it will be strange not to see him at the end of the table, although he assures me that Bruno can carve like an angel. I think perhaps Mamzelle can stay with Cornelius, to keep him company. I am so glad she is coming, if only she feels well and is not in one of her cranky moods! She wrote me a most extraordinary letter explaining all the things she felt she required, such as cotton blankets that she will use instead of sheets as she is afraid, apparently, of catching cold. A waste basket by her bed! A long list of what she can and cannot eat! Poor old dear!

For so many years she was a faithful servant, never thinking of herself, absolutely there for the children. For her, old age has provided a reversal of roles all right. She now commands and demands, and behaves like Queen Victoria, and, because she loves me I suppose, has become frightfully critical. She will be sure to notice the paper napkins and lament the decay of our standards. Oh, well, who else is there who still treats me like a child? I must remember to put some French books by her bed.

The house may be an ancient ark but at least it was built in easier times and there are plenty of bathrooms. The grandchildren have the whole top floor, what used to be the servants' floor, to themselves, and can bang away up there. John has warned me not to be shocked at how they all look—like tramps, he explained. But that is really how we used to look in the days of middies and bloomers. Blue jeans shredded and coming half way up the thigh are just another version of the same thing. I should hate it, really, if they were too elegant. They are such splendid people! Much better informed and more concerned about the world around them than we, God knows, ever were—and they will be gentle with Cornelius. They'll see what a battle he is fighting. At least I pray they will. We are all such blunderbusses, really, in this family. Even Mamzelle could never quell the fierceness in Olivia.

My Olivia—I had hoped so very much that she would marry, but she has fallen in love, with immense bravado, always with the impossible man, suffered, and held to her own way. Now she has become a magnificent aunt. Her nieces and nephews adore her. Somehow it is she who can speak their language.

John has gone over now to see Jane Tuttle. It is sure to do him good, for I think he feels the depression lurking again. He and Cornelius played cribbage for an hour last night while I washed up. They hardly talked, but I felt, right through the walls, the peace of it.

I have come to the conclusion that John, perhaps because of all he has suffered and his own sense of failure, is an extraordinary human being. Cruel world, for which this is not enough! Besides Bruno, so solid and sure of himself, John is like some rare refined creature—a camelopard, a unicorn—useless, to Bruno's way of thinking! Sybille—dangerous subject!—has tamed him too well, I sometimes think. But I have to remind myself that she has had to bear a great deal, and has done so with immense patience and lovingkindness. She just always seems so unimaginative, like a rather starchy nurse. I suppose that has been good for the children. They needed a sort of absolute person in authority. But I always feel she looks on us as a weird and rather unpalatable tribe. I know I am a snob about her and her air of suburban virtue. Luckily she seems able to "see" Cornelius. I have always baffled her completely. It's fire and water, I suppose. But away with such thoughts! Tomorrow is Thanksgiving. I am so deeply thankful for my family.

CHAPTER 9

While Christina put the turkey into the oven, washed the big Canton platter, and set the table, John got his father downstairs, settled in the armchair by the fire. And now the two men were having a smoke while they waited for the multitude to arrive. Cornelius, flushed from the effort of getting downstairs, looked almost like himself, especially in profile on the side that did not show the slight disfiguration temporary paralysis had left around his mouth.

"Well," he said, "here we are, John."

"Here we are, Father."

They looked into the fire. It was, no doubt, in each of their minds that both had had a brush with death since last Thanksgiving, and perhaps Cornelius had wanted to say something about this. He gave a little grunt, often the preface to something he had been ruminating. One of the logs crackled and sent a shower of sparks out into the room, and John stamped them out.

"I haven't the foggiest notion what it's all about—life —death," Cornelius said. Then, "Sometimes it seems as if we were mere sparks, like those. Yet life is precious. I must tell you, John, life has seemed to me infinitely precious lately—the marrow of it, I mean—just being alive, not dead. Being able to see trees, the mountain—I'm overwhelmed by love, John. It's as if it were all new—your mother and I . . ." But he could not go on. John was amazed to see the tears shining in his eyes.

"You've given your children a great thing—a happy marriage. Maybe we envy you a little." It was said with a smile, but Cornelius gave his son an intent look, then looked away. They had never talked like this before.

"If you can just hold out, marriages ripen."

"If they don't wither away."

"You and Sybille?"

"No, that's too harsh. We are forbearing—Sybille has been very forbearing," John said. "I guess that's the gist of it."

"Sad," Cornelius said. He pondered this. Then, "There are lots of things I have not understood." Now that he was feeling anxiety, the speech became blurred again, and John leaned forward to catch the words. "I want you to know that. I've had time to . . . to think."

"It's all right, Father." John felt terribly nervous suddenly, as if a secret wound were about to be unbandaged. He got up and stood looking down into the fire. "Don't say anything."

"I didn't love you well," Cornelius said after a moment's silence. "I didn't really listen. Lately I have come to the conclusion that the real trouble is that no one listens. We impose ourselves. We are so busy trying to be heard."

"Well, let's face it—I wasn't exactly the son you had imagined."

"No—no—" Cornelius made a gesture of pushing something away. "It's not that . . ." But he had no time to finish, for at that moment they heard the car brake to a halt on the gravel drive. Christina ran out to the porch, and John quickly followed to help the fragile Mamzelle safely up the steps.

In a few moments the Ark, which had seemed so silent, was filled with clamor—the thundering steps of Robin and Comfort carrying bags up to the top floor, and Mamzelle's whispery old voice greeting Cornelius, then demanding to be shown to her room.

"Yes, darling, come with me." Christina took her arm, and slowly they climbed. "You're in the blue room, with your own bathroom."

Halfway up, they met Robin and Comfort coming down.

"Oh, it's so wonderful! I found my rock collection." Comfort beamed. "Oh, Gram, you *are* an angel to have us all, even though . . ."

"Nonsense! It's heaven for me!"

Mamzelle, standing two steps below the landing, surveyed Comfort's leather skirt halfway up her thigh, her long blond hair down her back, and shook her head.

"I am dreadfully upset to see that child looking so . . . so . . . *ridicule*," she said. "What is it you wish to resemble —a girl from the chorus?"

Comfort blushed and Christina rushed in. "No one is to be criticized, Mamzelle. Darling, you are showing your age," she teased. "Come along, you must have a little rest to prepare for all the other monsters you will have to face at dinner."

Robin provided a diversion by sliding down the banisters.

"Good Heavens, Robin!" Christina said in dismay, for though the banister had held his forty pounds when he was small he now weighed three times that. It did look rather dangerous.

"It is terrible—John's beard," Mamzelle murmured.

Now Sybille, who had been talking with Cornelius, came up behind them.

"We like it," Sybille said. "It makes John look positively ponderous." She laughed her bright, hard laugh. "Where do I go, Mother Chapman?"

Christina had never been able to tell Sybille how she hated being called that. She opened the door into the pink room. "Hope all those roses won't make you dizzy." None of the wallpaper had ever been replaced, and the pink room did have a very old-fashioned paper, she realized, seeing it suddenly through Sybille's eyes.

"It's delightfully quaint," Sybille said, laying her bag down and going to the mirror over the bureau to arrange her hair. "After all these years I think I know every rose by heart."

"I'll just see that Mamzelle is all right." And Christina departed thankfully.

It was irritating to fall into the pattern of mother-in-law with this woman who managed to act on Christina like sandpaper on an abrasion. The word "quaint," for instance, disposed of things nicely.

Mamzelle was, characteristically, sitting on the bed still in her overcoat, a worn moleskin that she had bought in Paris eons before and that made her look rather like a mole herself, with her eager sniffy nose and small piercing eyes. She had taken up *Le Fanal Bleu* that Christina had placed on the bed table, and was already absorbed.

"Darling thing." Christina ran to sit beside her and

116

kiss her. "The journey was not too much for you? You must have a little rest now. Let me hang up your coat and tuck you in under the quilt—a little snooze with Colette."

Mamzelle laughed her silvery laugh. "You give me a strange bedfellow."

"Oh, it's a work of genius."

While Christina deftly hung up clothes, a wrapper and the coat, Mamzelle watched her.

"Why do you limp like that? All this is much too much for you. I told you that you must have servants if you came up here alone with Cornelius. Now, you see."

"But, darling, this is just my old arthritic knee, and the best thing I can do is to be forced to keep moving!"

"Humph," Mamzelle sniffed. "If you enjoy martyrizing yourself!"

"Now rest. I have to go down and baste the turkey." And Christina leaned over to kiss Mamzelle's cheek. How much she preferred the old woman's astringency and carping to Sybille's always-somehow-false politeness!

"I shall take off my skirt. No use crumpling the only decent garment I have left."

By this time Christina had to go, for she heard Olivia calling, "Mother, where are you?"

"Coming! I didn't hear the car—so busy getting people settled. Oh, darling child!" And there at the foot of the stairs they gave each other a warm hug.

"You're all right? You've managed all this alone? What can I do to help?"

"Don't you want to unpack?"

"Heavens, no. That can wait." And they went, arm in arm, to the kitchen, where Christina basted the turkey and turned the creamed onions out into a casserole and melted butter for the crumbs that would decorate the top, while Olivia opened a tin of nuts and began to wash celery.

"Where are the children?"

"Outdoors, I expect. Only Robin and Comfort are here so far. You know how they have to go out first, just like animals—smell the old smells. They are probably in the barn looking for a barn owl or something. —Oh, yes, the olives too. John brought them—over there."

"I brought champagne—three bottles. Do you think it will be enough? I'd better go and get that and put it on ice."

117

"Champagne! How marvelous! What an extravagant creature you are!"

"Mamzelle loves it, you know."

But Olivia looks tired, Christina thought. She's going on nerve. Olivia was tall and thin, elegant in her always-plain, beautifully-cut suits, her hair worn short these days, almost like a boy's, or rather—Christina corrected herself—shorter than most boys'. Her face looked a little gaunt under the reddish curls, her gray eyes deep-set—that was where the fatigue showed.

"French champagne! Good heavens!"

"We couldn't offer Mamzelle American champagne, lovey. She would turn up her nose!"

"She's more like a mole than ever. Oh, dear!"

And while they laughed and talked Christina punctuated the conversation with cries of "Wherever is the gravy boat?" "Champagne glasses—they'll have to be washed. On the highest shelf—yes, you'll need the stepladder."

John came in to get sherry and glasses, and he and Olivia stood for a moment in the pantry while Christina went out to be sure Cornelius was all right.

"The beard's great," Olivia said. "You really are a distinguished critter."

"It's a wonderful mask. I feel I can't be seen. I look out but I'm invisible, you know."

"I can see that it might be a kind of protection. I wish I could grow one."

"You don't need armor, do you?"

Olivia and John had always been able to connect at once. More than once it had been Olivia who was instrumental in bringing him back from the worst depressions.

"Who doesn't?" she parried.

"You look dead tired, girl."

"I am." She leaned against the counter, facing him but looking down. "The hard thing in this job is to keep a balance between caring and showing that you do, and yet being impersonal enough. Somehow I find it harder than I used to. It seems as if more children were cruelly treated than ever before. I see too much suffering. Some of the judges think keeping a family together is everything, and will send children home when we know it is dangerous. Last week a ten-year-old boy was brought in with a broken arm—broken by his father. At last we have been able to place him with foster parents."

"I don't know how you keep at it, year after year, and don't get emptied out."

"I do." Then she visibly shook off her self-pity. "But it's never boring. People do what they want, John, however much they may complain."

"Maybe . . ." John considered this. "No, I can't say that I have. Most of my life I've done what I ought to do. Jane wants me to write a chapter on the natural history of Willard for the bicentennial."

"Marvelous! That's something you want to do surely?"

"Yes and no. I dread the effort. I dread getting back into those old dreams of being a naturalist—but I guess it will be fun after all. And I want to do it for Jane, of course."

Olivia sighed. "Middle age is awful."

"Beleaguered from every side. Middle age is Atlas with the world on his shoulders." As John resumed the exaggerations of childhood, they laughed.

"It's good to see you, John. It's good to laugh."

"Well, back to the wars," he said, picking up the tray. "How is Father really?"

"Very gentle. It sort of makes one ache."

Then they heard the shouts, and Cathy, fifteen, pushed through the pantry swing door and rushed at Olivia.

"Aunt Olivia!" And she threw her arms round this "magnificent aunt," as the nieces and nephews all called her because she listened to everything they said as if it really mattered, and also (perhaps) because she could be counted on for a loan if things got really desperate. "After dinner will you come for a walk with me—alone?"

"Try to. Things on your mind?"

"Sort of . . ."

Christina hurried past, bearing the mince pies Marianne had brought, and Olivia vanished to join the others in the big room. They had settled like a flock of starlings around Cornelius, all, it seemed, chattering at once. Christy was taking his flute out and practicing by the big window. Alan, who had suddenly shot up like a beanstalk to over six feet, though he was only eighteen, owlish in his round spectacles, sat on the sofa with quiet Dorothy, the oldest of Marianne's children, beside him. Cathy sat on the little bench in front of the fire, and Marianne on the arm of Cornelius's chair. John stood at the other end, sipping his sherry. Bits and pieces of conversation floated about: "We saw a deer!" "Where?" "Down by the bog." "You're looking splendid, Father!" "Cared for like a pasha, why shouldn't I?"

Cornelius had got Marianne's right hand firmly in his. It stirred him to see her, so like her mother thirty years ago—the same brilliant blue eyes flashing out under dark hair, the same high color.

"Only you're too fat, girl," he said.

"Middle-aged spread."

"Middle-aged?" Cornelius laughed. "Never!"

"I'm forty-eight, like it or not."

"Nonsense." He would have none of that. "Even time doesn't fly that fast!"

Christina reappeared to warn them that dinner would be served in an hour. "I'll need help in about a half hour —minions to carry in plates. Olivia and Marianne can help me serve."

"Yes, Mother, but first sit down for five minutes and have a glass of sherry."

"I will," and she sank onto the sofa between Dorothy and Alan. "Where's Bruno? I haven't even seen him."

"He took the bags up."

"People vanish in this house like animals in an ark," Christina laughed. "Mamzelle is asleep."

"She can't be, with all this brouhaha," said Christy, taking up his flute. "Shall we lead her in with a song?"

"Oh, splendid! Yes! What shall it be?"

"Where's Comfort? We need her voice."

"She must have gone out. Someone go and call."

Cathy and Christy made a rush for the porch and raced away.

"Well," Alan said, "peace at last."

Alan was a physicist, studying at M.I.T.—he and Dorothy, the two quiet ones.

And then Bruno and Sybille came down together, and greetings and laughter picked up again. Olivia came out of the kitchen to pour herself a glass of sherry.

"Good to see you, Bruno—unofficially." They were on a committee together for urban renewal.

They all lived near or in Boston, yet hardly ever met. There was so little time. All of them had obligations and work, so an occasion like this was in every sense a reunion. At last they settled down and there was a silence.

John looked around at all the faces, amazed, as he always was, by the family resemblances—Alan's wide forehead so like his grandfather's, Marianne's eyes so like her mother's—and also by the fact that they were such extreme individualists. A stranger walking in might not fit them together at all as a breed or clan, might think they were strangers, met here by accident in a family hotel. He caught Olivia's eye.

"A penny for your thoughts, John."

"We're quite a family—that's what I was thinking."

But whatever he really had in mind was never said, for Cornelius had got Bruno over to discuss the market. And the two men were leaning close together, nodding, exchanging their mysterious language that interested no one else in the room.

"What I want to know," Dorothy said across the room to her uncle, "is what's going on in Willard. You've been here a whole day, Uncle John. Tell us the news."

John moved across to their end of the room as Christina and Olivia disappeared again into the kitchen. He told them about the history, and about Nick and the owl. And these morsels were devoured and commented on with the greatest eagerness. Marianne announced that she must go down and see Ellen, if only for a moment, after dinner. Alan was especially interested in Old Pete. "Has he got any coons this year?" Dorothy questioned her uncle closely about the history.

"Mother is writing a chapter about the women."

Sybille picked this up. "It certainly has been dominated by women around here."

"Yes, that's what's so interesting," said Alan. "A matriarchal society all right. And what does that do to the values?"

Cathy dashed across the room and upstairs to fetch her guitar, and was followed shortly by Robin, Comfort, and Christy, who had run to find her.

"There's a windowpane out in the barn, Grandpa," Robin shouted excitedly. "I can put a new one in if there's any putty around."

Cornelius lifted his head. "What? What's that?"

But the pane had been left open on purpose. It had been Cathy's wish because she hoped an owl might nest in the barn.

"Leave it," Cornelius said.

Here at Willard, John thought, it was as if they were always surrounded by shadowy beings, the wild creatures never very far away—raccoons, deer, owls, skunks. Wherever the talk strayed, even as far away as Wall Street, it

121

would come back to the not impossible owl, a link in the endless chain of natural happenings that every single person here, except perhaps Sybille, picked up as soon as he or she came in the door, even to the stuffed moose head, shade of Cornelius's father's pride as a hunter, that stared moodily down from the hall landing.

Christina appeared briefly to send Dorothy up to wake Mamzelle, while the others organized themselves to sing— what? "The Marseillaise," *Il était une bergère*"—suggestions poured in. But as Cathy ran downstairs with her guitar she had the final word.

"Au clair de la lune," she said, "because it's the only one I can play."

She sat down on the little bench again and strummed a few chords while Christy gave a tentative toot and Olivia slipped in and opened the baby grand in the library and played the old song through once, then changed the key.

"Better, much better!" Christy called, and ended by standing beside her. So they all flocked into that room and gathered round the magnificent aunt.

> *"Au clair de la lune*
> *Mon ami Pierrot*
> *Prêtes-moi ta plume*
> *Pour écrire un mot*
> *Ma chandelle est morte*
> *Je n'ai plus de feu*
> *Ouvres-moi la porte*
> *Pour l'amour de Dieu."*

Bruno's rich baritone and Marianne's alto sang out clear and loud among all the other voices.

"That was just a run-through—and not too bad," Olivia said. "Now hush, and when we hear them coming down we'll do it again."

The suspense was terrific. But at last, just as Cathy got a fit of giggles, they heard Dorothy saying, "Now careful on the stairs, Mamzelle, they're slippery!" and launched into the haunting old song again.

Cornelius, alone in the big room, listened to their voices with acute pleasure.

Mamzelle was surrounded, kissed, congratulated on her presence like an old princess, brought in to sit beside Cornelius, and given a glass of sherry.

"Yes, I'm quite overcome," she said, sipping it. "Thank

you, *mes enfants, mille mercis pour cette attention*—such an old woman."

"And such an old man," Cornelius murmured.

"Old?" Mamzelle laughed her musical, highly trained laugh. "You cannot be old while I am present. *I* am the old one."

"You are looking very well, I think," said Cornelius. He was courtly but maintained his distance. He and Mamzelle had never been intimate. He was ill at ease with her boarding-school manners and extravagant speech, and regarded her as a harmless old dodo. In the old days, when the children were small, she had been jealous of him, had attached herself to Christina with the implacable strength of a limpet to a rock, and appeared to feel that a husband was simply a burden sent by God.

Cornelius looked at his watch—past two. He felt hungry and tired.

And as if she guessed it, as if she felt his loneliness only for her in the midst of the voluble, overwhelming family, Christina was at his side, her hand on his shoulder, bending to kiss the back of his neck and whisper, "We're all ready, darling. Marianne and Olivia have taken over—chased me out of the kitchen!"

"I'm hungry," he said.

"Ravenous—so am I." The words meant nothing. But they rested for a moment in each other.

And then it was time to walk into the dining room—Christina on Bruno's arm, for he was to sit at the head of the table—all singing "We gather together to ask the Lord's blessing" as they went in, not in a hurly-burly but quietly because they were singing. So it had always been. It was a hard moment for Cornelius, left high and dry with Mamzelle while all the life and the laughter were across the hall in the next room.

"Champagne!" Cathy cried. "Great!"

While Bruno carved and Alan poured the Burgundy and Cathy and Comfort passed the vegetables, John asked for their attention, and Cornelius leaned forward to hear.

"Listen to John." Christina quelled the din. "He has a tale to tell."

"Not exactly a tale—something Old Pete told me—I thought it might interest you. Did you ever hear of the turkey round-up?"

123

"Did it happen around here?" Robin asked.

"Around here and all over New Hampshire."

"Tell!" Comfort demanded.

And while Bruno carved and sent plates down, John described the round-up—how weeks before Thanksgiving the turkeys were gathered and walked in a slowly increasing multitude from distant farms to Faneuil Hall in Boston to be sold.

"A river of turkeys," Cathy murmured.

"More turkeys, Pete said, than there were cattle in the West." John was warming to his tale. "How to water them? Where to stop for the night?—Nowhere near house or barn, for if a hundred or a thousand twenty-pound birds tried to roost on a barn roof it would collapse. Imagine their arrival in Boston—all traffic stopped, children standing on the street corners to watch this nervous, gobbling parade of birds pour into town!"

"It sounds horrible," Cathy said. "Those poor birds!"

"They're really so stupid," said Christy, "no one can waste pity on any member of the hen or turkey tribe."

And now they were off on the never-finished argument about animals versus people, voices raised, passionate involvement. No one listened any longer. Everyone appeared to be talking, and Mamzelle whispered to Cornelius, "Do you understand them? Your grandchildren?"

The question took Cornelius by surprise. He was waiting for his dinner. He wanted to be alone to eat it in peace. And the last thing he wanted was to be quizzed by this formidable old person.

He coughed his brittle cough. "I don't understand most people," he said. "The human race in its wild diversity is a total mystery."

Mamzelle shrugged. *"Naturellement,* but surely it is very queer to be as they are—no attention paid to how they look!"

"Do you remember how Olivia used to look when she was twenty?"

"Oh, those blue jeans!"

"You see?"

She shrugged. "Well, out here in the country, of course . . ."

"Willard . . ." Cornelius murmured.

He preferred to follow his own thoughts and leave Mamzelle to hers. They had always taken Willard for granted, like daily bread, but since his illness Cornelius

124

had come to think of Willard and what it had meant to three—no, four—generations, for he must include his father and mother and his brothers too. What it had done for "us Boston provincials," as he put it, was simply a miracle. All the trips to Europe, all the concerts and art courses, had not so civilized the Chapmans, he thought, as this obscure little village in the New Hampshire hills.

"If you must know, Mamzelle, Willard has civilized us."

"I don't understand. Christina has civilized it. She would civilize any place where she found herself . . . but . . ."

"No." Cornelius felt very cross suddenly—cross and excited at the same time, and hungry. "I will try to tell you," he said, his voice grown a little thick as it still did when he was upset. "My father came here as a rich man, secure in what he was and in who he was, but he didn't know half what Old Pete does about the natural world all around us. Even he had to learn that we would be respected only insofar as we could keep to a standard set *here*—a standard of behavior in the woods, for instance."

"I think you are exaggerating. *Noblesse oblige?*"

At last Dorothy came in with a tray for Mademoiselle, and Christy with a tray for his grandfather.

"Thank you, boy." Cornelius was glad to see that Mamzelle had not lost her appetite, and for a moment each was entirely absorbed in eating.

"Christina's stuffing!" Mamzelle gleamed. "She has not lost her skill."

"Why should she?"

"She is tired and no longer young."

It was the old refrain—meant to make Cornelius feel like a clumsy and life-devouring male who sucked the marrow out of a woman. But this time he was not to be drawn. He wanted to make a point.

"Over four generations we have become a little more than summer people—that is what I mean about Willard. Far more than the house in Boston can ever be, this is the root for the children and grandchildren. The first thing Christy did was to go and look at the mountain. There is something here that draws them. Thank God, we have it still to give!"

But Cornelius was now carrying on a struggle to cut his turkey.

"Let me help you."

"Please." He swallowed the groan of despair at his helplessness. Inside he had drawn strength from plunging into the question of Willard, but outwardly he was still a cripple. Now he had to watch a pernickety old lady ten years older than he cut his turkey up. Also, he needed to go to the bathroom, but this was clearly not something he could ask of Mamzelle.

They sank into a silence when she had handed him back his plate, half listening to the voices across the hall.

"We'll save toasts for the champagne, shall we, Christina?" It was Bruno's deep baritone.

"By all means. Let's eat."

The voices were talking about Nick, and again it was Bruno.

"The man sounds cuckoo to me."

"Why?" Christy's question to his father.

"Yes," Robin joined in. "Why is it crazy not to want to see wild animals butchered?"

"The man's a kind of saint," said Dorothy, and then everyone was talking at once—about wars and what they did to people.

"Nick came out gentle," Christina was saying, "almost too gentle. But I suppose it all got bottled up . . ."

"He's harmless, surely," Alan said judicially. "I can't see what all the talk's about. He got mad and socked some smart alecks from New York who couldn't shoot straight."

"Well," Bruno countered, "you've left out two things. From what John said, he had been lying in wait for hunters—he planned to attack them. And secondly, he was trespassing just as much as they were, only, one might say, he knew better."

"He was defending our deer, Father, that's what he told John."

"Yes, but . . ."

"But what?"

"When people take the law into their own hands, even in a good cause, it's the start of anarchy."

"I'm going to talk to Old Pete," Christy said. "Can I take him some turkey, Granny, and some stuffing—that stuffing is great. Does it have oysters in it or what?"

"Chestnuts and oysters," Christina said. "I had the most awful time shelling them. Luckily John helped me. What would I have done without you, darling?"

"I want to talk about it," Comfort was saying. "Why it always happens. Men come back from the wars and tell us war is hell. But they go right on, generation after generation. Why?"

"This generation is different," Alan said. "They may be loons but they don't want war."

"Except with the local police maybe?" Bruno teased.

"In self-defense."

"Yes, wars are always in self-defense—that's what each side believes."

"So men are brutes—is that what you think?" John asked. "We just have to accept that we're worse than animals—far worse—and not try to change?"

Cornelius woke out of a doze. "They're still at it, I suppose." He sighed. "World War I—what illusions we had!"

"It was no illusion to fear the Germans," Mamzelle hissed.

"Well, the Civil War then—could it have been avoided? What a waste it was! Here in Willard, how many men died or wasted away in prison? And that, after the best of them had already picked up and gone west, left the town crippled for generations. Where are the men around here?"

"Well, here's one." It was Christy, sent to ask whether they wanted second helpings. When they refused seconds, he gathered up the plates, went back to get wine and refilled the glasses, and Cornelius asked him for help to get to the bathroom.

It was a slow process, and while Cornelius took step by step, most of his weight leaning on Christy's shoulder, they talked.

"I've about decided on the Peace Corps, Gramp."

"Yes, I . . . I understand . . . better than killing. Or so it looks."

"College just doesn't seem relevant."

"It might when you come back. What does your father say?"

They had reached the door of the toilet downstairs.

"Father tries to let us do what we want to do. But the effort." said Christy with a smile, "sticks out all over him." Then, "Will you be all right? Shout and I'll help you up!"

Meanwhile Mamzelle was escorted across the hall to be present when the champagne was opened. Christina ran out to be sure Cornelius was all right, and found him and Christy coming down the hall.

"We can't have champagne without Gramp. Can't we move his chair in?" Cathy asked.

"No, we'll put him in Bruno's chair, at the head of the table."

Christina had missed him there. It had seemed all wrong. Bruno had done a lovely job of carving, but this was Cornelius's house.

"It was awful without you." She squeezed his hand, she and Christy helping him together.

"Let me take the weight, Gram," Christy said anxiously. He had only just realized what strength his grandmother must have to have managed alone.

Everyone rose as they saw Cornelius approaching. Pink with the effort of walking the few yards, even with Christy's help, he sank with evident relief into the armchair at the head of the table and asked for a glass of Burgundy he had left in the big room.

"Can't waste that," he murmured. "I take it we have to thank you, Bruno, for an exceptional wine. Far too good for such savages!"

And all the voices, children and grandchildren, rose around him in an ovation of pleasure that he had come back to them.

"For Christ's sake, sit down," he said, smiling across at Christina (Oh, how she had missed that smile at the other end of the long table!), "and let us eat some pie."

Everyone wanted a little piece of each—a piece of pumpkin pie and a piece of mince pie. Plates of cheese squares appeared from the kitchen. Marianne and Olivia were proving extremely efficient. In fact, Christina, a little dizzy now, had gladly given them all the responsibility.

"Coffee cups," she murmured to Olivia as she deftly cut and sent down the table one plate after another. "Put them on a tray. We'll have it in the big room."

Mamzelle had been squeezed in at her right.

"At last," Mamzelle breathed. "I have been trapped with Cornelius. At last I have you."

"We're here," Cornelius was saying to John on his left, "and what exactly does it mean to be here—all of us—in Willard?"

"Two kinds of pie," shouted Comfort.

"With cheese," Robin added.

"Well, that's two of you written off as Philistines," Cornelius chuckled. "Let's go round the table."

It was, Christina thought, amazing and wonderful that now that he was there a kind of harmony had come to them, a rest from pullings and tearings in every direction. He might have to lean on a grandson to get to the head of the table, but once there, Cornelius held them like an old lion. The table was magnetized at last. He turned to Sybille on his right.

"You're next, and your view—dispassionate perhaps— is especially precious."

Sybille was shy, never more so than when she found herself overwhelmed by the Chapman verve, the Chapman hilarity. But she had had two glasses of a great claret, and she too felt Cornelius's majesty.

"Shall I tell you?" Her eyes met John's for a second, a deep look. "When I first met John and came up for a weekend before we were engaged, I couldn't understand why the Ark, as you call it, had to be so dark and old-fashioned, and why John was so crazy about Willard. My idea of a summer place was somewhere on Long Island or Mount Desert in Maine. At first Willard seemed like a forgotten island of scrubby woods and poor people. I counted the roses on the wallpaper in my room and wondered why no one painted it white. Now, today, when I came back—how many years later?—and Mother Chapman led me to the pink room, I longed to lie down and go to sleep. I suppose for me it is an unchanging precious world, given me by chance. I have come to love it."

So that's Sybille! How I have misjudged her, Christina thought, exchanging a speaking look with Cornelius as she dispatched the last plate, with two pieces of pie, mince and pumpkin, down the table to him.

"A word from the noble minds of M.I.T.?" Cornelius said to Alan. "We'll change the rules to make the game more difficult—one sentence is all you are allowed."

Alan frowned, then said in his judicial way, "I'm not sure, but I think maybe the most important thing is living with a mountain—a mountain you can climb."

"It's the presence, isn't it?" Marianne burst in, "something that's always there, making us redefine what we are and what we mean—a god, I suppose you might call it, as the Japanese do Fujiyama."

No one waited now for Cornelius to call on them; they were absorbed in the game, even though Christina noticed the pies were vanishing with amazing rapidity.

Christy raised his hand (shades of school) and broke in. "No, it's people," he said. "It's Old Pete and going fishing and hearing some long tale about seeing a moose in that very place, or how his father got almost hugged to death by a bear but he held it by the tongue."

"Don't tell us." Cathy had her hands over her ears.

"That's a sentence, you've lost your chance," Christy teased.

"Don't be mean." Cathy blushed and looked down. "I've been preparing. It's meant to be a haiku," she said. "But I've been doing it in my head so I'm not sure—

"Asleep
In the long grass
A ladybird lights on my hand—
The long sweet summer."

"That's beautiful." Christina beamed, and a murmur of approval ran round the table, while Cathy stroked her long hair shyly.

"It's no fair for an investment broker to follow a poet," Bruno said. "I pass."

"No, you don't. It will break the magic circle," Comfort called down the table.

"Very well," Bruno said in his Board of Directors voice, but it was clear he was laughing at himself. "I'd just like to say that your father, Cornelius, made a damned good investment."

"But it's not really the house we think of, is it?" Dorothy broke in. "It's the whole place—the mountain, the pond, the woods, the village, ourselves and so many other people all mixed together. Willard is not just Chapmans. It's a whole world."

"It seems to me," Olivia said, turning toward Christina, "that it's a place where people can still be judged for themselves, for what they truly are, not what they have been given by chance. I see the opposite every day in the city slums—the poverty that is worse than mere lack of food and heat and decent bathrooms—the poverty of feeling one is no one and that nobody cares. When I come back to Willard I take a deep breath. Oh dear . . ." She turned to Cornelius, the arbiter. "I've run over my sentence, but I must say it better: Willard is a place where people are still cherished."

130

She turned to John sitting beside her, handing him the last word; but he, in turn, glanced down the long table to where Mamzelle sat beside Christina, looking, he thought, like a fretful old monkey, plucking a bit of fluff from her sleeve. And Cornelius caught his glance.

"Mamzelle!" he called. "Give us your wisdom!"

"*Moi?*" She looked startled. Christina reached over and took her hand. "You've all grown up," she said plaintively. "What can I say? The Ark is full of memories for me—and the wine has made me sad."

"We'll give you until after the champagne," Cornelius said firmly. "And now John."

"I have listened," said John. "I feel that everything has been said and nothing has been said, because each of us has his secret Willard, and that is what counts. But let me just say for now that it seems to me that we are together here in a very special and freeing way just because it has been for each of us a place of secrets." He smiled inside his beard. "Mine happens to be moths—moths and a very old lady called Jane Tuttle. Where else in the world would they have come together to give a small, lonely, difficult boy a sense of his identity?"

Olivia got up, and as she went by, laid a hand on John's shoulder.

"Yes, the champagne!" Christina cried out.

For the moment there was a pause. They felt replete —replete with dinner and with all the intense evoking of the last half hour. A kind of sigh passed over them as Olivia came back to ask for John's help. In the pause Christina asked Cornelius with her eyes whether he was too tired. The answer was *no*. Cornelius was flushed—flushed with the pleasure of all he had heard, not only about Willard but across and through all that had been said, what he had heard about the children and the grandchildren. In his heart was thanksgiving.

And when the champagne was poured he said, "I can't get up, but I hope you will stand, all of you, for I want to make a toast." As so often now since his stroke, his eyes shone with tears that did not fall.

"I drink to love," he said, holding Christina in his eyes, "deeper and better than you can know. I drink to Christina!"

Even Mamzelle rose to her feet for that toast, and chimed her glass with Christina's.

"But I can't drink to myself!" Christina said, putting

her glass down. Then she lifted it again.

"To Willard that brings us together. To Cornelius who makes it all happen!"

And so the tension was broken. Cathy and Comfort began to clear the dishes away. The talk resumed. They had reached a peak (they all felt it)—a moment that might not happen ever again—and now there was only going down to the normal routines of life, like washing dishes. The grandchildren flocked out to share in that chore, and Sybille, Bruno, John, Marianne, Olivia, and Mamzelle were left to finish the champagne with the grandparents.

"We're not going to let you off, Mamzelle," Marianne said. "Do you remember the dead mouse?"

"Do you remember my sneaking out the window and down the porch after we were supposed to be in bed, to help John find moths?" said Olivia.

"I remember everything," said Mamzelle. "I remember your saying in a fury, 'When I grow up, I'll never go to bed!'"

"Oh, dear me," Olivia sighed, "how wrong I was! Heaven is bed at nine!"

"Heaven is being young," said Sybille.

"No," Cornelius said with a fierce intonation, "no, it is being old and crippled and coming to see again everything so fresh, every person so precious."

But Mamzelle would have none of this. She bridled. She would not look at him.

"Willard," she said crossly. "Your Willard—a miserable, abandoned countryside full of second-growth woods and untilled fields, and a village where, whether you see it or not, poverty cramps. It's a wilderness," she said. "Only this house has some civilizing influence about it, perhaps."

No one was surprised. They were used to Mamzelle and her crotchets, but every one of them remembered her with fondness, and knew very well that her crossness was only her way of showing that she cared—just as she used to call them "dreadful savages" while she mended a pair of torn blue jeans or helped find just the right piece of red satin for a doll who was to be Lady Macbeth, while scolding them roundly for coming to the table with hands black with pine gum.

"I wonder what Ellen really feels about it," Olivia said, pondering Mamzelle's estimate.

"And when do summer people become really part of things?" Bruno wondered.

"When they become winter people," Christina answered, laughing. "But as for Ellen, she talks just like Mamzelle, and I suspect that under the talk she feels the same way. She's always saying she won't spend another winter in this hell-hole. She's always dreaming of somewhere else."

"She can't get away," Olivia said. "If one were caught here, year in and year out, no drugstore, no movie, no real community house, a dying church, too many women —and especially too many old women—well, there *is* another side. Mamzelle is right."

Christina saw that Cornelius had reached the edge of exhaustion. One eyelid drooped. He was making a visible effort to pay attention, and she suggested that he go upstairs and have a nap without waiting for coffee.

"We'll bring you a cup, Gramp," Christy said.

Mamzelle admitted that she too would be glad to retire for an hour. Olivia went out to the kitchen to help finish up. It was in her mind to suggest that she and Cathy walk down to the village and look in on Ellen. So, when the coffee was finally brought in, only the two couples and Christina were sitting by the fire. It was nearly four, and dusk was falling.

"He is so much better, Mother. It's a miracle!" Marianne was sitting on the arm of Christina's chair. "But aren't you getting exhausted?"

"If you stay all winter, you must have help," Bruno said firmly. "It's absurd to go on like this alone."

"Don't be silly." Tired as she was, the old flash came and went in Christina's eyes. "It's the best time Cornelius and I have had for years. It's precious. I wouldn't have a stranger in the house for anything in the world."

"You could get Ellen. She's not a stranger," John ventured.

"Well . . ." Christina faltered, hesitated a second. "There's a slight rift in the lute about Nick. I wouldn't want to ask her. I couldn't bear it if she refused."

The fire was nearly out, and John got up to put on another log. After all the words and the laughter and excitement of the past hours, they felt the need for a lower key.

"I haven't spent a winter here since I was eleven and stayed at Ellen's. I've longed to."

133

"But who'll shovel you out? How can you be sure you can get out?"

"Good heavens,"—Christina smiled—"we have a telephone. Old Pete will help, maybe Nick. You know one thing about Willard—when there is real need, help comes."

"Besides," John said, "I'll be up and down if I really do that chapter with Jane on natural history. Mother's right."

So they left it. Bruno, John, and Sybille went off for a walk, "to catch the light" Sybille said, and they must hurry to do that. So, finally, Christina was alone with Marianne.

"Perfect peace with loved ones far away," Marianne said after a moment. It was a family phrase that had come down from Cornelius's father.

"Bliss!" Christina closed her eyes for a moment and leaned her head against the back of her chair. Perhaps she slept for a few minutes.

Without the brimming light of her eyes, open, her face looked drawn and suddenly old. The delicacy was all there in the bones themselves, but the skin was parchment white; the throat, so much admired, had wrinkled under the chin. Marianne felt that shyness that one feels before a person exposed, and turned her eyes away.

But not from the truth this sleeping face drove home. Her mother would not always be there. She felt tight with the realization of this. Marianne was a doer, not a thinker. She plunged into life with reckless energy, spending herself on every cause that came to her attention. How rare it was to find herself alone in a room, with time to think—a little frightening. The children, so grown up now—even Cathy on her way to fifteen—had secret lives. At table she had watched them, felt pride, a kind of respect as if they were not hers at all; and Bruno, so tranquil and commanding a figure at the end of the table. It would never have occurred to him that she had decided years ago to go away, to leave him, when the last child left home—and that would be in five years! But I shall never have the courage, she thought. And wondered if her mother had ever had such wild ideas—the need to discover a self buried under family life, to reach right outside family to something mysterious—not love, not self-knowledge. What then?—fulfillment of something the child, the summer child at Willard, had glimpsed and thought possible. At night, when Bruno came to her with his need, did it ever cross his mind that she was not there

134

at all—that she had left that bed years ago, whatever in her was true to itself?

Not so for her mother and father.

"Eben is here," Christina said, opening her eyes and unaware that she had been asleep. "It's good to have an old friend around."

"But you haven't seen him for years, have you? I thought he was in Germany."

"He came home when his wife was dying."

"He was in love with you . . . once . . ." This was not a thing Marianne could have said even five years ago. Now it seemed natural to be talking with her mother as an equal, as a friend.

Christina smiled, a suddenly mischievous smile. "He makes me shine. You know, it's childish, but I found his admiration quite intoxicating the other day, the more fool I!" But then she looked into the fire and the mood changed. "Nothing ends, Marianne—it only keeps changing. Your father has become very lovable since the stroke. *That* is what I want to keep as long as I can—*that* is the point of staying here all winter."

"Do you think the pattern of a marriage really changes?"

"Oh!"—Christina was vehement—"every day. Every *hour*. A week ago I was so angry with Cornelius over Nick I could hardly speak to him!"

"I wish I could feel anything as violent as that."

"Bruno can't match your fire. But the children can, surely."

"The children are almost grown up."

"Then what?"

"Then we begin to face the cold reality—the funeral baked meats, as it were—of a marriage." It was said lightly but they knew each other well enough for Christina to catch the anguish.

"Yes," she said quietly, "perhaps at your age I felt that."

"You *did?*" Marianne leaned forward. One screen between her and her mother had just slid silently away.

"Of course. At a certain point a marriage has exhausted its nourishment. The man, if he is lucky, finds the nourishment in his work. For the woman, I feel sure, the forties and fifties are the greatest challenge to her authentic being. One just has to break out somewhere, somehow."

"How did you?"

"I threw myself into the Civil Liberties Union. McCarthy was rampant. I painted more seriously than I ever had—but of course I never had any real talent." She looked into the fire. How far away and long ago that period now seemed. For now when she looked back it was to her own childhood, when Ellen and she played in the hay in the barn. "It was at that time that I really came to know Ellen again—we used to take a picnic and just get out for a couple of hours."

"I guess she had her own problems. Rufus can't have been an easy man to live with."

"No,"—so absorbed were they, each in her own thoughts, that they were hardly aware of the silence, a companionable, comforting silence, as the fire seethed and sank into a crimson glow.

Out in the kitchen Christy filled a plastic bag with turkey and stuffing for Old Pete and put half a mince pie in a box. Once he was safely out of the way, and while the others dried the last of the dishes, complaining roundly that there still was no dishwasher in this old-fashioned kitchen, Olivia whispered, "Come along," and she and Cathy managed to slip out.

They seized any old jacket from the hall where the accumulations of three generations hung on wooden knobs for the taking.

"Delicious air," Olivia breathed as they stood a second at the top of the stairs. "It smells like metal, that winter smell I love."

They looked down over the pale brown grass to the group of white birch on the right and away over dense woods, the papery beech leaves still hanging here and there, silvery trunks against the dark green of hemlock and spruce and then, away off, a formidable dark gray, the mountain standing against the last pale green light in the sky.

"Yes," Cathy breathed. She was really saying *yes* to the mountain itself, that always seemed to affirm something, though it was never clear to Cathy just what.

After all the talk and noise, it was good to walk briskly without a word for several minutes, until they swung on down through hemlocks and outside the gate. It was not rational, but each had the sense that the atmosphere of the Ark was so powerful they would talk freely only when they were outside on the impersonal road, winding down past the cemetery.

Every now and then Olivia gave a sidelong glance at the girl at her side—the tattered blue jeans with velvet patches sewn on here and there, the Indian moccasins, no socks, and her hair lifting slightly in the air off her slender shoulders—a rather ragged waterfall of hair. Cathy held her head down, to avoid rocks in the road and because she was thinking.

"Aunt Olivia?"

"What?"

"I'm miserable at school. It's just like a jail."

"I thought you liked your history teacher—that Miss Beaver."

"Oh, she's O.K. I guess—it's just the whole atmosphere is so straight. We have to wear *dresses!*"

"Well, it's a city school. That seems a fairly reasonable rule."

"I don't feel like a city person," Cathy said. "Why should I be made to go there?"

"Have you talked it over with your mother? Maybe you could have your two last years somewhere else. There's a good school out in Colorado."

"Oh, Aunt Olivia, I might as well ask for the moon. They would say they can't afford it."

"Mmm . . ."

"They treat me like a dunce because I'm the youngest. No one but you ever listens." She kicked a stone ahead impatiently. "I guess I am a dunce. I get awful grades."

"That's a pity, because you won't get into a good college. That is rather stupid of you, angel."

"I *am* stupid, that's all," Cathy said crossly. "Besides I don't want to go to those old stuffed-shirt colleges—ugh!"

"I can't see that you have to."

Olivia was thinking hard. Cathy was certainly not cut out to be an intellectual. She seemed to have grown up late. She still hated dances, tagged along with her brothers because they, at least, took her for granted. What if she came up here for the spring term and went to the public high school in town? It might be a real help to her granny, good for Cornelius, too, to have someone young about. And Cathy had always been self-sufficient. Olivia hesitated to speak because Bruno was sure to receive any such suggestion as mad. Willard and all that surrounded it was just wilderness as far as he was concerned.

137

"You're hatching a plan," Cathy said. "I know that look, like when you persuaded them to let you take me out to Wyoming that time. Oh, Aunt Olivia, please help!"

"We'll see. I can't promise, but I do have a hunch. It will take some doing." She looked at Cathy, appraising her. "What's your life as you see it ahead? What do you really want?"

"Oh, a farm around here. Have sheep, cows, chickens."

"Hard to make a living around here farming."

"The Lovelands do!" And she added, "I could bring children from the slums for the summer."

"You've got it all planned, I see." Olivia smiled. This had been, though Cathy mustn't know it, the dream of all Chapmans at a certain age. Willard had a reality for them that nothing else had. But none of them had any idea how romantic a "reality" they carried around in their heads, nor what keeping a farm would mean of slave labor, their own—a different kind of prison from school but a prison nonetheless. She restrained comment of this kind. Life takes care of these dreams—dreams of escape.

"My guess is you'd better stick it out. It's only two years, Cathy."

"Two years! Thats' more than seven hundred precious days of my life *wasted!*"

They had come out now on the village green. It was almost dark, and most of the houses, including Ellen's, were lit up. Cars here and there showed that Thanksgiving guests were still lingering on, perhaps staying for supper. Cathy and Olivia stood a moment, feeling how small the village looked under the huge sky, lit only by stars.

"How peaceful it is," Olivia said. "Want to come in with me to see Ellen?"

"No, I guess I'll go for a walk, maybe up to the Lovelands'."

"I promise I'll have a talk with your mother."

"It's *Father*, Aunt Olivia—you have to talk to *him!*"

Olivia watched the slim figure move off, hands in pockets, into the dark. How is one to know, she was thinking, when revolt comes from the central being and when it is only part of growing up, sloughing off a skin like a snake? Probably Cathy would never have a farm, but there had been a tone of realistic self-estimate too. We must try to let people be themselves, she was thinking. And in this case there seemed to be several reasons why Cathy's presence here might be a good thing all around. After a half year she could still go back and graduate. The trouble with being the youngest, as Olivia well knew, was that the family never really considered one a person in one's own right. Well . . . she stood there alone in the center of the village and looked at the stars. There was no car in front of Ellen's, so the children must have left early for the long drive northward.

The welcome, when she finally crossed over to knock on the back door, was warm.

"Olivia! Come in. It's Olivia, Nick!" Ellen called as Nick vanished.

"I'll be down," he said.

"Forgive the mess," Ellen said. The kitchen sink was full of dishes, but the table had been cleared.

"Oh, it's *lovely* here!" Olivia said. She felt it, looking around at the geraniums on the window sill, the white muslin curtains, the sewing basket beside the rocking chair, the brown photograph of Willard fifty years ago, with carriages and horses drawn up in front of the general store that used to be right there in the middle of everything where the green now was.

"Sit down," Ellen said, and they sat opposite each other. "How are things with you?"

"I don't know really. These big family parties are such a jumble. I'm not sorted out yet."

"Neither am I," Ellen smiled.

"They all came? How is Micah?"

"Everyone's fine, but I'm tired . . . it all seems like a lot of work for a few hours . . . the children . . . I just can't get used to the queer way they dress. They're too far away for me to know them now."

"But they love coming here—you know they do."

"I suppose so." She shrugged her shoulders.

"It's the end of a long day."

Olivia saw how worn-out Ellen looked, just skin and bone. She had always been thin, but now her eyes seemed to have sunk into their sockets, bruised by fatigue, ringed in shadow, yet still so bright! It came to her as she talked that this was the person she could speak to about Cathy. After all, Christina herself had spent a year here in the country when she was only eleven, four years younger than Cathy. Ellen was the one person, perhaps, who knew both sides. Even her resentment of Willard would now weigh in the delicate balance, as well as her understanding

139

of Marianne. Bruno, of course, was hardly aware of what Ellen meant to the family.

"Ellen, I need your help." No words could have been more golden. What exhausted Ellen when she saw Micah and her divorced daughter and the children was just that they never said that. Everything, it seemed to her, was taken for granted. They came and ate like locusts and went away. Afterwards she felt resentment, felt exhausted and at a loose end, as if a lot of doors had been opened, a glimpse of something allowed, and then the doors slammed shut in her face.

"I need your help about Cathy," Olivia went on. She explained that Cathy was miserable at school and suggested that it might work to take her out, let her stay with her grandparents and go to the town high school for a semester. What did Ellen think?

Cathy, the youngest of the Chapman grandchildren, had never been Ellen's intimate, and it was not she whom Ellen now considered—it was Christina.

"Your mother feels that sore knee of hers more than she will allow."

"Yes," Olivia said. "I know that. But there doesn't seem any possible direct way to help. She says herself that not giving in to it is what the doctor recommends— and I gather that she and Cornelius are having a second honeymoon."

Ellen did not reply to this.

"I know Cornelius behaved badly about Nick. You have to forgive him—he's a sick man, no longer in control as he was. I think the idea that people could come and go without his even knowing—on the place, I mean—made that anger. It was not against Nick. It was against his own impotence."

"Maybe," Ellen granted. Then, with that characteristic lift of her chin, "But the village doesn't see that. They see the rich, as always, getting their privileges and resenting any invasion. I have been humiliated."

"No," Olivia said quietly, "that is not true. *We* have been humiliated. I wish you could have heard the grandchildren talk about Willard and what it means. Nick, to the grandchildren, and to John too, is a kind of saint."

"Maybe," Ellen said without conviction.

"You can't, you mustn't, shut Mother out after all these years!"

"We all have our loyalties."

140

"Yes," Oliva sighed.

In the silence that followed, it seemed to Olivia that an abyss opened between them. How could one every *say* what Ellen meant to Christina! And whatever Christina meant to Ellen was forever hidden behind the barriers of class.

"Tell me what you think about Cathy," she said. For after all, Ellen had not answered her question.

"Your kind of people don't stay here," she said. "Give Cathy a taste of this and then take it away? What good will it do? Only make things harder in the long run—just as, if I ever had a vacation, I mightn't be able to cope."

"I thought she could help Christina. That was also in my mind—a way out of a period of revolt . . . and *that,*" Olivia offered.

"Well, marriages are not made in heaven, that's sure."

"I don't get it. What do you mean?"

"I mean maybe Cornelius and Christina need this time alone."

"Yes," Olivia had to assent, "perhaps they do." But she couldn't push Cathy's anguish aside altogether. "But Cathy . . ."

"Cathy has to learn maybe that about half of life is spent doing things that seem irrelevant."

"Sometimes they are irrelevant." Olivia leaned her chin on her hands, trying to sort out what Ellen was saying. "I suppose you think we are sentimental."

"Well, no . . ." Ellen smiled her secret smile—the smile she gave when she was pleased by something. She smoothed down her apron and Olivia again noticed, as she had many times before, what beautiful hands they were, thin and brown now but with long, sensitive fingers. Their eyes met as Ellen said, "But, you see, there are always choices for you. Poverty means having no choice. I might dream of going to Florida in the winter, but I stay here. We have to make do with what we have."

"I know," she said.

"No, Olivia. You think you do but you don't."

"I see a lot in my work," she said, a little on the defensive now. "A lot of cruelty and hardship . . . and waste . . ." But why go on? The point was Cathy. "Maybe the whole trouble with Cathy is that her school in Boston is too rich."

"Well, she won't be slumming at the high school."

They were talking at cross purposes, the old resentment

141

flaring up. When Ellen was in this mood, it was better to change the subject. Olivia had experienced it before. It had to do, she surmised, with the children. Something hurt Ellen. Of all her children, only Nick really shared anything with her. The other two had fled their father and cut themselves off early. They had, as a matter of fact, made choices and gone up a step in the world, both Micah and his sister Sarah, who had a good job with the telephone company in Laconia. The thing Ellen longed for could not be uttered. She needed cherishing, Olivia thought. But she was a hard person to help. Put out a hand and, like as not, it would be slapped down. But one thing could be said for Ellen—she didn't treat grown-up people as children. Olivia had had many serious talks with her when she was in high school and college. In some ways she felt more at home here than even up at the Ark. So now she sighed and went on thinking in the good warm silence—warm even in disagreement, for the wonderful thing about Ellen was her tart honesty. I guess I can say just about anything to her, Olivia was thinking. Was there anyone else, except maybe John, of whom she could say that?

"I guess what I really think," Ellen said as if she had been meeting Olivia through the silence, "is that maybe Christina needs this quiet time right now—this time with Cornelius, alone." Then she added, "And maybe Cathy has to go through with something she thinks she hates."

"Well, that's the question. And anyway her parents would have to decide. It's none of my business, as a matter of fact."

"Oh, families!" Ellen laughed.

"What does that mean?"

"Getting in each other's hair, but maybe that's what it's all about. Sarah thinks Nick should go back to the hospital and have a talk with a doctor there. I flew off the handle—but she may be right. We just have to do the best we *can*, Olivia."

"I often feel as if I had been born to see everything and be able to *do* nothing," Olivia said.

"Still, in your work you must be able to do a lot for people."

"I wish I thought so. Half the time we are caught in some law, or lack of money, or one of the infinite coils of the damned bureaucracy." She pushed her hair back. "Oh, Ellen, it's good to talk with you!"

142

"I don't know why."

"Because you listen; so few people do. And because you're honest; so few people are."

"An onery old critter," Ellen said as Olivia got up to go. "But I guess I wear well, like an old sap bucket."

This typical image of Ellen's made Olivia laugh with pleasure, and reminded her to tell Ellen about one of the old women she had to call on, a particularly difficult old creature who said one day after complaining that she was lonely, "The trouble with me is I don't wear well."

And on that Olivia went out into the dark, to climb the hill homeward under the stars. She felt what being in Willard always did for her—stretched and rested at the same time. She took a deep breath of the damp, chill air smelling of earth, wondered whether Christy and Old Pete were still at it in the shack, where a light burned now, and whether Cathy had taken comfort in burying her nose in the donkey's fur up at the Lovelands'. How much Willard gives us, she thought, and how can we ever give it back?

CHRISTINA'S JOURNAL—*December 2*

Here I am again at last. Monday morning. Cornelius is still fast asleep. These last days have taken it out of him, but it was such a happy time! There was a moment after John, the last to go, finally took off yesterday when I could hardly bear to go into the silent house. No more thundering feet on the stairs, no fierce arguments going on in the study, no singing round the piano. I felt I was walking into some great gloomy cavern. Knee has been acting up, poor old thing. I feel compassion for this dying carcass of mine that really manages to serve very well, considering. Growing old is so strange because *inside* one feels just the same.

It's a dark morning, looks and smells like snow. The children are so concerned about my staying here alone. If only I could make them understand how I look forward to it! But there is just a chance that Bruno can be persuaded to let Cathy come here for the spring term—she wants to badly—Olivia's idea. How the nieces and nephews adore her! On Thanksgiving Day she and Cathy went off for a walk, and before that I heard her out on the porch surrounded by them. Ten years ago I grieved terribly that she was not married, grieved over those love

143

affairs, bound to be unhappy. Now I feel somehow that she has come through into her own. It is wrong to believe that marriage is always the answer for every woman or man. Some people are just natural-born solitaires, and I think perhaps Olivia is one. She is, at any rate, greatly loved.

If Cornelius and I can have two months now of real solitude, then it would be lovely to have Cathy come for the spring. She is so vehement in her desires; she reminds me of myself at her age. The family is really too high-powered for her. She is not up to them yet, and feels left out. But after the two days here she was radiant, hugged me so hard when they said good-by, I felt that a good hard hug is one of the most comforting forms of communication ever devised by man.

John too seemed at his very best, somehow lifted up on the problem of helping Jane write the chapter on natural history. He jokes about it—the lame helping the halt—but I can see he is pleased.

Only Marianne troubles me—such turmoil underneath that apparently safe and even placid marriage. But she is sustained by something of Cornelius's strength and stoicism—his daughter more than mine.

Yes, they are gone—and that is what I wanted to say. Thanksgiving had loomed before me as rather an effort, I must confess. Now I feel fulfilled, ready for the next step with Cornelius. We are truly blest.

PART TWO

Winter People

CHAPTER 1

After Thanksgiving the last summer houses were closed up for good. Even Old Pete had been commandeered here or there to cut pine branches to cover exposed sills. The Lovelands were putting up storm windows and dragging earth up like earthworks before a battle and piling it against their ancient farm. These were iron days, windy and cold, under pewter skies; only a few blond, shriveled beech leaves still clung to the boughs. Even the mountain looked grim—a dark, slate-colored presence, towering against cloud and often invisible now in the early mornings, hidden in mist. The only living thing in the landscape was water. The lakes were dark blue, and sparkled when there was sun; the brooks ran swift after days of rain; the bluejays came back to the feeder outside the porch and screamed. It seemed to Christina that they were all marooned in a long pause, waiting for the first snow.

The arrival of Dinnock Corey with the mail became important, and Christina sometimes walked down to the box at the gates to wait for him, drinking in the cold dank air, glad to get out, to hear the village news, and to get advice. It was Dinnock Corey's idea that Nick might be willing to shovel them out when the time came.

Christina looked at his shrewd old face, in which the

eyes were so crinkled up one hardly saw them, and wondered.

"I'm a little shy of asking," she confessed. "There was that trouble about the deer."

Dinnock smiled his crooked smile. "Well, if all the grudges around here were piled up in one heap they'd bury the village. I wouldn't let that trouble your mind. One thing about Nick, he's kind. Good for him to do a little work for a change."

"You ask him," Christina said. "Then he can. say no and no one will be bothered about it."

"I'll do that," Dinnock said.

Next day when Christina went down to the store for milk, most of the able-bodied men in the village were busy raking around the church and getting it battened down for winter. The last service had been at Thanksgiving, and Christina was sorry she had not been able to attend. On the road down she noticed that most porches, if they had had screens, were now boarded up. The village had a queer, closed-in, abandoned look—a little threatening. And for the first time she felt winter in her bones and that slight uneasiness before approaching isolation. Those who stayed on through the bitter cold and the snows would need each other. She almost turned in at Ellen's door on the way back, but thought better of it. Cornelius had not been feeling well. The tug, even greater than that toward her old friend, was toward home.

As she ran up the steps calling, "Hello, darling. I'm back," she turned a second to glance up at the mountain. The air was so still it seemed as though time itself had stopped. She lingered, taking in the leaden sky, and looked down at her garden, safely covered with pine branches, for the stillness felt ominous, not at all like the stillness before a summer storm. It smells like snow, she thought. And sure enough, weren't those a few flakes, whispering down through the concentrated, silent cold, one by one, hardly noticeable on the ground, just a dusting of white powder that had no substance?

"Cornelius," she said, "Cornelius, it's snowing!"

"I could have told you that," he answered from his chair where he was sitting wrapped in a car rug, with boxes of old photographs around him. "You don't have to see it. I felt it—the silence."

Christina, standing at his back, bent down and kissed him.

146

"How exciting," she breathed. She couldn't express what she felt exactly, but it was a kind of anticipation as of some moment of truth. It said "we are going to be alone."

But first there were things to do—if it was real, not just a flurry. She put the car in the barn and closed the door fast; then looked up at the brown-shingled fortress. The storm windows should have been put up. Old Pete had promised to get one of the Lovelands and do it, but he put things off. Never mind; the big porch protected the house. In summer it opened up the outdoors; now it provided shelter. And she felt grateful for the standards of the carpenters and masons in those days early in the century. It had been built to stand and to withstand. She noted the carefully stacked wood on the back porch off the kitchen. It had a new meaning—not pleasure but an elemental need. If the time came when the oil truck couldn't get up the hill, she could keep Cornelius warm. There were snowshoes in the attic, she remembered suddenly. Strange how the seasons always took one by surprise. Change was in the air—change and challenge.

"We're winter people at last," she said, laughing, as she brought in a tray with tea and cookies a half hour later. "Isn't it a dream?"

"I still wish you would get a housekeeper," Cornelius said.

"But she'd be around all the time! I'd have to cope with her."

They had been over this a hundred times. Christina's knee was stiff in the morning, and an invisible creature who could be summoned to help get Cornelius down would have been a help, but a person of flesh and blood, isolated here, needing to talk? No.

"Ellen, I suppose, wouldn't come?"

"Oh, she'd come in a trice if we were in real trouble, but I can't ask for regular help. She has her hands full."

There were other reasons—another reason. Her relationship with Ellen must remain that of equals, Christina sensed. Something might be endangered if they became master and servant. Eben could do it because he was part of the village, and Mrs. Goodnow regarded him as family, or nearly. But she and Cornelius were set apart. It was a hard fact, but true. Only for a few years when she and Ellen had been children together, money, social position —all that—had not counted. But you don't leave the

147

world even in a village like this. And the world creates barriers that only passion or death can break down.

They sat in a comfortable silence now, drinking their tea.

"Have you found what you wanted?"

Jem had asked Cornelius to see what old photographs he could hunt out, and this had seemed an ideal task when Cornelius felt up to it. Lately he dozed off, Christina noticed. Either that or he went down deep into himself to some private meditation; memory, so much more vivid, took the place of the browned, faded, crinkled photographs in his lap.

His answer was to lay down his cup and hand over a bunch he had selected out.

"What extraordinary clothes they wore!" she said, taking out a photograph of Cornelius's father and mother beside the Pierce Arrow. Mrs. Chapman had on an immense hat and a shirtwaist with a big bow under her chin. "And what a tiny waist your mother had!"

She had picked up another photograph, of a team of eight horses pulling what looked like a huge garden roller across a snowy road.

"That was the snow roller. Kept the snow down hard for pungs and sleighs." But he was impatient now. "Look at my father on Baldy."

There was Judge Chapman in his splendid riding clothes, on the gray he was riding when Christina first came to visit.

"Yes, I remember Baldy," she said.

There was a wonderful procession of long-skirted ladies with straw hats tied under their chins against the wind, and boys and men carrying picnic baskets, crossing a field. And Cornelius as a boy playing a foursome of tennis with girls in skirts to the ground.

"Good heavens!" Christina said. "How did we ever manage?"

"Put them away," Cornelius said. "They make me sad."

"Why, darling?"

"Strange, I suppose, how houses outlive people."

"Oh, yes, if only we could see them dancing, hear the laughter—*be* there again!"

"I miss my parents." He sounded cross. Christina recognized the family trait. She had thought Judge Chapman was angry when their engagement was announced. But he was actually moved and on the point of tears, so

148

he had blurted out, "Damn weddings!" and turned on his heel.

Christina took the tray into the kitchen and stood there for a moment looking out the window. It was snowing hard—thick, soft curtains coming down relentlessly, silently. Already the ground was white. It was catching along the pine boughs. She couldn't see to the road. Slowly, inexorably, they were being enclosed, carried off into winter. She would be alone with Cornelius, darling old man who mourned his parents—alone with him in a new way.

Around noon Ed Taggart, the road agent, turned up, insisted on bringing in more wood for Christina when he saw the woodbox was low, then sat and talked with Cornelius while she was out in the kitchen getting lunch. Now and then she caught a word. They were making plans about plowing. The snow drifted heavily on their hill, and she caught the suggestion "snow fences." When she came back into the study in her apron, she was amused to find the two men playing cribbage.

Ed didn't rise, just smiled at her and went on playing. Christina had always liked him, a rather stout man in his late fifties with very clear blue eyes, father of a family of six, who had himself been one of eleven children. No road agent is popular with everyone. He is inevitably the target of jealousies and complaints, but as road agents go, Ed Taggart was more acceptable than most of the half dozen or so the village had elected in the past twenty years. At least Ed took care of the plows and graders and trucks.

"You look very calm and cozy for a man who may be out all night plowing," Christina said.

"First snow—it won't last," he said, and "Yes, thanks," to her offered glass of sherry. He concentrated on the game.

While it continued, Christina picked up the pack of photographs and went through them again. It was a happy, peaceful feeling altogether. The change she had felt in the air for the past week was now here at the hearth where Ed Taggart would never have sat down before. Was Cornelius aware of how momentous an occasion it really was? Clearly he was enjoying himself, and when Ed rose to leave they agreed to play some more on another day.

After lunch, snow still falling fast, they talked about

Ed, and then about Cornelius's mother, who had died a few years after their marriage.

"I wish I had known her better," she said, the photograph of that slim elegance in her hand. "But she always made me feel uncouth—too large or something."

"It was shyness. She was really awfully shy—my mother." He reached for the photograph and held it in his hand. "I guess she was always a kind of prisoner, first of her own formidable family, then of my father and his world. When we first came here for the summer, the grandparents ruled the roost, you know."

"We may mind the world of our grandchildren, but it's so much more open than theirs, or even ours, isn't it? Imagine the road agent playing cribbage with your father!"

Cornelius chuckled. "We've graduated, haven't we?"

And Christina knew what he meant. They had moved into a different category—winter people at last.

"Not having servants makes a big difference. Your mother was always behind a barrier of servants. That's partly why I want to try this alone, just we two."

"And what's the other part?"

"Oh, you know, darling—to have you all to myself."

She held his hand hard in hers for a second, then left him to take a nap while she washed the dishes and then lay down on the couch beside his chair with a pillow under her head. From there she could see the dying fire and, through the window at the side, the soft white curtains of snow falling now incessantly, thick and fast. Could Ed have been right that this wouldn't last? It held a sort of forever in it. It might never stop, she fantasied, and the old Ark be slowly covered up, buried under this soft wool, this whiteness, this wonder.

Meanwhile, as long as it lasted, they were in a timeless place.

CHRISTINA'S JOURNAL—*December 5*

Ed was wrong. We have had more than two feet, and we heard the plows roaring by early this morning. Woke to a world of pure magic, dazzling sunlight, the mountain standing up there, bright dark-blue, with an air of great distinction. The pines are suffering—some branches have come down. Otherwise it is just pure beauty, that made Cornelius gasp when he opened his eyes, late this morning, and say, "Not bad, is it?"—an understatement of massive proportions. We are snowed in!

The phone began to ring by late morning, and I realized in a new way what this little thread between the hills and woods does to bring everyone close. Hannah called first for Jane, to see whether we were all right; then Ellen, bless her heart, to say that Nick would be up as soon as the road up the hill was clear, and would be glad to shovel out. That is a relief, I must say, as my darned old knee has seemed a little worse. Cornelius has invented a way of getting downstairs, putting most of his weight on the banister, so we can manage I'm sure, but it is wonderful to feel the dear concern and care of all the neighbors. I have such praise and blessing in my heart today for all this winter is. If only Cornelius can feel a little better! But whatever happens we shall have had this, and no one can take it away. As I write that, I am aware how often in the last years we have been pulled apart or distracted from the only really important thing—or so it now seems.

I forgot to note that Eben called just before noon. He has found a packet of letters from his great-grandmother to her husband in the Civil War—just what I had so hoped would happen. In the next days I must make a real plan of work and try to gather my thoughts together and get going at the chapter. There are also the women missionaries to be considered, and for that I must get hold of Miss Plummer. But since it is impossible to move at the moment, and more snow may come upon us, as another storm is brewing in the west, I have no care this brilliant day but to be with Cornelius in peace.

CHAPTER 2

It was two days before Christina was mobile. Nick got the big barn door clear of the tons of snow the plows had pushed up against it, and she decided to go to the village for milk and a few staples, and to stop in to see Ellen while he cleared a path to the porch and to the further woodpile out by the barn, and shoveled snow off the porch roof. If Cornelius needed something he could ring the old dinner bell she had unearthed from the attic.

She found Nick's presence restful. He was as silent as an animal, but he noticed things, suggested, himself, that he might keep the woodbins indoors filled for her as a regular thing, said he would put up snow fences for her and corral Old Pete for the storm windows within a few days. It was just plain comforting to have Nick around. Elusive creature that he was, Christina felt she had never really seen him before—tall and lanky, with a slow, secret smile and shadowy blue eyes. It was a mystery to which she had no clue—that violence of his of only a few weeks ago.

The brilliance was such when Christina crossed over to the barn that she had to shield her eyes. White reflected white, and only the distant view of pines and hemlock, bowed down under ermine, broke up the diamond facets—on the trees one could rest one's eyes.

The road was slippery, plowed but not yet sanded way up here, so she drove as if on tiptoe, almost skidded once, and finally went into first at the steepest part of the hill, noting as she passed that the gravestones were nearly

152

buried, the whole cemetery become a vast white bed.

It was heartwarming to get down into the gathering of small houses, to be in the village itself, where a geranium in a window and smoke coming out of chimneys, the sound of a jeep plowing out drives—all meant human concerns and human aliveness. And by the time she knocked gently at Ellen's door Christina was elated.

"Oh," she said, sitting on the steps in the hall to take off her boots, "we are so grateful for Nick's help. He's an angel."

"Good for him to do some work. Heard him whistling this morning when he got up."

"I just ran away, I was dying to see you."

"I sort of hoped you might drop in."

Christina noted at once that sewing had been put aside and books and papers laid out on the table.

"You're working for Jem, I bet."

"Well, it haunts my mind that there is a job to do. Wake up at night thinking about how it seems as if we more or less educated ourselves in villages like this."

Christina was wandering around the room, taking in, like a charm, the smell of coffee and a stew or something on the stove, the warmth and dearness of the shabby old kitchen, the cat under the table, paws tucked in.

"Sit down. I'll pour a cup of coffee. Made blueberry muffins."

"I'm just happy to be here," Christina said, finally sinking into the rocker with a sigh. "Winter is wonderful."

"It's early anyway—wonderful, I can't say. Seems like we get closed in."

"But it's so beautiful!"

"Hard on the birds," Ellen said, crumbling up a muffin and throwing it out the back door. "Nick worries about them, says an early storm like this kills hundreds—I don't know."

"Tell me about the schools. Have you started to write?"

"Wish I could talk it out. I'm no writer. Those sentences run through my head at night—then in the morning, I can't catch them. Seems like when I sit down with a pencil I haven't a notion what I meant to say."

"But you're way ahead of me. I have to get up to Eben's somehow and go over letters he found. You know, his great-grandmother took in half the village during the Civil War. It should be interesting."

"Dropped in here the other day just before the snow.

153

Must be snowed in up there today still. He talked about you."

Christina drank a sip of coffee and waited. Ellen knew as much as anyone about Eben and herself. But as Ellen did not volunteer more than this, she spoke.

"He's lonely, I expect."

"Never have been able to fathom him. He keeps himself to himself, then he turns up and talks my head off—just like a bottle of pop that fizzes up."

"Talk about the schools," Christina said, accepting a muffin.

"They weren't good enough—how could they afford good enough teachers? Once in a while a genius like Miss Morse came along, but after that we had Ben Torrey and hardly learned a thing."

"Why not?"

"He was only twenty and the girls teased him. The big boys were after him, too, to get him mad and see what he'd do then. He kept the children spelling, taught them a little arithmetic—whatever was in the books. He just plain didn't know enough. Seems like Miss Morse knew what she was talking about. First thing she did was to have us make a bookcase. Then she brought up her own books from Boston—a big Webster, an American history, a real one, not just one of those textbooks—and she told wonderful stories, made us learn poems. I guess my chapter will be about the teachers."

"And about yourself as one of them?"

"I was about as ready to teach as a hen to lay a goose egg, Christina."

"I can see you now, stern as a preacher, and you had such a pack of kids that year."

"I made them keep still." And the familiar secret smile came and went.

"How? Those big boys must have been a challenge—they were taller than you. That Higgins boy! Why, I should have been scared to death."

"Well, you know, I followed on a real brute. Captain Schooner, they called him, but as far as I know the only ship he ever commanded was the schoolhouse. He punished the children terribly—drew blood from a small boy's head with his ruler, threw books and even logs at the big boys. And finally there was a mutiny and they got together and threw him out bodily, head first, into a snow-

154

drift. I guess by the time I came they were grateful for milder ways."

"Can't imagine you mild, but go on—how did you keep them still?"

"I remembered Miss Morse. All she did I tried to do. For instance, we ended the day either with a spelling bee or with a story. If there had been noise, they had no story."

"What kind of story?"

"I told them true stories, sometimes, out of history; sometimes I made something up, but tried to get facts straight. The boys were crazy to hear about the wars with the Indians. I told them stories about the Underground Railroad and about things that had happened right here. I wanted them to feel they were part of history, right here in Willard."

"What a person you are!" Christina said, looking at the worn face and the dark shadows around the eyes.

"Don't know about that. But one thing's sure—if I could have kept at it—the teaching, I mean—I might have got myself an education. Nothing like teaching to make you learn. Got married instead." She looked out at the snowy world outside and sipped her coffee for a moment. "I wasn't the marrying kind, you know. Never should've done it."

"I suppose more than a few women feel that at times —more than we know. I was the marrying kind, I guess. I just can't imagine not being married to Cornelius."

Ellen sighed; then the pinched look left her face and she lit up with interest. "Nick told me he can eat by himself—that's a step forward."

"Yes, he's better in some ways. He's putting up a terrific fight way down deep inside him. Never admits he's discouraged. By spring I'll know better. We must take him down to Boston soon and see what the doctors say." But Christina was not in the mood to talk about Cornelius. She pushed away thinking about the future, even from her own mind. "What else did you do to keep the kids learning and quiet?"

"I thought up games—games where they had to use their wits—like, how would you pack a covered wagon to go west? What would you put in it—tools and the like? What kind of food? Maybe a few lilac roots?"

"What a wonderful idea!"

"I still play that game sometimes when I can't sleep."

155

Then she laughed. "Sometimes I teased them by misspelling a word and seeing if anyone could catch me out."

"And did they?"

"Once I got caught out myself—misspelled 'recommendation'—left out one *m*. I gave them an extra ten minutes' recess as a reward for knowing better than their teacher!" But suddenly the laughter ebbed and Ellen looked keenly at her friend. "It was the halt leading the blind! They learned what they learned thoroughly, but not enough— not nearly enough, Christina."

"Of course the school year was awfully short—just seventeen or twenty weeks, if I remember. With the children helping on the farms in spring, summer, and fall . . ."

"Rufus told me he never did get to school in the summer term after he was seven. And he was one, for all his faults, who hankered after learning."

"Yet the amazing thing is how many boys from villages like this went on to Dartmouth, got law degrees, became doctors . . ."

"The bright ones got out—bright like Eben—or went west. What's left has grit and that's about it. Look around you—people who amount to anything in this town left and came back different. My own daughters never say so, but they've gone on—they're different."

"In what way?"

"Buy things instead of making them—even food. They wouldn't bother to bake beans in the oven. They open a can."

"Why is that better?" Christina was amazed that it could seem better.

"It gives them time to read, time to play too."

"But is it better to work all day in a telephone office like Sarah and earn enough to buy canned food rather than grow it as their father did and cook it as you do?"

"Independence costs a lot, Christina—my kind, Rufus's kind. I've never had a holiday in my life, and sometimes I wonder where it has all gone, and for what."

"For wisdom, for one thing. You're wise. Are they?"

"I guess wisdom is beaten into a person. Whatever I've learned, anyway, I've learned out of grief and pain."

Christina looked across at her friend, so proud and grim, so sure she had been cheated in some deep way by life, yet no word like "failure" or "defeat" could ever be applied to Ellen.

"How are we to know what it's all about? But you

156

know very well, Ellen, that your wisdom has served—served Nick for one thing, and Nick is rather special."

"Never amounted to anything," Ellen said with her bleak mood unshaken.

"I came here to get cheered up—all elated by the snow—feeling that life was good, so good I'm just about to burst. When you said 'grief and pain' you left 'love' out."

"No,"—Ellen lifted her chin—"can't think of a true love that isn't mostly pain." She glanced across at the cat under the table and leaned down to rub his ears. "Even animals. Get to love one and it dies on you. Rufus wept when Dander, the old horse, had to be put to sleep. He wouldn't have wept for me."

"You don't know," Christina said.

"Well, I didn't weep for him," she said quietly. "We just about wore each other out."

"But I love you," Christina said earnestly. "And surely grief and pain don't enter into what we are, and have been, to each other since I was eleven and you brought me your Swiss bear that first homesick night." She felt that she must win through to some joy, something less harsh and bitter than all that had been said so far.

Ellen got up and took the cups and saucers to the sink.

"When you went away to college and never came back all those years, I thought I had lost you. I had to close my heart then." It was said quietly, but the words hit Christina hard—so hard that tears started in her eyes. It was the truth. She had gone away, forgotten Ellen, caught up in the immense new world of college, in all she was learning; then in parties, weekends, trips to Europe, finally in Cornelius's life. It was true.

"I'm here now, Ellen," she said after the pause.

"Now we're old."

"Now we're true friends."

"Maybe," Ellen granted. And suddenly she smiled one of her rare, mischievous smiles. "I'm ornery today—don't know why. Winter on us so early . . . and . . . well, thinking about the poverty of the schools. I got a kind of ache about the life here—felt starved."

"But you forget Miss Morse—and so many others!" It was Christina's turn to get up and go to the window, look out on the white world, so opulent and so stark at the same time. "Jane Tuttle, dear old Jem, Eben, Dinnock and Orin, Old Pete—it's a rich variety of human beings, Ellen, you'll have to grant that."

"Well, I can see it looks good and kind of human if you've lived in a city all your life. Then you have the best of both worlds. Then you can come back and drink from the pure water of a village well—and it must taste good. I might have liked a glass of champagne now and then."

"Ah, you shall have one," and Christina laughed with the joy of it. "Next time I come down, I'll bring a bottle."

"It's champagne enough to have you around for a winter, I guess." The words came out stiff. It had taken an effort to say them—that supreme effort of giving away something of all the withheld affection. Ellen, Christina suddenly saw, hugged everything she felt deeply, just because it was so deeply felt. "I'm copying Eben—he said you were like a glass of champagne."

"He did, eh? No fool like an old fool, I guess."

"You be careful now," Ellen teased.

"At seventy-five one of the best things about life is that one doesn't need to be. I shan't be careful a bit!"

After all, the dour mood had changed, and Christina drove off to the village store, humming an old tune she and Cornelius had used to dance to in the days of the tango. Who could have imagined that old age would be so rich and full? Just to cap the morning she saw a flock of evening grosbeaks on her way home.

CHRISTINA'S JOURNAL—*December 7*

That precious packet of Sophia's letters! Eben sent it down by Dinnock and I found it in the mailbox when I got home. There the letters lay, tied up in red tape, the ink faded, the paper worn and torn, but as I read them aloud to Cornelius, such a person came vividly out to us that it was like bringing the dead to life. We had an extraordinary afternoon, reading, talking, fitting it all together, the huge farmhouse—up this very road, Cornelius thinks—where a group of women under Sophia's leadership lived and worked together as a community when the men had gone to war. What a novel it would make! The sheer adventure of it makes my heart beat faster. And what a person Sophia was! In spite of the genteel style she comes through as humorous, forthright, opinionated, passionate. I bet she enjoyed having her own way for four years! She pretends to ask Elisha's advice, but of course she knew very well that by the time his answer reached her she would have made her own decision. At first she has only the vaguest idea where his regiment is— the Seventh New Hampshire. Sometimes several months elapse without news. But in the last year of the war he was wounded and in hospital, and then, at last, she could be sure that comfits—dried apples and cherries—a quilt, warm socks and nightshirts would reach him. Her heart was torn by the decision as to whether to go down and nurse him—as many women did—or to stay in Willard and keep her hand on the plow. It is a moving letter where she tells him how fervently she has prayed for guidance and that she has finally come to believe that she must stay. She was responsible, the moving spirit of a large undertaking.

What would I do without Cornelius? My imagination catches fire, but he, dear thing, keeps me close to the nub of reality. While I read aloud, he took notes and could tell me at the end just who made up "the family." There were, Cornelius thinks, five women in their thirties, able to work on the farm, one old woman, Aunt Tabitha, who helped with the cooking, an old man, crippled in one leg but a good worker, who could teach the women a lot they needed to know. And among these five women, there were fifteen children—nine of them, fortunately, boys. Sophia speaks often of their own, True and Harlie, a boy and a girl, ten and twelve at the start of the war, and of how proud she is to see how like Elisha True is, "an earnest worker like you, who cares to do a good job. I heard him scold one of the little boys the other day because he had not dug a bed deep enough. 'Not worth doing something badly,' he said." She hopes Elisha will understand about a flower bed when there is so much else to keep going, "but it is such a joy to have a posy on the table."

Little things like that make Sophia so vivid! I could sit and dream about her for hours . . . how did she look? Tall, I think, big-boned and sturdy.

"Tall?" Cornelius teased me, "because you are tall? Maybe she was short and stout like Napoleon!" I must ask Eben whether he has a photograph.

Cornelius was most interested in a letter where Sophia discusses the question of children's wages. As usual the matter is phrased as a question, first as to whether Elisha remembers the sad story of a neighbor child who had managed to save $100 to take him to Dartmouth, banked it, and then one day his father simply took it out and used it for some purpose of his own. By law a child's wages belonged to his father, so there was nothing the boy could do about the money. What he did do was run away. This is Sophia's introduction to a plea that Elisha go along with her decision to pay each child a small amount for work done, a wage that he may spend as he wishes. Some of the children bought candy, but Harlie saved up for a Bible, with illustrations of the Holy Land, and True bought himself a hatchet that he wears proudly in his belt. It sounds so sensible, but apparently the Reverend Ellis did not approve of such radical measures as paying a child for work the Lord intended him to do humbly and for no reward!

I long to know more about these human problems. . . . Luckily Sophia does seem to have one real friend, Bridget, who appears fleetingly but always as a lifter of spirits and a forceful person. She smooths over hurt feelings. It is she who gets them to singing after supper when they gather by the fire to mend or weave, and one grand summer day it is she who leads them all to climb the mountain.

Sophia wrote these letters by candlelight after the household was in bed. She was tired, of course, and I have an idea that what rested her was to contemplate work done, and what she enjoyed most was telling Elisha everything she could about the farm—how many tons of hay got safely stowed away in the barn before a rain; about the foot disease that looked serious for two of the oxen, Star and Barry; about sixty lambs born late one January when the weather was bitter cold, thirty below zero; or, one summer, how raccoons got at the corn and ate a whole row, and when True and two other boys sat up all the next night to watch, they didn't catch one of the clever creatures. Such news of the farm must have been lifeblood to Elisha. . . .

I'm half asleep—have been sitting here dreaming for ten minutes. Cornelius is in bed and it is time I was. Only I keep thinking in the back of my mind about a sobering talk I had with Ellen—a talk that has been running under the excitement of the afternoon and Sophia like a small thread of pain. In Sophia's day, of course, the hard life was the regular thing, shared by everyone.

160

Sophia did not, as Ellen does, see riches and waste and carelessness all around her, so there is now an added psychological hazard to life in the village. It has never been an easy life around here, that's for sure, but in the old days everyone was, more or less, in the same boat. That is the big difference. Ellen carries the scars of generations of bare subsistence. It shows.

On my way home I looked over at Old Pete's shack. Smoke was coming out of the chimney, but how can he get through a winter here? He doesn't even have a proper woodpile from what I could see. "The winter closes in," as Ellen said. For me, an adventure, but for some, a yearly ordeal. Already I am learning more about the village than I ever dreamed. One real snow has changed the atmosphere.

CHAPTER 3

It had all begun like a fanfare of trumpets—pure air, delicious snow, and the changed world, but when the second big snow fell before the first one had melted, and then a series of lead-gray, bitter-cold days and high wind made the windows rattle and the house creak like a ship, Christina's joy gave way to a feeling of anxiety. She begged Nick to try to get hold of Old Pete, but Old Pete, it seemed, was not feeling well. His hernia was bothering him, and he spent the days keeping himself warm and drinking with anyone who would get him a six-pack from the store.

Finally, at Cornelius's suggestion, she drove up past Eben's to the Lovelands' farm to see if one of that clan of hard workers would be willing to get at the storm windows and storm doors, fix a leak in the attic roof, and perhaps also clean the house. John had promised to come up before Christmas to see Jane and to help out. All the children had telephoned or written, so the slight sense of fear Christina had experienced, "the wind at my back" as she described it, had gone for the moment.

She went in to kiss Cornelius good-by. He was drawing up a plan of Sophia's farm, listing the animals and all the facts he could glean from the packet of letters, in his small methodical hand. It was really a great piece of luck to have a task like this to keep him amused. When Christina bent to kiss the top of his head, he hardly noticed, he was so absorbed. "Pigs," he murmured. Then as she

162

turned to go, he admonished her to drive carefully. "Go up the steep hill in first!"

"Yes, darling."

They were entering a new phase, for Cornelius, who had been so patient, letting her make decisions, never cross even for a second, was now getting to the point where his awkwardness had become a constant irritation. Christina told herself that this was a sign that he was on the mend, but she hated being ordered around, and it seemed for the moment that his recovered sense of himself was taking the form of his treating her like a rather feeble-minded child.

"You'll freeze to death in that jacket. For God's sake, have some sense—wear your fur coat."

But Christina didn't want to wear a fur coat to the Lovelands'. She slipped out in a ski parka without being seen.

The wind was cruel, and her teeth were chattering by the time she was safe in the car. They had talked about a Land Rover, but it would be much harder to drive than the Ford, and without actually saying so, Christina had managed to delay a decision on this. Her knee was the problem. She never complained aloud, but at times it was rather like a constant toothache, and lately the pain had kept her awake—she who normally fell asleep as soon as her head touched the pillow. Any weight on her foot made it worse. She had had to discard heavy snow boots as well as ski boots, and wore lined moccasins.

It was a relief to let a machine carry her weight for a change, and she felt quite exhilarated as she turned out into the road. No doubt about it, a car was a sort of intoxication for the old and infirm as well as for the young. Lovely to feel so much easy power in her hands, so she speeded up, went into a slight skid, and slowed down again. After all, why hurry? She noted in passing that Eben was plowed out all right. She was longing to turn up and see him, but she resisted the temptation. First things first and, for the moment, storm windows came before history or, for that matter, an old flame.

The various abandoned cars that surrounded the Lovelands' had been buried in the last snow. But there was the usual lively disorder around Ma Loveland's children's houses, settled below the old farm like chicks around a hen. The final turn up the road to this collection of fallen-in barns and sheds, and the house with its ancient, sagging roof, was tricky, but she got a grip all right and was able to drive almost to the door. The Lovelands anyway had been beforehand about winterizing: the house was piled all around, and the porch was covered in two feet of protective earth.

As she got out, a rather menacing dog was barking, hackles raised, until a small boy got him by the collar.

"Anyone home?"

"Gramma's inside."

The child, one of the innumerable grandchildren, dragged the dog away and tied him under a hay wagon. The wind was flailing around in the high air. A piece of tar paper on the barn had come loose and was flapping. The whole place, low on the ground, felt terribly exposed. And this was only the start of winter, with a herd of cows to keep fed and watered, the big work horses—for the Lovelands still had horses, the only ones in the village— and God knows how many other animals. Christina made her way slowly against the wind and knocked at the side door.

"Well," Ma Loveland said, "if it isn't you, Christina. Never thought to see you. Come in where it's warm."

The tiny kitchen, crammed with a table, stove, and straight chairs, bulged with life and heat. Every window was filled with potted plants. There were two cats under the stove, fast asleep, and another dog, an indoor dog apparently, under the table. He licked Christina's hand when she sat down. It took a moment to get her bearings, to recover from the shock of dear Ma's face. She had aged in the last year—her face now a mass of fine wrinkles, only her dark eyes as bright as ever.

"How is Mr. Chapman?" she asked. The warmth of interest flowed out at once. The Lovelands were always courteous. Going down from their hill on the daily errands —to deliver milk, to work on the roads, and Jeane, the middle daughter, to work for various elderly spinsters in the village—they gathered in the news, wove it in and out in their talk—*cared*. Once, when all Christina's tulips had been broken off by cutworms, it was Mary Loveland who telephoned to say how sorry she was about it. These were *real* tragedies. They themselves lived fighting impossible battles—battles that never could be won in this climate. Frost came early, or raccoons ate the corn. A fox got in to the Muscovy ducks. Every harvest, every egg, it seemed sometimes, had been garnered "by luck and by Jesus," as Old Pete put it.

So Christina reassured Ma about Cornelius and about herself.

"We're in for a long winter, looks like. When that first snow didn't melt, I knew we were in for it," Ma said, rubbing her hands on her knees—worn hands, rough with hard work.

"You're all well, though?"

"I get kind of tired in the bones, but hard work never hurt anyone."

"Mary, I came to ask whether maybe March and Hannie could help Nick get the storm windows up. This early snow certainly took me by surprise—but Old Pete was to have come weeks ago."

"Guess he's not feeling too good. March gave him a lift in the truck the other day. He's too old to live in that shack. I can't imagine how he'll get through this winter."

"Where could he go?"

"He has family all over, but they don't get on. He's a loner—always was." Then she smiled her rare smile—a smile of complicity, and at once Christina found again the young face she remembered, fresh and sweet as a rose. "Fact is, he's the best of the lot. Old Pete's honest, even if he don't care to work. —I'll just call March. Out in the barn, I expect."

"Oh, I'll go out and see him." Christina was sweating in the intense heat and, besides, she loved the barn. Indeed the sweet smell of ammonia, milk, and manure in the midst of the frozen world was absolutely delicious.

"Smells good in here, March," she said to the tall, lanky man who was laying down fresh sawdust. She stopped to rub a greige cow's forehead. March must be fifty now she was thinking, but he looks like a boy. And he had kept the shyness of a boy, and went on working now out of shyness. But after she had looked over the herd and they had talked of the weather, when she came to the point, March stopped for a moment, took off his cap, and scratched his head.

"Don't see why not. We could get off on Thursday. I have some wood to bring in down at Nobels'. Promised to cut and stack it. We'd come after that, by noon, Hannie and me."

What a comfort the Lovelands were! Yet such a different breed from Ellen, although they must be distant cousins. Mary's name had been Lockhart before her marriage. These Lovelands had no wish to leave the village. They were truly rooted here, prizing every tree and bush and every animal they owned, as if they owned great treasure. They did not suffer from hungers and aspirations for something else. Why not? Christina wondered as she drove quietly homewards, waving to one of the in-laws, a stout young woman hanging out a wash. Maybe it was that these people were nourished in a rather rare way by each other. The family was everything here, and the atmosphere of love, of respect, was tangible in the air. It had shown in the way Mary herself would not speak for her son. Work was done on a co-operative basis, but each one had his own special tasks and responsibilities. And, of course, they were held together by the magnificent courage and faith that shone out from Mary's every glance. They were rich in themselves.

Full of all this good news, wanting to tell Cornelius all about the visit, Christina drove back home elated. Cornelius was asleep and looked at her with a troubled look when he found her there and realized he hadn't heard her come in.

"I suppose they can do it," he grumbled. "But Old Pete knows where everything is."

"We're lucky to get them. They'll do it in half the time —never saw such workers!"

"Have it your way."

And Christina disappeared into the kitchen to forage for lunch. It was wiser not to make an issue of the Lovelands. She knew that Cornelius's father had been furious with them for keeping on an old horse out of sheer sentiment. Perhaps Cornelius was remembering that. He talked about his father a lot these days, as if he were seeking some sort of inward security from the idea of that grand but limited man.

"What if I invited Susie Plummer up here for tea?" Christina asked when she came back with the trays.

"Why ever ask that woman?" Cornelius grumbled.

"Well, I want to get at the material about missionaries, for one thing . . . and I thought perhaps you were getting a bit bored by solitary confinement. I suppose Ed's been too busy with all the plowing to stop in for a game."

"I could do with a little masculine companionship," Cornelius granted. It was a graceless remark and unlike him.

166

"Eben would love to come, of course. Why don't I invite him to supper one of these days? Give Mrs. Goodnow a day off."

"Eben . . ." Cornelius repeated the name. "Well, why not? Do me good to get out of my rut, and do you good to have your old admirer." He had pulled himself up in his chair and his troubled eyes had grown bright.

"Well, I'm not too old to enjoy being admired, darling, I must confess."

"I've been churlish lately—sorry." He reached out to grasp her hand and held it firmly in his. "The trouble is I want to do more than I can. Sometimes I feel as if I were in a cage."

"You have been marvelously patient."

"Because I hoped patience would do it. Now . . ." He let her hand go and closed his eyes. "Getting better by inches just doesn't seem good enough. I'll be dead before I can walk or do a day's work. I made out that list for you, and I enjoyed doing it, but I was pooped after an hour."

"I want to get you down to Boston before Christmas. We must see what the doctors have to say."

"Yes," he sighed. It was clear to Christina that the effort involved, the idea of moving, dismayed him. She would ask John to come up and help. Dear John! What comfort that he was there and would be coming soon. Perhaps they could then all go back together.

After lunch she did invite Susie Plummer. The tête-à-tête needed a third now and then, if only to give them back the dear sense of intimacy after she should have come and gone.

So Miss Plummer drove up in her little red Volkswagen at precisely four, wearing a kilt, a sheepskin coat, and sheepskin boots, her head wrapped up in a long wool scarf. She carried a package of books tied together with string.

"Well, well," she shouted in her outdoorsy voice, "donkeys' years since I've been up here." She had the quality of charging into any situation, even a merely social occasion, as if she must take it by storm. "Glad to see that bear is still around," she said, hanging her coat on his outstretched paw with evident pleasure. "Where's Cornelius? Can I keep on my boots? Forgot to bring my slippers."

167

Christina led her into the study where a brisk fire was burning.

"Well, Cornelius, you look very snug in here, I must say."

Miss Plummer had the odd characteristic of always raising her voice when in a conversation with a man, as if she presumed they were all born deaf. Her own father had been very deaf in his old age, Christina remembered, so perhaps that was the reason. But she saw Cornelius, captive in his chair, a rug over his knees, wince at the trumpeted greeting.

Miss Plummer gave him no chance to respond, but went right on as she laid the books on the coffee table. "Brought these—all I could dig out about the missionaries."

"Marvelous." And Christina left them to talk about the weather, the unfailing breaker of social ice in Willard, while she went into the kitchen to fetch the tea tray.

"Golly, chocolate cake!" Miss Plummer cried when she saw the tray.

"And anchovy sandwiches," Christina murmured. "I felt ravenously hungry for some reason. No one needs to eat anything he doesn't want."

She caught the twinkle in Cornelius's eye as Miss Plummer dove into a sandwich, accepted a cup of tea with milk and sugar, and swallowed it down in two gulps.

"It's a scrumptious do," she said between mouthfuls. "Christina always remembers that food is an important matter."

"Do I? I suppose I must be very greedy myself," Christina laughed. Dear old Susie, why did she remind one of a small, barky dog? Beneficent, gay, just a little absurd, she was not someone who showed her age. Though she must be sixty-five, she looked forty, with her high color and bright gray eyes.

"You're looking fit, Miss Plummer," Cornelius remarked.

"Oh, I'm in splendid shape. Couldn't stand the climate out there in Manila. Now I'm back in these cold winters, my circulation responds. It's a new lease on life."

Christina had untied the parcel of books and looked them over eagerly.

"So many women missionaries! Why, if we made a map and had threads run out from the church into the world,

168

it would be amazing to see how many went and how far from this village. I'm surprised."

"A map would be a darned good idea. Why don't you suggest it to Jem?" Cornelius volunteered.

"Were they really so religious?" Christina asked Susie Plummer.

"Some were. For some it may have been the only way to get out and see the world. Of course some went with their husbands, as wives."

"Yes, I never thought of that," Cornelius said, interested at last. "Hard for a woman with any gumption to get away. Teaching, missions—that was about it, wasn't it?"

"And women teachers were underpaid and undereducated! Religious?" Susie Plummer shouted. "Of course! But what I did was teach children how to read; learned Spanish, taught 'em their own language and English as well. Tried to show what a Christian life is. Left it at that —then when they asked, I told them."

Who could fail to be touched by Susie Plummer's unself-conscious goodness? Christina felt abashed that she had laughed at her, never really looked past the brusque manner.

"You must miss it," Christina said.

"Well, I do. Those children were eager to learn, and they had so little. Here in the village I have to cajole the mothers to bring them in. Then when they do come, they have little respect for books. Why, out there in Manila a book was a treasure. We never could afford many, and most had to be textbooks. Crayons were scarce as hens' teeth. It was a treat to be allowed to draw. Still, there are exceptions—that little Buddy Townsend has taken out *Peter Rabbit* three weeks in a row."

Miss Plummer beamed, and they were all three smiling with the pleasure of a small boy who had fallen in love for the first time with a book.

"Just offhand," Cornelius asked, "could you name a few countries where missionaries have gone from here in the last hundred years?" And Christina was grateful for Cornelius's businesslike mind. He was going to see to it that they stuck to the subject.

Miss Plummer thought while accepting a second cup of tea and a piece of chocolate cake. She screwed up her eyes and meditated as she sipped and absorbed a large piece of cake.

"Well, some, of course, went south after the war.

169

There was great need of teachers for the Negroes. Some of the best teachers went south—female, I mean. Miss Price went to Burma. Then the Ruddocks. Remember them? Their son lived here for ages, then settled in Ohio finally, an M.D. The Ruddocks went to Ceylon, I think. In one of those books you can see how many went to China. And our Mrs. Simmons, who died last year, went to Turkey, of course; learned Turkish and Arabic, lived through the massacre of the Armenians, and sheltered children all that terrible time. Ever hear her describe a plague of locusts?"

"We hardly knew her, I'm afraid."

"She married out there. Some did. There was a woman truly inspired by Christ. Yes, Edna Simmons was a deeply religious woman. They pop up now and then. She was given to spontaneous prayer on almost every occasion."

Cornelius and Christina exchanged a look, quickly subdued. Mrs. Simmons's prayers had sometimes been a little hard to take, as when the small library in memory of Miss Portland had been dedicated. Miss Portland had been an artist, an original and powerful person, but she smoked at a time when smoking by a woman, especially the smoking of elegant, long Manila cigars, was not quite the thing. Mrs. Simmons had prayed aloud that "this beautiful memorial be unsullied by any vice, and that it contain only books of an edifying nature." Cornelius himself had been the chief speaker on that occasion, and had not been able to resist an old joke about how phoenixes did, it would seem, arise from ashes, and he devoutly hoped the village would still contain at least one phoenix and a little smoke.

"We have to take people as they are," Miss Plummer remarked. "Don't you think a village like this is a remarkable achievement of just that? We all have bees in our bonnets, I suspect. But what keeps everything on the boil around here is the idiosyncratic character." For once she was speaking in a normal voice. They were beginning to see the real, the sensitive person under the armor. "We *have* to be tolerant, I guess." She turned to Cornelius earnestly. "There's always some grudge building up, you know, especially in winter. Seems like people have to keep going, and anger is no doubt good for the circulation." She gave her sudden loud laugh. "I have my eye on Nick," she said. "He's going to come to a boil one of these days, the way he cares about the wildlife around here."

170

"He already has, hasn't he?" Cornelius asked.

"Oh, yes, that affair of the New Yorkers and the poor doe—well, . . ."—she realized she was treading on thin ice—"he's all het up now about a mountain lion on the old Sumner hill. Thinks someone will kill it."

"Those lions used to be a real threat," Cornelius mused. "I can remember when one decimated the Loveland lambs —years ago—traditional enemies."

"Men like to kill," said Miss Plummer with some bitterness.

"Maybe it's in their blood," Cornelius teased. "Men are brutes, Miss Plummer."

"Oh, I wouldn't say that." She withdrew, blushing. "You're baiting me, Mr. Chapman."

"Every small boy in the world at some stage pulls the legs off flies."

"And it's usually to dazzle some little girl, I expect," Miss Plummer said. "The human animal leaves much to be desired."

"But in a village like Willard we can somehow absorb more of the Old Harry than they can in cities—is that it?"

"I wonder . . ." Miss Plummer chewed reflectively. "There's more space to be wild in. A boy can go out hunting instead of breaking into a school and throwing ink around."

"Do they read at all?" Christina asked.

"Well, you can't have everything!" Miss Plummer said, and laughed. "No, they don't, much, and that's a fact. There's TV, alas, in every shack, house, and trailer. You know what that means—half paying attention—half there . . ."

But it was time to go. Cornelius, she observed—he who had been so alert a half hour before—dozed, and she and Christina exchanged a glance. He woke as he heard them moving about and thanked Miss Plummer for coming "to cheer this old wreck."

"Just beached for a while, Cornelius. The ship seems in fine condition once the tide rises."

"If it ever does," he murmured. But neither of the women heard him—they were out in the hall.

CHRISTINA'S JOURNAL—*December 11*

Miss Plummer's visit did tire Cornelius, but I think he enjoyed it just the same. He had a nap before supper, and when he woke he seemed more cheerful. We had a real talk with our drink, and I got back in that half hour what I felt we were losing—the precious chance to be together and at peace, to be together and have time to let the whole inner world come to the surface and flower. When I think of the time we wasted at dull dinner parties last year and the year before, and forever it seems!

When Cornelius goes off into a doze he is not really absent, just withdrawn, hasn't the energy to exteriorize. But as soon as I sat down beside him this evening, he began talking about Miss Plummer. She had made an impression. He found her ardors and hesitations endearing, and he ended by saying something I have to think about. "We are among extraordinary people here, Christina. What makes them so? I feel that we, in a way, are ordinary. We are full of inherited attitudes. I mean, I suppose, that there are hundreds of fairly well-off, intelligent —I must grant us a little intelligence—well-educated people who have traveled and taken part in things, who are not unlike us. But who is like Old Pete, Miss Plummer, Ellen, Nick, or Jane Tuttle—even Ed Taggart?" That is more or less what Cornelius said. And the question we tried to answer is: What makes them extraordinary? Maybe it is that whatever they are has had to be created from the inside out, and against great odds. They have had to overcome a lot to exist at all. Cornelius thought that explained also why it always looks as if the people of the past, the original settlers to start with, tower over what any of us can be now. But the most interesting thing from my point of view is that a village like this absorbs and can use failure—Old Pete, for instance. I understand better now why the children look up to him. He seems more real to them than, perhaps, we do. He is *sui generis,* the authentic natural man.

Failure—perhaps one has to have experienced it to grow truly strong, and to reach the deep inner person. Cornelius is becoming an extraordinary person now, because he has been stripped down to his essence here. I sense that he has reached a point of something like despair. He begins to believe that he may never really get over this stroke. We must get to a doctor soon, but Cornelius resists. Is it simply that he fears the effort? I trust his sense of himself. I don't want to badger him. When he gets tired or tense, his speech falters. Walking is still a supreme effort, to get him up and down stairs. More than

172

once I have been grateful for Nick's help. I am going to get a wheel chair, and should have done so before this. I feel so stupid often! I am slowed down myself, let the day go by just keeping things going—haven't the extra push to think ahead. But tomorrow I am going to town and get a wheel chair. With people who are ill, imagination is everything. I feel I have failed Cornelius often because I could not *imagine* myself into him. And he never complains. When he is cross with me it is only a sign that he is battling with himself, against depression, against—perhaps—fear. Even in this time of our greatest intimacy since my first baby was born and we spent a marvelous summer in France, there is still so much we can't talk about, so much that each of us must come to terms with alone, and in his own way.

Cornelius teases me about Eben, but I think it is only a way of telling me that he loves me, a kind of flirtation. Could it hurt? Should I not see Eben at all? No, that is absurd, truly absurd when we are all so old! What am I thinking of?

CHAPTER 4

The visit to Boston came upon them sooner than expected, as John suddenly announced that he would come up that very weekend, and the simplest thing seemed to be for Christina and Cornelius to drive back with him on Sunday afternoon. After so long a time, the idea of even a brief journey (they would be away only twenty-four hours if all went well) was agitating, and Christina was busy on the telephone making arrangements, first with the doctor, who was fortunately able to get a room for Cornelius at the hospital, then to have a chauffeured car available to drive them home.

John's visit, that Christina had looked forward to so happily since Thanksgiving, proved an uneasy and rather tense one. He found Jane Tuttle enormously diminished in energy since he had seen her last, only three weeks before, swallowed up in the ministrations of Hannah, no longer able to react as she used to do with humorous self-assertion. "She is slipping away," John said. "I find it hard to bear."

He had brought her a rough draft of the chapter on flora and fauna, but the effort of taking it in had been clearly beyond her powers. She had laid it aside with a perfunctory compliment, very unlike her.

"Thank you, dear boy, for doing my work for me," was what she said.

Christina guessed that it had been hard on John to be left high and dry when he had worked so hard to please Jane, and at the same time to have to be gentle and pa-

174

tient with Cornelius, who was irritable, complained about John's driving, and was generally cross the whole way down.

"Mother, you are a tower of strength," he had said that night after supper when Cornelius was safely in bed at the hospital where some tests were to be made the next morning.

"No! Good heavens, I feel so bumbling, John! I should have got your father a wheel chair months ago. It just seems as if each day got eaten up moment by moment."

"You should have help," Sybille said, as if that would solve everything.

"Yes, that is what everyone says," Christina said quietly, "but the village itself is our help, you know. The Lovelands will always manage to come if I really need them, and Nick—he has been wonderful. He's so *quiet*— we hardly know he is there, but we find the woodbox full and the paths shoveled when we get up. What we have is peace and quiet."

John gave her a penetrating look. Peace and quiet were not what his mother had ever seemed to want before.

Christina was firm about having a Christmas alone this year.

"Please don't be hurt," she said, "but somehow I feel this is the right thing."

She did not add that after one is seventy, Christmas becomes an increasing strain, a kind of yearly ordeal that must be surmounted.

"For once," she explained, "I can settle in to writing cards—Cornelius and I by the fire after tea. We talk about the people, so many we have failed to write to over these last years. You mustn't think of us as isolated or lonely," and she laughed suddenly, "or too queer. The fact is that it's a kind of late honeymoon and we savor every instant of it—at least I do. I'm not even giving presents, just cash." And she laughed again. "Do you remember that old George Price cartoon of the wild old woman making fake money and saying, 'This year we are just giving money'?" She leaned her head back against the armchair. "No wrapping up, no grim hours in the shops trying to find teddy bears or something."

"I see your point," John said, exchanging a glance with Sybille, who, only yesterday, had been complaining of the hell of so many nieces and nephews and aunts and cousins

175

who must be remembered. "And next year you can give the history of Willard!"

"Next year?" Christina realized she never thought that far ahead any more. Next year for some reason sent a shiver down her spine.

Before Cornelius left the hospital the next afternoon, she had a talk with the doctor. It was not really a surprise to learn that, although the patient had made progress up to a point, he seemed now to have reached a plateau.

"What impressed me," said Dr. Paget, "is that he himself doesn't talk about getting back to State Street as he did constantly in those first months. It is as if he had laid that aside in his own mind—abdicated, if you like. I believe this to be significant."

Christina's eyes filled with tears, but she said quite matter-of-factly, "His range has narrowed down. Willard, the village itself, absorbs his mind. He still has so much to give . . . he is . . ." she searched for the word "growing all the time."

"Your husband is a remarkable man—a man of very great courage, Mrs. Chapman. Not everyone can handle almost total disability in this way. Everything must be done to keep his attention alive, not to let him sink down, so to speak. He told me yesterday that he is worried because he dozes off. Don't let it worry you. Part of it is a healing process. He mustn't get overtired. But . . ."

"But?" Christina waited. She felt as if a sort of doom had struck in the last few minutes. What was Dr. Paget really telling her?

"But the more he can live the better; the more you can ask of him the better. The wheel chair will make him movable. That was a good idea."

Dr. Paget took a cigarette out of his pocket absent-mindedly and lit it.

"I think I have to know now," Christina said, her hands clasped hard on her knee. "Do you think he will have a second stroke?"

"I wish I could tell you. There has been some brain damage, without a doubt. He might go on as he is for years; on the other hand . . ."

Years! Christina realized she had been thinking in terms of months.

"It may be that you yourself will have to get help. This is a long business, Mrs. Chapman, at best. You must

176

plan for the tiredness of the long-distance runner, and that, perhaps, is what I felt you had better think about, and was chiefly why I wanted to have a little talk."

There was no time to think or to prepare herself. The chauffeured car she had ordered to drive them back would be there in a few minutes. When the real things in life happen, Christina thought, taking refuge in the ladies' room for a few moments, there is never time—birth, death, love—we are never prepared. And suddenly she longed terribly for Ellen. *There* was endurance. She longed for Willard, for the comfort of adversity, so to speak. She was going to have to readjust all her ideas, find the inner rhythm and sustain it somehow. Alone there, leaning against the washbasin, for a second she felt panic flowing in, so that she was dismayed to see that her hand shook. Would she have the strength? And what if the arthritis got worse? Then, she knew in her bones and marrow the strength of Willard, the strength of the old, patient mountain. I can do it, she thought, for if it is true that we have to meet every great event as naked as when we were born, it is also true that courage flows back in a great wave when it is needed.

When Christina and Cornelius were settled comfortably in the limousine, she held his warm hand fast in hers and said, "Lovely to be going home, darling!" And the warmth of expectation made her heart beat fast. "Tell the man to stop off at that florist in Peterborough, will you? Let's fill the house with plants."

It was Christina's way always to latch onto more life as a way of handling any problem. Plants would need care—one more thing to attend to, but the very thought of their secret life around the house set her blood dancing. Cornelius did not answer, but he held her hand very hard in his, as if the separation of twenty-four hours they had just endured had been a long one.

And when they were settled at last by the fire again, and had shared a bowl of soup and a glass of wine, and read a few pages of *Swann's Way,* just to resume the phrase of music, to feel themselves back in the intimate world, Christina went to the pots of cyclamen—two white and one scarlet one—that she had placed in the window of the library where Cornelius could see the sun shine through their petals, and drank them in with her eyes. It was a moment of pure joy. The dread had gone. And she was thinking that in this unexpected phase of

177

their life together, meeting illness and facing death, many forgotten things—lost things—had slowly to be found again and used in a new way. It was years since she had bothered with house plants. Now, already, her mind was moving toward seedlings in the spring, perhaps a little greenhouse, the centering of life here and the enriching of it in every possible way.

"Deep as a well," she murmured.

"What?"

"I was thinking, darling, that whatever we have lost in breadth, we have gained, and are gaining, in depth. Don't you agree?"

"It's so odd," Cornelius said. "I mean, it's as if all kinds of things I felt I could not live without—even the bank, even the club—have just vanished out of my consciousness. They feel so unimportant. Other things have come to the surface. We are in a great adventure, Christina." She saw that he was looking intently at the palms of his hands. "It is all written here, I expect—how we go on making ourselves to the end. I am a better man than I was a year ago, a richer man, a—" he glanced up at his wife as if to find the word in her face "—happier man. How strange!"

Next morning it smelled like snow. A dark pewter sky and a harsh wind. Christina felt unaccountably tired, and her knee ached. She lay in a hot bath for a half hour before getting Cornelius up, thinking. Perhaps, after all, she could ask Ellen to come a few mornings a week and help out. And she had better go down this morning if another storm was brewing. This thought got her out of the bath and helped her through the morning chores. Cornelius fell asleep in his chair in the library after breakfast. They were both recovering from the expenditures of the Boston trip.

Hannah phoned to ask how things had gone in Boston, at Jane's request. Jane, she told Christina, was about the same.

"She tires," Hannah said. "Just like a baby, she needs a lot of sleep."

"We are all hibernating animals this winter," Christina answered.

But when she put the receiver down, she felt dismayed, and decided on an impulse to try to get over to see Jane,

178

take her one of the white cyclamens—if not today, then tomorrow.

Then Jem called to ask whether she had started on the chapter about the women, as he wanted to bring her some material about his own aunt who had, he said, been a remarkable painter of nature and should be mentioned. Christina put him off for a week or so, explaining that Cornelius needed time to rest—but Jem's call made her feel cross and at sixes and sevens with herself. She really must plan time to work. And Jem was quite right in suggesting that women artists, of whom there had been several besides the formidable Miss Portland, must come into any chapter about the women of Willard. So she fled down to Ellen's before the dishes had been washed—fled from the telephone, fled like a bird to a haven, a shelter from all that life was demanding of her, for a moment's rest.

She found Ellen sewing by the window—curtains for Jem's kitchen windows, she explained. But she took off her spectacles and laid the work down as they talked, remarking that it was odd how the color red strained the eyes.

As always there seemed to be a lot of news to be related when one had gone away even for only twenty-four hours. Old Mr. Patten was at war again with the road agent, and Ed Taggart swore he wouldn't plow the drive, come the next snow. "Let him get someone else. He can afford to pay." Nick was off on his snowshoes to be sure the mountain lion was still around and alive. And Old Pete worried Ellen because Nick said that half the time he didn't keep the fire going at night.

"Nick's been over there two or three times to get it started for him, Old Pete lying there under a blanket moaning about pains in his legs."

"He can't survive the winter, Ellen. It's awful."

"Well, you can't persuade Old Pete to look for shelter now—he isn't well enough to do it."

"What then?"

Ellen shrugged.

"The Lord has kept an eye on Old Pete all these years. Maybe He won't fail him this time. But it's asking a lot!" And she smiled her thin smile.

"Asking a lot of Nick, if you ask me!"

"Oh, well, Nick seems to think he is the Lord himself

these days, at least where any wild animal is concerned. His eye is on the sparrow all right."

She turned her eyes to the window and up at the dark sky.

"Looks like snow."

"Don't you worry about him when he goes off alone like that?"

"Worry more when he glooms indoors—worry more when he gets mad at people. Nick is safe as houses outdoors alone."

Christina felt increasingly shy about approaching the ticklish subject of help. There was a pause; then Ellen asked about what the doctor in Boston had said, and it all poured out in a flood—the long term that must be faced, and how somehow Christina had not been thinking ahead.

"I've been living from day to day, Ellen—that's the trouble. A month ago Cornelius seemed so much better I had taken it for granted that we'd be out of the woods, come spring."

"Well," Ellen said drily, "doctors are a little like weathermen—they're not always right; and they may be dead wrong. We were supposed not to get that storm out of Canada this time, but look at that sky!"

It was a strange, suspended, white darkness when one looked out of the windows—ominous. The two women looked out, each meeting whatever was brewing in her own way. Ellen got up, as she so often did when she was thinking something out, and picked dead leaves off a geranium. Then she spoke with her back to Christina.

"You know I'd be glad to help out, Christy . . ."

"You would?"

"Felt shy about asking, but it's been on my mind, and now if I could help it would be just what I need. Get me out of the house!"

She turned now to give her friend a piercing look.

"Nick says your knee bothers you more than it did."

"Nothing escapes that eye of Nick's, does it? Frankly, I've been anxious. Can't afford to let it get any worse, and that's the truth. It would be a tremendous thing if you could come one or two mornings a week and dust around and straighten us up again."

"I get pretty tired sitting all day, and my eyes bother me, so I'd be more than glad. I'll come with Nick tomorrow. How's that?"

Christina felt the tears pricking her eyes. It was not

the first time that Ellen had been at her side when she needed help. There was the year, her eleventh, when she had come to stay at the farm. There was the time of Eben—when she could talk to Ellen and to no one else. And there was the more than once when she had been dreadfully anxious about John.

"That's fine," she managed to say. "What's the rate these days? Would a dollar-seventy-five an hour be fair?"

"More'n I make sewing, I can tell you."

And they changed the subject quickly because this talk of pay embarrassed them both.

CHRISTINA'S JOURNAL—*December 18*

Today Ellen was here to work for the first time. It has given me an enormous lift, especially as the dark skies hang over us and still the snow has not come, but it is surely on the way. At first we worked together, changing sheets and planning what she might do. I realized the instant I began to look around how much has been neglected! And finally, at her suggestion, she simply set out to clean the house from top to bottom, at least all the rooms we use these days. I had dreaded having anyone under foot, dreaded Cornelius's exasperation—he has become sensitive to any noise. But Ellen displaces so little atmosphere we hardly heard her moving about in her soft shoes. Her whole approach to this rough work is as subtle and rare as she herself is. She notices everything, even to cleaning a small silver ash tray in our bedroom. I hardly know how to explain the kind of presence I felt while she was here, so attentive to the house itself—perhaps it is that. She does not walk in as a stranger. She too remembers the past. When she lifts a framed photograph of Cornelius's father to dust the bureau, she does it so gently, and I was amused to note that (just like me) she sometimes murmurs something to an object with which she is concerned. "There," she will say when she has shaken out a rug and laid it down again, "that's more like it."

At eleven we all three had coffee together in the library. Cornelius hardly knows Ellen, I suddenly realized —realized by the way he looked at her, a penetrating look. He felt her distinction, and was much amused when she brushed aside the high and mighty Oldsens as "limited sensibilities," a phrase Cornelius surely never expected to hear from the lips of a native. It brought back so vividly—and we spoke about it after Ellen left—some of the people who worked for us in the Touraine one summer when we rented a house near Vouvray. Our cleaning woman there had such dignity and spoke such pure French it made ours seem vulgar. She used to say of the Baron who owned the chateau nearby, "He lacks distinction, one must admit." It was said in just the tone Ellen used about Mrs. Oldsen. It is not so much a matter of language as of values, I suppose. Ellen is an aristocrat by nature.

And somehow, because I waited for her to offer to help out, it is all right. She is coming not so much to work for us as to offer a neighborly hand in a time of trouble. So her pride, that fierce negative that censors so much of what she will or will not do or allow, is not in play.

But, strangely enough, it was after she left that I was most aware of her presence and what she had done for us. The house had a new serenity—order had been made out of chaos. Everywhere I looked I felt her hand, as if I had been given, suddenly, a fresh start, could take a deep breath without seeing dust under the table.

While she worked, Nick got us caught up on kindling and wood, took out the trash, then drove her home. I wonder whether he can be tamed to join us for coffee next time. The thing is that he is not articulate as she is— she is one of the most articulate people I have ever known. It is as if her creativity went into language, and into conversation. Yet it has had so little play, first while living with her boor of a husband, and then left alone with her withdrawn child. So I think it will be almost as good for her as it is for us to do some philosophizing with Cornelius.

"You know," he said just before his nap, "I have never really understood your feeling about Ellen before. Now I begin to. She is quite a person."

He had forgotten that she was Town Clerk for years and is a permanent member of the trustees for the library. I told him how she had fought to get first-rate reference books.

"I am having to give up my prejudices one by one," he said, and laughed at himself. "Where will it end?"

He has always taken it for granted that we and people like us were the civilizing influence; now he begins to know that it has always been an exchange. We have enriched each other immeasurably is my thought about it.

182

It led me to speak again of Eben, a good example of how the local quality came up and finally flowered—and that couldn't have happened without financial help from old Judge Chapman when Eben was a boy.

"Father had the right idea, but he was such a swell! He did it badly.—Yes, we must invite Eben over. I want to have a talk with him."

Dear Cornelius! He has been thinking a lot about the past. He is re-examining everything. It makes me so proud.

CHAPTER 5

Christmas was as quiet and beautiful as Christina's dream
of it—a tree decorated simply with a few red and white
balls, brilliant sunshine on the snow outside, so Sybille and
John were able to drive up unexpectedly for an hour or
two, bringing presents of records and books, and two
light, fluffy mohair throws in stained-glass colors, drawings
and poems from the children; and Christina enjoyed the
sweet sensation of feeling that she and Cornelius had become the cherished ones this year. The day ended with
listening to Christmas music alone together, drinking a
glass of champagne, and then eating a duck *à l'orange*
that Cornelius pronounced as good as that at the Tour
d'Argent in Paris. Long before midnight they were in bed,
reading poems aloud from the *Oxford Book of English
Verse*—Thomas Hardy, Herbert, and Traherne. Peace and
joy, Christina thought, falling into a seamless sleep.

For the following days snow piled on snow. For the
first time Christina felt really walled in for twenty-four
hours. But she was beginning to understand the winter
rhythm—if one did not panic, the plows did come finally,
and when the lights went out for a few hours, candlelight
cast beautiful shadows on the walls, and Cornelius and
she went to bed at seven and lay in the dark and talked,
hand in hand, startled when all the lights went on again
at three in the morning.

As soon as she was movable again, on the Saturday after Christmas, exhilarated by the brilliance of the morning, Christina did what she had promised herself for ages

184

—she left the car at Eben's driveway and walked up to see him. It had been weeks since that first visit. But she felt lighthearted and at ease this time. They met halfway, as he was on his way down to pick up the mail. He would fetch it when he took her back to her car, he said. His orange cat sat licking her paws on the porch beside the storm door. Molly waved from the kitchen window, and the low-ceilinged, dark study felt welcoming after the stunning light outdoors.

"Well," Eben said, "what about those letters? Find them interesting?"

"Not only I did, but Cornelius has been happily employed making all sorts of lists and charts so we can try to visualize exactly what livestock they had, what tools, how many oxen, and what they harvested."

"Do you get the sense of a person at all? When I first glanced through them, they seemed so impersonal—so very impersonal, I tried to relate them to the portraits."

Eben got up and moved piles of papers about on his desk, finally laying his hands on a small filing envelope tied with a piece of string. He laid it in Christina's lap.

"Take a look at her!"

"Strong face. I'm not surprised."

In the first photograph Christina took out, Sophia was standing in front of a barn door, in a tightly buttoned double-breasted jacket over a full skirt or, perhaps, apron —beneath it another skirt showed through. Her hair was parted in the middle and drawn tightly back from a wide brow. It was a strong, good-humored face, for although she was not smiling, her glance was warm.

"She does look in command of the situation."

"That she certainly must have been."

Christina went through the packet, about twelve photographs in all. In one the two children sat beside their mother, the boy remarkably like his mother, even to the mouth; the girl smaller in build, slighter, with rather pale eyes.

"It's so funny," Christina said, smiling at the children, "how they dressed children like small adults in those days. How did they ever manage in those long skirts?"

Then she laid the packet down, one hand over it, palm open, as if she were thinking with that hand as well as with her whole body, bringing alive what she had just looked at.

"Of course what the letters don't tell is the hard times

185

—the times when a crop failed for not enough sun, the times when it snowed and snowed, the times of panic or when a dog died. Of course what one longs to have is the other side of the correspondence."

"My guess is that his letters were full of advice that was rarely followed. One wonders how long a letter took to reach a regiment in the field."

"What was he like, Eben, do you think?"

"Well, here he is in uniform—a captain."

"Heavens, how young he looks—far younger than she! Was he?"

"Just two years, if the dates in the family Bible are correct."

"And what was it like when he came back and found his wife so powerfully in command? What then?"

They had plunged right into the whole subject as if nothing else existed. Now Molly came in with coffee, and they laughed spontaneously.

"We're way back somewhere about 1870, Molly. We're ghosts."

"Nothing like the past to make one feel alive, I always say," said Molly.

"Join us, won't you? Bring in a cup, Molly—do."

But Molly excused herself, to do the ironing she said. Christina guessed she was indulging Eben, being sensitive about his needs. No doubt they did have coffee together as a usual thing.

"Well," Eben said when he had taken a sip, "Elisha came back with one arm shot to hell, and he had spent a winter in prison. For a time anyway he must have been pretty darned glad to have such a competent wife at home. My guess is"—and his eyes twinkled—"he just dwindled back into matrimony with a sigh of relief and let Sophia run things her way."

"I wonder . . ." Christina was thinking of Cornelius, who hated to let her take hold wherever real decisions, even about storm windows, must be made.

She felt Eben's eyes resting on her and looked up to meet his piercing glance, which since their first meeting had seemed to probe her in a rather relentless way, just because the focus was so sharp.

"Don't," she said, putting a hand over her eyes.

"Don't what?"

"Don't look at me like that."

"Can't I be bold enough to try to see you, Christina—

186

the real you—now we are so old and wise, you tell me? May not wisdom look at beauty in peace at last?"

"Ridiculous man!" Christina smiled, but she felt a queer pain in her heart—too absurd.

Eben got up and paced up and down, his characteristic action when he was moved or thinking hard.

"When you came that first time—and I have been chewing over every word ever since, you must imagine— we touched on the subject of the strength of women in Willard. It is, perhaps, to be the theme of that chapter of the history?"

"I feel awfully confused at the moment, Eben—in a whirlpool of facts and intuitions—nothing sorted out. Susie Plummer came the other day and regaled us about the missionaries. There is a tribe in itself!"

But Eben seemed not to be listening. He was off on one of his private tangents, she sensed, and she waited, stimulated, excited by the liveliness of this mind at work, by the something fiery and original in this old man. He was not judicious like Cornelius, or even, perhaps, wise in the way of Cornelius. His quality was mercurial, intuitive. His mind ranged about in a large orbit of speculation, she felt. He looked now like an old hawk. There was, she realized, no kindness in the way he looked at her—the probing look that had made her blush. No, it was the look of a hawk.

"Ever since you were here—some weeks ago, Christina . . ."

She caught the shade of bitterness in his voice.

"I wanted to come, but the days flow by in a timeless river of keeping Cornelius and me going. It is a full-time job, Eben."

"Of course. I'm not complaining—lucky to see you at all. Anyway what's on my mind is this: why Jem looks back with such nostalgia and wants to make the history a work of piety toward the past is, no doubt, because of those old virtues—the pioneer virtues of hard work, courage, a variety of skills, a way of coping with the impossible, humor (that Scotch-Irish blood boils up into laughter as well as anger, you know). But where did it all lead? The men petered out finally because there was too little for them to get their teeth into. The women flourished because women thrive in just this atmosphere of make-do, of daily creation of life itself. Men, I believe, wither away if there is no challenge to the mind. Physical hardship

187

creates character, Christina, and that is what we still see around us and treasure—in Ellen, in Old Pete even, in men like Orin Gregg, the old stock still clinging to a kind of frontier life in the middle of the twentieth century. But what was the culture? The Genteel Tradition with a vengeance. Who in this town *reads* these days? Who ever heard of Faulkner or Malamud, to say nothing of Sartre or Kierkegaard or Marcuse?"

"It's a country village, Eben, for heaven's sake!"

"Well, take a look at the equivalent in England or in France. I remember having a hot argument with a tobacco-seller in an English village about G. B. Shaw—years ago, of course. The missionaries did go out and find a larger air—some of them did. Some of them transplanted the Genteel Tradition and its emphasis on 'how beautiful and interesting' it all was, even to China! Good Christ, it's been a thin air around here for half a century!"

"But people did things. You did, Eben. There's nothing thin about you!"

"Maybe not, but my father, the grandson of Sophia Dole, for all his intelligence, had none of her edge, or strength of character for that matter—a farmer who spent half his life drinking and telling stories with his cronies."

Christina looked thoughtful. "It's a rather grim picture."

"Well, isn't it a bit grim that people go wild about collecting what amounts to crude peasant furniture—early American, they call it—as if it had a character? But what was its character? Crude, often actually ugly, having the virtue that someone had made do with what he had around. Some savage tribes do better!"

"The women did make beautiful quilts, Eben, and hand-woven materials."

"Maybe. But nothing to compare with Scandinavia or any of the Middle European countries. Why worship a past so lacking in original pith? Of course Jefferson had it. Thoreau had it. Yes, here and there. But right here, in Willard, the most inventive man we ever had around invented a spindle for machine weaving. And the greatest statesman, I suppose, was down the road a piece in Hillsborough—Franklin Pierce."

Eben flung himself down in his chair, his eyes twinkling with savage glee.

"I ask you! Just about the dullest President ever elected

188

—he could hardly wait to get home again from Washington."

"I see no flaw in loving one's home," Christina flashed out. "You chose to come home yourself."

"Yes," he sighed. "I did—for Olive. A hell of a lot of people come home to Willard to die, that's a fact. But how many come here to *live,* I ask you? City people, maybe—people who bring their books and their ideas with them."

"Americans, I suppose, are pragmatists, Eben."

"What I hate," he said, "is the awful sentimentality about it all. I don't look at the broken-down stone walls with admiration; it makes me sick to think of all that hard work for nothing—fields grown over to brush in fifty years or less. What was it all for?"

"To make a person like you, maybe," Christina said.

It was moving to see how much this old man cared. Here, living alone on the top of a hill, he was still wanting to change the very heart of the matter.

"What am I? Nothing much, I can tell you. I had it in me to move mountains . . . ah, Christina,"—he looked over at her again, but this time the look was tender—"what I could have done with you at my side!"

"What makes you think so?" she countered at once, for this was simply not the truth, she felt. "We did nothing but torture each other, Eben."

"You would have made me spur my horse. Don't misunderstand," he added, seeing her grow tense and half rise as if to go. "My marriage was just about perfect, if one thinks of happiness. Just as yours, I expect, may have been. I'm talking about challenge—you challenged me very deep down."

"It's all so long ago, Eben. Please, let it lie there."

"Like some ship full of gold and mystery at the bottom of the ocean in my mind," he murmured.

"In spite of your sharp edge, what a romantic you are!" And now Christina did get up, for she was suddenly anxious about Cornelius. She had stayed far too long. "I have to go, Eben."

"Very well," he said testily, and added, "Where is that cat? I need some comfort."

"Don't we all? On the way back from Boston I stopped to buy plants. It seemed as if I just had to have something —something alive around. Maybe we should get a cat.

189

Cornelius would like that. He spends a great deal of time dozing."

"So do I, if you must know, and a cat's a fine personage because a cat purrs while one dozes. I can recommend the experience without reservation."

As Eben helped Christina with her coat, he went on. "You don't see me as I really am—an old wreck—because when you come, life flows in. I wake up!" he said with a grin.

She watched him in the car mirror as she drove off, standing there, following her with his intent gaze. And only when he was out of sight, did she allow the past to overwhelm her for a moment. Strange boy he had been— more intense, more sure of what he wanted than anyone she had ever met. For a brief, dangerous summer that intensity had nearly driven her mad with longing, although she was engaged to Cornelius at the time. Was it fear that had held her back, or, as Eben would say, the Genteel Tradition? But as she turned into the drive, feeling unaccountably anxious, she had no regrets. Good marriages are not made out of such wildfire. Only it was strange indeed to find it still had such power. Perhaps it was untrue that the old live less intensely. She felt the hour she had just spent with the fierce old hawk burning in her like some fuel.

CHRISTINA'S JOURNAL—*December 28*

My Puritan ancestors, I suppose, turn in their graves at the very idea that an old woman like me can still feel elated and renewed by an hour with an old flame. But I am sure that we were not meant to marry and then go through life like a horse in blinders. I must remember to ask Cornelius what he feels now about that girl—what was her name? Violet? No, Prudence—and whether he ever sees her. I feel sure that we are meant to love many people in many different ways, beginning with our parents, who cause so much pain because one almost inevitably loves one of them too much. I don't suppose I shall ever again feel quite what I felt about Hans, the riding master when I was at camp. Or, for that matter, the *sehnsucht* that inhabited me over Miss Finch, the head of my school. All the time, through them, and so many others, the knowledge of love was growing in me. Eben came at a time when I was in revolt against background, against

190

money—and, of course, he represented adventure, challenge. I know now that I did not choose an easier path with Cornelius. As I look back, it seems to me that we hardly knew each other for the first years of our marriage. Cornelius was so intransigent, knew what he wanted and imposed it on me. During that period I gave up painting seriously forever, and threw myself into causes. Well, it is a long time ago. But isn't life mysterious? It is surely true that he and I are only harvesting the fifty years of our marriage now, in old age. What was it that each of us withheld before? Perhaps it was just our own weakness that we withheld, out of pride. Both of us had been brought up to be reserved about feeling. And we had not, God knows, had much—or any in my case—experience with loving in a physical sense. It was ten years before I felt any real fulfillment in bed with Cornelius, and by then the children had been born. We never never could have talked about that. It happened in both a physical and metaphysical *darkness*. How absurd we were!

Now it is acknowledged weakness, dependency, that has finally opened all the doors between us. I am closer to the physical man than I have ever been because I had to wash him the first weeks, because I knew his every muscle and stiff place as if they were my own. And in that time some warmth began to flow through him. I shall never forget the way he clasped my hand when at last he could use his hands again—the strength of the love in that handclasp! After that, and in all these weeks, we have moved into a deepening phase where we are closer as souls than ever before. Sometimes the communion is through words—we have talked and talked about everything under the sun, including ourselves, and our parents, and very often about Willard and all it means. Cornelius turns Willard over and over in his mind as if it were a kaleidoscope and the pattern shifted and reassorted itself as he is aware of new elements in the design. Heavens, how little we ever had time for talk of this sort until now! Partly, I suppose, because his chief concerns were beyond my understanding, and didn't, *au fond,* interest me enough—the bank, the state of the market, the trends —all that. The very words bore me as I write them. I have never found money a fascinating subject, only an embarrassing one. But at last we have been able to talk even about that—about being rich, and how it both enlarged us in one way and in others, certain human ones especially perhaps, has been a limiting thing, a kind of enclosure.

Oh, it is so wonderful to have time to talk at last! Sometimes I feel that it is pride that has been peeling off, like the skins of an onion. We now, for the first time in our lives, depend on others. We could hardly manage without Ellen, without Nick, without the village. But, on a different level from that one of physical dependency, we are learning so much about the human beings here. I am so moved by the way Cornelius listens—to a dear thing like Susie Plummer, for instance, whom he would have regarded as a figure of fun even a year ago.

Must we be weak and accept our weakness to begin to see? Is it in just this sense that power corrupts? (Money is power, of course.) Is it only when power goes, ambition in a worldly sense, that driving need, as in the old Cornelius, to manage, instruct, dominate everyone, including his own children—is it only when one becomes humble—humble as a cripple—that one begins to *live?*

I started this long sermon to myself because I felt so lit up by Eben. Then, as so often happens, it became something else—it drew me back to Cornelius, the deep, fulfilling center.

CHAPTER 6

Twice in the next few days Christina picked up Old Pete and Flicker on their way to the general store. He complained a lot of pain in his feet, looked dirtier than ever. But when Christina wondered aloud how he would manage all winter and in the January cold, he recited with a flourish, " 'Now the days are getting longer and the cold is getting stronger!' Well, Ed promised me I could have a couple of big trees they just took down, back on the Long Hill Road. Maybe Nick will help me." There was something touching about the old man's faith that he would and could manage. "I've spent a good many winters here in Willard, and, come spring, I've come through. No one's going to scare me out of my first trout this May!"

"I'm not trying to scare you, Pete, but do be careful, and don't go to sleep on these cold nights without being sure the fire will last you through to morning, will you?"

"You teach your grandmother to suck eggs!" he teased.

But Christina did feel anxious. There was no electricity in the camp, just a kerosene lamp. So she rummaged around in the attic and went down next day with extra blankets and a quilt, also some old boots of John's that he would surely not mind parting with in such a good cause. It was a scramble to get up to the shack from the road over a snowdrift. She knocked at the door, tied together with a leather strap, but there was no answer, so she pushed it open to leave the things inside. In some ways the shack was a mess, but it was clear that every piece of junk had its place: a tin tub hung on the wall; there were

193

two pails of water standing just inside the door; Old Pete's best suit and shirt hung on a hanger beside the bed. Christina laid the blankets and quilt on top of a crumpled old army blanket, set the boots down where Old Pete would see them, and then went quickly away. She felt as if she had intruded on the lair of a wild animal.

Strange, strange creature to choose to live such a hard life! The only luxury, the only sign of pleasure, was a small transistor radio and a pile of old Western magazines neatly stacked by the bed. These, and the enamel coffee pot beside the stove, and the frying pan hanging on a nail behind it meant Pete's winter life. The greater part of it must be spent simply keeping alive—getting wood chopped, keeping the fire going. Cornelius would be eager to hear all about this adventure. But she had determined to get up to see Jane Tuttle before another snow and while the road was still passable. It had been an indulgence to see Eben and not push on up the steep hill the other day.

Now, in deep winter, Jane's little house looked even more isolated than in summer. Without the telephone, no one could live here, surely not two women. But of course the road agent, the mailman, and all of them kept an eye on Jane. The village did not forget its own.

She could see Hannah peering out the kitchen window as she turned the car round ready to go back. This sort of maneuver was hard on the knee, but she managed it this time without mishap.

Hannah opened the door, her finger to her lips.

"Miss Tuttle's asleep," she whispered. "You're a sight for sore eyes, Mrs. Chapman. I'll wake her in a moment. She'll be so happy to see you—was speaking of you only this morning, worrying about how you were making out without help."

"Ellen comes in twice a week. Nick is there every day. We are doing splendidly!"

Then she took a real look at Hannah's red, ugly, worn face. It was clear that she had been crying.

"How is Jane?"

This was answered by a stifled sob and by Hannah wiping her eyes on a kitchen towel.

"She won't last the winter, Mrs. Chapman. She's as weak as a kitten."

"Well, she's ninety, Hannah. Perhaps she's ready to go.

Sometimes we must realize that, I guess. She's had a good long life." Christina blamed herself for the false cheer. "You must get pretty worn out these days."

"I don't mind the work," Hannah said. "I get a nap in the afternoon when she does—dozes off these days. I mind that Miss Tuttle isn't herself—too gentle for her own good—used to tell me to be quiet when I talked too much. It just ain't natural how she never complains."

Christina slipped out of her coat and sat down to take off her boots in the formal parlor.

"She does get up every day?"

"Sometimes she does. Sometimes I can't bear to get her to make the effort. She's up today though—all tuckered out, sitting in the rocker by the window. I'll just go and tell her you're here."

"Good strong coffee, Hannah dear," Christina heard a faint voice asking. "I do want to be myself."

But when she was allowed to go in, Jane Tuttle held out a thin but surprisingly warm hand, and at once asked Christina about Cornelius. Her face looked hollowed out, the bones of the forehead as thin as those of a bird. But her eyes were as clear and attentive as ever. While Christina told about life at the Ark, Jane pulled threads in her skirt straight, just as she always used to do. Christina felt that any real talk they might have would come after the strong coffee Hannah was preparing, for until then Jane was obviously listening for her approach, a little anxiously.

"Has not life been good to send me Hannah when I needed her most?" she asked when at last Hannah and the tray appeared.

"I notice that Willard has a way of providing," Christina answered.

"All the old babies get proper attention?" Jane asked with her old twinkle. But when Hannah had left, she sighed.

"That is what I have become, Christina—a little weak baby." Then she looked quite mischievous for a moment and whispered, "At last Hannah has me where she wants me, completely under control."

"It can't be easy," Christina murmured. For this was, without doubt, the real ordeal of very old age—consciousness without power, the cruel truth about life, that we suffer most from seeing without being able to do, carried to the highest magnitude.

"It was hard when I struggled against such dependence,

and against being babied. Then one day I just gave up—gave up the ghost, you might say—just decided to rest on the strong arms God has provided." She gave Christina a tender look. "It's good to have a little talk. Sometimes, deep down inside, it has been lonely, except for dreaming. I think I am most awake these days in my dreams—wonderful dreams, Christina. I have seen my mother as clearly before me as if she were sitting in that chair."

"That is what Cornelius says. He says he is wide awake when he is dozing—he just seems not to be there. But he is very much somewhere else."

"Dear man, it must be awful for him not to be able to move about freely. He was such an outdoorsy person."

"The odd thing is that he doesn't mind. He lives within the limits—what he can do he enjoys."

"Sometimes I think Brother Ass is the wise one. Finally we are forced to listen to him and once in a while he leads us to wisdom." Jane smiled mischievously. "I used to get very cross about things that didn't matter at all in my fifties. If Hannah had been with me then we should have had some fearful battles. But the Lord spared me, for then I could live alone, took out my angers by weeding and botanizing. Well, now, you see, I am a very old lady indeed, and I have given up anger. It just isn't in me. Strange, isn't it?"

She drank thirstily from her demitasse and set it down.

"Coffee is my liquor now," she said with a smile. "Alcohol, even a sip, makes me dizzy." She reached over then and took Christina's hand in hers. "Hannah's goodness has taught me a great deal."

"I should have guessed it was the other way around."

"Well, you'd be wrong," Jane said with some of her old tartness. "That woman is clearly a saint."

"You used to say she was a dragon."

"Perhaps," Jane said with a smile, "I was the dragon myself." She let Christina's hand fall and looked thoughtfully down at her own hands. "I was an awful egoist."

"Nonsense, you are a great person, and always were."

"I had illusions. One thing about very old age, all the illusions wither away. I had illusions that I might do some first-rate work in botany—on ferns, you know. Well, I never did."

"What you did was educate a village. Think what you did for John! Without you he might not be alive."

"Oh, I had my triumphs," Jane said with a lift of her

196

chin. Then she sighed. "It's been a good life, Christina. I have no regrets. And now," she added in a murmur, "I am learning to die. You know, it is a great adventure—but one can't help being sometimes frightened by the immense Nowhere, the immense leap into darkness."

"Or into light. How can we be sure?"

"We can't. All I seem to know is some blessing to come. I want to be ready to be blessed." She gave a low laugh. "And that means giving up one thing after another with grace—if one can. The hardest thing has been giving up reading. Lately my yes blur in a queer way. So I manage a poem a day, and that is it."

"Would you like me to come and read to you for an hour now and then?"

"Darling person, you have enough on your hands. No, thank you, I should fall asleep, I fear, before the hour was up."

"I mustn't stay too long. This has been heaven." Christina got up and bent down to kiss Jane's hands.

"Yes, Hannah," she said as the kitchen door opened cautiously, "you are right, and I'm just going."

Did she imagine that Jane murmured, "Oh, let my joys have some abiding!" But Christina's back was turned. She waved at the door and went quickly out.

"Good gracious, your eyes are so bright they're like stars, Mrs. Chapman!" Hannah said. In the half light where Christina was being helped into her coat, the tears must have shone.

"Thank you for coming," Hannah said warmly. "It has done us both good, believe me."

"I'll be back soon," Christina said, but somehow it felt like a lie. She knew in her heart that she would not see Jane's dear transparent face again, nor the old, veined, sensitive hands plucking a thread off her skirt. Jane was outward bound.

CHRISTINA'S JOURNAL—*January 8*

The winter skies! The winter light! It is dark now in the village by four, but up here on the hill we get the late light—the mountain sometimes purple against a perfectly clear, amber sky until about half past. Cornelius can wheel himself to the windows, and often we spend a half hour in silence watching the sunset and the afterglow. It is a world of sharp contrasts—black trunks of trees making patterns on the snow, all perpendiculars, and then something rich and baroque when the great pines are covered with ermine. When the sun is out in the morning, the world is so dazzling we might be living inside a great brilliant jewel. Squirrels dart down to the feeder, one hanging upside down very cleverly to feed. He jumps from the branch of the big pine by the porch and swings there by his back feet, holding a nut in his paws. The jays crowd in screaming, making their flash of blue like a note in music. Exhilarating birds! "Gangsters," Cornelius calls them. He objects to them on moral grounds, it would seem, because they are thieves, and I tease him about this. "Who made them?" I ask, "and who are we to impose ethics on Creation?"

This evening I told him about Jane and Hannah, and we had a long talk as the fire bubbled and sighed—about death. Cornelius has come to feel that people make their deaths as they make their lives, but I wonder. Sometimes a final illness is so cruel it feels unfair. There is no chance to make anything, only endure as best one can. My father's death was like that. He was so drugged at the end that he was no longer really a human being. But Jane, the blessed creature, is dying in wisdom as she lived. She calls herself a baby, and it is true in one way—her eyes have the absolutely clear, deep look that a baby's have, a transparency that seems to open to things we can't see. There is nothing of the dying animal about her except weakness. And one must hope that she will slip away in that sleep that she told me is more awake than waking for her these days.

Cornelius was most interested in this. He has told me before that when he dozes off he feels as if some door below consciousness opened very softly and he "gets in touch," as he puts it, with the past in a new way. Cornelius and I are one, and can share everything, but what seems miraculous about Jane is that she has had to prepare herself with the help of dear good Hannah, with whom she cannot share the whole of herself by any means. It is just this that moved me so deeply—the way she has managed to take Hannah in, the laying aside of the struggle as not really important. That marvelous twinkle in her eyes when she speaks of Hannah as a saint! For she really means it, yet she *knows*. We have not thought of humbleness, of abnegation very much, Cornelius and I, as part of a good life. I guess we have both been rather arrogant until now. Now we are learning. There is sweetness in it.

It is time I opened our bed and got Cornelius upstairs. Ellen has been here today. The whole house feels "swept and garnished."

CHAPTER 7

In mid-January the great snows began. If winter had seemed something of an ordeal in December, it was something else now. The day began with feeding the birds— Christina was ordering a hundred pounds at a time, and sometimes the delivery van trundled up the hill long after dark. It was bitterly cold. The Ark proved less windtight than they had thought, and Nick spent a day lining the cracks of the windows and tacking felt strips under doors. Cornelius waited impatiently for an hour Ed Taggart could spare for cribbage, but Ed was often out plowing all night. Now Christina began to understand why Ellen dreaded the winter and the snow. At first it was all excitement and gaiety, and getting plowed out and movable was a kind of game against the elements. But as more and more snow fell, the old heaps towered along the roads. Getting down to the village, one drove through a labyrinth of white walls six or eight feet high on each side of the road. Every now and then Christina experienced a bad moment of claustrophobia, as if they were being buried alive by inches. She learned to have plenty of food stored away. Twice they were not plowed out for forty-eight hours.

But the rugged weather had one positive element. She and Cornelius felt more vividly than ever what those Civil War years must have been like for the women, old men, and children left behind to meet these hard winters alone. If someone was ill, it meant harnessing up and driving, sometimes through a blizzard, to the doctor down in the village, and hauling him up out of bed. Had there even been a doctor? But Ellen reassured them about that at one coffee hour, for, actually, he had lived in her house, a Dr. Fitzsimmons, known as "Dr. Fitz." His stable boy lived over the horses, and when Dr. Fitz was called, the boy harnessed up while the old doctor got into pants, boots, and a coat. Dr. Fitz was much loved, but he enjoyed a little nip, and especially on his way to a hard case there was the risk that his sled might turn over en route—as it once had, with all the medicine bottles strewn about on the snow, so the story went, and the horse galloping off in a panic. In those days a doctor had to be prepared to operate or diagnose there and then, without the help of X rays. And perhaps it was not too surprising that Dr. Fitz needed to feel a certain fire in his stomach.

In one of Sophia's letters mention was made of a terrible accident when one of the children lost a foot when the ax slipped. Sophia herself made a tourniquet and saved him from bleeding to death, for that day it took Dr. Fitz some hours to reach the house. He had been delivering a baby in the next village and had been up all night.

On these January evenings when the dark came down like a curtain before teatime, Christina and Cornelius drew in to the fire and sensed around them an imaginary town—the town of a hundred years earlier. It was the time to begin to write. While Cornelius dozed over *The New York Times,* which was now delivered by mail and came a day late, Christina labored over a large lined yellow pad.

"What was that long sigh all about?" Cornelius asked without opening his eyes. "It sounded like the end of time."

"I never knew how hard it is to write!" Christina had chewed off the end of her pencil and crossed out the first paragraph three times. "It all seems so clear in my head. I know just what I want to say, and then the minute I try to set a single word down, it all goes blank."

"Want to read me what you've got? Sometimes reading aloud helps. That's what Copey used to say."

It was absurd to be so shy of reading what she had written, but Cornelius suddenly loomed as he pulled himself upright and turned toward her, all expectancy, and she felt before him as she had before the formidable Miss Carstairs at Vassar—a perfect fool.

201

So her voice came out wobbly and uncertain as she read:

"Willard can be proud of its women. From pioneer days onward, the town has bred courage and character in all its residents, but often women bore the brunt, and sometimes they were the ones to make the great adventures, as did those who went to China, Turkey, and the Sandwich Islands as missionaries, or to Paris to study painting, in one case. But those who stayed home were expected to be the strong root of an arduous life for the men."

"That's all right. The last sentence needs a bit of thinking about, maybe—the whole thing is to plunge in, darling."

And plunge in she did. The case would rest, she decided, on missionaries, Sophia, Erica Portland the artist, and Jane Tuttle.

"Jem would prefer that I concentrated on the early years," she thought. "But I can stuff in a few paragraphs about that later on."

If there was comfort, it lay in the fact that Ellen had bogged down completely. She, who was so articulate when speaking, stiffened into trite phrases and stilted sentences as soon as she put pen to paper. And they both decided that Jem had been extremely clever to concentrate his powers on dates and tables, and leave the real work to others.

"The trouble, of course," Christina said after struggling along for what seemed like hours and was less than one, "is that when you start to write you discover how little you know. I have a sense of the structure of the house, so to speak, but it is bare of furniture, rugs, all the things that make a house the personal thing it is, that would make a person walking into it sense what sort of life had been lived in it. Oh dear!"

"Well, surely you have a pretty good idea about the sort of life."

"Yes, but what I realize more and more is that it is the small details that count. It's all very well to talk about Sophia's pluck and imagination, but I need facts—facts and more facts, Cornelius. And I need to know so much more than I do about the period itself. I get stopped all the time by ignorance."

Christina laid down her pad on the pile of books she had been dipping into and had then set aside in a sort of desperation. Anyway, it was time to think about a drink and supper, time to draw the curtains against the bitter-cold dark outside.

"Strange," Cornelius murmured, "but that sound of the curtain rings being drawn always brings Mary to mind. You remember how she used to come in on her silent feet and draw the curtains after dinner. Those were summer nights. My mother played Chopin. My father read the Wall Street news and smoked a cigar."

Christina stood there a moment, one hand on his shoulder.

"My mother . . ." Cornelius murmured. But whatever he had meant to say sank down into silence, and Christina tiptoed out to the kitchen.

Later that evening the phone rang to tell them that Jane had slipped away in her sleep. She had not, after all, been able to make her great journey lucid. For days she had been unconscious, while the doctor came and went, but there was nothing to do but wait for the weak heart-beat to stop. The minister would spend the night in the house, and he assured Christina that Hannah was all right. Luckily the doctor had left her a sedative on his last call that afternoon.

"She died as she had lived, in perfect gentleness," Dr. Park assured Christina.

Before she went upstairs to tell Cornelius, Christina flung on a coat and slipped out onto the porch to look at the brilliant stars and the dark outline of the moun-tain. Tears flowed down her cheeks and froze there. Then the absolute stillness touched her, and a strange sense of peace and—how to name it?—fulfillment flowed in. It is all so much greater than we are, she thought. And for this little time, this night, she wanted only that huge, impersonal sky. Tomorrow would be time enough to tell John, to do all the things that death brought in its wake —the human things. It was a strange moment—a mo-ment of awareness beyond the personal.

"Warm my hands, darling, I'm cold," she said to Cor-nelius when she was safe in bed beside him.

"Where have you been?"

"Out on the porch. Jane is gone."

Cornelius held her two hands hard, so hard it hurt. She felt the shock in that hard clasp, the shock and then, as he let go a little, the wonderful warmth of life, the mystery of it. Like that they fell asleep, her last conscious thought how steady and strong Cornelius's heartbeat sounded, and that on this small, indefatigable engine her own life was suspended.

On the day of the funeral it became clear that although Jane had no family—an only brother was too frail to come—the village had become her family, and the village mourned. Boys appeared from nowhere to shovel a path up to the church, no easy task because of the huge drifts against steps and door. Dinnock and Orin got the fire going. The women of the Ladies' Aid swept the church and made a balsam wreath. Someone remembered that Jane's favorite hymns had been "Rock of Ages" and "My Soul There Is a Country." And Dr. Park was prepared to read the twenty-third and the hundred and twenty-first Psalms. Had there ever been a funeral among these hills without their being read?

Long before the service was to begin, people stopped by—partly out of curiosity. The florist drove up with innumerable baskets and vases of flowers, and these were discreetly commented upon as they were taken out one by one and carried through the cruel icy air. But the village, usually so taciturn, a village where people did not pay calls often or exchange many words with each other, now seemed to have opened itself to the heart. There would be no eulogy at the service, but Jane's name was on every tongue. Dinnock was two hours late with the mail, because at every door or mailbox someone wanted to speak of Jane. It seemed as if each person had a special memory that he or she wanted to share. One remembered bird walks when he was a small boy in school, another remembered going berrying and how they had seen four bluebirds on a sumac bush, another that she had scolded him for shooting woodcock.

"The village just won't be the same without her," they said. And they got into cars and drove up the steep hill to the house to pay their respects to Hannah, and to comfort her.

But Hannah did not need comfort now. She was in her glory; dressed in a black suit, a white blouse, she held court in the empty house, served cups of coffee, sat down with her friends and with Jane's friends, and talked incessantly, as if she had held back this torrent of words for years. Over and over she told Christina and Ellen and Jem and Eben—the world at large—how Jane had failed, how gently she had ebbed away, what a saint she was, how she loved to laugh, how the last thing she recognized at all was an evening grosbeak at the feeder, how she had asked for a cup of strong coffee that day but fell asleep before Hannah brought it in.

No one sat in Jane's chair. It stood there, empty, in the window, the presence that had sat there for so many years looking out with such seeing eyes still vivid, still a *presence* to be reckoned with.

John had arrived by eleven and went straight to the house alone. Fortunately, there was no one but Hannah there when he pushed open the door, as if he had been running and must get there in time—in time for what? The emptiness hit him like a slap in the face. The man in his fifties who had always been a boy here sat down once more in the little chair in front of the rocker with his head in his hands. And Hannah, for once, was silent. She went into the kitchen to cry.

Until now she had been lifted up on the drama of death —played on this stage where she was, for today, the heroine, the one who could tell the story. Now John had brought it all back to the human scale; she was suddenly bereft and at a loss; she trembled as she put coffee on again to heat. Or would he prefer sherry? Yes, the small cut glasses Jane had always demanded when he came.

"Here," she said, "Miss Tuttle always asked for the best glasses for you."

"Sit down, Hannah. You need a glass yourself."

And she did—on a straight chair.

"We knew it would happen, didn't we?" he said gently. "But it's worse than we could know."

"When the breath stops and there's no one there," Hannah sobbed, "it's so lonely!"

But kindness was such a built-in part of the ugly old woman sitting awkwardly on the edge of her chair, that she managed to pull herself together and tell John what comfort it had given Jane to know that he had really got going on the chapter, and, although she had been unable to read it all, she had sat, Hannah told him, with the pages of manuscript in her hands for an hour, looking content.

"It will be better now," he answered. "Because I can speak of her, and now it will be a memorial. Oh, Hannah, the worst—isn't it?—is that we can do so little—nothing really—for the dead. So I am happy I can do this one thing."

What would Hannah do now, he longed to ask, but sensed that it was too soon.

"Yes, I slept a whole night through for the first time in years," she said. "There was no reason to wake."

Then Hannah slipped back to her kitchen where she felt at home, and washed up the cups and glasses while John sat on, his hands clasped between his knees, thinking. Pure love, he thought, inhabited this house, so for once there is no guilt. No one of us can feel remorse for things not done or things not said. Every wound had been healed by those small strong hands long before Jane died. Why was it? Perhaps because she never asked anything—never expected more of people than they could give, and wanted of them only what they could be, not what she herself might need. So, even with Hannah, she had ended by accepting possessiveness, tyranny even— and had not asked for what was not there, but had managed to make everything all right for Hannah too. It is not so easy as it looks at first sight to accept the fierce love and protectiveness of an inferior, not to let it become a burden to take such a one deep into the heart. But that was Jane's way, John thought, lighting a cigarette and puffing on it. The sense of loss that had nearly overwhelmed him when he walked into the room and saw the empty rocker had gone. He felt almost as though he and Jane were silently talking—one thing he had loved about her was that she could be silent. Twice, when he himself was close to despair and felt utterly useless, a prolonged silence between them had seemed to be a kind of wordless balm. Once after such a silence she had said gently, "There is such a thing as soul, John. You are out of touch with your own soul. Come, we'll go for a little walk, shall we?"

A little walk with Jane meant that one found oneself looking at everything. John remembered that what struck him that day, as if he had never really noticed it before, was light through leaves, the shivery way it had in the branches of a white birch. And that day they saw a woodcock and an ovenbird. Jane had never once said, "Lift your head and look out of that little self of yours, teeming with devils and nightmares," but being with her, he found that for almost an hour he had forgotten to be desperate.

206

And as he sat in this room alone for the first time, it was not only memory that held him so quiet. It was coming to John that when the great people in one's life die, one is forced to be more oneself. One is forced to grow up. All these years, he realized, he had leaned on Jane. Even when they did not meet, he knew there was one person around who fully understood him and, at the same time, expected him to be able to handle his demons, and never doubted that he could. His own parents cared too much perhaps, and felt his afflictions as attacks on them . . . yes.

John got up and stood at the window looking out, as Jane so often had done in his presence. Not the least of Jane's gifts was her realism. She had talked about Christina and Cornelius more than once, had reminded the rebellious boy before her that it was not easy to live in the world. "Far easier to be me," she had said, laughing. "Why, I have just one hat! Think of the time your mother has to spend just buying hats and dealing with servants!"

She had laughed, but she had not been critical. In fact she had made John see just what a toll a life such as the Chapmans' must exact of the inner person, and how much of it was spent giving in one way or another. John must have been fourteen or fifteen when this conversation took place. He was helping Jane paint the big wooden armchairs that she set out on the lawn every summer. It had simply never occurred to him before that grown-up people could not do exactly as they pleased, that his own mother, who could make a roomful of people light up and become animated by her mere appearance in a doorway, lived a life given almost entirely to things that could be called chores.

"I want to be like you," he said passionately.

But that too, he had learned, was not so easy as it looked to a boy. Jane had made herself what she was by following a consuming passion for nature, and by choosing that at the expense of a lot of things he still wanted. One had to have a strong character to do what she had done, and a rich nature to achieve happiness within such a limited area. Had she ever been in love? How secret our lives are, John thought, even a life as apparently open as this one had been!

Well, I'll never know, he thought, turning away. It was time to go home. It was time to say good-by to

Hannah, upon whom this huge capacity for loving had been concentrated for so long. That's it, he thought: even the love of an animal or a poor ignorant, faithful servant can teach us all we need to know. Like grief, it is not the thing itself but what we do with it.

In spite of all the memories and the love gathered in the church before the tiny coffin standing on trestles under the pulpit, the funeral service was curiously dry. There was a feeling of anticlimax, as if there had been no real discharge of grief, and now the people of the village were eager to get away. Nevertheless they gathered in small knots, blowing on chilled hands, plumes of congealed breath coming from their mouths, while the men got cars started and the women talked in subdued voices. A gang of small boys went sliding down the hill, shouting with relief at being released from so much gravity.

Christina met Eben outside and, on an impulse, begged him to stop at the Ark on his way home.

"Cornelius will want to hear all about it," she said. "Come, Eben, and cheer us up."

"I'll be along," he said.

He was standing in the snow, hatless, talking to Old Pete, who had taken up his station leaning against the back of a jeep. There Old Pete was holding court—the person everyone knew and who knew everyone. Christina saw Jem walk over to join them, and Jim Heald and Orin, and felt as she had so often felt as a girl when the boys went off in a gang. They would be talking their own talk, full of profanity and laughter, a special kind of laughter. Old Pete must be telling some tale about Jane, and Christina was hungry for talk. What is there to do when people die—people so dear and rare —but bring them back by remembering?

She waved at the Lovelands, just getting into their old truck, then stopped her car to say a word to Ellen and Nick, walking soberly home.

"Never saw the church so full," she said.

"Oh, well, I guess Jane had more influence in this town than God," Ellen said, with her thin smile.

Nick walked on, his hands in his pockets, head down.

"He's taking it hard," Ellen murmured. "Of course Jane was on the side of the wild animals. I guess Nick feels like his side is let down. He's worried sick about the does on this hard crust. Says the dogs have been after them. Jane cared about that."

"Extraordinary how she made herself felt, though for years no one saw much of her."

"But she was there," Ellen said. "Seems like the heart has gone out of the town."

Those were the words Christina carried back to Cornelius. She found him with John at his side, and hurried out to the kitchen to put coffee cake in the oven and get out cups and saucers.

"Eben's stopping by on his way home," she called out through the door.

She felt happy that she had thought to ask Eben. This was the right occasion for the ice to be broken between him and Cornelius. And about time too!

A half hour later he walked right in. In the kitchen Christina heard the door close behind him, and heard John introduce himself, and Eben's shout—

"John, my boy! Good heavens! I would never have recognized you in the beard! Where is your father?"

When she went in with the tray, Eben was standing, back to the fire, his eyes so bright undr his thick white hair that she felt herself kindled by them.

"People who read the Bible as if they were launching an attack on the Democratic Party ought to be run out of town. Where did that awful old man come by that harsh voice anyway?"

"Poor old Park," Cornelius said, "he lacks something as a minister, it must be admitted."

Christina knew by the way he smiled that he was enjoying himself, that it was all right about Eben.

"But why must he sound so angry?" Eben asked the world at large. "I never go into the church without feeling *non grata,* a sinner publicly brought to book. What ails the man?"

"What ails him is that Jane, dead, can fill the church that, when he, alive, conducts a service, is empty," John said, passing cups of coffee around.

"Sit down, Eben. Stay a while," Cornelius commanded.

"The man looks far too young," he said to Christina. "It's unfair to old people like us, Eben. Try to bank that fire a little. After all, we've endured Park for twenty years."

But Eben did not sit down. He walked up and down restlessly.

"There wasn't a wet eye and we all *wanted* to weep, Cornelius. We had a right to mourn, damn it! I feel deprived."

"What did Old Pete tell you?" Christina asked. "I could tell just by the way your heads were bent, you and Jem, that things were being uttered."

"Complained about his feet hurting. My guess is he'll not survive this winter. Town should get him out of that shack."

"Try to do it!" Christina answered. "I've taken quilts down and scolded him for letting the fire go out. He can't admit that he's older than he once was. Says the winters are colder, but the fact is that he hasn't the strength to do what he used to do."

"We're on the road to ruin," Eben said darkly. "The town's falling apart."

He sat down on the big sofa and laid his cup down.

"Well, if you must make a drama out of it," Cornelius jibed, "you at least haven't changed, old boy. Still at it, eh?"

"At what exactly?" Eben asked crossly.

"Wringing the last drop of emotion out of things."

But Eben was not rising this time. He leaned his head back and closed his eyes. "I've lost a friend, Cornelius. Let me mourn her."

"Yes," Cornelius sighed. "I know."

And for a moment there was silence, while Christina looked over at John, who was sitting where he could watch the bird feeder and the squirrels' gymnastics. She did not often have a chance to look at John, and she felt startled to note how solid he had become, a middle-aged man with an alert, yet somehow wary, or perhaps tender, look about him—one on whom, she realized suddenly, one could depend. The change was not to be defined in anything as obvious as his beard (really very becoming, she decided); it was something inside—something that he had from his father, that look of solid warmth. Never, never would she have believed that the temperamental, difficult, often desperate boy would grow into this kind of strength. Was she imagining a change since Jane's death?

"Influence," she murmured, "isn't it mysterious? I mean, there Jane was, up a lonely dead-end. We had hardly seen her for years, not as a regular thing anyway, yet her influence was felt. It touched everyone in the village—or almost everyone. Yet she was totally unassuming, and would have been astonished, I think, that she could be mourned in the way she is, that you could say, Eben, 'the town's falling apart.' Why, she would have laughed at the very idea."

"I was trying to remember when I last saw her," Cornelius said. "It must have been last summer at the party the Websters gave. She sat in a chair on the lawn, and we talked about old times, about my father. I thought she was about the prettiest old lady I had ever seen—engaging woman. One never thought of her as an old maid—that's odd, isn't it? She seemed so . . . unrestricted . . . so free."

"Authentic," Eben interposed. "There are never a great many authentic human beings around at any one time. But she was one. And we all felt it." Then he gave Cornelius one of his bold bright looks. "And what did Jane Tuttle have to say about Judge Chapman?"

"You know, I've forgotten," Cornelius answered with a slow smile. "I remember an atmosphere—an atmosphere of subtle amusement. She did say that his character showed in the way he handled a horse."

"Mmm . . . I should have said that his character showed in the fact that he handled people as if they were horses."

John looked up and leaned forward. "What do you mean, Mr. Fifield?"

Christina heard these remarks with her every antenna raised. John and his grandfather had never been able to communicate at all, and she sensed that he was, consciously or not, reacting now to years of childhood suffering, when he had been sent back from the table to wash his hands or put on a presentable shirt, and called a coward when he refused to jump a balky horse and said, "Sam's just as afraid as I am. What purpose does it serve to force him—or me?" He was eleven or twelve, and it must have taken a good deal of courage to stand up to that towering force of command, his grandfather.

"You always resented Pop, didn't you?" Cornelius answered with a quizzical look. He was not, Christina realized, to be put out or on the defensive. He was simply interested. This was only one more sign of what had happened to Cornelius lately. Beside him, Eben suddenly looked a little cheap. Alive, oh yes—terribly alive still to hurt, to old hurts, to grudges—burning, but not wise.

"Yes," Eben shot back. "I resented his arrogance. He thought that people had to be mastered, not really understood, just kept in their place. He couldn't help feeling superior."

"Father was no saint, that's sure," Cornelius answered. "But he was no fool when it came to judging people. He had, I might say, the greatest admiration for you and was always holding you up to me as an example. 'There's a young man who knows what he wants and is out to get it,' he used to say to me."

"Whew!" John grinned. "Not exactly the way to cement your friendship."

"We were never friends," Eben shot back. "We were rivals."

"Do you really think so?" Cornelius swallowed this and seemed to be chewing it over. "I suppose it is true in a way. But I always thought of you as having everything I lacked."

"Yes, you said it once: 'I wish I had your ambition,'" Eben said bitterly. "I don't suppose I have ever been so angry in my life—and that is saying a good deal—as I was at that."

"But why?" Cornelius now leaned forward, totally alert. "I meant it as a compliment."

"I know, but it hit me in the stomach just the same. It implied that you felt that ambition was it—ego, the driving force—not intelligence, not a capacity for unremitting hard work. You could afford to be wise. I couldn't. I had to push my way up, you see."

"Well, I'll be darned," Cornelius said, looking Eben straight in the eye. Then he suddenly laughed—a rueful laugh. "Old men can afford to tell the truth, Eben. I enjoy being old, and that's one of the reasons. Thanks for telling me this. It explains a lot that has puzzled me, I must confess. I would have given a great deal if my father had given me the faith he gave you." Then, with a shy glance at Christina, he added, "Well, here we are, fifty years or more later—and it's about time we had it out."

"I wonder . . ." Eben said thoughtfully. "Money, privilege—they act like acid on people like me. No one's fault," he added, "just a fact."

"But not on Jane," John said gently. "They didn't act like acid on her. I wonder why."

"Oh, Jane was a saint." Eben shrugged it off.

"Jane was a woman. Women are different," Cornelius added.

"No, people are people," Christina said firmly. "Ellen feels as you do, Eben, and now and then I get it from her like a whiplash."

"Ellen is a fine woman," Cornelius said, "but after all she has not made her way up in the world as Eben did. Pride keeps her warm, I expect. No, Eben, when we first knew you—when you used to come over to play tennis with Christina, you seemed on fire in such a splendid way. You made us all look like the end of an era; you were the new world, the one that would take over, that has taken over." But Cornelius clasped his hands and it was clear that he was thinking back, reliving it, that he was after some clue. "Then you went sour, were out to pick a fight with me at every turn. What did it?"

"Very simple. I was a native. When your cousin got married here that summer, I was not invited to the wedding. Things like that. You were summer people. I was a native, to be picked up and helped, but to be kept at a distance . . . oh, you know, Cornelius."

Cornelius exchanged a discreet glance with Christina as if asking for her interpretation. He looked a little at a loss suddenly.

"I don't believe it, Eben," Christina answered him. "There must have been something else."

"You," Eben said bitterly, but recovered himself before the word could really land, got up and went to the window. "If you must know, I guess it was the way your father lent me that money for college. And the fact that, in spite of his condescension, I took it."

"You paid back every cent, as I remember. And that too my father rubbed in—I was always in debt at that age," Cornelius said. "This is all very interesting, Eben, I must say."

"Mother, you spoke about influence just now," John said into the rather tense silence—Eben was standing back to them. He had lit a small cigar.—"It's so much more powerful than we know, or have any idea of really. Sometimes I think every meeting between two human beings is a collision."

"Especially where class—forgive my using a forbidden word—enters in," Eben said to the window. "You could take everything for granted. I couldn't take anything for granted. I felt crude, inept. I didn't know how to dress."

"As if that mattered." Cornelius brushed this aside. "We all went around looking like tramps, as I remember."

"Tramps in white flannels for tennis, tramps in good old riding trousers made by Brooks Brothers; even those round white sailor hats you wore—I could never manage to look like you, casual and elegant. Well, I was jealous, let's face it—jealous and humiliated."

"You had a chip on your shoulder," Cornelius said. "But you never realized that I felt inferior, man—inferior. And Father certainly rubbed that in, I can tell you."

"Grandfather seems to have been a rather inhuman person," John said. "It's a relief to say it now. I'm sorry, Dad. I know how you admired him."

"He was all of a piece, hard but generous. He couldn't help what he was." And suddenly he sat up, all alight. "That's what Jane said, bless her. She said Gordon Chapman was great because he was simple. 'All of a piece,' she said. She implied this was something a horse reacted well to." And Cornelius chuckled. "People, on the other hand, bolt. My mother, if you remember, often did, by withdrawing with a headache—a headache that sometimes lasted for days." Then he sighed. "My father humiliated *me*, Eben. That's what you couldn't know. But he also taught me a great deal. I suppose I might say that he taught me to be a man."

"Whatever that means," John put in.

"Not to complain, for one thing. To take it on the chin, as he used to say."

"I suppose what he did for me was to challenge me— challenge me because I was bound to show him I could win at his game, be someone in the world," Eben said. The anger had gone.

"Whereas Jane—oh, let us come back to her—challenged me to be myself," John said, "really against the whole climate around here."

"Gordon Chapman," Eben said, "created enormous pressures in all those around him. Some of it was salutary —spurred the horses on, you know. But Jane—well, I must agree with you, John—Jane somehow took the pressure away so one could see oneself naked."

"The difference, no doubt, between a great gentleman —for you'll have to grant my father was that—and a saint," Cornelius said.

214

"Yes,"—Eben came back and sat down—"I'll grant you that, Cornelius. And I suppose the best thing that can be said about Willard is that it could contain them both—nourish them both—accept them both for what they were." Then he looked over at Cornelius, really looked at him, Christina thought, for the first time. "You've changed, Cornelius."

"Have I?" Cornelius returned Eben's look, and for a second the glances locked. Perhaps even Christina, who was pouring out more coffee, didn't catch it, a fleeting second but a momentous one. It was not a collision. It was as if in each of these men a door that had been held locked for fifty years opened. Cornelius turned away first, lifted a hand and let it fall. "Old age tames us, Eben. Still," he teased, "it doesn't seem to have tamed you. You're still a tiger pacing about and growling, aren't you?"

"Yes, I am." Then, very unexpectedly, he added, "I need you, old boy. I need your wisdom—for you have somehow achieved it, and I, God knows, have not."

"Well, you haven't got knocked over and pretty nearly knocked out. This . . ."—he coughed before the word and perhaps chose a different one—"incapacity of mine has not been a wholly disastrous thing. Perhaps it is that we become what we have to become to survive."

It was now as if the two men were alone in an arena, and, feeling this, Christina and John, on the excuse of taking out the tray and on the understanding that Eben would stay for lunch ("just a sandwich and soup, Eben —no trouble"), withdrew into the kitchen.

After they had gone, there was a silence. Eben bent down to put another log on the fire. He slouched down in the big armchair opposite Cornelius. Was Cornelius asleep? His eyes were closed, and Eben wondered whether the conversation had been too great an effort.

"I'm not asleep," Cornelius murmured. "I find when I close my eyes these days that everything becomes a good deal clearer. Go on, Eben; we haven't got much time."

Was he referring to death, in the wings already, or to the simple fact that Christina would not be gone long?

"I'm 'incapacitated' too, in a different way. I have no wife."

"I can't imagine life without Christina," Cornelius said, opening his eyes.

"One doesn't imagine it. Perhaps if Olive had lived—

she died just when we might have had some tranquil years after all the strain and expense of our life—I might not be such a tiger still. Oh, well . . ."

"You know women are very personal, Eben. That is their great quality, and I sometimes think their one defect. Sometimes I feel cooped up. It would be a real boon if you dropped in now and then and we could talk —about politics, for instance. I get wind of things. This chap Marcuse, for instance—can one take him seriously? The young seem to. I'm an old-fashioned man, more so than perhaps I once was, but the old bean still gets stirred up by ideas." He paused to smile a mischievous smile. "Christina will be jealous, you know. She thinks of you as *her* friend."

"No, we were never friends," Eben said quietly.

"Why not? Let's clear the decks, for once, Eben. It would do us both good."

"I was in love with her, of course—fifty years ago."

"And still are a little perhaps?"

"We light each other up—always did. She was the unattainable for me, Cornelius. The unattainable haunts. Not a bad thing for an old man to be haunted. The past is alive."

"People think the old have no feelings. Why, I feel so much more than I did as a boy that there's no comparing it. But it doesn't hurt so much—odd thing."

"When I was twenty, you knocked me down one day in the woods. You were engaged then."

"Then I saw red. Now we can talk about it. There are great advantages to being old. For one thing, one's idea of the past, especially the personal past, changes. I must confess I thought then that you were a cad."

Eben laughed.

"By your standards I guess I was. No hard feelings, Cornelius. But how does that past look to you now—and the native who had the arrogance to try to take your girl away from you?"

"I think I was damned lucky. You had more to offer than I did then."

"Such magnanimity!" Eben said ironically.

"No, just common sense. But it wouldn't have worked, you know. Christina would have eaten you up, and I suspect that Olive nourished you."

"Yes, she did," Eben said. There were tears in his

eyes. He hoped that Cornelius would not see them. "That is just what she did."

Cornelius had closed his eyes again.

"There aren't so many people left who can remember back fifty years with me. Old friends, even old rivals, get to be rather precious, don't they?" And he added, "It must be damned lonely up there, Eben. You must come down and see us often. Will you?"

"I will."

When John and Christina came back bearing trays of soup, the two old men were discussing Marcuse's ideas of revolution.

CHRISTINA'S JOURNAL—*February 10*

It seems years since I have had time to write anything in this journal. The children have been at us to go on a cruise, but Cornelius and I feel exactly the same. The winter is a terrific adventure, and we are getting all the cruising we need learning about being winter people at last. I must say February is the worst yet as far as the weather goes. There has been sleet and freezing rain on top of the packed snow. Driving a car has been really nerve-racking. Nevertheless Eben has managed to come down in his jeep once or twice a week. Who could have imagined even a month ago that I would be just a little jealous of Eben, and Cornelius not at all jealous! He and Cornelius have long talks about philosophy, politics and things. Eben brings books over and sometimes reads aloud. Then they go at it like two college boys, and it's very clear that they are just as glad if I absent myself. Of course each has been starved for just this sort of conversation—starved for another male, in fact. Anyway this unexpected turn of events has given me time to have some good long visits with Ellen. I am anxious about her. Quite suddenly she looks so frail, so tired. And she reacts to feeling low by being more than usually critical of everything and everyone, so occasionally I get exasperated. She had quite a set-to with Jem about the school chapter. He is pressing us to get those chapters to him by Town Meeting Day. That is the deadline. But, good heavens, he has just "passed the buck" as Ellen says bitterly, and expects us to do his work. She is cross partly because she, like me, has discovered that it is quite easy to criticize a piece of writing (Ellen has a keen critical sense) but very hard indeed to produce something even halfway as good oneself. I wonder whether she will ever finish her chapter. She polishes one or two pages over and over, and then gives up. Cornelius is helping her now. He is constantly amazed at her wit and intelligence. Dear man, it has taken him all these years to take the village in. But now he is making himself felt in all kinds of ways. Last time Ed came to play cribbage he nearly persuaded Cornelius to run for Selectman. It's a splendid idea. He would do it so well, and he would enjoy it. But would the village elect him? Cornelius thinks not. And I can feel, too, that he is not sure enough of himself. He still tires very easily. When Eben comes, I put Cornelius to bed before supper and take him a tray.

The days are getting longer. Amazing what that five or ten minutes more of light does to lift our spirits. Now the sun is setting at teatime. We sit by the window and watch it go down behind the trees. The skies have been very luminous, a marvelous pale green above, then orange, and the hills a brilliant purple. I never realized how much color there is in winter. Some beech leaves cling on, pale yellow. The trunks of trees look almost red at times. Whatever color there is—a blue jay's wing— stands out against all the white, and I wear a red shirt myself because Cornelius tells me it makes my eyes look bluer than ever.

We have given up Proust. After *Swann's Way,* the best of the book I have always felt, it became faintly incongruous. The elaborate sentences, the rich tapestry of feeling, and, alas, the endless hair-splitting about class, began to be tedious. Willard and all that concerns us here fills our minds now. It seems as if we have been making a journey into Willard, and it never ceases to be interesting and illuminating.

But winter takes its toll. First Jane slipped away. And now poor Old Pete is in the hospital with both feet frozen and one leg up to the knee. He hailed my car a week ago when I was on my way to do the shopping, said I had to take him to the hospital right away. Fortunately I could go—Ellen was up at the Ark. He had let his fire go out, of course "under the influence." Said the chimney smoked and he was choking to death so there was nothing else to do. I must confess that I didn't take him seriously, thought he was just feeling dispirited, but we went to the emergency room, waited an hour, and finally they unwrapped his poor feet from the old rags he wore, and told me the truth. It looks as if he will lose them both. How awful! Whatever will he do? How will he manage?

When I go to see him he is always cheerful, looks so clean for a change, shaved and dressed in a hospital nightshirt. It is something to know that he gets warm meals and is cared for. The nurses are very kind. He is not a complainer, that's sure. Takes a huge interest in his fellow-patients, who come and go, plays cards with anyone who is well enough to join in a game. We have Flicker now. He's a dear dog and Cornelius already loves him. So at least Old Pete knows his friend is in safe hands, always asks about Flicker, and bemoans the fact that we can't hunt him. "He's a good dog," he told me last time. "Tell Ed to take him along when he's hunting hedgehogs. Flicker will turn them over with his nose. Tell Ed." But poor Ed is so badgered by people complaining that he hasn't plowed them out, and so busy trying to keep the machinery going (we need a new plow badly, he says) that he hardly gets a night's sleep. We had three new snows in succession two weeks ago, after Jane's funeral, and that was bad enough, but then the sleet followed. Where will all the snow go when it melts? I sometimes wonder whether I shall ever see a patch of earth again.

So we are deep in winter, and deep in Willard. Except for my kneee, which acts rather like a toothache when the weather is damp, I feel wonderfully well. Ellen teases me, says I look ten years younger for all the hard work, and blames it on Eben. "You have a light in your eye," she says in her dry, mocking voice. But it's not Eben. It is that I feel brimful of life—real life. By that I mean waking up to the mountain, waking up to Cornelius and a whole day together alone, doing things that really matter. I suppose it is a kind of escape. If so, we shan't have it forever. Marianne has written me a long letter about Cathy. She is doing badly at school and seems to be on the verge of a sort of breakdown. They feel it might be good for her to come next month, go to the town high school, if we can get her in, and, as Marianne says, help me out with the cooking and housework. Olivia is back of this, I think, for she also wrote me. Oh dear, the awful truth is that neither Cornelius nor I really want the darling thing. Yet, we can't possibly refuse.

John, bless his heart, says not to think of it. "You're old enough to do what you want to do, Mother," he said on the phone last night. "Cathy is not your responsibility. You have enough on your hands."

So I am back again weighing *should* and *ought* against Cornelius's needs, against what we have found here. And suddenly I remember how I felt the year they sent me to Ellen's family and how I bloomed and was renewed. Can I deny such renewal to my own grandchild? Cathy and I are real friends. She will be very understanding. And I tell Cornelius that, after all, we know everything —or almost—about Willard except the young people. Cathy will bring young people into the Ark. I do not believe in segregating the old, or in indulging myself, for that matter.

Oh dear, how complicated life is! But in my heart I know we must welcome Cathy, and that we only quail as one does before any great influx of life because it brings demands as well as joys with it.

We still have a month, or nearly—a precious month. After all, that's *ages*.

PART THREE

A Stranger
Comes to Willard

CHAPTER 1

Cathy would have the attic room where the old rocking horse stood in one corner, only a few hairs on his tail left. There was a big oak table there, a bookcase, and a bed right by the window, facing the mountain. Christina had prepared it all with joy. She found an old patchwork quilt in one of the blanket chests, threw a red corduroy pillow on it, and took the Persian rug up from the guest room because it was blue and red and made the whole room suddenly warm. The faded, torn shade had been replaced with a new one. And she and Cornelius had spent an hour choosing books from the bookcase in the hall—Kipling's poems, Louisa May Alcott, an American history and a child's encyclopedia, the *Oxford Book of English Verse*, a bird book. Cathy would find them old-fashioned, no doubt. Later, on an impulse, Christina took up a book on American Indians, a book about woodpeckers, *Ring of Bright Water*, and a book on Tibet. As she arranged them in a row on the desk in a little wood bookstand that one of Cornelius's uncles had carved, she realized how little she knew of Cathy, the inner person. Now in late March it was time for some new life to come into the Ark. The very idea of spring pulls one forward, and here in Willard they had to hold the idea of spring a very long time before any hope of being out of winter hazards and winter tedium could be realized. So this new element, fifteen-year-old despair and fifteen-year-old hopes and fears, was, after all, welcome.

Cathy was to arrive March twenty-first, by bus. She had firmly refused Marianne's offer to drive her up. But although it might be the first day of spring even a hundred miles south in Boston, here in Willard the only sign of spring was the dangerous crust over soft snow—hard on the does heavy with fawn. Christina had gladly accepted Eben's offer to drive her down to town in the jeep. One day she had skidded right off the road into a tree, and ever since, her knee had troubled her more than usual—she must have given it a twist in trying to right the car.

So by two when Eben drove up, and Christina, in a round fur hat and sheepskin coat and boots, went in to kiss Cornelius good-by, she was flushed with excitement.

"Oh, darling," she said, giving his hand a squeeze. Absurd to feel as though she were saying good-by. But it was good-by to their long, rich tête-à-tête—there was no avoiding that. How peaceful they looked, Flicker lying on the rug by the fire and Cornelius with a book open on his knee. For a second she wished devoutly that Cathy were not coming. But then life swept her on as Eben blew the horn, to tell her to hurry, she supposed —yes, there was just time. Flicker ran out to the hall, wagging his tail and barking, "Let me go with you."

"Not this time, old boy. You stay here with Cornelius," she said firmly.

Eben, nervous and impatient, helped her up the high step into the jeep.

"You know this thing can't go sixty miles an hour, Christina. We're late!"

"So is the bus, no doubt," she answered. "We are not going to hurry. We are going to enjoy ourselves."

They had not been alone together for weeks, she realized, giving a quick look at Eben's face, frowning as he concentrated on a slippery corner. And it was fun to be setting out on this expedition together.

"For once," she said, "I have you all to myself."

" 'The voice of the turtle is heard in the land,' " he

222

said with his mischievous smile, his eyes on the road.

They heard a series of short excited barks to the left below the cemetery.

"Those damn dogs!" Eben said. "They're after deer, I expect."

"Can't the town do anything about getting Mrs. Croswell to restrain them? I just don't understand it. Nick is making himself ill again over this."

"The selectmen are a bunch of cowards. They pay calls on that woman and she laughs in her sleeve. One of these days Nick will go out with his gun and that will be that! Good riddance!"

"It wouldn't be the best way to solve anything—start another feud in the town. No, I hope he holds onto himself this time."

"He's a strange critter—reminds me sometimes of a sled dog—those pale blue eyes, mild and dangerous."

"Ellen worries."

"Ellen would worry if she were in heaven with God's hand on her shoulder. Worrying keeps her alive."

"You're cruel, Eben."

"No, just realistic in my old age."

They passed several cars, and each time Eben lifted a hand from the wheel in salute. It was one of the things winter had brought to Christina—the pleasure of being greeted by everyone, for everyone recognized you. Now they had come out onto the school road that followed a winding brook all the way down to town.

Reveling in the sound of water, the rush and roar as the snow-rich brook tumbled down past rocks and blocks of ice, a thundering, joyous aliveness, Christina said, "That's the only sign of spring, yet it is March twenty-first."

"Looking forward to the change?"

"If you mean the weather, yes."

"I meant Cathy."

"Oh, Eben, I don't know." But for some reason she didn't feel like talking about Cathy. "Do you think you are more realistic now—whatever that really means?"

"Maybe all I mean is that I am more able to accept people as they are, to accept—maybe—that their faults go to make them what they are. I'm eager to see this little person and what she is like. The only trouble with Willard—our Willard anyway—is that it is composed of the elderly. Good for us, don't you think, to be stirred up

223

again by someone young enough to be in revolt?—for I gather that is what she is."

"She wears dreadful clothes—her skirts are halfway up her thighs and she hasn't the legs for that. Her hair falls down straight over her face as if she were an English sheep dog. She is doing very badly at school. She loves animals passionately, and plays the guitar really quite well, and sings in a strange piping voice that, for some reason, catches my heart in an absurd way. She writes poems. . . . I just can't imagine what it's going to be like, Eben. I'm scared, I guess."

"You don't really like women, do you?" It was a typical thrust from Eben. He liked to make Christina rise.

"Don't I? Olivia and I have always been very close, it seems to me." Then for a moment Christina thought this statement over. "I guess you're right. Olivia is more like a man really. Women are so damned personal, Eben, and girls are always worrying about how they look."

"Well, Cathy doesn't seem to err in that direction."

"She's wild and elusive and doesn't know what she wants."

"She wanted to come here."

"Because Willard lets her out of all the things that bother her now—boys, her high-powered schoolmates with their ambitions, and, above all, her bewildered parents. She thinks of me, I presume, as an all-purpose object to lean on—one who won't criticize."

"Nonsense, she adores you."

"How do you know?"

"Cornelius told me so."

"How strange it is, Eben, that after all these years you and Cornelius have become friends."

"Do you mind?"

"A little." At that they both laughed. "Oh dear, we're almost there and I want to *talk*."

But, after all, the bus was late, and they had a good ten minutes sitting in the jeep, waiting. Now Eben could turn in his seat and look at Christina, and reach over and take her hand.

"You know," he said, lifting an eyebrow, "it's no fair at all that you grow more beautiful every day."

"I'm afraid I hoped you'd say something like that—absurd old creature that I am!" She pulled her hand away. "But I'm getting to be a wrinkled old apple, and you know it as well as I do, Eben."

"Don't look into mirrors, look into people's eyes."

"I can't. It makes me blush."

"After a certain age mirrors lie."

"How?"

"They give the bare facts all right, but they leave out all the poetry."

"It is lovely to be appreciated at any age—you are a dear."

"I'm safe. Fifty years ago you wouldn't have called me a dear, would you?"

"You weren't a dear. You were a threat."

He sighed. "Yes, I expect I was. I wanted to be, anyway." Then, mercurial as ever, he ceased to be a teasing admirer and looked thoughtfully away. "It *is* rather fine that Cornelius and I have become friends. It has made the winter for me, Christina. For at last I understand why you love him. I never could get behind the bank, don't you know—the bank and all the family looming behind him. I never really saw him until now."

"He's changed."

"Changed or simply become able to show himself."

"I'm finding old age full of miracles, Eben. I suppose that's why I dread Cathy's coming. This winter has been a journey inward. I want to continue the journey."

"Well, here comes the bus! So I guess you can't."

"Life does have a way of interrupting philosophy," Christina laughed, not even waiting for a hand to help her out, clambering down and running to the huge, bumbling monster that contained Cathy.

Eben stood by the jeep and watched the meeting with some amusement—the meeting of these two, so different —Christina so tall and distinguished; Cathy, short and awkward, guitar case held in one hand—but so alike in the warmth of their hugs.

"Can't believe it, Gram! I've escaped!"

"Come along. You know Mr. Fifield, don't you?"

"Hello, Cathy. Any luggage I can get for you?"

"Oh God, yes—an awful lot, I'm afraid."

There were two huge suitcases.

"What have you got in these—geological specimens?" Eben asked as he lifted them in.

"Ski boots and stuff."

There were also three coats that Cathy had left in the bus and rushed back to find, and a carryall filled with books.

"Now, is that really all? You haven't forgotten anything?"

After the clamor of arrival, there was silence as they drove up along the winding brook toward home. Every now and then Cathy leaned forward from the back seat and put an arm round Christina's neck to whisper something.

"It's so beautiful, Gram! In Boston the snow's old and dirty. I knew it would be wonderful here, but I never imagined the brook like this—castles and icebergs, that marvelous green—look, there!"

Then a little later, "I can *taste* the air, Gram."

The approach to Willard from the town was different from that by road from Boston, and Cathy noted that they were climbing steadily—"climbing into our world," she said.

Nothing could have been fresher or more invigorating than Cathy's delight, yet somehow Christina felt it as an invasion, and as they drew nearer home she felt she must speak a little about Cornelius—his tiring easily, his suffering from any loud noise, the fact that Cathy was coming into an intimate and silent house.

"But all I want is to write poems, Gram. I'll be quiet as a mouse."

"School doesn't begin for a week, so you'll have time to settle in."

"Oh, hurrah! School's the only thing I dread."

"It does seem like a great interruption to life, doesn't it?" Eben remarked. "When I was your age I learned more from the hired man than I ever did at school."

"What was he like?"

"Josiah? Well, he was laconic, but there wasn't anything he couldn't do, and those were the things I thought I needed to learn."

"Like what?"

"How to kill a porcupine, track a deer, how to make an ax handle or a little box for my special treasures; where to find Indian flints and the first arbutus; how to skin a woodchuck and cure the skin for thongs and things."

"Real things," Cathy said dreamily.

"You come over in April and I'll show you a bank of arbutus I have kept a secret till now," Eben said.

"Thanks." Cathy withdrew. She felt the old man was being rather intimate when they had only just met. Cathy

226

found people a trial. Mostly she wanted to find things like arbutus for herself. She didn't want to be *shown*.

Whatever Christina's anxiety had been, within three days Cathy had become part of the household, and, far from being a problem, was hardly ever visible. She disappeared into her quarters at the top of the house for hours at a time. Sometimes they heard the guitar, faint and haunting. Often she went out with Flicker, having promised not to go far into the woods alone—but Christina was aware that this promise was occasionally broken. Cornelius had given her a police whistle to wear round her neck on a string, and she was to blow it if she got lost—so even he did not take that promise too seriously, evidently. Cathy spent a lot of time at Ellen's, but when Christina asked Ellen whether she was making herself a nuisance Ellen just smiled and said, "No, she's a great talker and I listen and sew." This was the more surprising because Cathy did not talk much at home, or only in short bursts when she and Christina did the dishes after supper.

She proved to be almost overanxious to help. John had apparently whispered in her ear that it would be a splendid idea if she brought breakfast up to the two old people on trays. After a rather disastrous first try at this—when the coffee was spilt, the eggs hard-boiled, and the toast cold—Christina helped her plan things the evening before, found a thermos for the coffee, set the trays—and she had to admit that it was luxury not to have to get up till an hour later than usual.

Cornelius, meanwhile, was quietly making his own plans for the granddaughter. He suggested that they read aloud every evening for a half hour after the dishes were done, and Christina was aware that he took this responsibility seriously. Sometimes he chose a passage from the Bible, sometimes it was poetry—Cathy, they discovered, hardly knew Wordsworth or Keats. Once in a while it might be a short story by Sarah Orne Jewett or Willa Cather. Cathy and Flicker lay on the bear rug by the fire, and Christina put her feet up on the sofa and felt very much at peace. Sometimes she stole a look at Cathy and rested her eyes on the purity of line of the unformed face, so vulnerable, with the hair flung back over her shoulder—no wonder she hid behind all that hair!

Occasionally Cathy said something surprising. She always kissed them both before she went upstairs to bed. Once she said, "I wish people kissed each other more. No one does at home." And Christina sensed that Cathy was moved by the tenderness she herself showed Cornelius—moved and a little disturbed. She blushed when she came in with the breakfast trays and found them, like as not, Christina leaning against Cornelius's shoulder as they greeted the mountain from their bed.

"There's so much love in this house, Gram," she said once when she was standing on a stepladder to put dishes away.

"Well, there is, darling," Christina answered. "Is that strange?"

"In summer we're outdoors. I guess I never thought much about the house. It seemed rather dark when I was a child."

"All that oak—when I first came here as a bride I wanted to paint it white or something. But I've got used to it. Now I'm glad I didn't change anything here. It *is* an ark, and arks have dark wooden walls. Is that it, do you suppose?"

"It's more intimate," Cathy observed. "And it has a good smell. I love the smell in the closet in my room —a smell of sneakers and tennis rackets and old clothes. New houses don't have any smell."

"Could you write a poem about that?" But it was the wrong question.

Cathy looked surprised. "My poems are about feelings," she said, and made an excuse to disappear.

What *were* her feelings, Christina wondered? She fitted in almost too well, but so far there had been no revelations of her inner self—only the evidence that she was delighted to be here and that she dreaded school. The week was flying away already. And somehow, in relation to them, Christina felt, Cathy was rather like a passionate bird-watcher, observing a fascinating pair of old birds and keeping her thoughts to herself.

On the Sunday night before the first day of the new term, Cornelius asked her whether she could bring her guitar down and sing for them. "Would you like to? We hear lovely sounds—but rather faintly—from your attic."

"All right," she said, and ran upstairs.

"No more breakfasts in bed, darling," Cornelius said while they waited. Cathy would have to leave the house at a quarter to seven to be picked up on the green by the school bus, and would not be home again till half past three. If the weather was too bad, she would take refuge at Ellen's and phone from there and Christina would drive down the hill to fetch her, or Nick might bring her up when he came to fill the woodboxes.

"I do hope she'll find her way at school. That is the big question, isn't it?"

"Well, she'll be a new girl, and I expect the boys at least will be interested."

"I hate boys," Cathy said, catching the last phrase as she came back. "That's what I dread most."

That evening, for once, she had put on a skirt—a very short red-and-white kilt—her legs were concealed in black stockings and she had on a black turtle-neck sweater. Her remark was odder because she looked so attractive.

Cornelius coughed.

"But they won't hate you, my girl. So you'd better watch out!"

"It's just going to be hell," she said, sitting cross-legged on the floor facing her grandfather, her back to the fire.

Now, with her instrument in her hands, she looked at ease, bending her head over it so they couldn't see her face, and listening to the few chords she played to warm up. It was an unexpected song she chose first. "I brought thee flowers to straw thy way," her small flute voice sang, "but thou wast up at break of day/and broughtst thy flowers along with thee."

When she had finished, Cornelius and Christina exchanged a glance. But Cathy was absorbed and did not look up. She sang "I Know Where I'm Going" and "The Riddle Song" and ended with "The Times They Are A-Changin'."

"She can sing," Cornelius said. "Bravo, Cathy!"

" 'The times they are a-changing,' " Christina hummed. "It is a good song."

"I didn't expect you to like it."

"Why not?"

"Well . . ." Cathy hesitated. "Oh, you know, it is sort of against things as they are." Then she asked, "Shall I sing 'Bonnie Prince Charlie' now?"

"Well, don't write us off as absolute old fogies," Cornelius said. "Sing what you like. After all, we are in sore need of an education!"

Cathy paused, laid down her guitar, and hugged her knees.

"You're so different from my parents. They just don't pay *any* attention! They sneer at songs like that. They can't seem to see how wonderful life is!"

"I expect that's what your Uncle John used to say about me. The times may be a-changing, but parents and children seem to change rather little—so it's very pleasant to be a gramp instead of a father." Cornelius laughed. "Isn't it, Christina?"

But Cathy was not to be put off. "You don't seem so safe. My parents are so damned *safe!*"

CHRISTINA'S JOURNAL—*April 1*

I wonder what Cathy meant when she said that we're not *safe* like her parents. Anyway, *we* seem to be getting good marks, and there is no sign of that depression and withdrawal Marianne has worried about. My guess is that Cathy needed to have time alone—time when she was not under pressure even at school. She came back yesterday afternoon after her first day quite elated. She likes her English teacher. Two girls proved friendly and helped show her around, one, I am glad to say, from the next town—Betsy Sullivan—so perhaps we can invite her over now and then. The boys, so far, have kept their distance, but there is a square dance this Saturday in the town hall and then perhaps she'll feel more in her element with them—the grandchildren have gone to the summer dances since they were eight or nine years old. I don't feel that I know anything about what goes on inside her, except that her love of Willard is passionate. Sometimes she comes in, her cheeks flushed pink, and just hugs me without saying a word. That is our best form of communication at present.

As for Cornelius, he is plainly bewitched, says she is like me, bless his heart, "wild but tamable," as he puts it. Everything will depend now on what boy she falls in love with. How precarious to be a woman! Perhaps Cathy's fear of boys ("I hate them," she says) comes from her awareness of how vulnerable she is and how dependent, in spite of all her outward swagger and her capacity for being alone. She is such a loving child! When Cornelius asked her what she wants to do after college, she said, "Work with children, Gramp—with poor children—with Blacks if I can." Here I see Olivia's influence. Olivia is the one in the whole family whom she truly admires, and Olivia must have talked to her about how much there is to be done. "But there's so little time!" Cathy added half to herself.

Yes, I remember that feeling—so little time to do all that has to be done! It is strange how narrowed down our world has become since Cornelius's stroke—but even stranger that it doesn't *feel* narrow, for if it is narrow it is also deep. It is as if we were on an island. Willard is an island. Our imagination and concern reaches to its borders—which reminds me that I must go to the hospital this week and see how Old Pete is getting on. Cathy would like to see him, too, so perhaps I can pick her up at school one afternoon.

I do long for an end to snow. Ellen says this is the hardest season. We're all pent up and pindling after the winter's struggle to survive. There are times, I must confess, when I feel dreadfully tired. The old animal complains. I feel caught in my body, which will not move fast even to a stern command, and which ties the spirit down. But how much worse for Cornelius! I massage his legs at night—they get terribly stiff.

A flock of evening grosbeaks comes to the feeder and my spirits lift at once. For inside all the weakness of old age, the spirit, God knows, is as mercurial as it ever was. Nick brings in wood, or Eben stops by for a talk, and suddenly all is well. At sunrise I am so elated, often, that I want to sing.

CHAPTER 2

On Wednesday afternoon Cathy stopped by at Ellen's when the school bus dropped her off. She and two younger boys were the only passengers to Willard, the last stop. It had rained all day, dreary downpour on top of dirty snow.

"But at least it's taking some of it away, Mrs. Comstock."

"Yes," said Ellen, going to fetch a glass of milk and cookies.

"It's good to be home," said Cathy, sitting in Nick's chair and looking around the familiar kitchen as if she had been away a long time. "School's another world."

"I expect it is."

Ellen sat down again in the rocker and picked up her sewing. Cathy munched and was silent. One thing she had found out about Ellen was that they could sit like that and not say much, and it was strangely comforting.

"I'd never go back, if I could. Everyone says one has to know things, but I think I'd know more if I just went to work in a nursery school."

"You might, but it would take longer. School's a short cut."

Cathy pondered this.

"Well . . . but . . . *you* were quick and clever, weren't you? I don't do very well, and especially at French—and it seems so useless."

"School was escape from home for me—just the opposite of a jail, as you seem to find it. I couldn't wait to get there, and I had quite a tussle to get my parents to let me go through high school, I can tell you."

"Why?"

"They needed me at home. A family in those days took a lot of children to keep it going. I got up at four and did chores."

"Gosh, you were brave!"

Ellen smiled grimly.

"Not brave to do what you have to do to get what you want."

"I have considered running away—till I came here."

"Every child worth his salt runs away sooner or later. If you're over that, you've started to grow up. That's my view."

"Did Nick run away when he was little?"

Ellen laughed.

"He was hardly ever at home. Got licked I don't know how many times for trying to find a beaver dam or something. Had us scared stiff more 'n once."

"Nick's lucky."

"I wouldn't be too sure."

"He does what he likes, doesn't he?"

"I wouldn't call that lucky. Nick's a sick man, Cathy."

"Sick?" Cathy was unbelieving.

"You might as well know, it'll come out sooner or later. He came back from the war—World War II— kind of queer in his head. Saw too much, I guess. Suffered things we'll never know."

"Oh." Cathy watched the nimble fingers fly in and out, in and out with their needle—it was the only sign that Ellen Comstock was tense.

"Like living with a volcano," she said, and bit off the thread. "Good for him to work up at the Ark. First steady work he's done. Know why he does it?"

Cathy shook her head.

"I don't know myself. Maybe he feels sorry for them up there. He's eaten up by pity, Nick is, the way some people are eaten up by anger or money."

"But that's wonderful," Cathy murmured. "Why do you say it that way?"

"It's not natural, that's why."

"Then," Cathy said firmly, "we have to make a world where it is natural. Nick's just way ahead of the rest of us—that's how it seems to me."

Ellen gave her an ironic look.

"Nick couldn't afford pity unless I worked ten hours a day on other people's sewing."

"Oh." Cathy frowned. "I didn't think of that."

"No, I expect not. . . . How's your grandfather? Last time I was up to clean he seemed perkier. Good for him to have you around."

"Gramp's great," Cathy said with enthusiasm. She was relieved to be able to change the subject. Sometimes when she and Ellen talked, an awful kind of darkness seemed to well up, and Cathy didn't know how to cope with it. She withered under the bitterness of it, and sensed that somehow she was set outside, would never really know what this life cost. In her poems she called this darkness a membrane that she had to get through to be human.

"I never knew how grand he is before. His being sick has changed things at the Ark."

"They're up against something they can't change and have no choice about. First time, I guess."

"Sometimes when I walk in and they're sitting by the fire, each reading a book . . ." Cathy hesitated, not knowing how this feeling could be said. "—Oh, I don't know . . . it's as if they had a magic circle round them. I feel I'm breaking into something. Mrs. Comstock, do you think that's usual? I mean . . ." She frowned. "I never wanted to get married. Maybe you have to be very old to enjoy it."

Ellen laughed.

"Very old or very young maybe."

"Maybe." Cathy considered this point. "My parents . . ." Ellen paused a moment and glanced up, but as Cathy seemed to have decided not to say whatever she was going to say, she bent her head over her sewing again. "Oh, I guess they love each other—but it's not like Gram and Gramp. . . . You've known them forever, Mrs. Comstock. Was it always like this—their marriage, I mean?"

Ellen laid her sewing down and looked out the window.

"I sometimes think marriages are like plants—they have their hard years when it seems like they'll never bear another flower, just look so puny and worn out. And then —you can't tell why, but that bush suddenly perks up."

"Was that the way with you and Mr. Comstock?"

"Mr. Comstock and I?" Ellen looked startled. "We never understood each other, not from the start. Rufus was a hard man to understand—and I was a pretty spiky young thing. Takes two to make a marriage as they say, and when there isn't even one really trying . . . well . . ."

"Why did you marry him then?"

Cathy was entirely unconscious of how painfully she probed, just because she was so transparently honest herself. But, much to her own surprise, Ellen found herself trying to decide how to answer this child, instead of biting off the thread as she would have done if Christina, for instance, had asked any such question—found herself trying to meet the honest wish to learn about life with an equal honesty about what she herself had learned the hard way.

"I guess I shouldn't have asked that," Cathy said into the silence. "You're about the only grown-up person I know who will answer rude questions like that."

"No, I was thinking. . . . I didn't know Rufus very well. I never saw his temper till after we were married. I didn't know he was a hard man. When a man's in love—well, sometimes you don't see what he's really like."

"That's what scares me," Cathy confessed. "How does one *know*? I think I'd rather be like Aunt Olivia than anyone—free to be myself—and trying to help poor children instead of having any."

"Women get caught."

"Aunt Olivia isn't."

"Maybe not."

"You mean she's in love, but can't marry him?" Cathy said with evident alarm. Somehow it seemed important that Aunt Olivia *not* be in love. The reason Cathy could accept her grandparents was, she knew in her heart very well, because sex was somehow not the point. The very word "sex" made Cathy terribly uncomfortable. She couldn't say it without blushing, and one of the reasons she hated school in Boston was that the girls in her class seemed so sophisticated and aware about things that just made her blush and the palms of her hands sweat.

"It's none of my business or yours," Ellen said firmly. "All I mean is that we know very little about each other really. Your Aunt Olivia is a splendid woman, I can tell you that."

Nick came to the door then in his outdoor boots and stood there waiting.

235

"I'm about ready if you are," he said.

"You're going anyway?" Cathy asked. "I can walk."

"About time the woodboxes got filled."

She climbed up into the truck and off they went, and never said one word the whole way. But neither of them noticed the silence. Cathy was thinking hard, and Nick was used to silence. That was the thing about Willard, Cathy said to herself—you could be what you felt. Nobody minded. Besides, she was sure that Nick was a saint on earth, and she hadn't an idea how to approach a saint.

CHRISTINA'S JOURNAL—*April 11*

I suppose this is mud season—a long-drawn-out, colorless, wet, gloomy waiting for spring to come. We snatch at every smallest sign that it is on the way—somewhere down in the Carolinas, no doubt. The willow branches are turning a brighter yellow. Cathy came in the other day, her eyes shining, with a bunch of pussywillows for Cornelius. The skies are water color—by which I mean, I suppose, softer than the brilliant skies of winter. And we have had some great sunsets after rain—I drink in the crimson and orange and those pale green reaches above the clouds, as if color were a needed vitamin. But too often Cornelius and I wake to a wall of fog—the mountain is elusive these days. Driving is hazardous—I wouldn't dare drive up to the Lovelands' or to Eben's, and even he has twice stuck fast in mud in his jeep, and once walked down here to call for a wrecker to haul him out.

My garden is still under snow, although here and there a patch of black wet earth shows, or dank grass—it seems impossible that it will ever turn green and dry out around here. Only the brooks give us hope—and we can hear the roar of ours even inside the house at times.

I am making a sustained effort to finish the chapter for Jem. Now I begin to wonder whether I have been wrong to concentrate on the exceptional women. In some ways I have come to sense that the ordinary farmer's wife was the real heroine. But it's too late to go back now and change the whole point of view. I have chosen to write about those who escaped the grueling chores and extremities of farming on poor land, to write about those who escaped into an art or into travel as missionaries—all except Sophia, who found her adventure at home.

I find myself thinking a great deal about women like Ellen. Of course we forget that just because families were large and villages isolated, there were a great many events that brought people together—some seasonal like sugaring off, apple bees, quilting parties in winter and church suppers in summer, an occasional dance. Weddings and even funerals were social gatherings when hard cider flowed, among the men anyway, and talk flowed too. Villages like this were extraordinarily self-contained—when I think that there was a general store on the green one hundred years ago!

Whatever Jem pulls out of this helter-skelter book of his, he has made every one of us engaged in it look back and do some thinking—and I feel grateful to him.

Cornelius is deep in town histories these days. He's always coming up with a fresh insight. The other evening he and Eben were discussing how it was that, despite the hideously poor education in the village schools, so many boys had the ambition to go to Exeter and then Dartmouth, and so many families managed to make it possible for them to do so when it meant not only finding cash, always scarce, but also losing a man from the farm. Yet Willard spawned lawyers and doctors well into the nineties, and those who went off to the cities come back, with remarkable fidelity, on Old Home Day. Eben jokes about it and says they got educated out of sheer desperation, as a way of escape. That's his story. Cornelius argues that respect for learning was there from the start, came over with the Scotch-Irish. Eben takes the negative, out of a sort of pride, I think. Calls Cornelius sentimental. Deep down he is proud of being a country boy, but he is complex, and sneers more often than not at what he cherishes in his heart. He contends that there's no vision in villages like this one. They stick to the wrong ideas out of sheer ignorance, won't vote for zoning because they think it attacks independence, the right to build what one wants where one wants—and so the village will be overrun by trailers before we know it. Eben fought hard to get a zoning law passed when he was selectman, but the hardheaded natives never would go along with him. The exceptional person, Eben insists, has to get out to be able to get a large view of anything at all, from politics to farming. He points out that it's a stranger to these parts who is experimenting with Scotch Highlander cattle for meat, as his own father did long ago. So maybe I am not wrong to devote my chapter to the ways in which women found a way to escape into the world. I wonder . . .

Yesterday I took Cathy to see Old Pete in the hospital. He looks well. Amazing how delicate and fine his face looks now he is shaved and one can see it. He is wonderfully cheerful, the pet of all the nurses. But he showed us the terrible swollen black feet and legs, black to the knee. Apparently they hope to save one foot by a new method. It doesn't look hopeful, alas. Cathy was very silent all the way home. It was more of a shock than I had foreseen for her to see those poor feet.

I was touched to learn how many people go in regularly to call on him. Even Reggie Planter, who must be near ninety, had thumbed a ride the twenty miles in with a paper bag of fruit and a pencil and pad for Old Pete. It is in times like this that the village is at its best, and my guess is that it has always been so. People leave each other alone until there is a real crisis. Then the ranks close and help is forthcoming.

Old Pete is worried for fear someone will break into his shack and steal his treasures, and I promised to go and be sure that the lock has not been broken. Must remember to do it tomorrow.

Now I must quickly write a word to Marianne and tell her that Cathy really seems happy and is doing well at school as far as we know. So far she has not wanted to bring anyone home, but we are not pushing that. I think she doesn't want her friends to know about us. She is very sensitive about our being rich, talks about it as a wall, or, as she said once, a membrane. She wants to be taken for granted as herself. Cornelius teases her gently about this. "I can't see any special virtue in being poor," he said the other night, "or in being rich for that matter."

"You don't even know how different you are from other people, Gramp," she said tenderly. But when Cornelius tried to get her to tell him what she meant, she clammed up and retreated to her attic. And when he pressed me to try to tell him whatever she was talking about, I couldn't seem to.

High time I went downstairs and put that casserole in the oven. Cathy talks about learning to cook, but I notice that she doesn't show up very often when I am in the kitchen! Perhaps a woman needs to be in love to want to learn to cook—and even then! . . . Now and then I'm tired of thinking about *food!*

CHAPTER 3

At night the center of the village was as still as the grave, inhabited as Willard was chiefly by the old. Ellen and Nick rarely had lights on after ten, and then the only sound was an occasional car, a worker on his way home from the night shift at the mill a few miles down the road, or one of the big trucks routed through the village to avoid the town. And of course the snowplows at it all night after a blizzard. But on this night in mid-April Ellen could hear only the brook roaring down below the meadow. For a half hour before she went to sleep she lay there in the dark thinking about Cathy. She couldn't help worrying, because any human creature as open and vulnerable as Cathy is bound to get hurt— that is for sure. And all this talk of working among the poor could lead to no good in Ellen's view—cities were dangerous places these days, especially for a girl alone. People who set out to change the world only got hurt like Nick, and often did more harm than good. If everyone looked after his own, the world wouldn't be such a sorry place. But that was the trouble these days with the whole world coming right into the house and all the suffering with it. People knew more about children starving in Africa than about the neighbors a few miles away, and that's an upside-down, roundabout state of affairs.

Ellen sighed a deep sigh and turned over to shut out gloomy thoughts. "Cart before the horse" was her last lucid comment to herself.

It must have been an hour later when she opened her

eyes in the dark, wide awake. Had she dreamed it—a voice? No, there it was.

"Please someone . . . turn on a light."

The voice sounded thick and strange. Some drunk on the loose, no doubt.

But then it shouted again: "Please someone, turn on a light!"

And when the eerie cry repeated itself once more, Ellen was up, calling out, "Nick! Nick! Did you hear that?"

She felt her way downstairs. Nick was too fast asleep to know what was going on. She didn't dare put on a light, just stood back of the door, listening.

She could hear footsteps on the road, crunching the snow, and then again the desperate, lost sound. This time she felt sure it was a young man's voice, and, against her better judgment, Ellen turned on the hall light and shoved back the bolt on the door. It wasn't more than a few seconds before whoever it was pushed his way in without even knocking and fell headlong onto the kitchen floor.

By this time Nick was aware that something was happening and came down in his bathrobe, his hair standing on end, bewildered as an owl.

"What's this, Mother?"

"You're asking me. This man has been calling for light —sounds drunk or crazy."

The man lay on the floor on his stomach, but when Nick turned the kitchen light on, he lifted his head, still not seeing Ellen or Nick, peering at the stove through long, fair hair, as long as a girl's.

"Christ, where am I?"

"Not in heaven, anyway," Ellen said.

He twisted around, frowning, a young man in a navy coat and jeans, loafers, but no socks. He took in the two faces looking down at him and gave a bewildered smile as Nick bent over to help him up. Then he staggered to the chair by the table and put his head in his hands, rubbed his eyes with the cuff of his coat, and stared at them silently.

"You were asking for a light out there. What happened?" Ellen asked sharply. "What's wrong?"

"I don't know," he said. "I'm so tired."

"You didn't come here on foot," Ellen prodded.

"Oh," he groaned. "The car . . . turned over . . . awful

241

sharp curve . . . couldn't see very well. Oh," he groaned again, feeling his shoulder as if it hurt.

"Nick, go out with a flashlight and see what's happened. Too late to call the police. Better wait till morning. I'll give him some coffee—there's some on the back of the stove—and he can sleep in the parlor."

"Sleep . . ." the boy said. "Sleep . . ." and laid his head on his arms again.

"If the car did turn over, you're lucky to be alive. What's your name?" Ellen asked.

"Joel—Joel Smith," he said, without lifting his head.

"Where you going? How did you come this way—it's off the main road."

"I don't know . . . New Jersey . . . left Hanover sometime . . . ten maybe."

"You a student?"

"I was yesterday . . . not today . . . today I'm a civilian," he said, "discharged from that army."

Ellen did not comment on this.

"Your family expecting you?"

"Christ, no."

"Here, drink this and leave Christ out of it."

Ellen was furious with herself for obeying an impulse and getting this problem thrust at her, willy-nilly. He drank the coffee slowly, and when he had set the cup down, he looked a little more normal. His eyes anyway could focus.

"Didn't know there were rooms like this—warm. Where am I anyway?"

"You're in Willard."

"Never heard of it."

"Not many people have."

"Geraniums," he murmured. "Water from a pump."

"You won't taste its like in a city. Want a drink?"

She handed him a tin cup full, and he drank it greedily. Ellen observed him closely. If you could forget the girlish hair, he had quite a strong face, blue eyes, long legs in tight jeans.

"Take off your coat," Ellen said. "You'll have to stay the night."

He sat hunched over now, looking as if he might be going to throw up. His teeth were chattering, and Ellen thought "shock, of course."

"Don't know as I can. Shoulder—it hurts."

Nick came back, sat down on the stairs in the hall to

242

take off his rubber boots, and said quietly, "The car's total." Then he peered in at Joel. "Don't know how you got out."

Ellen helped the sore shoulder out of the coat arm carefully.

"Nothing we can do tonight. Take him in to the couch in the parlor, Nick, and I'll fetch some quilts. Cold in there."

An hour later the house was dark and silent again. The moon had come out from behind the clouds, and Ellen looked at the path on the floor, filled with anxiety and dismay.

"I'll get Christina over in the morning," she thought. "I feel all upset." Yet at the same time she was curious, as if a strange bird had flown in.

Next morning Cathy stopped by, early for the school bus, and found Joel there in the kitchen eating a corn muffin with bacon and egg. He had on a clean shirt of Nick's, but he hadn't got his bag out of the smashed car and hadn't shaved. Ellen introduced them, explained the situation briefly, and poured Cathy a cup of coffee, which she drank standing with her back to the stove.

"What are you going to do now?" she asked Joel, going right to the point.

"Hey, wait a minute." He grinned. "I'm not awake yet."

"Guess the first thing is to get the car towed away, and report the accident," Nick said.

"Oh, there's the bus. Have to run!" Cathy grabbed her satchel and was out of the door without waiting even to say good-by.

"Willard has pretty girls," Joel said, lighting a cigarette.

"She's from Boston."

"What's she doing here then?"

"Going to school."

"She's only fifteen," Nick said protectively.

Joel absorbed this information, then rubbed his forehead.

"So what am I going to do now?" He took a worn billfold out of his hip pocket and peered into it. "Looks like I have twenty bucks and some change."

"Maybe you should tell your father what's happened," Ellen volunteered.

"Don't have a father."

243

Joel leaned back in his chair so it was tilted and rested rather precariously on the back legs. Nick and Ellen drank coffee in silence. Cathy might ask questions, but this was not their way, not with a stranger.

"My father got killed in the boondocks of Korea, poor guy. My mother works in a dentist's office—married again, of course. My stepfather thinks I'm a bum and I think he's a bastard, so we're quits. I'm flunking out of Dartmouth . . . and just totaled my car. I doubt if I shall be welcomed as the Prodigal Son at this point, and I have no idea of going home. Not now."

Having said this much, he let the chair right itself and looked at the two silent witnesses and around the room.

"If I could stay around for a few days . . ."

Ellen had begun to clear the table and Nick was sitting, his hands between his knees, his head bent, in the attitude he took so often. Neither answered, and Joel swallowed, frowned, and asked, "Any sort of job around?"

Nick looked up.

"Maybe at the sawmill down the road—or the road agent—you could try him."

"I'd pay my way," Joel said to Ellen's back.

Ellen had to make a decision now and her whole instinct rose against taking in this perfect stranger. What was Nick thinking? But on the other hand, how do you turn away a boy in as bad trouble as this one? In the old days it was taken for granted that a stranger would be put up at any house in the village, his horse baited and given a stall.

"We don't turn people away from the door," she said. "That's not the way here in Willard."

Nick, who felt perhaps that this was rather a thin assent, added, "You're welcome, Joel."

"A little island of humanity, are you—in the middle of the so-called affluent society?" The tone was ironic, but Ellen, much to her astonishment, saw tears in Joel's eyes.

"Time you men got going," she said. "Dog hasn't had his breakfast, Nick. Where's he at?"

"Spring fever," Nick said, scratching his ear.

She watched them go from the window, then went to the sink to wash up, thinking about what she could rustle up for supper. Maybe a pot roast—they'd have one down at the store, and Dinnock could bring it up if she called before he got started out with the mail. She had onions and there must be some carrots down cellar—potatoes too. Well, you never knew . . .

When she had finished the dishes and swept the floor, she went to the phone and called Christina and told her what had happened.

Christina was, as always, reassuring. "He sounds all right. Of course it's a risk, but Nick has his head on his shoulders. I just hope Cathy doesn't get interested. He sounds like just the sort of crazy lame duck she might think was in need of help."

"Doubt if he stays long. I have an idea he's never done a day's work in his life. When he's got some good blisters on his hands at the sawmill he'll light out."

"You are good to do it, Ellen."

"Couldn't see a way out. Every Lockhart would turn in his grave if a Lockhart turned a stranger from the door. Can't say as I wanted to, exactly."

"Well, maybe that boy will learn something—'a little touch of Willard in the night.' "

For Nick it proved to be an entertaining morning. He had never in his life come across a boy so ignorant as this one. Joel had never handled a scythe or a buzz saw, and hardly knew which end of an ax would cut, but after the business was done and the car had been towed off—and that took half of Joel's cash—and when they had made a report to Johnny Dole, the town policeman, they drove around a while looking for the road agent.

"I'll have to wait a day or so till this shoulder stops aching," Joel said. "Say, could we stop a minute?" he said when they were off somewhere in the woods on a dirt road and had seen no sign of the grader. Nick eased the truck to the side of the road without a word.

"That policeman doesn't even wear a uniform," Joel observed, "or carry a gun."

"Nope."

"Why not?"

Nick scratched his head.

"Only gets paid fifty dollars a year by the town. It's hardly a job around here. Johnny does it in his spare time, and kind of likes arresting people on the through road. It's a game. Anything serious, the State Police come in."

"All these dirt roads—where to?"

"Houses up most of 'em. You'd be surprised how many people live around here."

"What do they do?" Joel asked, incredulous.

"Oh, summer people mostly."

"Who lives in that big place we passed a while back?"

"Chapmans. You met the granddaughter—she was the one at breakfast."

"Rich?"

"Uh-huh."

"It's weird," Joel said. "Gives me the willies—all these woods. It's sad. Lonely."

"The deer and raccoons wouldn't say so."

"I feel as if I'd landed at the end of the world. What has it got to offer, man? I mean, rich people . . ."

"Lakes, mountains, rivers . . ."

"All we've seen is dirt roads, dirty old snow, old stone walls, undergrowth, so far." Joel pondered. His head ached.

"I can't seem to get adjusted," he said, frowning. "I feel I'm in a dream ever since last night. I feel crazy in the head—tired."

"Well," Nick proffered, "time for dinner soon. Take it easy today. We'll find the road agent tomorrow. O.K.?"

Then they sat silent for a while. Nick wanted to ask this odd duck about himself, but he didn't know where to begin. If Joel had never been in a place like Willard, Nick had never come across a boy like this one. In his experience, Dartmouth boys were skiers and outdoor men. This one seemed like another breed.

"You ski?" he asked tentatively.

"Couldn't afford it."

"But college—must be a lot going on there."

"Maybe. But I'm interested in living—and I don't mean acquiring a mind like a computer." It was Joel's turn to feel needled. "I did well in high school, but I couldn't get turned on at college. Those professors—a bunch of stuffed shirts. Grades, grades . . . the point is they don't seem to realize that a revolution is going on. I bet not one of them has ever been in a city ghetto. They have a few specimen Blacks, you know, just to be able to show the visiting liberals. People live in cities, Nick. That's where the problems are."

Nick nodded.

"I should have gone into VISTA, but my stepfather,

the bastard, said that was for rich boys—and where would it lead?"

Nick turned this idea over in his mind. "Seems like those people in the slums might not want people to barge in."

Joel gave him a haunted look. Under his bravado, Nick could tell, he was running scared. Touch him and he would leap like a frightened animal.

"In Willard, we live in a way," Nick ventured, "if you're interested in living."

But Joel let this pass. And Nick turned the truck round and started for home. He had done an awful lot of talking, it seemed to him, and he was feeling the strain. His instinct was to pass the problem over to his mother. She was the talker after all.

After the noon meal, Joel sat down cross-legged on the floor, his back to the stove, and had a long talk with Ellen. She may have balked at the idea of this uninvited guest but Ellen absorbed life through conversation, and she rarely had such a strange specimen to investigate as this curiously uncouth, sensitive boy. After a while she forgot about the hair and found she could talk to him, because he listened in a very intent way, as if it really mattered what she had to say. He was unlike her own grandchildren, who, she felt, never really heard anything, wild to get out and run, or go to a movie or a game. This was a new breed of critter to Ellen. When he asked about Cathy, he talked about her with surprising insight. She never felt that he was out to talk about her just as a girl, a piece of potential sex—he seemed to think about people as persons, regardless of sex. Their exchange had been brief enough, but she suspected that Cathy had sensed his interest. Well, one never knew.

So while she talked and sewed, turning the cuffs and collars of one of Cornelius's fine shirts, she was thinking all the time, and was startled out of a thought by the question Joel now posed.

"It's hard to be a rich girl. How will she manage to stay real?"

Ellen put down her sewing with a suddenly impatient gesture.

"I'm sick and tired of people who seem to think poverty is real and being well enough off not to worry about

247

where your next meal is coming from is not. I never saw a realer person than Christina Chapman, Cathy's grandmother, if you want to know."

"Go on," Joel said, turning over to lie on his back, full length, his arms under his head, looking at the ceiling. "Still, Cathy herself, from what you have told me, wanted to get out of that rich school and come here."

"She's young for her age, Joel. Maybe she imagined that here she could stay a child—a wild child—a little longer. I gather she is afraid of boys."

"No boys in the high school?"

"Well, it's different from Boston society. But maybe she just needed some time away from home. Grandparents are easier on a teen-ager than parents, I have a hunch."

"What are her parents like?"

"Father's a banker. I guess you'd call him a square." And Ellen laughed. "Marianne, her mother, is a handsome woman. Looks like her mother, but she's always seemed less of a person than she meant to be. Works hard at her life. I don't envy her, having to entertain and all."

"That's what I'm against."

"Against just what?"

"I mean people doing what they ought to do when there's no joy in it. That's what's the matter with this whole damned rotten society—a lot of people doing what they think they ought to do."

Ellen swallowed a smile. "Yes, I thought as much."

"Are you for it?" Joel sat up, hugging his knees.

Ellen laid her sewing down and looked out the window. Joel simply floored her with a question like that—a question that looked simple till you tried to figure out what was wrong with it.

"Well," she said slowly, "I guess maybe there is always a good deal of hard work attached to what one *wants* to do."

"Who wants to give a lot of parties where everyone is so drunk by the time dinner is served there's no conversation anyway?"

"You're talking about a different breed, Joel. The Chapmans would never allow such a thing."

Joel raised an eyebrow. "They're pretty rare then."

"Seems to me you base your judgments on a lot of . . . stereotypes—is that the word?—that don't mean anything when you take a look. What if everyone felt as you do, Joel—we'd have no doctors, just to take one example. If everyone just lived like Old Pete—that's the village tramp who's in the hospital now with frozen feet —where would we be? No doctors, no one to man the telephones, or deliver milk, or mend cars."

"Your ancestors didn't have any of those things, and from what I hear they were real people and led real lives —even without the telephone!"

"My ancestors got up at four and worked till ten or eleven at night. If they were to have light they had to make candles. Know how long it takes to dip one candle? Well, I can't tell you myself, but it was a long and tedious job. If they had clothes they had to have sheep, keep them alive, card the wool, weave the cloth. Most of what they ate they grew and harvested themselves. Whatever worked for them had to be fed too—oxen, horses—had to be shod, looked out for. My ancestors lived hard lives, dread-fully hard."

"Didn't they ever have any fun?" Joel said gently. "You're painting a pretty stark picture."

"No point in painting a rosy one. Wouldn't be true. But I'll grant you they did have fun—sewing bees, apple-picking, dances, all sorts of gathering together to get some piece of work done."

"Work . . ." Joel sighed.

"Don't know what you have against work, Joel." And Ellen picked up her sewing with a smile.

"What's so good about it?"

"Some kind of satisfaction hard to explain."

"Helping people—I can see how that might justify hard work."

"Well, pretty nearly every job I can think of helps someone."

"I suppose so." Joel gave a deep sigh and when Ellen looked up next time, he was fast asleep.

So at last she managed to finish Cornelius's shirt and could wrap it up to give to Cathy when she dropped in after school. And Ellen would have been ready to bet a considerable sum that she would drop in today.

Ellen was shy of looking at the boy's sleeping face, and turned to rock a few minutes and look at the hairy woodpecker greedily eating suet. Such a bold, beautiful bird! She had always been fond of woodpeckers. The zestful way they had of going about getting a living!

. . . She had to admit that a lot of what Joel said made some sense—not exactly sense, but she understood his feelings of hatred at the way the country was going— toward more and more things and less and less of what he called "life." But the trouble was that that word seemed to have no definite meaning. It was just an idea in his head, poor boy. He seemed to know what he was against but not in any clear way what he was *for*. His whole generation had been wounded by the war in Vietnam—that was part of it surely. And she supposed that if he dropped out of college for good he would face the draft. He had not spoken of this, but it must be in his mind—one more reason why he didn't want to go home.

Cathy burst in eagerly to interrupt these thoughts, then stopped at the doorsill when she saw Joel lying there.

"What's wrong?" she whispered. "Is he sick?"

"Only asleep."

Joel opened his eyes and, from the floor, looked up into Cathy's. It was a long straight look.

"So it's Cathy," he said, getting up rather clumsily. "You caught me napping."

"I'm sorry if I woke you."

"Want me to walk you home? Looks sort of nice out for a change."

"O.K."

"Put on a coat, Joel. You'll catch your death in this wind," Ellen said dryly. "Take that navy coat of Nick's— on a hook in the hall."

"Thanks."

"And wear your boots," she added.

Ellen gave Cathy the shirt to take home, and Joel carried her books. Watching them go slowly across the green, heads bent, apparently not aware of anything but each other, Ellen shook her head and sighed. It was not exactly what had been planned for Cathy, but then life, Ellen had observed, rarely followed human plans.

CHRISTINA'S JOURNAL—*April 22*

At last the snow has melted. I went out and uncovered a piece of shady border where I found daffodils showing about five inches of yellow shoots, poor things, longing for sunlight. Spring is not yet on the ground, but it is in the sky—such tender washed skies, a pale, acute light that sets the sad, muddy earth in relief but overhead plays out a continual theater of cloud—April skies. Only the October ones (so different) move me as these do. New birds are coming to the feeder every day—yesterday purple finches. We hear the phoebes. How Cornelius loves them! It seems incredible that we have lived through the long winter, that we are really emerging into a new world at last, a world where every tender young thing can come into flower; soon it will be the maples. I feel so full of hope and energy suddenly, it's wonderful.

Cornelius gets quite cross because I try to do too much, and I suppose he is right, but there is some sap rising in me just as it did in the maples when they were sugaring in March—and it makes me want to clean out cupboards, polish the silver, get curtains washed. "What does it matter?" says Cornelius. "The curtains have been dusty for twenty years." "Yes," I answer, "but we have not lived here for twenty years. We camped out in summer. Now we are *living* here!"

But why do I write about all this when the happening here is something entirely different and a little frightening. That hippie—or whatever he is—Joel Smith, seems to have moved in on Ellen for an indefinite time. He tried working at the sawmill but he is not cut out for hard physical work and now he helps out at the store in the mornings and on holidays and, as far as I can make out, waits for Cathy to get home from school in the afternoon. Ellen complains but does nothing to make him go. The fact is that he and Nick have become friends, and that is certainly a good thing for Nick. But how long can Joel keep the news from his parents that he is not a Dartmouth student? Cathy says he plans to tell them soon. He has a stepfather who seems to be rather hard to persuade of anything not absolutely "square"—and who would surely shudder, from what Cathy says, at Willard and whatever it represents to this rather lost character. We invited him to supper. Cornelius and Eben have a real specimen now to examine, in regard to all that reading they have been doing of Marcuse and whoever the other people are this generation goes for.

But we can't be anything but kind, as Cathy is so on the defensive. She expected us both to react against Joel, and it was quite funny to see her astonishment at Cornelius's extreme courtesy and that we both treated Joel as we would any one of our friends. It was rather a stiff occasion, but at least there were no fireworks. Joel is a great asker of questions and almost incredibly naïve. He has us pigeonholed and was visibly surprised that I had gone to college. He has some kind of stereotype of the rich, Cathy says. He seemed quite upset by the stuffed animal heads in the hall. "Why kill them?" he asked Cornelius. And for once Cornelius was stumped. The ethos of the hunter is not something Joel can understand, it appears. Finally they dropped the subject.

So far Cathy has been willing to talk, and assures me that they are not in love. I gather that Joel is companionable and not, it would appear, highly sexed. I have talked with Marianne on the phone about him, and her attitude is that it's high time Cathy lost her little-girl attitude to boys as the enemy. She doesn't worry—at least not yet. And it is lovely to see that child opening out. She is suddenly merry, sings all the time, and she and Joel spend hours upstairs singing together while she plays her guitar. Amazing that Cornelius, after a moment's violent reaction, has accepted the facts of life. He would, God knows, never have allowed a young man into any of his daughter's rooms for any purpose whatever.

The most interesting thing about it all is to see the effect of Willard on Joel. His curiosity is endless; he is ready to listen indefinitely to anything about the village. The other day he went into town with us to see poor Old Pete. The decision has finally been made to amputate. Old Pete takes it wonderfully well, insisted on showing us again his terrible black stumps. "But I'll be back," he says, dear old optimist. "I'll be as good as new." After that visit Joel insisted on seeing Old Pete's shack. That perfectly useless life seems to him romantic and lovable—as Nick seems to him a hero. Cathy takes this all in, wide-eyed. And the queerest thing about it all is that even I have to admit that Joel creates a loving atmosphere. He listens so well! A harmless critter, but a very young one still. At what point will iron enter his soul? That, I suppose, is a very old-fashioned question. What do I mean? Something about responsibility perhaps. It is just not a loving world full of gentle souls who do not have to work for a living, and to wish to make it so leaves out too much. As it leaves out too much, I feel, to make an ideal of love without responsibility. Am I a dodo? We have to keep the door open. That is all I know. We have to try to understand each other, and in some ways Joel's coming feels like a challenge we needed.

I can't help thinking of Eben, and how different this boy is. We grew up in a safe world. Eben reacted with ambition and drive. He knew what he wanted. He wanted to prove himself in the world, to get ahead. What Joel wants is very different. He appears to have no ambition except to "live," as he says. But what is life without purpose? Even when she was over ninety Jane's life was molded to a purpose—to understand all she could about the natural world and to teach what she knew. I'm mystified.

CHAPTER 4

"Couldn't sleep all night . . . there was a noise," Joel said as he and Cathy trudged up the hill after school ten days later, a rivulet of water running down each side of the road and the mud keeping them in the middle, not able to hold hands for once.

"What sort of noise?"

"Oh, bells . . . or something . . . I got scared, thinking it was in my own head. But then I knew it was a real noise."

"Peepers most likely." Cathy gave him an amused glance. "You *are* a city boy!"

"What in hell are peepers? Little folk? Sounds like something in an Irish fairy tale!"

"They're tree frogs," Cathy said. "It's the first sign of spring around here . . . 'sound like sleigh bells. Nick says when you hear them you know you've made it through another winter. I heard them first a month ago."

"No kidding."

One of the nice things about Joel was the way he absorbed pieces of information like this and savored them. After a while he asked Cathy what the big furled bright-green leaves were he had seen by the brook on the way to the store. And he laughed when she told him skunk cabbage—"they stink like skunks!"

"Lucky I didn't try to eat one. They looked good."

"You really like it here, don't you?"

He reached over and took her hand. For a moment he didn't answer.

Then he let it go and rubbed his head.

"It's an island. But I'll have to get back to the mainland one of these days."

"Why not stay and live?"

"I'm a city boy, Cathy—you just said that. It would be just running away for me. . . . Jeez, what I wouldn't give for a joint!" he said, kicking a stone ahead of him in the old childish game.

"Why? What would that do?"

"Calm me down."

Cathy swallowed this in silence. Her communications with Joel were oblique on his side and direct on hers, and she had to take time to understand what he was not saying.

"What is it really like—smoking those?"

"It's cool. Kind of like floating, and while you're floating, everything seems unbelievably clear and beautiful."

"That's how I feel now because you're here," Cathy said.

She pushed her long hair back and stood in the road facing him so Joel would have to look at her. They had long looks, and this was something she found terribly moving, as if their eyes were screens and little by little all the screens slid away one by one and she felt touched by Joel in some deepest place in herself.

"Look at me, Joel . . . please look at me."

But Joel pushed her aside and walked on, stubbornly kicking his stone.

"Sometimes I think I'd better get the hell out of here and quick," he said.

"It's because you won't make love to me, isn't it? . . . Oh dear,"—for suddenly she had tears in her eyes—"it's my fault. If only I were really old like, say, twenty-two or -three. Then we could—you wouldn't be scared. But, Joel, you know I think people should touch each other more. I want to be hugged and that's something no one does in the family except Gram. Oh, I wish you would hug me!"

"Wouldn't be a good idea," Joel said, but for the first time he laughed. "If the wolf hugged Little Red Riding Hood he'd end by eating her up in one big mouthful."

"Maybe Little Red Riding Hood would like that."

Cathy felt the blush rising in her throat after she had said it. Whatever is happening to me? she thought, and quickly changed the subject to what seemed safer.

255

"I can get you some grass. There's a boy in school who sells it."

"It's against the law."

"Whose law? We didn't make the laws. They were made by people who don't understand."

"Sure, they get soused and we get stoned. What's the difference? But you can't tell that to the judge."

"You're awfully good, Joel. Good to me, I mean."

"Shit."

They had reached the big stone gates into the driveway at the Ark, and there, as if something held them outside, as if going in were in some way dangerous or difficult, they stood. Joel leaned against a huge pile of snow, his arms folded, and Cathy watched him, wondering what to do or say next. She felt they were reaching some hard place. She felt as if happiness were slipping through her fingers like sand. But she didn't know how to hold it back. Only poetry, perhaps, she thought, could hold it.

"Your hands are cold. Come up and I'll make you some cocoa."

But as soon as she had said the words, she knew they were all wrong. Joel was not a child to be comforted by cocoa.

"O.K.," he said somberly. And they walked up the drive in silence until they were high enough to see the mountain, standing up there, marvelously dark blue and sharp against a pale sky.

"Cities may be all right but they don't have mountains," Cathy said. "It's great, isn't it?"

She took a deep breath. Joel was looking at her with a hard, intense look, not at the mountain. Neither of them noticed Christina, raking snow off one of the lower borders, flinging a pine bough off and peering down at a patch of lavender crocus in flower. But as she stood up, she saw them and waved and called, "Want some tea?"

"Thanks, Gram. I'm going to make cocoa. We'll have it upstairs."

Christina watched them go, two slight figures, up the porch steps and out of sight. She had the strange impression that each was, in some way, burdened. How hard to be young, she thought! To find your way, step by step, through the maze of feeling and the clouds of unknowing, shot through as they were, at least for Cathy, with radiance, and yet so intangible, shifting all the time.

Was Marianne right not to be alarmed, to wish Cathy to be "involved," even with this confused boy? Whatever happened would be costly for Cathy, Christina surmised.

While Cathy made cocoa, Joel stopped a moment to speak to Cornelius, who was getting impatient for Christina to come in and give him his tea.

"Oh, it's you, Joel," he said with evident disappointment. "Not Christina."

"Sorry, Sir," Joel said. "Shall I get Mrs. Chapman?"

"She'll come, she'll come. She just gets completely cuckoo in the garden, forgets where she is and all about time! My advice to you is to keep away from women who are gardeners, Joel. There is bound to be a conflict of interests."

"I don't expect I'll ever meet many gardeners."

"No . . . well . . ."—Cornelius scratched his eyebrow —"perhaps not."

"Cathy wants a farm," Joel said, realizing too late what a giveaway it was to mention Cathy in this context.

"Oh, Cathy is a poet, a chameleon. She'll take on the color of whomever she loves—at least for a while. Women do that. But let me tell you something, Joel—that malleability is only an illusion. Women have hard centers. Cathy's a stubborn girl."

"She's a genius, maybe," Joel said quietly.

Cornelius raised his eyebrows.

"Really? What makes you think so?"

"Have you read her poems?"

"One or two. I'm afraid they seem rather formless and obscure to me, but that's the generation gap, no doubt."

"I think they're cool. She has things to say. She talks about loving, for instance, in a wonderful strange way—she knows so much."

Cornelius gave him a rather piercing look, coughed, stirred in his chair.

"Yes, I expect she does. It's sex that throws girls her age. That's why I regard my generation—old fogies now, of course—as lucky. We didn't have to go the whole way the first time we took a girl out." He coughed again. "It's loving, old boy . . . I mean, as you say . . . Cathy . . ." But he felt he had already spoken far too frankly, reached down and patted Flicker's head, and was relieved when Cathy called Joel to come along.

It's their world, he thought, and we can't really help them make it. He longed for Christina; he longed not to be struggling to understand absurdities like the word "genius" applied to Cathy's clumsy, touching little poems; he longed to be safe in his own world.

Upstairs in the attic room, the world of Cathy and Joel was not the perfect bubble of joy they had carried so carefully in their hands for ten days or more. Joel was lying on the floor on his back staring at the ceiling, and Cathy was kneeling at the window to watch the sunset and the pale gold sky back of the pines.

"Joel?"

"What?"

"Do you remember the first time you came up here and we held hands for a long time, as if we had arrived at the end of a journey?"

"And we sang 'Where have all the flowers gone?'— The thing is, Cathy, that my stepfather will say I have to go in the army; it's that or Dartmouth again. I have so little time to live!" he cried out. "I feel so pent up and caught every way I turn."

Cathy looked down at him and slowly slid over to where she could brush the hair back from his eyes and "really look at him" as she said. But this time Joel pushed her away roughly and sat up.

"Leave me alone!" he said. "I'm not an animal to be petted."

As Cathy made no answer but returned to the window, her back to him, Joel groaned.

"If only you were away from your grandparents, somewhere, it would be different."

"I don't see why. What I do is none of their business."

"Come here then," Joel said roughly.

He took her in his arms and kissed her hard, so hard her mouth hurt. Then he kissed her again in a way she had not been kissed before, and Cathy suddenly gave a sob and pulled away.

"What have I done now? What is it, Cathy?"

"Nothing," she said, trying to hold the tears back. "I just . . . didn't know . . . I mean . . . Oh, Joel!" and she buried her face in his shoulder. "Don't go! Don't leave me!"

"Come here and sit down," he said gently, "you little

fool, you darling idiot child." And he drew her to the bed and wiped her eyes with a Kleenex.

"I am an idiot, Joel . . . but I don't know what I feel anymore. I'm scared of myself—of you—of the whole thing we are in, whatever it is."

"If only we had some grass," Joel said plaintively.

"I suppose it does help people get over being scared."

"You'd take a puff or two and you'd feel so easy and happy, Cathy. Sex is good for people. It's what we're all about."

"But, Joel, I wouldn't want to do it that way—I mean, if it happened because I wasn't really myself." She was half hidden behind her hair and pulled it over her eyes like a screen. "Don't be angry."

"I want to feel you all over, to be with you deep deep inside," he said, holding her hard against him. "Don't you see?"

"We might have a baby, Joel . . . I wouldn't know what to do with a baby."

"Good Christ, Cathy, I have some sense. Give me credit for a little sense. You won't have a baby," he said, suddenly furious. "We'll be careful."

But Cathy had now begun to cry and couldn't stop.

"It was . . . so good . . . before . . ." she said. "Why can't we be as we were?"

"Life doesn't stay where we were. Life keeps moving. Where we were was two children playing at love."

"But you said the poems were . . . serious."

"That's it! Don't you see? You've been pouring love into me, Cathy, and you expect me to take it all and not *want you!*" He got up and walked restlessly up and down. "I'm a man, after all. I've got some feelings myself."

"What feelings?"

"Oh hell, I get all uptight and crazy. You want to know what John Donne says about it? '. . . else a great prince in prison lies.' "

Cathy lay down on her stomach and pressed her face into the pillow. After a while she said, "I'm not ready, Joel . . . for the prince. You'd better go now. I have to think."

It was as if she were melting away into Joel, as if she were no longer altogether herself. She wanted to hold onto herself. She didn't know how to handle all the feelings inside her.

"I'll see you tomorrow?" Joel asked meekly.

"Of course."

When Joel bent down and kissed the top of her head she didn't move. She heard his feet running down the stairs and heard the door slam. I've failed him, she thought. I let fear of the unknown get in the way of love, for I do love him. But not that way—not yet.

It was wonderful to go downstairs for supper and find Gramp sitting there with Flicker by the fire. It felt like a reprieve, so safe and warm there. No one mentioned that she'd been crying or asked why Joel had left the way he did, although they must have heard the door slam.

But when she lay down in the dark she couldn't sleep. It's so awful to have to go through this alone, she thought—like dying, I suppose. Whom could she ask? Talk with? Would Betsy Goodwin know? There was "the pill"—but how did one get it? For Joel it just seemed natural, and he talked so much about how society kept people from being themselves, made them produce things they didn't need and consume things they didn't need, like some big cruel machine. But what if sex were a kind of machine too? And once you got caught in it, you couldn't go back ever. Or was it more like taking a horse over a jump, and you just had to grit your teeth and do it or fail? All Cathy knew was that her body was doing things to her she couldn't understand, and had ceased to be the friendly, affectionate thing she wanted it to be. Now her body had become the enemy, for when she remembered Joel's tongue in her mouth she felt all prickly and strange, and, most of all, not whole, for one part of her liked it and some other part, deep down, was revolted. I'm having to suffer powers in me I didn't know I had, she thought—powers I can't control. That's what is so frightening.

"Oh please, God," she murmured, "tell me what to do and how to be."

CHRISTINA'S JOURNAL—*May 8*

I am having the most horrible struggle trying to get that chapter finished for Jem. The deadline is May twentieth. All I want is to get outdoors, and instead I sit at the desk upstairs and struggle along, and it just isn't good. Even with Cornelius's help it turns into a mass of detail and none of it feels alive. And I feel I am letting down those great women who should come alive and take the reader with them to China or into the heart of their adventure during the Civil War. The only one I manage to come to terms with is Jane. Because I knew her, I suppose.

Out of doors the world is so alive! The warblers are starting to come—so exciting! There are only patches of snow left, although even a week ago I thought it would *never* melt, and we'd be lucky to see grass in July! The thing is that spring doesn't come and doesn't come, and suddenly it is here. All at once. The daffodils are glorious in the lower beds, but it does look as if the mice have eaten most of the tulips. A few tiny shoots are showing, but I planted two hundred. The yellow rose by the porch steps is showing tiny frail green leaves. And the maples are suddenly in flower. Cornelius sits out on the porch wrapped in rugs like a Chinese philosopher, and soon I am going to take him on drives. Eben will help get him in and out of the car. There will be expeditions! The whole world is opening out for this festival of spring—and it seems very poignant to me that we cannot be renewed in the same way. We are old—there's no help for that.

Yet I feel sorry for the young. Cathy looks pinched. Joel puts pressure on her, I suspect. And soon he will be gone. At the end of the month, he tells me—to the draft. He finally did have the courage to go home and see his family. His stepfather was apparently impressed that he had been working at the store and agreed to let him return here as long as he would come home at once if and when he is drafted. I suspect that it has been in Joel's mind to take some stand about the war, perhaps even refuse to go and take a jail sentence. But when it comes right down to it, are his convictions firm enough for that? It means five years, Cornelius tells me. No wonder some of the boys have chosen exile.

Joel is an unlicked cub, Cornelius says, a mass of good intentions and good feelings that have not jelled. We feel that it's too bad he left college when he did. On the other hand, people grow at such different speeds, and it may be that, if he survives, a few years in the army will help knit him together. It is all rather worrying, I must confess. We have agreed, Cornelius and I, after much heart-searching, to put no pressure on Cathy, to

261

keep hands off. With the one exception of drugs. From what she has told me there are some children at school who smoke occasionally—but she assures me that she doesn't want to. Does she talk to Ellen, I wonder. She must need to talk with someone, and I can see that just because we are family, *in loco parentis,* we are the last people she can talk with. It might be a good idea to ask Olivia up for a weekend soon. Yes, that's it. And I'm going to call her right now . . .

She'll come May seventeenth, she says. Cornelius too needs a change. And by then that horrible chapter about the women will be finished—and spring will have *really* come!

CHAPTER 5

When Cathy got off the bus that Tuesday afternoon, for once there was no Joel to meet her.

"He's gone off with Nick somewhere. He'll be back soon, I expect," Ellen said. "Sit down, child." Ellen laid down her sewing and got up. "My back's stiff—been sitting here all day trying to get this mending off my hands. Let's have a cup of coffee or something. There's a muffin still warm in the oven."

The child looks peaked, Ellen was thinking. High time Joel left. Can't understand why Christina has let this thing go on.

While Ellen made the coffee, Cathy wandered about, looking out the back door for any sign of Joel, then back to the front windows.

"Things all right at school?"

"Oh, I suppose so. I like geometry. But chemistry is so weird, half the time I don't understand the textbook, and Mr. Grant seems so nervous about explaining, we don't dare ask. But Mrs. Huntington is great. She lets me write poems instead of themes, every other one."

Suddenly Cathy had no more to say. She sat down in Nick's chair, her head in her hands. The trouble was that she really couldn't communicate with grown-ups at all these days. The dear, cozy room she had always loved felt confining now.

"Oh dear, I feel so dull . . ."

"Spring fever," Ellen nodded. "I'm as restless as a

swallow myself. By the way, they should be back any day now."

"How is Nick?" Cathy asked politely.

"I never know. What goes on in Nick doesn't show on the surface. Seems like every season has an ordeal in it for him." Ellen smiled grimly. "At least so far he hasn't taken it into his head to defend the trout against the fishermen! But I wouldn't put it past him. He's that set against mankind and on the side of the wild."

"Joel will mind leaving Nick and you as much as anyone," Cathy said.

"Nick and he are just a little crazy in the same way."

"Joel is the sanest person I ever knew!" Cathy said.

"Here, drink this and have something to eat—no one's attacking Joel. He's a good, kind boy. Never thought I'd get used to that long hair but I have. We'll all miss him."

"I guess he never imagined a place like Willard. He feels just the way I do about it."

"Yes," Ellen sighed, and took her coffee back to the rocker where she sipped it. "I expect he does."

"I wish I knew what he really wanted," Cathy said.

"Maybe he doesn't know that himself—he's full of grand ideas but I haven't seen more'n a vestige of practical good sense in any one thing he talks about doing."

"Do you think women keep men back by being practical?" Cathy asked solemnly.

Ellen laughed. "Somebody has to."

"I hate myself," Cathy said miserably.

"What are *you* keeping Joel back from?"

Ellen did not have a clue as to what Cathy was talking about. So she was unaware that it took some doing to decide to answer that. Cathy looked at the worn, lined face and thought of all the living that had gone to make it so, like a beautiful worn piece of wood.

"Me," she said. Tears stood in her eyes, and she just prayed they wouldn't fall. She couldn't start crying—that would be the end.

Ellen picked up her cup and turned it in her hands, not looking up.

"Yes, I expect so. High time he got out of here and left you alone."

"Sometimes I want him to. It's just so hard right now. I mean, I feel all crooked and mixed up and . . . somehow *less*. When he first came, I felt so much *more* than I had ever been before, or imagined being. Why is that?"

"Don't ask me, child. But if you'll take a good hard look around you in this village, that you and Joel see as some sort of paradise, you'll see more'n one marriage not made in heaven but right here on earth where two innocents got caught. And some of those marriages go on for fifty years, all wrong, paying for some girl's letting herself get pushed. Times may change, and fashions, but human biology remains pretty much the same, as far as I can see. So we still have to deal with it, even though *sex* is no longer a dirty word."

"But . . . but . . ." Cathy felt miserable. This was why you couldn't talk with grown-ups—they made it all seem horrible. ". . . why isn't it good for two people to be wholly together if they love each other wholly?"

"It *is* good . . . could be, I guess. Don't ask me." And Ellen picked up her sewing as if to close the subject.

Cathy observed her and was silent. There just didn't seem to be anybody who could help. It was hard to imagine Ellen and her husband having the slightest resemblance to herself and Joel. Maybe it was just that each pair of lovers had a great secret which couldn't be talked about or shared, the entity they were together, without words.

She jumped up as she heard a car drive in, but it was only Mr. Grindell, who got out of his station wagon and came to the door carrying a long thin sign in his arms.

"Well, if it isn't Jem with the marker! Lord sakes!" And Ellen ran to the door.

Jem was beaming with the pleasure of at last having got to the action after all the meetings and talk.

"Here," he said. "Like it?"

And Ellen read: "Dr. Reginald Foster, 1803–1877."

"I expect Dr. Foster would be pleased," she said dryly. "I feel kind of shy about being labeled."

"Come now! This is a house of the greatest historical interest—one of the oldest in the village, you know."

"It's come down in the world, hasn't it?"

"Not at all, not at all. Rufus Comstock was a yeoman farmer in the great tradition. The village honors his name. Only these markers—they are to show original sites."

You just couldn't tease Jem, he was too pleased, and he had worked hard.

So far he had been too full of his errand to notice Cathy. But now he saw her and greeted her warmly.

265

"I understand you are hibernating in Willard," he said jovially. "I'll be up to see your grandfather shortly."

And after Jem had tacked the sign up on the maple and had stood back to admire it, Cathy accepted a lift, almost glad that Joel had not come back after all. But she waited a while, sitting in the front seat, while Mr. Grindell and Ellen talked and talked in the doorway.

"I don't know as I can do it, Jem. Bit off more'n I could chew," she was saying. But Jem would have none of this, and finally she agreed to let him read whatever she could muster of the essay on education by the end of the week. By that time Joel and Nick were walking in from the road and Cathy felt caught.

She pulled down the window and called out, "Mr. Grindell's driving me up. I have homework, Joel."

"Well, Mr. Smith, a good afternoon to you," Jem said. "Have you enjoyed your stay in the village? Made yourself useful, anyway. Off to the wars, are you?"

"So they tell me," Joel said glumly.

"Good luck!" Jem waved as he got into the driver's seat, turned the car with jerky, erratic motions, and they were off.

Cathy didn't look back, but she knew Joel was standing there, watching her go, and she felt miserable—too miserable to go up to the attic alone. So, instead, she offered to make tea so Gram could talk with Mr. Grindell. It was good to have something practical to do.

When Cathy came in with the tea, they were "deep in Willard," as she put it to herself, and she was happy to sit down on the bear rug and listen. It felt like a reprieve— like all she had known of peace and contentment before Joel.

"I think you had a fine idea, Jem, about the signs," Cornelius was saying. "Make people aware of all that went on here two hundred years ago. Going to mark the mill sites, I presume?"

"And where the blacksmith shop was, right there below Ellen's," Christina broke in before Jem had time to answer.

"And the general store." Cornelius took up the refrain.

"And the gristmill over by Lovelands'."

"Well,"—Jem scratched his head—"I had been thinking more in terms of the cemetery, so people could find out where everyone lived, who they were, and so on." He looked momentarily unhappy, but added, "We have had

266

to choose, Cornelius. Couldn't do everything. It has fallen mostly on me and—thank you, a little sugar, no milk"— he interrupted himself to take the proffered cup—"I've worked hard to complete the record. Don't know of a town around here where the cemetery has been so completely mapped."

"Wish we could make the village come alive though, as it was," Cornelius said. "I notice the strangers always think of it as a quiet place, whereas, from what I've been reading, it was just the contrary—lots of bustle and noise, hammers pounding and saws screeching, mill whistles blowing, men shouting at teams of oxen, the blacksmith's hammer clanging."

Jem cleared his throat. "I count on my wonderful aides to complete and touch up the picture. Christina, are you about ready to deliver yourself of 'The Women of Willard'?"

Christina laughed. "It has been a rather hard delivery, Jem, since you put it that way—labor pains awful; result, a poor mite. But you shall have it—as soon as I've drunk my tea."

"No hurry. But by May twentieth I must have them all in. You don't happen to know when the Websters come back, do you? Their place is still all closed up. Big drift of snow up against the back door in the shade there."

"Houses must get lonely in the winter," Cathy said.

"The mice come in," Jem answered, "and squirrels too now and again. Bad for the chimneys, that."

"Maybe they just creak and settle in and go to sleep— the houses, I mean," Cathy went on, enjoying her fantasy.

"And dream," Christina said. "The Websters' house must be full still of those two mad sisters who lived there so long, the Misses Townsend. Remember when Ella came to vote, carrying a sack of hedgehog noses to get the bounty? The Town Hall practically had to be fumigated."

"She was quite a woman," Jem said, unwilling to be critical, "going out on snowhoes at more than eighty, I hear, after hedgehogs."

"How much was the bounty?" Cathy asked.

"Twenty-five cents a nose."

"Only twenty-five cents?" Cathy tried to imagine how it could be—how *many* noses anyway—and how ghastly a mess they must have been in.

"They imagined they were down to their last pennies," Christina said. "You were asked to look into matters

267

when you were selectman—remember, Jem?—and reassure them that they could still afford to eat?"

Christina was happy to remember it all. One rested in the past.

"Poor dears," Jem sighed.

Cornelius chuckled. "Jem, you are a charitable man. I must say I could not manage to call either Ella or Pauline 'dear'; Ella could hold up Town Meeting for hours on a point of order, so I have been told."

"Well, she was up on parliamentary procedure. More than once I had to eat crow, I must confess. She was good Yankee stuff, Cornelius. I admired her. That woman wouldn't be downed."

"Mmm"—Cornelius pondered this—"the struggle for survival. Amazing what people can endure if they have to. So many around here have died hard deaths, lonely . . ." His eyes were bright with tears, Cathy noticed. Amazing how Gramp felt everything so these days.

Flicker stirred and came to have his head stroked.

"And why is it that when we *remember* things, evoke the past, it is always someone *old* we remember?" Christina asked. "I've only just thought of that, but it's true, it seems to me. Why don't we think of the young?"

"You're always talking about you and Ellen when you were young," Cathy said, ". . . sliding down the hay in the barn and getting scolded, and running away to try to see the wildcat they said was up Stone Hill."

"Maybe it is that we remember ourselves young and everyone else as old," Cornelius said, rubbing his hands together as he did when he was enjoying himself.

"Or maybe the old make a strong impression because they have become themselves. They have more character," Christina said. "We're always, it seems to me, younger than the world we live in. And it is the old that give a place its atmosphere, make it what it is—Willard and Jane Tuttle, Willard and Erica Portland."

"By the way, I trust you have devoted some pages to Miss Portland?" Jem said.

"I did, but it was hard. You know what happens when you begin to write something—it all slips through your fingers in some queer way. I thought I knew *all* about Erica Portland but it took me hours just to track down where it was she studied in Paris and when she came back. I saw her so clearly—huge in old age, with her loud, happy laugh and her white hair cut like a man's, her air

268

of being a queen, but a happy queen who enjoyed being rich and royal and talented and all she was."

"And that is what did not get into Christina's essay," Cornelius teased. "Christina was so impressed by being an historian that she developed an academic style—a Victorian academic style at that."

"Don't tease me," she begged, but she was laughing. "Jem, Cornelius corrected nearly every word, and before I was through I felt like a schoolgirl who had just managed a C for the course."

She got up, obviously feeling her knee.

"I'll just go and get it . . . or . . ."—she looked over at Cathy gratefully—"you could run up for me, darling. The darn thing is in a folder on my desk. You can't miss it."

Cathy was rarely in her grandparents' room alone, and when she got there, out of breath from taking the stairs two at a time, she stood for a moment, feeling like an intruder. Christina's old Jaeger wrapper was flung over a chair, and Gramp's red leather slippers were by their bed. The folder was under a pile of letters from Europe and all over the place, and when she had found it, Cathy went to the windows for a long look at the mountain. The foreground was a mist of red maple in flower and frail greens among the gray trunks, and above it all the mountain was dark blue against a pale blue sky where some wispy clouds were turning gold in the setting sun.

"It's there," she whispered, "always."

A jay flew across and into the pines, giving a loud scream.

Joel, who had been miraculously absent from her heart for a whole half hour, was there again like some burden. How could she bring him and Willard together? For surely, she thought, they are wrong and Willard is not for the old. It's for us to go tramp in and look for arbutus—she hugged herself at the very thought. Tomorrow . . . yes . . . she would go with Joel into the woods. There, they would be safe. There, they could find everything they had lost these days . . . surely . . . surely . . . and Willard is forever, she thought, but we are *now,* just like the arbutus that only comes once a year and must be celebrated.

"Oh, Joel," she breathed. Dear Joel, who might have tried to eat the skunk cabbage. Dear Joel, as innocent and wild as a deer. Love flooded her eyes. Her heart was beating too fast. How could she run away from love?

269

Now that spring has come, it's hard to keep at this journal. Perhaps it served its purpose. I have been glancing back, quite astonished at how faithfully I managed to write at least once a week. It is the record of, in some ways, the happiest winter I can remember. It seems like years, not months, ago that Ellen and I took off into the woods on that memorable walk . . . and now Jane is gone, and Old Pete, who watched us go and come back, is knocked out for good, I fear. He is determined to come home to his shack, to his treasures that look so desolate as the snow melts—an ancient rotting canoe, God knows what trash, rusting and dying.

There are violets out by the front steps, and daffodils and every sort of narcissus in the borders, just glorious. I bring bunches in for Cornelius so he can see the light through the petals. He walked down to the garden where I was working, with the help of two canes, to surprise me yesterday. But I could see the strain when he panted up the hill again. However, he is determined to get about, as he says, now that he has accepted that he may never be able to walk without canes. He says he is in training now. The sheer courage of him! He thinks he'll be able to drive before summer.

We are all *en fête* waiting for darling Olivia, who comes on Saturday. Joel is invited for dinner, and Eben—it may be one of Joel's last times, as I gather he goes back to New Jersey any day now. I am terribly anxious to see what Olivia will think of him, and about this whole affair that seems to be turning Cathy from a child into a young woman with frightening rapidity. Anyway, she looks less pinched and miserable, so I must believe they have come to an understanding.

Ellen is quite torn about Joel, I can feel. She was here yesterday doing her usual quiet, wonderfully calming job of cleaning, and we had quite a talk upstairs in the bedroom, away from Cornelius, who has come to enjoy Ellen's wit at the coffee hour and looks forward to seeing her. It seems years since she and I have had a chance for a talk . . . Joel has been a good companion for Nick and has kept him from disappearing, as he so often does, into his strange spells of anxiety and inward-turned anger, and Ellen is grateful for that. Also he is amazingly helpful around the house. "Never saw a man who washed dishes before," she said with her wry smile. "Couldn't stand to marry a man who was under foot all the time, but I must admit he's handy."

On the other hand she is well aware that Joel, as she says, believes in "people getting together." "What is touch but a way of saying love?" he told her. "Why be scared of it? The more people we can know the richer we are, and this is one real way of knowing." Ellen is so wonderful. Apparently she told him that here in Willard we try not to know too much about each other, and that's what makes it a good place to live in. I gather she greatly enjoys the running fire of her conversations with him. Heaven knows they are both articulate beings! Nick, I imagine, drinks it all in and smiles his secret smile.

We all like Joel in spite of ourselves. Despite his revolutionary ideas, his behavior is exemplary. He is a truly gentle person—Cornelius says so. And if Cornelius can accept such a "weirdo," as he called Joel at first, that does prove something—something about them both.

Is it partly that here in Willard there has always been room for the eccentric? It is hard to imagine his coming to tea on Beacon Hill—partly because we just wouldn't know him there.

Oh, I see Nick coming up the hill and must run down and ask him to help me with raking leaves away from around the rose bushes!

CHAPTER 6

That Friday afternoon turned out to be one of the spring days when the air itself is so exhilarating that it acts like an intoxicant—a blue sky with flecks of small white clouds racing across it, and sometimes a sudden darkness as one covered the sun, only to bring out, it seemed, the strong bitter smell of wet earth and sodden leaves. Overhead there was a thin veil of green, and, at the roadside, grass in patches looked brilliant green again.

"We're going to look for trailing arbutus," Cathy said, "down by the pond. Nick told us where."

She left her satchel of books in Ellen's kitchen, and Ellen came to the door and watched Joel and Cathy break into a run—like two colts, she thought—as they passed the green and disappeared down the road and out of sight. For a moment she stood there, feeling the sun on her face, and feeling the pang the old must feel when they witness young lovers in spring, especially when one of them must go to war. Cathy had surely looked radiant, and she noticed how Joel laughed when he saw her—the laughter of amused recognition, of pure joy. Cathy had caught the laughter and laughed herself, and neither of them, she surmised, could have said what was so merry about the moment except being together again after a whole long twenty-four hours.

"What's happened to us?" Cathy asked as Joel took her hand and swung it as they walked. "We're all right, aren't we?—Look, there's a robin!" She broke away from him to stand and watch the absurd short run, then dip of the robin's head as he pulled out a worm on Miss Plummer's lawn. "If the robins are back, the mayflowers will be out."

"How do you know?"

"I just made that up!"

"And how many other things have you made up to tease a city boy?"

"None, Joel. I tell you the absolute truth," she said, solemnly pushing her hair back so she could look into his eyes. But coming this close was still hard. Somewhere at the back of their eyes, there was hesitation now.

"It's a singable day—let's sing."

"Well, we'll have to slow down. I'm out of breath."

"No, let's just walk and be silent," she said as he took her hand again, "and look at everything."

"It's quite a world," Joel said, looking up at blue sky through the branches.

"Those are beeches. See how tightly furled the leaves are still—little brown needles. But any day now they'll open like tiny hands.—No," Cathy corrected herself, "that isn't right. A leaf isn't like a hand. My English teacher says I have to look harder at things to get them right. You know what, Joel? She says poems are made with words, not with feelings—but maybe you have to have the feeling first to want to find the right words."

"Stop talking, will you?" Joel said. "Let's drink the air."

"Let's see how many birds we can hear!"

"I don't care how many. I just want to *be!*"

It was hard for Cathy to keep still, bubbling over as she was with things to say and to ask Joel, but she managed it for some minutes, partly because he was holding her hand so hard.

"There," he said gently, "now we've landed. You can't just talk your way into landing—you have to let it happen, give it time."

This was a new concept for Cathy and she thought about it before she said, "Yes, I see. You're so wise, Joel."

Joel took a deep breath. "I feel immense," he said.

"We're huge," Cathy agreed. "We're as high as mountains and as deep as rivers. We're all natural things rolled into one."

"And just what has happened to us? Do you know? You said we were all right."

"I don't know, Joel. I think you've been making magic.

I feel so . . ." She hesitated before the word "safe" and did not, after all, utter it.

"Where are these flowers, anyway?"

"Just a little farther. We're almost there."

"Doesn't seem as though anything could flower. It's all so sodden on the ground."

"They're under the leaves, Joel, and sometimes even under snow. That's why they're so wonderful."

They had turned off the road now, down a woodsy path that led to the pond, and for the first time since they had started out, with the sense of being out of sight of anyone, in a secret spring world, Cathy suddenly felt self-conscious and slipped her hand out of Joel's, almost running as they neared the arbutus place.

"Don't be in such a hurry, Cathy," Joel said sharply. "We have to talk."

She stopped short then.

"After all, I haven't seen you for ages."

"But everything's all right, isn't it?—now, I mean."

She caught the slight wince on Joel's face, usually so open.

"I want to talk," he said gravely. "You and I are more important than that flower."

"Oh, yes"—she nodded like a good child—"of course."

"I just feel that you are so far away, Cathy . . . as if . . . as if . . ."—he lowered his eyes—"some door had closed between us."

"I can't help it, Joel," she said, near to tears now. "But you said just now we had landed."

"I thought we had." He looked up then through the haze of buds and flowering trees overhead, a gauzy canopy between them and the sky here in the woods.

"I'm sorry I'm making it hard," Cathy said.

"Kiss me then," and he pulled her roughly to him and kissed her on the mouth, but not in the way she had found so disturbing. "Cathy, Cathy," he said, laying the palm of his hand against her cheek, as if it were a leaf, she thought—such a cool, composing hand, so dear. "When you're seventeen, I'll be back. Will you wait for me?"

"Can't we just *be,* as you say it . . . be all we can *now*?"

Joel gave a wry little laugh. "I guess I'm learning that being never stays still. We're on our way, Cathy, toward being more or being less for each other."

"Now it's all become difficult," she sighed. "Please, Joel, come and look for the mayflowers. You'll see . . ."

His answer was a groan. "Sometimes it seems as if Willard—the whole place, the people, even the weather —were some strong magic . . . and it's all on your side."

"How?"

"When Nick talks about animals, the young does, or even about birds, the silent way an owl flies, he's always saying, 'Leave it alone, let it be itself.' I've learned a lot from Nick, Cathy."

"I know."

"Nick sees the young things as always in danger. The tenderness of that man, Cathy! Oh well, I suppose all his love goes there. He's made me think a lot about men and how they ruin everything by wanting to possess it—shoot the deer to possess it, shoot the woodcock as if they could only really have it by killing it."

"Nick isn't Willard, though. Willard is more cruel."

"Yes, half the girls marry because they have to, I understand." It was said harshly and Cathy took it like a blow.

"Just like the slums you talk about, isn't it?"

"Oh, Cathy wouldn't it be great if we could go somewhere together, into the city together, and do something about the mess?"

"Why not here?"

"Because this is a dream world, Cathy. The action is somewhere else."

"I wonder . . . that's what *you* say."

Suddenly Joel's mood changed. It was as if he had been able to abstract himself from the place and the time, draw back and look at Cathy—the way she frowned and pushed her long hair back when she was puzzled or interested, and see himself, leaning against a tree trunk, and all around them the gauzy, fresh May day—and hold it like a bubble again in his hands.

"The thing about Willard for me—it's like love. I mean it feels outside time. No one hurries here. That's what I find so amazing. The place itself seems to lay a hand on my shoulder and tell me to take it easy, not to hurry anything."

"Oh, yes," Cathy breathed. "Oh, yes . . ."

"So we'll go and find those flowers now," Joel said gravely, and this time she didn't pull her hand away.

275

"People come here who are not like us," Cathy said, dragging an old beer can out from among the leaves.

"Summer people?" Joel asked, teasing her.

"More likely the toughies and their girls."

But then she became wholly absorbed in feeling among the dank, wet leaves to follow a branch of arbutus, and pulled out a single frail, waxy, pink flower. "Here's one!" she cried out. "Give me your knife, Joel—otherwise I'll tear out the root!"

"There," she said when she had carefully cut it off with a short stem and two leaves, "here's the spring, the early spring of Willard. Smell it."

"Mmm!" It was truly an amazing sweet fragrance, like nothing Joel had ever smelled before. "I see what you mean."

"It's a secret," she said. "Keep it for me." And he gathered in her smile and her long look with the flower. But there was nothing to say.

Together they spent a half hour of this wet, exciting treasure-hunt, dragging out pieces of crockery and beer cans, their hands scratched, nails broken, but drawn on by the not-impossible treasures to be seized on, one by one, most of them still waxy white, only a few deep pink, star-shaped, perfect.

"We've got to stop," Cathy breathed. "Gram will wonder where I am!"

Joel gathered together the bunch and buried his nose in it.

"She'll be grateful when she sees this!" He straightened up and grinned. "Well, I surely never imagined I could get this absorbed in tracking down a flower!"

They walked back to the village and up the hill fast, and mostly silent. Every now and then Cathy glanced over at Joel as if to be sure he was there at her side. And once in a while he smiled back at her.

"Oh, I forgot to say that Gram wants you for supper tomorrow. Eben Fifield will be there, and my Aunt Olivia. Oh, I am so anxious for you to meet her, Joel. She's the one you'll like!"

"I like your grandfather and your grandmother," he said a little formally. "Guess I just like your family."

"You didn't at first."

"I know. Then I was young and foolish," and he laughed. "Seems like I've had a college education in a month."

"Joel, you are so dear," Cathy said, looking up at the trees and the sky as if she were speaking to them, including the world in the dearness of Joel.

"Going to miss me?"

"Don't."

"We'll write. You'll write poems, Cathy . . . won't you?"

"Don't," she said again. They had reached the gates. "Joel."

"What?"

"It's nearly suppertime, and I guess I'd better go in alone."

"O.K." He put the arbutus into her hands roughly. "See you tomorrow." And he ran off into the dark—happy? angry?

And Cathy stood there for a moment between worlds before she climbed slowly up to the Ark, to the firelight, to the familiar and safe. What had Joel meant about "landing"? They had not landed. They had stayed in suspense, trying to feel as they had felt a week ago. They had not mentioned the army. That word was a sort of taboo, Cathy felt. It was what they had to keep away, not to melt into one great tearing, terrible good-by.

CHRISTINA'S JOURNAL—*May 16*

I'm writing this on my lap by the fire. Cornelius is safe in bed, but for some reason I wanted to come down here alone. The Ark is very still. I am longing so to see Olivia. . . . Cathy seemed very subdued at supper. I wonder whether I have kept hands off unwisely. I felt—and Cornelius agreed—that it was her first real love and we did not want to loom over her. Now I wonder whether she would not have been relieved to have some limits set. I notice that she hasn't asked Joel up to her room these last days, and if she has been the one to make that decision, it is hard, of course.

This afternoon they went arbutus-hunting and came back with an exquisite bunch. Cathy gave it to me, but she didn't look happy and ran upstairs almost at once instead of coming to be with Cornelius and me while we had our drink.

How hard it is to be young now! I had really forgotten about the pressures and bewilderments. And who would wish to go back to a time when one was only getting acquainted with one's own body and how treacherous it can be? Sometimes I wonder whether all the touching that goes on now may not be a good thing. When I was young, any touch, just holding hands, was so momentous that it rocked my whole being. But even if they can hug each other now and walk around arm in arm, and hardly give it a thought, there is still the immense leap that sex means, that taking in of the stranger. Especially for a woman, how disturbing it still must be! I feel that Joel would not force anything, but one supposes that he is in love, or thinks he is. After all, he came here in such a strange way, saw Cathy first when he was in a state of shock, and I feel that perhaps all of us, Willard itself, and especially Nick and Ellen, have provided shelter for that confused young man—a sort of innocence that he truly appreciates, for which he feels a great deal.

Why do I say "innocence"? Whatever it is, it is not suburbia here. A haven for the very old and for the very young; for those in between—a shadowy nowhere, maybe. Joel talks a lot about "Being Now" (Cathy evidently capitalizes this when she utters the phrase), and that is just what Willard has been for him these weeks. He has had the peculiar joy of being both inside and outside, an irresponsible observer. Well, we shall know more after tomorrow night.

It is strange that spring has never seemed to me a happy time. It is too poignant. Poignant for me and Cornelius because, although we never speak of it, I know that he must, like me, feel a pang that everything around us is being born again . . . every old tree is putting out frail, fresh, tiny new leaves, but we cannot be renewed. We cannot be born again. We have begun an inexorable descent. It is the one thing I cannot talk about with Cornelius. Sometimes I am frightened—frightened of what the end will be. Then I think of Jane and remember how intensely she lived till the very end, and how wisely! She gave up everything not essential, but she kept the essential. So till the end she could look at a mushroom or a bird or an autumn leaf with total joy. Dear God, I say to myself, remind us to pay attention. This it is in the power of the very old to do. For them too, just as for the very young, life can still be full of miracles—and a miracle is a stone with a special color, or a flat fungus growing out of a tree trunk. But for that one must not allow oneself to get cluttered up.

It is odd that I have begun to pray again after many,

many years when prayer did not mean a great deal to me. I have no intimate sense of God's presence, but somehow when I can pray, I feel transparent again. Light flows through me. I am no longer a thick substance composed of lists of things to do, small anxieties, pains. I wonder whether this is what Joel means by "Being Now"? That thought just occurred to me.

CHAPTER 7

Nick and Joel had decided to go on a last walk, deep into the woods to a place where Nick thought there might be beavers, but for once he had taken a false bearing and instead they came out at mid-morning near to a hard-topped road that wound along an artificial pond.

"I could do with a pause," Joel said. He didn't like to admit that he was dead tired, but the rough walk, over old stone walls and for a time along a brook, the pushing branches back, the uneven footing, and Nick's pace had about done him in. "I'm out of breath," he said, sitting down on a round piece of granite. . . . "I suppose this rock got smoothed out by the glacier."

While he sat and felt the sun on his back and took in the pale blue shimmer of the water, Nick wandered off and began poking under leaves along the bank. After a time he came back with a small bunch of arbutus in his hand and sat down silently beside Joel.

"You'll have to learn to walk further'n a couple of miles in the army," Nick said after a moment, giving him a sidelong glance.

"You're right, I'm soft," Joel said, his head bent. "Fact is, I'm scared of the whole thing."

Nick gave him a hard look. He'd be shorn of more than his long hair, this city boy with his gentle ways and loving heart. Nick spat. It was the only way he could express his feelings.

Joel wanted to ask whether Nick had been scared. He was longing for some support from this man who had

280

been through it all—the worst, judging by what he had gathered from Ellen. But that was years ago, and that war had made some sense.

Joel kicked a stone with all his force.

So they communicated, these two. Sometimes. At other times Joel talked and Nick listened. But today they were both on edge. Any change disturbed Nick, and Joel's leaving was a worry. He didn't want to think about it, but it was always there, like the war itself, like a curse on the spring world.

"Amazing," Joel said, "how the leaves have burst out. When did they do it? It just happened."

"Always thought I might be there when the beeches unfurl—but I never have been. Always takes me by surprise, like now. That's how it is."

"It's so groovy here," Joel breathed.

"Later on that bank where the arbutus is will be a mass of flowers—checkerberry, a little purple flower; and, just above, lady slippers. Gets the sun, and shelter from wind. Just about ideal."

Joel tried to imagine that sodden bank of dirty old leaves and beer bottles as a mass of flowers. He would not be here to see it, that was sure.

"I wish I could stay!"

"It'll keep," Nick said with his secret smile.

But just then they heard the horrible roar of the road grader in the distance.

At first Joel didn't know what it was, although he noticed how tense Nick became, lifting his head like an animal who senses a threat. He got up at once and walked off toward the sound. Joel knew enough by now to know that there was no love lost between the Taggarts and the Comstocks. Ellen had told him about the fight that Rufus had had with Ed's father. But that seemed like ancient history. Was it possible that people could hold a grudge so long? Nick never said much about Ed Taggart, but he was always pointing out things Taggart and his big machine had done to the landscape. There was nothing Joel admired more about Nick than his minute knowledge of, and caring about, the whole natural world of Willard. Nick was a one-man conservation society—that was what it came to, and Joel found this admirable. At the store he had occasionally heard gossip about some fight Nick had had with New Yorkers over a deer last fall, but it was treated with amusement rather than censure. And by now

281

Joel had learned that all such tales got embroidered in the telling, so he had not taken Nick's reputed violence on that occasion as a fact. No doubt he had had a fit of anger, and now the village was busy making a mythical assault on five men out of it, with half of them left sprawling. It was a quaint image when one looked at Nick, gangling, silent, and so unaggressive.

But it did seem a little odd, this violent feeling about Ed Taggart. Joel saw Ed now and then at the store, a heavy, quiet man who complained about being overworked and had a hard time getting help on the roads. Once when Joel had been up at the Ark with Cathy, Ed was there playing cribbage with the old man. All this added up in Joel's mind to a decent person, not the monster Nick made of him. Of course the work was rough, and sometimes the heavy machinery tore out precious wild things. Even Cathy had been upset when, on one of their walks, they came on the whole bank of a dirt road torn up to widen it. It looked terribly raw and disorderly, gashed-up earth and piles of rough stones left helter-skelter, and the stumps of trees. They had stood and looked at it in dismay, and then Cathy had shrugged. "Oh well," she said, "in a few years it will all grow back. The wilderness wins around here. You'd be amazed."

"But why do they have to do it?" Joel had asked. This seemed such a remote road, leading nowhere as far as he could see.

"Because of the plows," she had said. "There are two houses down there, one of them inhabited in winter, and besides, in mud season it's hard going. They'll pour gravel on those deep ruts and get it packed down hard."

It had taken more than a week before Joel became aware of how much feeling coursed along just under the surface in the village, how many people barely greeted each other, what grudges remained generation after generation. Ed had been a boy when his father had had the fight with Nick's father—now he was past middle age. Must it go on?

For a second Joel thought the big grader might not be making the turn into their road. If only Ed would move on! But no, in another minute he saw the huge yellow beast come trundling along, and Ed sitting in the high seat, towering there, a cigar in his mouth. It was strange how, on the machine, Ed had become suddenly threatening. The very sound grated as he swung along by the shining pond.

"Nick!" Joel called, suddenly worried. "Nick, where are you?"

"Nick around here?" Ed leaned out to ask, a little anxiously—or did Joel imagine that?

"Yes, he's been picking mayflowers," and Joel waved an arm in the general direction where Nick had disappeared.

Now Joel could see that the grader was being followed by a bulldozer with a big shovel attached, and this was driven by a stubby, grizzled man with very blue eyes and red cheeks, who gave him a cheerful wave.

"Might as well get going," Ed called to the man. "You can start there where all the beer cans are. Clean it up. Take off about two feet. Plow got stuck there twice last year, where it dips down. See what I mean?"

The bulldozer was backed off and turned while Joel watched uneasily and kept an eye out for Nick. Where in hell had he gone anyway?

The grader was now stationary, and he went up to speak to Ed.

"You're not going to tear up that bank there, are you?" he asked. "I mean, Nick says it's a great place for wild flowers . . . I mean," he bumbled, getting the cold stare from Ed. "After all, there aren't so many places left."

Ed shifted the cigar to the other side of his mouth and spat.

"My job is to keep the roads open, fella."

"I know, but . . ."

Ed now opened the door of his little tower and climbed out clumsily. "Get going!" he shouted at the man on the bulldozer. "We haven't got all day!"

But just as the bulldozer was pulled gingerly up into position and the big shovel lowered like a grunting, unwilling animal, Nick came out of the woods. Instinctively Joel ran to his side.

"Oh, there you are, Nick."

"Get out of the way!"

Joel took one look at the white, tense face and stepped aside. Nick took up a stand on the bank, facing the bulldozer, about four feet from the menacing shovel. From there he talked over his shoulder at Ed, who was now leaning against one of the huge grader wheels, looking grim.

283

"Now listen, Ed," Nick said quietly, "you'll have to shovel me up with it if you touch this place."

"Sacred, is it?"

"Yes, if you like, it *is* sacred."

"Who says?"

"Anyone in his right mind says. *I* say. You're going to destroy things we can't get back if you tear up this bank —it's a mass of flowers. You know that as well as I do."

"Flowers! Good Christ, the woods are full of 'em! Go ahead, Chuck—he'll move!"

Chuck scratched his head. He was not about to shovel a man up, and the man standing there had a pretty determined look about him.

"Come on, Nick," he said cheerfully. "Some things have to go—you know it. We all know it. Give us a break, man."

He put the machine in first and crept a few feet forward. They heard the shovel grinding up earth and rock.

"Go *on!*" Ed shouted, suddenly in a rage.

He was across the road before Joel knew what had happened and had grappled Nick and swung him out of the way.

"God damn you!"

"No!" Joel shouted. "Leave him alone! Don't you touch Nick," and he hurled himself at the two men, not knowing where or how to get a hold.

"Keep out of this, long-hair," Ed muttered between his teeth.

Just then Chuck got going and the bulldozer roared forward, pushing a slice of the bank before it, and with that sound Nick went berserk. He managed to get one arm loose and socked Ed hard in the jaw. Chuck looked back then, stopped the machine and jumped out just as Joel managed to get a grip on Nick from behind, and before Ed had caught his breath Chuck had him too. For a second all four stood there breathing hard, facing each other.

It seemed an eternity to Joel, and he wondered how long he could hold Nick back. But suddenly, as suddenly as it had blown up, the storm of anger dropped.

"Let me go," Ed muttered, and Chuck, feeling the man gone slack, took his hands off.

"Shucks, I got hired for road work"—Chuck tried to laugh it off—"not to supervise a boxing match."

"Shut up," Ed said, wiping blood off his mouth. "This

time you go to jail, Nick—or to the state hospital. Take your choice."

"It's only because he *cares*," Joel said passionately. "Can't you see?"

"Cares enough to give me a bloody mouth."

"Nick, Nick!" Joel pleaded, "say something!"

But Nick was beyond speech. He had become a furious, bewildered animal, head down, panting long panting sobs.

"He's having a spell—crazy," Ed said. "Can't you see? He can't even hear what you're saying."

He turned back then to the grader, as if he found some comfort in the inhuman beast that he could control, and climbed into the seat. From there he talked to Chuck in a whisper, told him to go down the road a piece and come back and do the job after they had got Nick away.

Joel meanwhile had put an arm around Nick and was just standing there.

"I can't . . . stop . . . them," Nick said. "It's all being taken away."

"No, you can't alone," Joel said gently. "But it was a good try."

He felt sick to his stomach. Everything was in a whirl in and around him. Even the pond, as he looked at it, seemed like a hallucination, so peaceful, still, not a ripple to break the mirror of the surface where the birches were reflected, as white, as innocent of man and man's furies and miseries as ever.

They walked home to Willard along the hardtopped road in silence. The day had begun as a holiday, a last day of freedom for Joel, and because he would soon be gone, it had all had a particular brilliance. He didn't suppose he would ever forget the look of the lake and the delicacy of the birches reflected in it, the wakeful stillness of everything, as if they were present at a silent explosion of life at its purest and best. And now the whole mood had changed. The sun might as well have gone behind a cloud, there was so much darkness in him and in the thin, stooped man walking beside him like a sleepwalker, head down. Joel had seen his friend turn into a brutal animal, out to kill if he could. It had been so sudden—so unexpected—and so terrible, really—different from the scuffles he had witnessed at school. For Nick, he knew, it was pretty nearly a matter of life and death; for him the destruction of the wild flowers was as much murder as if

285

they were people. Was this wrong? Who could blame a man for being that sensitive to the world around him?

Yet, it had been ugly. The ugliness of it hurt Joel. Anything that makes a man behave like an animal hurts. And it was pretty clear to him now that a man who might be unable to control such fury was not safe to have around.

"He's never been right in the head since the war," he remembered a man saying at the store. So . . . what now? And how would Ellen handle this?

When they were about a quarter of a mile from the village, standing on a hill where they could see the church spire below, Joel spoke for the first time.

"You had to do it, I suppose," he said, feeling his way. "But you can't change things as they are, Nick."

"Someday, when they've wrecked it all and there aren't any wild flowers, they'll be sorry. Someday they'll learn." He wiped his mouth. "Too late by then." There was only weariness in the tone, and in the way he dragged his feet.

How speak to a wound? Joel felt young and vulnerable beside the iron in the man beside him. He himself had never felt anything as fiercely as Nick felt about the wild in nature. Nick would not hesitate, he was pretty sure, to kill a man for the sake of a deer or a woodcock—or, maybe, even a flower. This was the ground of Nick's being. But all I am, Joel thought, is a kind of loose energy, undirected. How can I say anything to him? Pity would be out of place.

They had reached the door. Joel let Nick go in alone and went off to the barn to sit there on a chopping block and think. After a while, Ellen called out to him, "Joel, where are you?"

The kitchen was empty. No Nick.

"He's lying down," Ellen said, rocking, and keeping her hands busy with a piece of sewing. "What happened? You'd better tell me."

Joel noted the glass with a bunch of arbutus in it on her table. So, whatever his state, Nick had somehow brought it home to her; must have stuffed it into a pocket. Joel had tears in his eyes. He felt weak. Here he had found shelter, been treated kindly, surely more kindly than he deserved—and now he was the messenger with bad news.

"I'm afraid the road agent is pretty mad," he said, "I think he means to go after Nick."

"I suppose they got into a fight." Ellen watched Joel

put his head into his hands. "You'd better have a cup of coffee. If you've never seen Nick in one of those spells, it can be scarifying. How badly was Ed hurt?"

"A bloody mouth—nothing serious."

She nodded and bent her head to her sewing.

"How can one care too much?" Joel blurted out, making a helpless gesture. "But Nick does. I mean . . ."

Ellen laid down her sewing and went to the stove. Her gestures were mechanical. Her mind was clearly elsewhere. After she had poured two cups of coffee, she stood and looked out at the maple and the tiny perfect umbrellas of leaves, some quite pink like flowers, that had appeared on it overnight.

"Seems like man isn't ready for the beauty of this world." Then she said quite calmly, as if she had been ready for a long time, "You can drive a car, can't you? Yes, of course"—and she smiled—"you arrived here in a car. Well, Joel, it would be a real help if you could drive me and Nick in the truck to the state hospital."

"When?" It was in Joel's mind that he was expected up at the Ark for supper.

"Soon as we have a bite to eat."

She went out to the pantry and brought in the remains of a stew and put it on the stove.

"It takes only a little over an hour. You won't be late up at the Ark."

"It doesn't matter."

"Now I'll go and have a talk with Nick. You sit there and calm down." She had noticed that Joel's hand was trembling so much he found it hard to get the cup of coffee to his mouth. At the door she turned round and said quietly, "I've known this would happen for a long time. Now it has. Now I don't have to be so anxious any longer. It's a relief."

"They'll help him?"

"Keep him out of mischief." She shrugged. "Who knows?"

If Joel had expected Ellen to weep or react as some women would to tragedy, he still had much to learn about her. The only way she showed the effect of shock was that she moved slowly and with more dignity than usual about the tasks of the moment.

When she came down again after a half hour, she set a packed suitcase in the hall ready to go. Then she phoned Christina, suggested that she get hold of one of the Lovelands to do the chores Nick had been doing. "Glad you won't have snow to worry about anyway," she said. "Joel is expecting to come up tonight. He'll see to the wood."

"Don't forget the wood, will you, Joel?" she said when she came back to lay the table. "Olivia will be coming today. They'll want fires in the downstairs rooms. I feel bad letting Christina down this way."

"It's you," Joel said, "I wish I could do something."

"Trouble's no stranger," Ellen said, with that characteristic lift of her chin. "It's one thing I can handle, I guess."

"Mrs. Chapman too, from what Cathy says . . . about her son."

"Yes—John." Ellen paused a moment, considering this. "Only difference is John tries to kill himself. Nick tries to kill other people. But it all comes from the same root maybe. Not being able to take things as they are."

"Sometimes I think what my generation wants is to make a world where people like John and Nick could live and not despair," Joel said passionately. "There's something awfully wrong."

"The best fail—is that what you mean?"

"The best get caught in the machine. When that big grader came down the road, it looked prehistoric. I hated it."

"Maybe. But we have to have roads."

"I don't know," Joel said. "Seems like I know less every day."

"Someone has to be responsible. Someone has to pick up the pieces. Someone has to make shelter," Ellen said sharply. It was the first sign she had shown of strain. "That's what you people haven't learned yet, Joel."

"I guess you mean you did it for me—shelter and all."

"Well, you've paid for it, haven't you?"

"You don't pay for what you and Nick and Willard have given me. You can't."

"You're a nice boy, Joel, I'll grant you that." Then she sat down at the table for a second and faced him. "It's only that somebody pays for Old Pete and Nick and you and John . . . and what looks free and innocent, everything you thought you found here, costs a lot."

That was when Nick came in, and there was no more talk—only Joel's blundering attempts to make the meal less strained.

I had come upstairs to lie down and think, but I can't stay still with so much happening, so much to be sorted out. Ellen just called to say that Nick attacked Ed Taggart and she has decided that this time he has to go back to the state hospital, at least for a while, to see whether they can do anything about his violence. Luckily Joel is there and will drive them over. I offered to go of course, but with six for dinner I feel rattled, so I was relieved not to have to. Olivia will be here in a half hour—such a blessed thought. It seems as if all the little threads that bind us together here have got hopelessly tangled. God knows what is going on with Cathy and Joel, or, for that matter, when he really will leave. I suppose it might drag on for months, his waiting to be drafted.

Ellen is so staunch when it comes to the real rub. I know she has fought off facing this illness of Nick's, and she was so violent about his attack last fall just because she had doubts. But when she once makes up her mind about something, she is like steel. It was like her to worry about us. We'll miss Nick awfully, not just the work he did but his gentle ways. It seems ironic that he went berserk, apparently, when the bulldozer began to tear out that bank along the pond where all the wild flowers are— there of all places. He is so like John in so many ways— Jane, if she were alive, would be right at Nick's side. But Ellen faces the fact that he is dangerous. I feel all churned up. I guess the thing is to go down and get scalloped potatoes ready. Ellen sews; I cook—and so women have met crisis from time immemorial.

Cornelius wheeled himself out onto the porch. Cool as it is, he said, he wanted to look at the mountain. This business about Nick has come as a shock for him. He's broody and on edge, too, waiting for Olivia. No wonder human relations are as difficult as they are. Everything we do, every move one of us makes, affects the whole fabric. . . . No, it is more like a stone thrown into a pond— the ripples widen and widen until they reach the shore that bounds us all.

Why are words such a comfort? I feel better just because I have scrawled these out, no use to anyone—a way, I suppose, of putting some distance between me and events. I see more clearly when I have been able to say what is happening.

Darling Olivia—how wonderful to have a child like this! Her voice sounded so alive on the phone. I felt it like a cordial, coursing all through me, the other day. She brings balm.

CHAPTER 8

It had been Olivia's idea that she and Cathy set the table and get everything as ready as possible before six—"and then we can all sit down with a drink and not worry, Mother," adding, "and I'll serve, so for once you won't have to keep running out to the kitchen."

"Yes, darling," Christina said meekly, but her eyes were dancing, "you're the boss."

It amused her to see Olivia's way of ordering everyone about when she first arrived. She came bringing with her a whiff of the office, and it took a day or so before this masterful manner became subdued by family life. The time was sure to come when Cornelius would roar, "Sit down and stop ordering your mother about!" But until then, until the metamorphosis had taken place, Christina had to admit that it was very restful to have the endless "things to be done" taken right out of her hands.

Cornelius had insisted on staying out on the porch, wrapped in rugs, to see the sun set. It was, Christina guessed, his way of resting and of preparing himself for the rare event of six people sitting down at the table. And while Cathy and Olivia worked, she herself slipped upstairs to lie down for ten minutes and to change into something suitable for the occasion—it had been ages since she had worn anything but tweeds and sweaters. Something festive, springlike, was in order, she felt. Also it might be a fine idea to let Olivia and Cathy have a little talk alone before Joel arrived, full of the painful drama of the afternoon, no doubt.

"You've been having adventures?" Olivia asked, laying forks and knives down on the mats, not even looking up. Wild creatures like her niece felt easier when something besides talk could be going on. "You're not sorry you decided to come?"

"I'm alive, Aunt Olivia! It seems years ago that I was in Boston. Everything's changed." She was standing, back to her aunt, at the corner cupboard. "Wine glasses, do you think?"

"Of course. No, not champagne glasses. I brought some Burgundy."

"These?"

"Yes." Olivia stopped a moment and leaned on the back of a chair while Cathy brought out the glasses carefully and set one at each place. Alive this fifteen-year-old surely was, but she looked white and strained.

"By 'everything's changed' I suppose you mean you've changed—into something rich and strange?"

Cathy gave her aunt a wary, sidewise glance from under her hair.

"I'm all mixed up," she said. "I'm in love . . . I *think* . . ."

"If you're not sure, that's enough to mix anyone up. And it's this boy who dropped down into Willard like someone from the moon, I presume?"

"Gram told you?" Cathy visibly winced.

"Well, it hasn't been exactly a secret, has it?" Olivia went back to table-setting, getting out damask napkins from a drawer. "Might as well be as glorious as we can." She folded each napkin carefully. "Tell me about Joel."

"He's—he's awfully like me, really," Cathy said. "I mean he ran away from Dartmouth just the way I did from school . . . only he had no place to go like this . . . so it was rather wonderful that he ended up in Willard. That's what *he* thinks."

"How serious is this, Cathy?" This time Olivia did not avoid a straight look at Cathy.

"I don't know," Cathy breathed, sitting down, as if she had to rest the burden she carried these days.

"Yes . . . well . . . from what I hear he's going to be drafted. You don't have to make any terrible decisions right now, do you, darling? I mean, can't you take it easy? Time solves a hell of a lot of things, I've found."

"I'm *so* glad you're here, Aunt Olivia!" It was heartfelt, the one certainty in what had been said so far.

Olivia laughed and came round to lay an arm around Cathy's shoulders and give her a good warm squeeze. "I'm dying to see him," she said. "I just hope he won't be overpowered by Father and Eben."

"He won't," Cathy said, "even though I think they look on him as a specimen of something or other—the younger generation, I suppose."

"Yes, well, no doubt he looks on them as specimens?"

"Oh, yes, he does," Cathy said, smiling mischievously. "He's never seen anyone quite like Gram and Eben. He can't get over how they talk about real things, as Joel calls them."

"His own family doesn't?"

"His stepfather is an absolute straight, you see. He and Joel never did get on, and now, of course, this Dartmouth business has made it all worse. And his mother—" Cathy hesitated, twirling a glass in her hands, then setting it down—"I guess she's one of those women who complain all the time, and is terribly anxious about Joel, so she always needles him. They sound *awful*."

"Lucky thing for him that he landed at Ellen's, I must say."

"He just adores Nick."

"Good heavens, Mother told me to be sure to look at the potatoes—and the roast." Olivia fled to the kitchen, followed by Cathy. "Just run out and see if Father wants to be wheeled in, will you, darling?"

Cornelius insisted on wheeling himself in, but then the fire needed a new log, and Cathy went out to get a few more from the shed. The time for any intimate talk was past.

Eben walked in without knocking just as Christina was coming downstairs, in a long, soft, blue dress she had unearthed from a cupboard. He stood looking up at her, quizzically, and murmured, " 'She walks in beauty like the night.' "

"Don't be absurd. It's an old thing—years old."

"Not the dress, Christina—you."

Just then Olivia came out of the kitchen. "Oh, hi, Eben!"

"You and I," Eben said, slipping an arm through hers, "know beauty when we see it! What young girl can hold a candle to that?"

"She does look rather grand, doesn't she?"

Christina, still only halfway down the stairs, laughed her boyish laugh and felt awkward.

"I'm emancipated. Olivia has commandeered the kitchen. Come in, Eben, take off your coat, and come in to the fire. Cornelius will be wildly impatient!"

Eben insisted that he could at least be allowed to get the drinks, and for a few moments Christina and Cornelius were alone. He made no exclamation, but took her hand and kissed it as she sat on the arm of his chair, flushed and sparkling. They were caught like two lovers when Cathy staggered in with two huge logs.

"Goodness, child, you'll strain your back!"

"No, it's fun! Let me," she begged as Christina moved to get up. "Don't move, Gram. You and Gramp look so nice there." For some reason Cathy had tears in her eyes. She felt queer and shaky inside, and seeing her grandparents together in a moment of intimacy like the one she had witnessed by accident sent a tremor, a sort of pang, through her.

At last they were all settled with drinks, Eben standing back to the fire, Cathy on the bear rug as usual. She had been allowed a glass of sherry at Eben's insistence. "The child needs warming up," he said, giving her a keen look. "Spring air—it has a chill in it."

Olivia had stretched out her long legs on the sofa—slacks and the blue tunic she wore suited her. But Christina noticed how much gray there was threading through her red hair, and the lines of fatigue round her eyes. She was as tense as a coiled spring. They were all really suspended on the moment, waiting for Joel.

Before anyone else in the room heard the truck, Cathy had scrambled up and run out into the hall. The front door banged shut behind her. Christina got up from the arm of Cornelius's chair and went to sit beside her daughter. Cornelius and Eben exchanged an amused look, and Eben turned to Olivia to whisper, "The stage seems to be set. Where are the actors?"

"Don't make them into actors, poor dears," Olivia said with a quick frown. She was thinking that it must be hard on the young, the way grown-up people looked on love at this age—with something like merriment, with, at any rate, a superiority of experience hard to swallow.

" 'Poor dears'!" Eben picked it up with a flash of his old impatience. "They're young and in love. Must we *pity* them?"

294

"Where are they?" Cornelius asked crossly.

"Here we are, Gramp!" Cathy called as she opened the door.

She came in holding Joel's hand and took him right to Olivia, with a look of such shining happiness in her eyes that it was as if she came into the room bearing a treasure.

"This is Joel," she said. "My Aunt Olivia."

What Olivia saw was someone tall, very thin, with long fair curly hair over his collar, dressed in blue jeans and a red lumberjack's shirt. He gave her a quick, shy smile and went the rounds, shaking everyone's hand rather nervously.

"I'm sorry to be late," he said, "but we had to wait at the hospital—all sorts of papers to sign. It was hell."

"You could do with a drink?" Eben asked.

"Thanks. I'm rather shaken up. Bourbon on the rocks —but I'll be glad to get it, Mr. Fifield."

"You stay there!"

"Did Nick mind terribly?" Christina asked. "I mean, he didn't fight about going, did he?"

"He seemed bewildered, subdued . . . oh, I don't know." Joel sat down on the rug beside Cathy, leaning on one hand, rubbing the fur with the other. "How can you know what's going on in his head?"

"Will they be able to help him, Olivia?" Christina asked.

Eben caught the question as he came back with Joel's drink.

"How can a man be helped who's fighting the battle of conservation alone, and in a village that couldn't care less?"

He handed Joel his drink and took his own back from the mantel. Eben faced them now, his white hair like a crest, and dominated the room.

"The drugs will help," Olivia whispered to Christina. "They'll get him calmed down."

"But he has a *real* problem," Joel said intensely. "I mean it isn't exactly madness to care so much"—he was looking straight at Cornelius—"or is it?"

"Well"—Cornelius turned his glass in his hands—"my answer has to be that sometimes to care *too* much, beyond all reason, is madness."

"Why?" Joel asked.

"Because—at least in Nick's case—it leads to violence."

"It was very frightening," Joel admitted. "It happened

295

so fast. Nick, mild Nick, picking arbutus for his mother, suddenly like a wild animal. I suppose they've dug up that bank by now—he couldn't stop them."

"What you people forget," Eben said, "is that here in Willard wilderness has always been the enemy, from the beginning when the first thing a settler did was cut down the primeval forest, burn the stumps, drag the rocks out, and plant corn and potatoes."

"There were no potatoes in the eighteenth century, Eben," Cornelius said dryly.

"Right—you have me there. The point is that maybe it needs some violence to reverse what has been going on for two hundred years. Now we are beginning to pollute the clear waters of the lakes. Half the brooks are unfit for fish or soon will be."

"But you must admit, Eben, that Nick gets nowhere by attacking people!" Christina said.

"Yeats would answer you: 'Even the wisest man grows tense/With some sort of violence/Before he can accomplish fate,/Know his work or choose his mate.' "

As Eben looked around him in triumph, Joel got slowly to his feet and faced him.

"Say that again, will you?"

And Eben repeated it.

"I don't know," Joel said, rubbing his eyes as if to rub away what they remembered—Nick, savage, dangerous, not himself.

"I can't see why you have to be violent to choose a mate," Cathy said, and everyone laughed. "Why are you laughing?" she said. "It wasn't meant to be funny."

"Why are we laughing?" Olivia asked herself. "A good question, and, to be quite honest, I don't know why."

Cornelius leaned forward. It was the kind of conversation he most enjoyed, where some real idea got a grip on people and they spoke up. "Well, Eben, my interpretation of that passage of Yeats—and, by the way, I note you omitted the deliberately shocking first two lines, which run 'You that Mitchel's prayer have heard/"Send war in our time, O Lord!" '—my interpretation is that a man has to be knit together, and what does it is strong emotion."

"Oh, don't water it down!" Eben shot back. "I prefer to believe that Yeats meant exactly what he said."

"Can't a person be knit together by love *without* violence?" Joel asked.

" 'Some sort of violence,' " Christina mused. "That's not just *any* kind of violence, clearly."

"But violence," Joel said, "tears things apart—I really think so. It's . . ."—he searched for a word—"devastating. Nick doesn't want to be like he was. It's as if he had a seizure, I mean. He's not *more* himself, he's not himself at all!"

Olivia had been observing Joel closely. He was not all the "unlicked cub" that her father had described. In fact, he held himself well. He had a kind of natural dignity. For a second her eyes met Cathy's and she smiled, trying to say in a smile that she liked Joel, that she understood, but then she entered the argument.

"Gentleness won't preserve the wilderness," she said. "That's the trouble. So what will, Eben?"

Eben gave a short laugh. "Organization, hard work, going to meetings, writing letters—all things the good citizens of Willard flee from. The only time this town ever gets together as a whole is at Town Meeting. And why is that? Because every person there is out *against* something that may come up in the Warrant."

"You have a sour view, Mr. Fifield," Joel said with a smile.

"You're a tourist," Eben shot back. "Tourists see what they want to see."

"Joel works in the store—he's not a tourist." Cathy came at once to the defense.

"But he's in the first stages of love," Eben proceeded; then, seeing Cathy's blush, added, "I don't mean that personally. I mean he's in love with an imaginary village which he has seen, if I may venture an indiscretion, chiefly through the eyes of what we call summer people —young Cathy, to be precise."

"Don't tease, Eben," Christina said quite severely. "Let's have harmony and another drink—and someone had better have a look at my roast, by the way!"

"But why have harmony?" Eben flashed at her as he collected the glasses on a tray Olivia handed him. "Disharmony makes for better conversation!"

Olivia followed him to the kitchen.

"Yes," Cornelius said half to himself, "things have to be fought out to get them clear. I buy that. I'm for a certain amount of dissent and controversy. It's healthy."

When Olivia went out to the kitchen, Cathy moved over

297

to sit on the sofa beside Christina. Joel put another log on the fire, and Cornelius went on thinking about Nick.

"Isn't it, partly at least," he said, "that Nick is helpless because he feels very strongly but hasn't quite the capacity to think things out, to organize, to get some effective action going?"

"He's the natural man," Joel said firmly. "That's what makes him so great."

"So, for that matter, is Old Pete. I can't quite see the validity of the word 'great,' " Cornelius grumbled.

"But they're *real* and they really *live!*" Joel said passionately.

"What do you mean by really living?" Christina asked.

Joel frowned. "They notice everything," he said. "Nick knows where every owl and fox in the region lives—he can find them."

"He means," Cathy explained—for she could tell that Joel was about to get into deep water—"that most people never see the world around them."

"I mean most people lead joyless lives. Old Pete and Nick know how to enjoy."

"Maybe," Cornelius answered, "but someone pays for those joys. Irresponsible people have to be carried either by society, as in Old Pete's case (I understand it is costing the town and state welfare five thousand dollars to get him on his feet again) or by a single responsible person. Ellen sews her eyes out so Nick can follow an owl to its roost."

"But surely," Christina broke in, "it's possible to be joyful *and* responsible. They're not mutually exclusive, do you think, Joel?"

"Most people worry about paying off their car or their frigidaire, about the mortgage, God knows what! The middle class, as I know it in New Jersey anyway, hasn't any time for joy, they're so busy thinking about things they want."

"And the things are just a substitute, *ersatz* food, so they think they have to have more and more," Cathy said. "Don't you see?"

"No one as far as I know has posited that responsibility lies in having things," Cornelius said dryly.

"But I do see"—Christina turned to Joel—"that Nick and Old Pete represent something *real*. You know they do." she said to Cornelius. "Think what Old Pete has meant to the boys!"

"Escape," Eben said, catching the last sentence as he came back and laid the tray down on the coffee table in front of the sofa.

"Why is that bad?" Joel asked innocently. "Escape into something real like this country. Why do you say it with a sneer, Mr. Fifield?"

"Why do I?" Eben lifted a Machiavellian eyebrow. "I suppose because these are failed lives. We have got to a pretty pass, it seems to me, when the heroes of a generation (forgive me for the generality) are tramps or the like"—there was a moment's pause while Eben remembered just whose glass was where and handed it back to its owner. Christina shook her head at him as he handed her hers—". . . and I will not pull my punches, dear Christina."

Cathy and Joel exchanged an amused look, and she said, "We can take it, Gram!"

Cornelius stirred, lifted himself a little in the armchair.

"I want to hear what Joel has to say. After all, you came here out of the blue, Joel. You fell into Willard, so you see it with a naked eye. Ours are filmed over by years of contending with the local apathy. But you would make a great mistake if you imagined that we do not love it passionately. You do understand that, don't you?"

"And that although we grumble a lot," Eben added, "we really do not want anything changed. You find yourself in a nest of old conservatives."

Joel was feeling the effect of a drink after a day of emotion and anxiety and had sat down on the bear rug again, his knees clasped in his hands, rocking as he thought how to make his answer.

"You see"—he turned to Eben—"one thing is that we don't believe in heroes. We believe in people, just plain people, having a chance to live their real lives—as they don't, for instance, in the slums."

"Hear, hear!" said Olivia, coming back.

"What Willard is to me . . ." He leaned back now on his hands and stared at the ceiling. Then he smiled. "You have to remember that I am a city kid. At first the silence nearly killed me. At night I would jump out of bed when a frog croaked, because any sound was unfamiliar. Cathy teased me a lot, didn't you?"

"He wanted to eat a skunk cabbage," she giggled.

"Then, Nick and his mother were unlike anyone I had ever seen. They took me in, a perfect stranger. I never

299

felt at home at Dartmouth, you see, but I do at the Comstocks'." Then he remembered. "Of course now, without Nick..."

"Yet there must be some things you can't discuss with them," Cornelius ventured. "You are educated..."

"There's nothing you can't discuss with Ellen," Cathy said vehemently. "You know that, Gramp."

"I enjoy that woman. She's an original, as they say. I enjoy talking with her. But there are tremendous areas that simply can't be touched on at all."

"Like what?" Cathy asked.

"Well, foreign policy, or history apart from local history, about which I think Ellen knows about as much as anyone alive; philosophy in a theoretical sense..."

"But how many women anywhere know about those things?" Olivia asked.

Cornelius smiled, catching a look half humorous in Christina's eyes. She herself hated abstract discussions and had suffered at innumerable dinner parties where, she thought, everyone showed off.

"Anyway, go on, Joel," Eben said kindly. He was again standing by the fireplace.

Joel rubbed one ear thoughtfully. "I don't know what to say. I don't have the words like Cathy in her poems, but I guess Willard has given me a glimpse of what life might be like if success wasn't the criterion and if the society were less competitive and cheap. There's room for all kinds of people. I saw a lot at the store, and heard a lot, too."

"And they didn't talk about buying things—fishing gear, boats?" Eben teased.

"Naturally, but those things are for pleasure in themselves—I mean not just to show off—that you have a Cadillac and your neighbor just a Ford." He looked up at Eben quizzically. "You went away and came back, Mr. Fifield. I suppose—I must suppose—that you came back for a reason."

"Oh well," Eben said in a casual tone that masked his feeling, "my family has lived in my house for four generations—six if you count the old farm that burned down and that this house replaced. There are roots, my boy, and when you get to be my age, their pull is stronger than one would have thought at twenty. At twenty, I can tell you, I had only one idea—to get the hell out!" He laughed his ironic laugh.

"Do you think you could come and live here now, Joel?" Olivia asked gently. "I mean before you've achieved what you want for your life?"

"I don't want to achieve. I just want to *be*," Joel said with perfect self-assurance.

This sentence was galvanizing. Everyone shifted in his place, and before the reaction could explode, Christina suggested to Olivia that she and Cathy might serve.

"Bring your drinks," she said. "We can go right on in the dining room."

Joel was placed at Cornelius's right with Cathy beside him, Olivia on her father's left, and Eben beside her with Christina at the end of the table, on his left.

"Somebody light the candles," Christina said.

She had been quiet during the discussion, but now, at the foot of the table, she was the most vivid and commanding presence among them. And, quite unconsciously, she drank in the homage of Cornelius, of Eben, and of young Joel, who had stationed himself for the moment behind her chair in a sudden seizure of gallantry that she would not have expected of him, blue jeans and all.

When he sat down at his place, Cathy squeezed his hand hard under the table. Olivia was pouring the Burgundy.

"Shall we conjugate the verb 'to be'?" Cornelius asked.

"No," Eben said, "we are going to toast Christina before we do anything else or say another word." Silently he lifted his glass, catching a swift glance, half amused, not giving him what he wanted, before her eyes and Cornelius's met down the table.

Everyone at the table felt this glance in his own way. Joel had Cathy's hand in a firm grip under the table, her fingers clasped in his. Eben pondered how a marriage such as this creates a sort of loneliness around it—at least there is a space no one should try to cross. He had wanted to toast Christina to bring her close to him, her dazzling look. But it had not been like that after all. And Olivia, faced by Joel and Cathy opposite, and with her mother and father on either side, was thinking about middle age and how it is swung between young and old, and may be the period of life that asks the most strength of any. But she wasn't feeling sorry for herself as a single woman, as she might have even a few years earlier. She enjoyed her singularity and her freedom. There was in it,

301

she felt, the openness of growth, of deepening a self she found more interesting than ever before. This had all taken thirty seconds, and now Christina was busy carving, and sending plates down the table.

But Olivia was still considering—considering Joel, a little flushed, his dark blue eyes very bright. It was clear that he felt quite at ease here and didn't mind being the focus of attention, or being needled. Probably he was enjoying it—enjoying saying his say before Cathy's admiring eyes. He was not exactly showing off, but he was at ease with himself. And this was, as one thought about it, interesting, for, after all, he had left college, had no real job, and was about to be drafted. He would have had some reason to be bitter, Olivia considered, but was not. But of course he was in love, a state of delightful madness when all values have to be revised in that brilliant light.

"I've been thinking of what you said about being rather than achieving. Am I right in supposing that for you and Cathy being appears so rare that it becomes a kind of achievement in itself?" she asked.

"Nuts," Eben said.

"Well"—Cathy looked shyly up and down the table— "you see, Joel means achievement as the world sees it— making money, getting ahead—all that. We would like to join the Peace Corps or VISTA and work together when he gets out of the army."

"All very well," Cornelius said, "I presume you mean to marry. What about the child or children? Is it to be dragged to some primitive village with its parents?"

Cathy blushed and gave Joel a rather desperate glance. The talk of marriage, quite casual, had taken her by surprise. She was not prepared for everything to be taken so for granted.

"We're not even married, Gramp."

Cornelius chose to change the subject.

"Christina and I have experienced a winter of what you would call 'being,' I suppose, and I grant you that it has been very rich and wonderful." He gazed down the table at his wife and smiled. "But I have a sort of feeling that we earned it, through a rather long life of hard work, bringing up children, keeping them afloat, and so forth."

"But we don't want to wait till we're old, Sir."

"Instant being is what you're after!" Eben said.

"It's not only that," Cathy said. "We're not afraid of being poor."

"Of course. You're the children of the affluent society," Eben shot back, and Christina picked it up.

"Ellen *is* afraid. She has seen life cramped by poverty. She knows that it can be a blight."

Joel had been thinking his own thoughts. "You know why my generation takes pot?" He looked around, waiting for the attention of the whole table. "It's to take things easier, to relax and look at the beauty of the world, not worry about things that don't matter. When I first came, I wanted a smoke terribly. I was haunted for a while by the idea that I must have one. I guess I was still in a state of shock over the car and everything—what my stepfather would say. Well, then I met Cathy and got to know Nick and Ellen Comstock and began to explore Willard, and after a while I forgot all about smoking pot. You asked me before dinner what it was that really happened to me here, Mr. Chapman, and I've been thinking that that is one thing. Just the tempo here, just the way people behave, made me loosen up and look around me, I guess."

Eben shot an amused glance at Cornelius and then laughed aloud.

"Willard has been celebrated in a great many ways, but never, I think, as a substitute for marijuana!"

"No," Joel said, for the first time just a little tense, "I don't mean to say that. I mean that marijuana is a substitute for some kind of real living that goes on here. It's just the other way round." Then he added, "Most people are so nervous and uptight that grass is a real help to some sort of sanity."

No one had yet said to Joel that he would change his mind in time, and no one now reminded him that he had taken Nick that afternoon to the state hospital. It was not so much kindness—Eben at least was not always kind to the young—as that Joel seemed curiously invulnerable. And that, Olivia thought, is what innocence is all about. It is experience that tears us apart—and for good reason.

Christina quite deliberately changed the subject now, and, anyway, the evening had reached its peak, and fatigue was beginning to show. Cornelius, who had been deeply interested, had nodded several times and finally consented to be wheeled into the drawing room by the fire while the others washed dishes and got coffee ready. After helping all they could, Joel and Cathy slipped away into the spring night.

"I thought it would never end," Joel said. "I love you so." He walked fast as if he were taking her away somewhere at full speed, as if he could not wait to get there, wherever they were bound. "They're all so kind, but they don't really understand, Cathy."

"I know," she said. "You were so great, Joel. I was so proud of you."

They had reached an old apple tree by a stone wall. Its fruit was wizened and good only for deer, but every spring it was covered with flowers, a basket of bees and sweet scent and tiny red buds that opened to show bright gold centers—even in the dark, it was there, a white presence. Joel took off his jacket and they sat on it, on a big boulder. He held Cathy's head against him with one hand and kissed her hair.

Then he felt the tears, hot on his other hand, clasped in hers.

"What is it? Cathy, darling, why are you crying?"

She couldn't explain. It was, she felt, that as love grows deeper it tears apart, makes openings in the flesh. All she could do was sob, "I don't know how to live without you!"

"You'll write great poems, Cathy."

But this remark brought on more tears. "I don't want to write, I want to *be!*" She wrenched herself away and blew her nose. "It's all so complicated, Joel—I feel I'm being left alone among st-str-strangers." The word came out as another sob.

"Your Aunt Olivia? You told me she understood everything."

"Yes, but . . ." For a moment Joel held her hard against him and they were silent. The stars had come out since they had walked out of the house. Now the sky was pricked with light as the air, hazy at first, chilled and cleared.

They looked up. "It's calming," Cathy said, "isn't it?"

Joel's presence, so firm and healing, lifted her.

"I meant about strangers only that you and I are so close . . . I mean, everyone else seems miles away, because they don't know—they can't.—Look, Joel, it's stars on earth and stars in the sky." And it was really that, as they looked up through clusters of white flowers to those distant points of light. "Olivia has had love affairs, you see. I think there's someone now—a doctor—he's married."

304

Joel nodded in the dark. It seemed amazing that any-one so old could be in love, but he was ready to grant that Olivia Chapman was no spinster aunt. "Their hang-ups are so different."

"Explain," Cathy said. She realized that, since Joel, she looked at everything in her life differently, even her magnificent aunt, as she always called Olivia in her heart.

"They don't see that we—our generation—are responsible but in a different way. They think of supporting families, things like that, while we are trying to change the ethos. It was so typical of your grandfather to talk about *earning* a little time with his wife, as if he couldn't make that time before he was eighty and had a stroke!"

"The trouble is they inherited an awful lot," Cathy said. "It's hard—maybe next to impossible—to lay aside that kind of thing—houses, I mean . . . oh, all that goes with their life."

"Could you?" Joel asked, suddenly aware as he had not been before that Cathy was part of this world and she too would inherit.

"Easily," she said, laughing suddenly, "but you see, Joel, I'm only fifteen. I mean, I'm still free to be myself. You've got to help me not to get caught, darling. Poets can't be rich."

"Wallace Stevens was."

"That's right. I'd forgotten about him."

"Kiss me."

Cathy leaned toward him and put her two hands along his cheeks—cool hands, like two leaves—and kissed him very tenderly. After a while words frayed out, she had discovered. They just had to be silent to find out what was happening.

Then Joel shivered. After all, they were sitting on his jacket.

"You're cold. We'd better go back."

They stood for a moment in the road, drinking in the spring sky. Somewhere a bird sang a brief song. Then it was absolutely silent.

"The silence of Willard," Joel whispered. "Listen."

The silence opened up, opened up the farthest line of woods, the hills, opened up the sky—it was huge. It seemed to absorb love and grief and parting into some great whole. They took deep breaths. Then, very slowly, they walked up the hill back to the Ark, hand in hand.

"No, I won't come in," Joel whispered. "I want to

305

leave you here, darling," and this time he didn't kiss her but hugged her very hard and ran away down the road.

He had not told her that this was good-by. He would be taking the bus to New Jersey early the following morning.

CHRISTINA'S JOURNAL—*May 25*

The spring is simply tearing us apart. There is something so naked about spring here in Willard—late to come, waiting on the threshold for so long. But all so gauzy now, veils of pale green leaves, the structure of trunk and branch still to be seen. I feel so vulnerable. It is quite absurd. We have come through the winter, but we feel rather wan. We are survivors rather than victors, as Ellen said. There is so much to do in the garden and no Nick to help! But John has promised to come, and the Lovelands will come, one or other of them, if I get desperate. I feel that they represent a rocklike strength in this community. When all else fails, there they are, ready to take on hard work, ready to "help out." What would Willard be without them? They are the old world, the world of Cornelius's father. Soon there will be no more of their kind, rare as some rare wild flower being bulldozed away.

Joel left the night of our party. He did not tell Cathy, and I think perhaps that showed wisdom. Cathy has been a sort of lunar-pale self ever since. Long letters arrive and she stays up till all hours, writing poems she says. If there is anything enviable about being young, it seems to me to be the possibility of concentrating all one's energies. It is dispersal and complexity that kill us, the huge web of life we drag around, feeling the tug at this point or that—"do this," "help me," "where are you?" . . . But who can complain in this heavenly spring air? It tastes so clean and fresh!

While I garden, Cornelius sits on the porch with bird glasses. We are together as we were when reading by the fire last winter. Yet, as the spring rises, he ebbs. I sometimes think that in old age all change, even seasonal change, enters the marrow. The spring has made me see it—how much older we are, he and I, suddenly.

But "sap rises sweet even in old trees"—who said that? Was it Cornelius? There are moments when I am flooded with happiness. One came the other day when I saw a

306

pair of bluebirds in the road as I drove down to the village to see Ellen. I suspect that Cathy sees everything now in a halo of feeling about Joel, and perhaps one of the gifts of old age is that nothing stands between us and what we see. The bluebirds gave me a lift like love itself.

Olivia approved of Joel and reported back to Marianne that all was well. Cornelius believes that he has made Cathy blossom and become a real person in herself, but he has no faith in this thing between them lasting. He thinks Cathy was just a part of the excitement of Joel's discovery of Willard, and that his whole view of life precludes commitment, at least at this stage. I wonder what the army will do to him. Some of that innocence he wears like armor now will get pierced, that's sure. I wish Cathy could go through college anyway before making up her mind to marry him, but I shall not say so!

The Websters turned up the other day, like swallows, eager for all the winter news. Old Pete talks about getting "home" by August. They will fit his artificial leg this month sometime. He is brave and doesn't complain, although I have been bad about visiting him. He was concerned about Nick last time I went and talked of little else. "I should have been there," he said. "That boy had never seen him in one of those fits, but sometimes I could make him laugh. More than once I turned the anger away." But I fear this is an illusion. Of course we all live on some illusion or other, and Old Pete's has been that he is immensely useful in ways that he makes up as he talks. What does it matter? The shack looks lonely and it would be good to see smoke pouring out of its chimney one day again. But how could he ever live there on crutches?

The strangest thing about this spring is that Ellen seems not unhappy about Nick. I think the strain of waiting and being anxious, knowing that one day he would get into real trouble again, was a great deal more than any of us knew. Jem drove her over to the hospital once, just to make sure Nick was all right. Her comment was characteristic. "You know what hospitals are. A person gets swallowed up and the hospital takes over. Nick is doing some carpentry and seemed very serene. Couldn't tell whether he was glad to see me or not. Seemed interested chiefly in his dog."

She seems to enjoy her two days a week up here. It gets her out of the house, as she says, and is a change from the everlasting sewing. How grateful I am for the help!

I don't know why I have written all this down, as if it were a letter to someone interested in all our doings. I suppose gathering it all up for a moment does make me feel a sense of the whole tapestry of life, and not just a thread here or there. What Joel and Cathy cannot see is the struggle, of course. They see the reality of it all as beauty, wildness, and freedom—"escape," as Eben would say. When Joel thinks of Willard, he thinks of wild animals and untamed people like Old Pete and Nick. He doesn't see Cornelius's fearful daily struggle to get himself up and going, or notice that I have to lie down on one thigh to garden because kneeling is just not possible these days, or Ellen's poor eyes red from fatigue, or Ed Taggart when he comes in here—so rarely these days—absolutely frantic because he can't get help, or the fierce struggle Eben makes not to let loneliness eat into him. We know Eben better now than we ever did, I think. Under that surface of bitterness, there's something fine, a keen edge to his mind still. Cornelius has come to value him.

There *is* a whole tapestry here and sometimes I get the feel of it very strongly. But it is not a place for romantics like Joel. Even these naked spring skies, so immense, windy, tower overhead and make demands on the spirit. And the prayer really has to be, "Dear God, keep us tough, ornery, and self-reliant enough to live here," for it takes some doing.

PART FOUR

A Celebration

CHAPTER 1

Christina woke with a start to bright sunlight on the curtains, rippling like water, and drank in the air, still cool at six, although it would surely be a hot day. There was some reason to register on the weather—what was it? Oh, of course, this was The Day, Old Home Day, and a very special one as it was also the celebration of the bicentennial. Goodness, Christina thought, we have been climbing up to this day for a year, and now, as usual, I feel quite unprepared. She glanced at Cornelius, still fast asleep, then slipped out and went to the window to look down at a dragon tail of mist on the meadow, and then up at the mountain, dark glowing presence as the sun turned the rocky summit red. Perhaps somewhere in a hundred years there had been a rainy second Saturday in August; if so, it was the exception. It looked like a perfect day, yet this height of summer, when the green pressed in from all around like a jungle, was not Christina's favorite season in Willard—this season when the trees looked breathless, smothered in their leaves, and even the meadow, hay still uncut, had a formless overgrown look about it. The design goes, she thought, and except for the sturdy outline of the mountain, we are almost stifled by our rich thick green world. But then, she felt the heat—it did not agree with her. Wonderful to have this hour of peace. Wonderful that Hannah was there downstairs and no effort need be made for a while. How quickly I have come to take her help for granted, Christina thought with a pang. It was only three months ago—less—in June, when Hannah, homeless after Jane's house was sold, had agreed to come and help out with Cornelius, and to cook. Christina wondered how she ever would have managed this summer without her, as children and grandchildren poured in and out. Keeping the garden watered seemed alone to take all Christina's strength these days.

Downstairs a door banged. It was not in Hannah's nature to do anything unobtrusively—when she got going in the morning the Ark shook with her presence, especially as she seemed to get her own motor started by a burst of fury each day.

"Where are you, darling?" Christina turned from the window to see Cornelius's hand reach out to find her. His eyes were still closed.

"At the window. It's going to be hot, but glorious."

"Mm . . . glorious, eh? Come and give me a kiss."

"Now open your eyes!" she said, after kissing the lids.

Cornelius's face when his eyes were closed looked old and worn, but as soon as the brown eyes opened, she met the delighted, expectant gaze of a boy. People just waking up look so new, she thought.

Back in bed, she leaned against Cornelius's shoulder, and they lay there, wonderfully at peace, looking out into the bright world, waiting for Hannah to bring the breakfast trays. It was not a time for talking. Cornelius swam up into consciousness slowly, as if he needed time to take possession of his physical being, bit by bit. But Christina was wide awake, resting on him with perfect lucidity, feeling his heart beat against her side.

"Old Home Day," he said after a while, and sighed. "Between the haying and the harvest—the men could take a day off then, and no harm done. Before the Civil War the militia were mustered, and it must have been a great sight, a family picnic and parade all in one."

"Good heavens, Cornelius, you never told me that before!"

"Only just remembered it. Heard my father saying it at breakfast seventy years ago . . . there were muffins, but Sarah burned them, and Father was angry. I had to

310

wear button shoes and a Norfolk jacket . . . a sweltering hot day. At some point I disappeared and took my boots off and sat with my feet in the brook—delicious."

"And Willard, dear Willard, is two hundred years old. I do hope we shall do it justice, this day—that it won't all peter out."

"Why should it?"

"Oh, you know—it's all so casual and helter-skelter really."

"Fiddlesticks! Willard is not fond of pomp and ceremony."

"It does seem a pity that Jem's history won't be out though—after all his work. I have a feeling that Eben is going to steal the show—either that or go off on some wild tangent."

Cornelius chuckled. "Absurd woman. No one ever listens to the speech. What does it matter?"

"*I* shall listen," Christina said. "You're not in a proper state of mind," and she laughed with the pleasure of Cornelius's teasing mood, his joy in the morning. "Still, I hope Eben does well."

At that moment Hannah knocked at the door and bustled in with Cornelius's tray, and Christina disappeared into the bathroom.

"Good morning, Sir," she said, "and a fine morning it is, I'm glad to say."

"Ah, you didn't burn the muffins!"

Hannah frowned. "When did I ever? I never burnt a muffin!" She had blushed dark red.

Christina came to the rescue. "No, but someone seventy years ago on Old Home Day did and Cornelius was remembering."

"God bless Hannah, the non-burner of muffins," Cornelius said as Hannah poured out his coffee.

"Is everyone up?" Christina asked.

Sybille, John, and Alan had arrived Friday afternoon. Marianne, Bruno, and Cathy would be coming in time for lunch, with Mamzelle.

"No one's up except Alan. He's gone for a swim."

"Good, you'll have time to catch your breath."

"Sandwiches to make. Eggs to stuff," Hannah grumbled.

"The children will help."

"I'll thank them to keep out of my kitchen," she said crossly, and left the room.

Cornelius lifted an eyebrow.

Christina leaned back on her pillows, her arms behind her head. "It's a hard day for her, poor old thing. She misses Jane."

"She shouldn't address you in that tone of voice."

"Oh, darling"—Christina shrugged—"think what she does for us! It just rolls off my back unless I'm in a cross mood myself."

Hannah came in glowering, desposited the second tray on Christina's lap, and departed without acknowledging the thanks.

So, as usual, the day which had begun with that moment of pure peace, with the mountain at dawn, was already entangled and entangling, as one little thread of human concern after another was drawn taut. But if Christina had learned anything in the last months, it was to try to keep the momentum from accelerating too fast. The hardest physical job of the day was getting Cornelius up and dressed; it took patience and good humor, and in preparation for it she drank a second cup of coffee and lay back again, "for a little think" as Cornelius called these moments of intimate reflection.

She curled her left hand into his.

"What are you thinking about so solemn?" he asked gently.

"I don't know. I suppose how much tragedy is woven into these days of celebration—and how lucky we are, darling." She looked over at him now, her eyes suddenly full of tears. "I was thinking about Ellen, and Nick still in hospital. Ellen, Hannah, Eben—how many lonely people there are! The trouble is that on a day like this the dead are very much with us."

"Can't see that as a trouble," Cornelius said. "Too bad if they were not woven through our lives. I woke thinking about my mother and how, reserved person though she was, she blossomed on Old Home Day just because it was casual and she didn't have to make an effort. I can see her sitting on the grass, a white parasol open over her head, looking happy."

And one day one of the grandchildren will remember us, Christina thought—will remember Cornelius in his Panama hat . . . Why did this thought make her sad? There was an old phrase about "bringing to remembrance." Already Jane was taking her place among the

312

shadows. We may bring to remembrance, but we also forget. Often she could not remember her mother's face.

"No more dreaming, we have to live." Cornelius gave her ear a gentle pull to wake her out of this revery. "I think I had better get going, love—if you would help me up. The old carcass feels like a ton of lead this morning."

From the vantage point of her house, facing the green, Ellen did not even need to go out to keep an eye on all that was going on. She watched John, Ed Taggart, and two of the Lovelands busy setting up logs for sawing, and the greased pole, of course, too. Rather characteristically Willard appeared to be about to celebrate a bicentennial simply by being itself. The only change—and it was hardly radical—was the discreet presence of Jem's markers tacked up on trees here and there, to date the building of a house and name its original owners.

As usual a whole posse of children materialized from nowhere. It never ceased to amaze Ellen how many children turned up on Old Home Day—usually the village seemed to be inhabited only by the elderly. But there they were now, racing around in jeans, screaming like jays, gathered in a knot to watch Ed pour a handful of pennies into a heap of sawdust in one corner of the field. Buddy Townsend came along just then on a pony, leading a second one. He trotted round the green and back of the church, followed by two little girls pleading for a ride. A gang of little boys had taken over the speaker's platform, facing the church; then they were chased off by someone testing the loudspeaker, and retired to the Civil War monument just behind it, to scramble about on the granite plinth.

Ellen looked at her watch—after ten. They'd better get the games started. She had heard that there was to be a greased pig as a special treat—that would take some arranging. Nervous, on edge as always, Ellen took a dim view of the organizers so far. But what did it matter? None of hers would be coming this year. Micah and his family were down in Maine, and her daughter had to work.

Well, at least she didn't have to make sandwiches. Christina had invited her to join the Chapmans for a picnic lunch in front of the church. The summer people gathered there, while the natives preferred the long trestle tables set up under the maples at the side. Smoothing

313

down her fresh blue cotton dress, Ellen had to admit to a whiff of excitement. It would be a pleasant change to be a guest, for once . . . but how would Cornelius stand the heat? The shrill buzz of a cicada told her to be prepared for a humdinger—that and the absence of dew early that morning. She went upstairs and put a dab of lavender water on a handkerchief, then came down again, restless as all get-out. When she looked out the window this time, she did see an unexpected sight at last.

"For heaven's sake," she said to Foxy, snoozing under the table, "the Healds have brought Old Pete!"

Jim was taking a folding wheel chair out of his big Buick. She saw him hesitate as to where to place his charge, and Old Pete lean out and speak to him. Apparently Old Pete had decided that he would take up his stand in front of the schoolhouse, and there, a few minutes later, he was settled in. Ellen ran out to speak to him, but was stopped en route by Miss Plummer's hearty voice: "Greased pig this year! For the bicentennial!" and she doubled over with laughter. "Who would have thought it? Such an occasion!"

"Going to be hot," Ellen said, and moved on, leaving Miss Plummer to chaff John Chapman, now busily knotting rope in one of the big maples for the children to climb.

Miss Plummer looked up at him merrily. "Need some help? I'm raring to go."

John smiled. "No thanks."

Miss Plummer, he noted, had dressed for the occasion in a red-white-and-blue blouse and a straw hat with a red ribbon round it.

"You'll make us all spruce up, you look so grand and festive, Miss Plummer!"

At this she blushed and laughed. "Made the blouse myself," she said, and added, "put the flag up over the library door, too. How is it we have never had a flagpole in Willard? It's too queer," she said. "People would think nobody cared."

"Isn't that Old Pete?" John called down from his tree.

"Yes, isn't it wonderful he could come? Jim and Sarie went to the hospital and got him out for the day."

Meanwhile Ellen and Sarie were standing, one on each side of the wheel chair, deep in conversation with the old

314

man. He looked a little wan, maybe because no one had ever seen him with a close shave and so clean before. But his eyes had the same old twinkle, and he was eager as a boy, waiting to be made much of, to be noticed.

When Sarie went to join Jim, whose business at the moment was to get the big guestbook out for people to sign, Old Pete proudly pulled up his trouser leg and showed Ellen his light plastic false leg. "I'll be walking in a month," he said.

"Now tell me about Nick before all the others get here," he went on.

"Well," Ellen said, "he's in there. I don't know what more I can say."

"Seems pretty cheerful?"

"I guess so. Nick doesn't talk. But he's *safe*, Pete— that's something.

"They have all these drugs now, tranquilizers—they should let him come home." Old Pete felt around for a package of cigarettes in his pocket and lit up. "They won't let me smoke my pipe in the hospital." He spoke into Ellen's silence. "Won't seem natural without Jane Tuttle . . . without Nick . . ."

Ellen wandered off, unable to talk about these things that lay heavy on her heart.

Mrs. Townsend was busy setting out pies on a trestle table in one corner for the pie-eating contest, and before she was through Johnny Dole and Ed Taggart's son had got the three-legged race started, and over on the far side of the green the smallest Lovelands and all the other little children were hunting pennies in the sawdust. It was an odd thing, Ellen thought, how suddenly what had appeared to be a casual chaos of activities was pulled together. She wandered up to the church, and from there saw Pete surrounded like an old king by cronies and children . . . but where was Flicker? On her way home she called out to John. And John promised to fetch him as soon as he could.

"We didn't know Old Pete was coming," he explained. "Nobody told us."

Then Ellen went in. There must be a hundred people milling around now, she thought, and half of them I don't even know by name—all those people from the cottages. She felt suddenly tired and depressed, and on an impulse went up to the attic.

She had not been up there since the fall, when she had gone to unearth her grandfather's school records and her own. It smelled musty in the August heat, and under the roof it was stifling. She thought maybe she would just sit up there for a while, surrounded by all the mixed-up relics of the past; just sit and think about Willard, the old Willard of farmers—Comstocks, Lovelands, Townsends, the Willard of before the summer people. She blew the dust from a wooden trencher that must have come down from nearly the start of things here and held the soft worn wood in her hands. Haven't the foggiest idea what I'm doing here, she thought. Maybe just getting away in a private corner like an animal that wants to recover from a wound. But what wound was she thinking of? What particular one? Rufus always got drunk on Old Home Day—but she certainly was in no mood to remember their life together with anything but relief that it was over and done with. Still, as she thought these thoughts, she had gone instinctively to his old hunting jacket and buried her face in it, smelling its smell of musty tweed and leather. The fact was that she felt lonely. Might as well admit it. When loneliness crept in there was some comfort in taking one's stand backed by all the ancestors —her grandfather with his prickly whiskers, his sweet, haunting chuckle, and those shy Loveland blue eyes. She never saw one of the clan without a start. They were still farmers, dirt poor, but somehow they seemed to have the best of it. At least on Old Home Day they came together as a clan, won all the prizes, and knew the village as their own. She, with her children, moving up a notch in society —and Nick a cripple—she came to Old Home Day very much alone.

Rufus had let himself be vanquished by hard times, but her grandfather, never. "If we have apples, we'll make apple sauce, and if we have turnips and a bit of mutton from our own sheep, we'll eat well," he used to say. "They haven't got us down yet, Ellen, and don't you forget it."

"Only, Grandfather, I never thought I'd grow old," she murmured, leafing through a mouldy book of New Hampshire history that he had treasured. "Who does?"

Her grandfather had lived to be very old—over ninety. And he had died in the hospital, the flesh worn off his bones, suddenly refined of all the tough hard muscle in him and in his spirit. Only his eyes never lost their intensity. "Take care of Alice" were his last words to her, holding her hand in a hard grip. And that she had done. She had taken care of them all—her grandmother, her own mother, then Rufus, the children. She had done it and she had not been vanquished, but . . . what did it all mean? A hard life with loneliness at the end, and children who took everything for granted and went their own way.

Ellen wiped her forehead. It was terribly hot, stifling, up here in the attic. And it had brought her no comfort. The dead don't help the living much, she thought. Only the living can do that.

Willard? There was Old Pete, who had never done a lick of real work in his life, lording it like a king out there on the green—and that was Willard, she supposed, at least to people like Christina and her children, who enjoyed him as a "character" and who could afford the taxes he and his like cost the town. But Willard was Hannah too, wearing herself out for love, a born giver, her poor knuckles swollen with rheumatism. And Willard—she had to admit it as she got up and went slowly back downstairs into the brilliant sunlight in the kitchen, and sat down in the rocker by the window—Willard was Christina. It was hard to imagine what life would have been like without that something grand, generous, 'the beam of light that had made a saving difference . . .

Where were the Chapmans anyway? It was nearly noon. As Ellen looked out the window anxiously, the big bus was drawing up with the American Legion Band in it. Nearly noon—greased pig, Chapmans, and the salute to the flag still to come. The conjunction made Ellen smile her thin smile.

The Ark felt more like one than ever when the Chapmans were finally assembled on the porch, Flicker on a leash tied to the porch railing so he wouldn't run away, Mamzelle and Cornelius already settled in the back of Olivia's car, John and Hannah handing baskets, thermoses, and paper bags down to Christina to put in the jeep.

"Alan! Comfort! Cathy!" Sybille called anxiously.

"They can walk down," Bruno said. "Maybe have already, for all we know. Let's get going!"

Marianne ran down to join them, bringing Bruno's hat. "You'll need it, Bruno. It's terribly hot."

"Mother, you come with us," Olivia commanded. "John will drive the jeep down, and Hannah can go with him."

"You'd think we were going to the moon!" Christina said as she got in beside Olivia.

At last the caravan wound down the road to the gates, and as Eben trundled past in his jeep he blew his horn in greeting.

"Look at Eben," Cornelius chuckled, "he looks like a character out of Turgenev in that deerstalker's hat—the country gentleman."

"Handsome!" Olivia said, blowing her horn in answer.

After what felt to Christina like hours and hours of preparation, they were really off. Now at last she could enjoy herself, let others be responsible. As they drove down the hill, they could see below them what looked like a huge crowd—parked cars everywhere, and clusters of grown-ups and children in the road and all around the green, where preparations were apparently going forward to release the pig.

"Come on, Hannah," John said, pulling the jeep to the side of the road halfway down the hill, "we've got to see this!"

"Land's sakes, is that a pig?" she asked as they heard hysterical squeals coming from somewhere near a knot of people at the far end of the green gathered round a small pick-up.

While John took Flicker over to Old Pete, Hannah ran down to see what it was all about, and Olivia edged as close as she could in her car. The Websters came to say good morning and were introduced to Mamzelle, Cornelius just a little brusque, for they were obstructing his view. "It's the greased pig," he said. "Excuse us, please, but we want to see it."

"Where's Alan? Where's Cathy?" Sybille asked for the nth time.

"Who cares? Come on," Marianne said.

The children were getting impatient. They were a form-less huddle at the moment, each one tense with anticipa-tion and, perhaps, just a little fear—as if the small ter-rified animal about to be released were a wild boar.

"It'll be one, two, three, go," Ed shouted on the bull-horn. "Are you ready with the pig?"

But a greased pig is hard to control. The two boys who held him let him go before Ed could give the official word. There was a wild scramble, the pig was entirely obliterated by the rush, and no one saw anything at all but a herd of children running. Then came screams of laughter and despair as the pig, intoxicated by his freedom, and terrified, slipped through their legs and made a dash out from the green, under Olivia's car and up the hill.

"After him!" Ed shouted, laughing so much himself that he could barely speak.

About twenty small boys went skedaddling away after the pig, while most of the little girls grinned and giggled and swarmed around to watch the chase, so the car was surrounded, with people leaning on the hood, turning to greet the Chapmans inside.

"It is disorganized," Mamzelle said crossly. "It is a fiasco!"

"You take a dim view of the escapade?" Cornelius teased. "Nothing makes for greater chaos than a greased pig. I call it a wild success!"

The leader of the Legion Band was now trying to marshal the crowd to stand at attention for the salute fo the flag. But after two tries for silence, he decided to give up till the pig was caught. And long before that Olivia had nosed the car around to the side of the church, so that Cornelius could be helped out and his wheel chair placed away from the hullabaloo.

Christina left Sybille and Marianne and Bruno to get everything settled and walked off to see Ellen. Halfway across the church lawn she stopped for a second, her painter's eye ravished by the scene—the bright dresses, a boy's red shirt in the foreground, the Legion Band in blue and gold, and, as background, the old red school house and the white Town Hall. It looked like an American version of a Breughel, even to the pig, now being hauled back on the end of a rope, he and the little boys charging down the hill together.

The roll of the Legion drum preceding the salute to the flag broke the spell, and she walked on quickly, anxious to get away to Ellen and not be caught, stopping only to look back and wave at Cornelius and the little group by the car and calling to them, "I won't be long!"

"Oh, Ellen," she said, pushing open the door, "I came to walk you over. But let's sit down for five minutes. It's been so long!"

"Do sit down. You must have been running all morning getting everything ready."

"Yes"—Christina sank into the rocker—"I'm all out of breath and in a whirl." She looked up and met Ellen's eyes—and held back an exclamation. Ellen looked ten years older, suddenly. I suppose I do myself, she thought. But we don't see ourselves. Not in the same way.

"You look peaked, Ellen."

"My eyes are tired. Finished up a tedious job for the Palmers last night."

"I wish you could stop. Can't you one day?"

"Wouldn't know what to do with myself if I did—that's the trouble."

"But when Nick comes home . . ."

Foxy, asleep under the table, pricked his ears and got up sleepily to wag his tail at the name of his master.

"No, Foxy, not yet, dear." Ellen patted his stout white side. "They don't tell me anything. How do I know?"

Christina got up and went to the window, where she stood looking out.

"Jem's day," she mused. "I'm so afraid he will be disappointed. He's worked hard . . . He's out there now, saluting the flag." She could see him, hand across his heart.

"Don't know what he expects," Ellen said quietly.

"A thundering good speech about our wonderful ancestors for one thing—and I doubt if Eben will see his way to producing that."

"You know why they asked him, don't you?"

"Any special reason?"

Ellen chuckled. "Just so they wouldn't have to ask the Governor! That's what I heard. The committee didn't want an outsider and especially not a politician."

Christina threw back her head and laughed. Then, after the relief of a good laugh, she sighed. "Oh, Ellen dear, I feel as if I had lived through the whole two hundred years myself, I'm that tired these days"—she wiped a tear from her cheek—"and I don't really know whether I am laughing or weeping. It's a queer sort of day, this bicentennial. I feel unaccountably depressed."

"What's it all been for, that's the thing," Ellen said, still at the window. "When I got up this morning, something made me go up to the attic—terribly hot up there these days—I felt stifled by the past. That's the word"—she repeated it with satisfaction—"stifled."

"What is it? They had so much hope and faith maybe . . . and we lack them . . . is that it?" Christina looked down at her hands, so like her mother's, even to the

320

thickened joint in the little finger. But it was of Ellen's mother that she spoke. "Your mother seemed to wake every morning to a fresh creation. How she looked at everything! Remember when she made us get up to see a ruffed grouse walking its stately walk across the grass? How bright her eyes were!"

"There was a kind of sparkle about her . . . I don't know . . . sprightliness." For a moment Ellen allowed herself nostalgia, then she cut across it sharply. "I feel depressed because it seems to me we're a whole lot less than they were . . . the way your mother took your father's breakdown . . . it looks to me as if we *manage* but they *triumphed*. I wonder why that is, Christy?"

"Oh, I've been famished for a talk!"

Christina got up and put an arm round Ellen's slight shoulders. She felt as slender and frail as a bird.

"We must go," Ellen said. "Cornelius will be wondering where you are."

"Let them finish the national anthem"—for "The Star-Spangled Banner" was opening the Legion's before-luncheon short concert. "We'd only have to stand at attention, so we might as well be here."

She was thinking about Ellen's question. "They saw things plain and clear in those days, maybe. They were simpler at heart. But then a lot got buried and festered, I guess. My father made himself ill trying to live up to impossible standards of honesty and good faith in a cruel business world. And now, I suppose, the psychiatrists would be able to help him, and all those drugs they use . . . Surely Nick will be sent home soon, Ellen. They know so much more now."

"Maybe—but he'll never get over caring about the animals, Christy, and I'll never get over worrying."

"Come along, what we both need is *food!*" Christina got up and took Ellen by the hand. "And we must find Molly Goodnow. Eben is here somewhere, but they may not have seen where we are."

It was strange, but as they came out from the darkness of the house into sunlight and leaf shadow, the checkered pattern of bright colors, and many faces, Christina felt a lift, was suddenly transported into the celebration, the sense of holiday she had not before been able to feel. She and Ellen walked fast, in spite of the limp.

From his station by the schoolhouse, Old Pete, who noticed every arrival, narrowed his eyes and watched them. It brought to mind that day in the autumn when they went off together on a walk up by the brook and over the hill and he had watched them go. They now stopped to talk to Jem a moment, then moved on up the slope of the church lawn, threading their way between the groups of people, and Old Pete turned to Eben standing beside him to say, "They don't make that quality anymore—they are the last. When they go, Willard won't be the same."

"But I can remember my mother saying that very thing about the crazy Miss Townsends, and I expect it's been said by someone in every generation since 1769," Eben said.

Old Pete chuckled. "But the Miss Townsends were crazy —crazy as loons."

As he chaffed with Old Pete, Eben's mind was really on Christina, as she and Ellen joined the group around Cornelius in his wheel chair. Watching her like this from a distance, he saw how much older she looked. And her limp was worse, too. He realized for the first time that he was looking at a frail human being who would not live forever, and it hurt.

"What are you going to do when they let you out?" Eben asked, his eyes following the band as they took up their stations at the other side of the church from where the picnic tables were set up.

"Where's Flicker?" Pete asked—perhaps he hadn't heard—"did you see him go?"

"No, but I'll have a look." Eben was glad of something to do. "Can't be far off."

Old Pete lit a cigarette. In spite of all the old friends, the children, the warm sun on the back of his neck, Old Pete felt low in his mind. The actual meeting with Flicker, to which he had looked forward as the true "Old Home" part of the day, had been a letdown. Flicker had barked joyfully and jumped up to be petted, but he did the same thing for nearly everyone he saw, and Old Pete was not at all sure he really knew his master. Then, instead of lying down obediently by the wheel chair, he had lit out for the hill road after the children and the pig and vanished.

"Darn dog," he said crossly. It ruins a dog to have too many masters; John had said that Cornelius and Flicker got on like old friends. Well, let them keep him then. Everything was at sixes and sevens. He'd heard Eben all right, asking about what he was going to do—well, he hadn't answered on purpose . . . For it was in Old Pete's mind to come back to his shack, only it would take some help and some thinking out. And he wouldn't be able to hunt Flicker, that was sure.

The cigarette didn't taste good and he threw it away. For a while he was alone as people gathered their children up for lunch and families got settled at the tables, opening thermoses and unpacking picnic baskets. Jim Heald was talking with Jem on the church steps . . . Had they forgotten him? And where in tarnation had Eben gone? No sign of him or Flicker. The old man felt nervous and on edge. That was the trouble when you looked forward to something too much—it never could quite come up to expectation. "Darn dog," he muttered.

"Must go down in a minute and rescue Old Pete. Don't want him to get sunstroke," Jim Heald was saying to Jem.

"It's hot." Jem wiped his neck with a huge linen handkerchief.

"A fine day, Jem. Couldn't be better. You must be pretty proud of having got this whole affair swinging."

"The book's going to be all right if the printers and binders ever get the job done. I've had my moments of anxiety, I can tell you—the prevarications, the delays. Luckily Cornelius's photographs alone will sell it even without the text. I expect to break even."

"And of course everyone in the cemetery will buy it," Jim said, putting an arm round his old friend's shoulders. It was only a way of speaking—of course he meant people with families buried in Willard, but it brought a twinkle to his eyes just the same.

"Still, it's an ornery town, Jim, as you and I well know. And as for today . . ." Jem shrugged. "No one on the committee asked my advice about anything—just went their own way."

"What about fireworks at the pond? Was that dropped?"

"Too expensive."

"Oh well . . ." Jim soothed, as was his way with his old friend. For under his ponderous manner and immense weight, Jem was broody. "The book will last. What's all this bustling about compared to that?"

They stood looking out over the green and were silent as the band struck up "Yankee Doodle."

When it was over, Jem sighed. "They're smart and all that, but I miss the old band. Remember? From Highfield. Half of them were elderly ladies, and it was just dandy to see one of them with the cymbals or the xylophone." Jem chuckled. "And the big brass wheezing out 'The last rose of summer'! Oh well, the Legion's smart, all right."

"Must go and get Old Pete," Jim said. And he went off, pushing through knots of people, to look for Sarie; found her spreading out lobster sandwiches, and told her he was bringing Old Pete up.

Just then Eben came around from behind the church and cried out, "Flicker, you faithless creature!" for Flicker was lying beside Cornelius's chair, his nose on his paws, asleep. "Old Pete's asking for his dog, poor old fellow."

"You'd better take him on the leash and tie him," John suggested.

"Will do."

"And then come back," Christina called after him.

It was really rather foolish to have decided to make a picnic out of it, she thought. Mamzelle looked exhausted already, sitting on a folding campstool, and she and Cornelius towered over everyone else, sitting or lying on two steamer rugs. John was pouring martinis into paper cups, which Alan passed.

"What is that?" Mamzelle asked, sniffing it suspiciously.

"Sh," Alan teased, "it's a secret martini. Dr. Park would not approve."

"Oh well, he's over by the tables surrounded by dear old hens," Olivia said. "Aren't they marvelous? The Misses Tucker look exactly as they did when I was ten years old. They haven't changed at all, except maybe to look a little smarter every year. Miss Ruth has on a magnificent hat. Did you see it, Father?"

But Cornelius was watching Eben approach, flushed by his exertions, the heat, and the excitement.

"Here the conquering hero comes!" Cornelius shouted, lifting his paper cup in salute.

"I'm a mass of nerves. Give me something to drink, Alan."

He stood beside Cornelius.

324

"Nervous about saying a few words to old friends?" Cornelius chaffed.

"Naturally," Eben answered. "What's more terrifying? There is hardly a person here who doesn't remember some awkward or foolish thing I've perpetrated in my time."

"No fool like an old fool," Molly Goodnow remarked.

"She puts me in my place," Eben said. "You see?"

"We might have done better to sit on the church steps," Christina murmured to Olivia. It was a moot point whether Hannah and Molly Goodnow would ever be able to get up again. "But we'll move to the benches for Eben's speech, after all."

"If this crew had sat on the church steps, it would look as if we'd taken over," Cornelius said. "Dr. Park would hardly have enjoyed that."

"Sit down, Eben, for heaven's sake," Christina admonished. "Cathy, will you pass sandwiches? That's a dear child."

"What time is it?" Eben asked. "My watch has stopped."

"It's just after one," Cornelius answered.

"Then it hasn't stopped. Time has simply decided to stand still. I feel it is mid-afternoon."

"Relax, Eben," Christina ordered. "You must save your strength."

There was now a pause in the banter while everyone dealt with sandwiches and cups of coffee and stuffed eggs. Cornelius, in his superior position above them all in his wheel chair, felt happiness flowing through him with the martini. He looked around, at Mamzelle, pink under a big straw hat (a pink mouse, he thought, smiling very sweetly at her), then at Sybille and Marianne, on one rug near her stool. Bruno, imperturbably "square" as always, had gone to sit on the church steps with his lunch rather than sprawl on the rugs. Hannah and Mrs. Goodnow were close to Christina, and Eben had now joined them. John was still moving about with Alan, seeing that everyone was served. And Olivia and Cathy were settling down on a rug a little way off. The big brasses caught the sunlight under the maple trees—the Legion was relaxing. Some of the men had unhooked their hot blue tunics, and the leader had taken his off. Beyond them, children were still running about in a rather fierce game of tag, in spite of the heat. Cornelius's happiness flowed from the sight of

325

so many dear people of all ages enjoying the day together. The Chapman group made a kind of island of their own, yet they were joined in spirit with all the other families and friends scattered about. It was a precious moment, and he savored it to the full, forgetting to eat his sandwich, looking across to catch Christina's eye and smile his joy in everything to her in a single beaming telegram.

Of course the wonderful thing was that Old Home Day *was* always the same. There might be a cruel, stupid war in Vietnam, but Buddy Townsend was taking his friends on pony rides, and under the maples the changeless old ladies traded a year's news. It was deeply nourishing, Cornelius considered, that in a world of such immense changes (he saw two girls in dresses well above the knee, crossing the green) a few things did not change at all. Was it only the old who wanted this sense of continuity? No—he looked across at Cathy, deep in conversation with Olivia, who had stretched out her long legs in white slacks and was leaning on one elbow chewing a piece of grass—no, he thought, my grandchildren have to have somewhere to come back to from the wars, and Willard is as good as any place I can imagine. But his happy moment of contemplation changed to anxiety as he noticed Eben pouring himself a second martini. That, Cornelius feared, was not a good idea. He caught Christina's eye.

"Don't have another, Eben," she said quietly. "Have a sandwich."

Eben lifted an eyebrow and obediently poured his second drink onto the grass. "A libation to the gods of Willard," he murmured, "and to the goddesses, Christina" —he sat down beside her—"even when one of them behaves like a nanny."

"I'm sorry . . ."

"No, you're quite right, of course. Two drinks never did a speaker any good. One is essential, but two . . ." He smiled. "I might praise the wrong things if I drank two martinis!"

"You might lose your temper," Christina said. "You know what an ordeal it is, with cars going by, children running about. You are prepared, I trust, for something less than total attention?"

"Oh yes," and Eben smiled quite happily. "I'll really be talking only to *you*, you know—no one else really matters—to you and Cornelius."

"Well, you'd better please Molly," Christina teased.

"Indeed he had," said Molly with dignity. "Goodnows have gone to every war since the Revolution, for two hundred years."

"Molly, don't make me nervous," Eben said, reaching for a sandwich. "All I can promise is brevity."

Now the groups from the trestle tables were starting to move onto the lawn and find places on the long benches in front of the speaker's stand, and among them several came over to greet Cornelius. Mamzelle too was congratulated on being there, by a woman she didn't recognize but who turned out to be "little Helen" whom she had tutored in French one summer thirty years before. Helen, it appeared, now lived in Cleveland and had a little Helen of her own. Her husband, the Reverend Harrington, whom she had met in Willard, had been asked to give the closing prayer.

"And you came all that way to join us?" Mamzelle asked in her querulous voice. "I must say it is admirable."

"We *wanted* to come, Mamzelle! Our dream is to buy a little bit of land here and build. We want to retire to Willard some day." She stood beside Mamzelle, looking out on the whole scene and smiling with pleasure. "It's so beautiful!"

"I can't see why these modest buildings set around a green excite such admiration. After all, they are not architectural treasures." Silenced, Helen moved off.

But Cornelius had caught the characteristically negative comment and couldn't resist teasing the speaker a little. "But think how cold a French village is in comparison! A long street of closed houses behind high walls, a hideous Town Hall, a few cafés—can you really call this ugly?"

"It has a certain rural charm," she conceded.

"Oh, Aunt Olivia," Cathy was saying, "what is wrong with me, do you think?"

They had been talking about Joel, of course. Cathy had read aloud part of one of his letters because she found it impossible to explain why she was dismayed by their endless flow of rapture, as if he simply refused to look at the experience of the army at all, gliding over it and talking about imaginary worlds he and she would make some day.

"Why? There's nothing wrong with not liking something."

"It seems disloyal." Cathy looked miserable.

Olivia glanced at her quizzically. "It's not a crime to fall out of love, darling."

"If he walked in now—came and sat beside me, I'd *know*. But his not being here is so strange . . . I mean what absence does . . . it's as if he were fading . . . fading away. That's what's so awful, Aunt Olivia."

"I have an idea it's not he who's been fading but you who've been growing up, awfully fast. It may be, dear heart, that you've outgrown Joel."

"But I don't *want* to!" Cathy said passionately. "Besides, he's four years older than I am. How can I outgrow *him?*"

"It doesn't have much to do with age." Olivia took a bite of sandwich and swallowed before she went on. "People grow up at such different rates—at such different ages . . . and stop growing, too, at different ages. You had an awful lot thrown at you for fifteen. Maybe it was all too quick. Maybe you have to catch up with yourself and haven't outgrown Joel at all."

But this reversal on the part of the magnificent aunt only added to Cathy's anguish. "How am I to *know*, Aunt Olivia?"

"Only by living it through."

"But that's so hard. He's upset now because I've stopped writing poems. He keeps asking for poems—and somehow it's stopped. I don't feel the way I did."

"How did you feel?"

"I felt torn up, my whole body opened, not mine anymore. I felt as if I were being born again."

Olivia gave her niece a thoughtful look. They were strong words and they had a ring of absolute truth about them.

"You were lovers then?" she asked gently.

"Oh no!" Cathy shook her head vehemently. "It all went on inside me . . . but I couldn't . . . I wasn't ready . . . I guess I was scared of having a baby."

She looked up then, terrified that this last remark might have been heard. But everyone was absorbed now in collecting cups or in talking with friends and neighbors. Olivia and she were the only two still lying on rugs.

"Joel is so warm—such a loving person, Aunt Olivia. How can I help wanting him, wanting to love him?"

"I guess you can't, angel. But you have time, that's the

328

great thing. I like Joel. You know that. But I felt he was terribly young still."

"If only he doesn't get killed!"

"Well, so far he hasn't even been sent over. Try not to worry till you have to."

"It's horrible not being grown up and not knowing."

At this Olivia laughed. "If you think love gets any easier after you're grown up . . ."

"I suppose you've been in love . . ." Cathy hesitated as if she were about to take a dangerous dive into unknown depths ". . . more than once?"

This was the thing she needed to know because of the absolute atmosphere Christina and Cornelius created around them and their faithful love. Was it just some terrible weakness of character or lack of depth that could make one change as she felt she had changed?

"Yes," Olivia answered crisply, "more than once."

"Didn't you feel guilty?"

Olivia frowned. "I suppose so . . . sometimes. We have been brought up to believe that any change of heart is immoral. But I am sure it is part of growing through a lifetime to love more than once."

"Not Gram!"

Perhaps fortunately, at this moment Dr. Park called out through the loudspeaker: "May I have your attention, please . . . please . . . the ceremonies are about to begin."

"Thank you," Cathy whispered.

Olivia lit a cigarette and didn't move for some minutes. She was thinking that perhaps the most painful part of growing up was the having to accept that there are no absolutes. Whatever her parents shared of loving partnership now in old age, she suspected that even they had been through some hard times, and she was well aware that Marianne, her own sister, had dreamed of escape. As for John and Sybille, theirs had been a crippled marriage from the start. Cathy was very young for all this to land on her. It was certainly a piece of luck that she had stood Joel off . . . and it must have taken some doing. But who am I to speak, Olivia thought, I who have made a mess of every deep relationship in my life? It was not the time to think of Sasha . . . or Will . . . or dear Ben. Once more she heard Dr. Park insistently calling for order.

"Order our thoughts if you can," she murmured as she got to her feet and joined the others, finding a place be-

329

tween John and Alan on one of the long benches. She sat, her hands clasping her knees, apparently listening, but she could not keep her thoughts away from the dangerous subject on which they had embarked—herself. One thing was sure, she was not intact. She was wide open to feeling, whether it came from some poor woman struggling to bring up a family of seven with a ne'er-do-well husband who came and went, or whether it came from Cathy, or whether it came from Ben, deeply in love but tied to a neurotic wife by weakness and by guilt. The flow of life seemed to be always in the hands of the sinners, those on the rack for one reason or another. The good, like her father and mother, but especially her father, were like deep wells, but brooks and waterfalls in their impetuous course were nourishing also, poured themselves into the main currents of life. Only very lately could Olivia have said such a thing. She had stopped castigating herself for what she was not and had begun to accept what she was—a sign of maturity perhaps.

"What's happening?" she whispered to Alan, who was sitting very straight and looking very owlish in his huge black-rimmed round glasses.

"Nothing, as usual," he grinned. "Dr. Park is apparently testing the loudspeaker."

Eben now made his way to the platform and sat down in one of the three straight chairs. Jim Heald was already sitting in one, riffling through papers in his hands. Three little girls sat on the steps in front of the speaker's stand, giggling. Christina hoped someone would ask them to leave before the speech.

It was very hot. Eben pulled out a handkerchief and wiped the back of his neck. Christina reached over to take Cornelius's hand. His wheel chair was drawn up beside the bench where she was sitting with Mamzelle on her left, and Hannah and Molly Goodnow were farther down.

People were still moving about, finding seats. The church steps were filled. A newcomer—at least Christina didn't recognize him—was busy signing the book. As a matter of fact there were dozens of summer people she didn't know. Many sat on the grass, and behind the speaker's stand children played, and some of the old men sat on the bench in front of the Town Hall, preferring their own tales to any speech they might hear. Would

Eben be able to hold the attention of this scattered audience, however brief his speech? At the moment, head bent, he looked so frail. Mamzelle seemed to be asleep under her hat. It was a moment of numb suspense—foolish to feel so anxious. Extraordinary how just holding Cornelius's hand in hers made the whirling world focus again, centered and balanced everything.

Dr. Park launched his prayer like a rather unwieldy boat, and little by little managed to hold it steady on its course. It was, as always, terribly long, and, as often, rather tactless as he begged them to consider and emulate the virtues of the ancestors, among them those who had taken up arms to defend their country in the Revolution, the Spanish War, the Civil War, World Wars I and II—unlike the present generation, some of whom at least had proved themselves to be cowards. Christina gasped. She couldn't think of a single conscientious objector in the village—the more shame, she thought. But even so, the bicentennial prayer was surely not the place for this. She exchanged a glance of dismay with Cornelius. Eben glanced up, caught her eye, and winked at her shamelessly across the bowed heads.

At last Dr. Park's boat reached its destination, the Lord's Prayer, which everyone repeated with him. Then heads lifted and a quickening breeze of relief stirred among them.

Jim Heald got up next. He praised Jem and the history still to come, and presented him with a scroll, emblem of the town's grateful thanks. Jem came lumbering forward like an elephant, rosy with the heat, fanning himself with his straw hat, while everyone applauded.

"Evidently he's not going to be allowed to speak," Olivia whispered to John.

"Jim Heald is a wise man," John whispered back, while people settled down again, a few stopping Jem as he made his way back to his seat, to shake his hand; others fanning themselves as they prepared for the chief event of the day, resigned now to sweltering in silence. Jim coughed three times, then brought his gavel down hard. A mother ran out to capture a wayward infant, and somewhere a baby gave a howl. Finally there was something like silence and he was able to introduce Eben Fifield, the local boy who had come home after bringing honor to Willard in a long and distinguished career. Eben listened with one hand covering his face.

331

Oh dear, Christina thought, the suspense is awful. Poor Eben. Suddenly she was so nervous she could hardly listen. But something in Jim's tone brought her attention back so she did catch his little joke at the end. The committee, it seemed, had voted unanimously to ask Eben to be the bicentennial speaker "because he is brilliant, indiscreet, and totally unpredictable. I have no idea what he is going to say, but I can promise you that, unlike many a bicentennial speech, it will not be boring!"

Eben roared with laughter and put an arm round Jim as he acknowledged the chuckles of amusement and the clapping. Standing there, his eyes very bright, he managed to exchange a look with Christina, as if to say, "the bad boy is going to have some fun, and you can't stop him now."

It was quite a send-off, Christina was thinking, but also a precarious one, and she wondered how Eben was going to handle it. But there was no time to worry—he was off and away before the audience had quieted down.

"One thing about Willard," he tossed into the air, hardly raising his voice to be heard, "we don't take any chances. Jim has covered himself against almost any eventuality except my sudden death."

His brilliant smile roved around the audience, and slowly faded as the laughter died down. Eben was facing the church, of course, and now he looked up at it—the sturdy white pillars, the strong façade—held it in a long, long look, a theatrical pause, to command attention.

It was perfect except that the three little girls on the steps below him were still giggling and whispering, and, in the silence, *they* controlled the atmosphere. Christina exchanged a look with Cornelius.

Eben glared at them, waited a moment, and then leaned down and told them icily to go somewhere else, and if possible somewhere facing the speaker. Children on Old Home Day were traditionally permitted almost anything. These looked amazed, but, recognizing a command, slithered off and sat down on the grass facing the stand. Christina glanced apprehensively around at the crowd, so scattered, disparate, and, above all, so hot. It was a perilous moment. Would he have antagonized his audience?

Eben himself was perfectly aware of the danger of a fumble. He gave a quick look in Christina's direction, but she had turned toward Cornelius. Well, he would make her listen, by God. He put on his glasses, then held the lectern firmly in his hands and began to read in a loud voice. It was rather like pushing a very heavy weight ahead of him, word by word, and he felt already exhausted, as if he hardly had the strength, the actual breath, to dominate the scene. Yet he must. Nothing in his life had mattered more. At first he spoke too fast and knew it. The words tumbled out—

"The celebrations to mark Willard's *centennial* closed with an adjournment for a hundred years. It was 1869. Thirty thousand New Hampshire men had left their homes to fight in a terrible war, and only half their number came back . . ." Did it sound like every other speech on such occasions? Yes, Eben told himself, it did. He hated the words he had written and wished he were anywhere but here, miles from the end of the journey, struggling to be heard.

"However brave the women had been, however hard they had worked, four years of neglect turns land back to wilderness." He lifted his head a second and met Christina's intent gaze full on. It was as if his lungs filled with air, as if he were lifted on her listening. His very tone of voice warmed.

"Not without reason did Erica Portland choose to design the window in our library as a phoenix. The little town of Willard has died and been reborn more than once." At last, at last, he was in the stream, carried along, and he felt it instantly in the kind of attention he could command. Now he could afford to pause as he turned a page.

"My theme," he said, taking them all in, "is change and essence. We have come together today from many parts of the country—Reverend Harrington all the way from Cleveland—and we are people of all ages. I see Mrs. Gramercy among us," and for a moment he looked lovingly at the very old lady in white, leaning on her cane, in the front row, as she smiled and gave a little wave. "She is nearing the century mark herself. And I see among us Peter Loveland, who is only a few months old." Some of the audience turned to seek out Anne Loveland with her infant son on her lap. "We are rich in them, and in all those we bring to remembrance—especially, today, Jane Tuttle, whom Willard has lost this year."

The name was greeted with a ripple of emotion. At that moment, one of the small boys scrambling about on the Civil War monument just behind Eben lost his balance and cried out. Christina held her breath. Eben turned sharply, took in what had happened, recovered himself, smiled, and went on:

"No doubt one of the small Alpine climbers behind me will grow up to bring us cheering to our feet for some great exploit to be. Jane Tuttle may have left us, but the young are coming on strong."

Spontaneous applause greeted this graceful way of handling a trying interruption, and at last Christina relaxed. Eben had got into his stride, had achieved his balance. He would be able to handle whatever might happen. It was going to be all right. She smiled—and he caught her smile before he turned back to his text.

"If memory binds us together, let us not allow it to fence us in. What was two hundred years ago a tight Scotch-Irish community, God-fearing, hard-drinking,"— Eben lifted his head with a mischievous smile, well aware that the town preferred not to admit how much drinking had always gone on here—"industrious, an agricultural community founded chiefly on sheep-raising—that community has changed radically. As I look at your faces, I rejoice that we have become, in the last hundred years, a far more interesting and varied society than we have ever been. The Willard I want to celebrate is not that Willard of two hundred years ago but the Willard that managed to absorb disaster, the failure of farms and then of stores, shops, mills; and, in its second century, recovered by welcoming an invasion of outsiders."

Here Eben paused and looked around him. What is he driving at, Christina wondered.

"It was fitting that when, in 1869, the centennial celebrations were adjourned for a hundred years, they had recorded chiefly, and paid homage to, the rural virtues of the frontier and to the courage of the boys and men whose names are engraved on the monument behind me. I believe that today, on the two-hundredth anniversary of 'this brave and beautiful Willard among her rocky hills' (as the centennial speaker called her), it is fitting that we celebrate the marriage of us natives with the world outside, the fertile union of the old stock with summer people." At this point Eben caught Christina's eye and gave a little laugh. "What would Willard have become without this rich influx of life at the turn of the century?" His eyes were full of mischief. "Isn't it true that these strangers met the ornery ways of us natives with superb courage and stamina?"

Eben gathered in the murmur of amusement and leaned on the lectern, relaxed and obviously enjoying himself. He was not reading any longer; he was enough at ease to forget the text.

"The summer people came, built big houses, employed local labor, cleared away second growth, paid taxes to keep the roads open—those charming dirt roads we curse in mud season but that many a horseman blesses in summer. The summer people gave Willard a blood transfusion at the critical time when—who knows?—without it the patient might have died. A few of them—I invoke Miss Morse, for one—gave years of their lives to bettering the village school. One of them, Erica Portland, endowed our library. Twenty years or more ago they helped Willard become a center for the revival of folk dancing, and longer ago than that one of them, Judge Chapman, helped a farm boy go to college. His name was Eben Fifield." Eben gave a quick glance in Cornelius's direction, then went quickly on. "The summer people enlarged the life of Willard in a hundred ways . . . What did Willard have to give them?"

Eben addressed this question to the row of Chapman children and grandchildren. Cathy leaned forward intently, and he caught her eye and smiled, as if they shared a secret.

"Well," Eben said, "some of you last spring made the acquaintance of a young rebel who turned up here by accident after totaling his car. Joel Smith was reversing the journey so many young men made in the nineteenth century. He escaped *from* Dartmouth *to* Willard." Eben waited for this little joke to sink in, as Cathy blushed and looked down at her hands. "This endearing young man fell in love with our town and found it a great deal more human than college had been. He seemed to believe that he had learned more in a few weeks here than he had in nearly a year in classrooms."

"Hear, hear!" someone at the back called out. And suddenly everyone was laughing and clapping with the pleasure of this quaint slant of Eben's. But now Eben was dead serious, leaning forward intently.

"You see it was not only the town's people who touched this city boy but, even more, the town's closeness to the secret world of nature. Joel could not get over the wildness of our woods, the presence of skunks, raccoons, deer, even a few wildcats—of woodcock, partridge, ruffed grouse. Joel came here with his eyes wide open and took it all in. And this boy (who is now in the U.S. Army, by the way) really made us all sit up and take notice of ourselves, of the continuing creation of Willard, of the *quality* of life here. There is the *true* history of Willard. Each of us carries a different version in his heart. It is a secret history, composed of—what?"

Eben stole a quick look at Christina. Was he going on too long? "No" he read in her intensely concentrated attention. And once more he let himself relax, slow down.

"Maybe you have an idea the old fellow is about to dig up some gossip, eh? Well, the secret history I have in mind *is* very personal, but not in that way. For instance" —Eben straightened up with a faraway look in his eyes— "there is a spring day sixty or more years ago when a boy caught his first trout, using a homemade fishing rod and having played hookey from school . . ."

There was no pause now, and Eben felt a wonderful flow of sympathy and attention, so he could take his time.

"Or the day when Jem's father at eighty climbed our mountain—or another day when two of the Lovelands chose to be married on top of it. Yes"—Eben nodded and smiled at the applause directed toward old Ma Loveland —"or the autumn afternoon when Old Pete met a wildcat . . . or the day when a spirited young teacher called Ellen mastered some pretty noisy boys, taller than she was, in the old brick schoolhouse behind me . . ."

Christina leaned over to catch her friend's eye but Ellen was sitting bolt upright, in her sheath of pride and shyness, and did not respond.

"Or the day when Susie Plummer came back from China and set to work to make our library a place where children would love to come and read . . ."

Eben gave Miss Plummer a salute with one hand and again applause broke out. It had become a game, Christina thought, of recognizing and savoring what they all suddenly felt to be precious and true—but now again the tone changed.

"Or the day," he said gravely, "when Jane Tuttle took four or five small boys and girls for a walk through the woods and taught them how to listen, and smell, and look, and eat a mushroom raw, so they came home hardly aware of all they had learned about the planet we live on, in a single hour when they had, perhaps for the first time, truly paid attention."

Now Eben hesitated. It was not a theatrical pause this time, and Christina, close to the pulse of his nature, guessed that he was deciding whether to leave it there or—

Suddenly he lifted his head and went on.

"Or let me call to remembrance the day when I brought my wife home. She had not long to live—we knew that. We were truly 'coming to stay.' For a moment before we went indoors, we stood and looked up at the house my great-great-grandfather built, then out over the meadow to our mountain. A pair of bluebirds flew in at that second to have a dust bath in the road not more than five yards from where we stood—one of those moments, you know, that one does not forget."

Eben coughed and wiped his neck with a linen handkerchief.

"Time I got back to my text," he said. "Must end things right"—and he shifted the papers around to find what he was after. "Here you are!" He looked up with a whimsical smile, then read:

"You expected me to speak of history today, but I feel sure that the way to Willard, the road in, so to speak, is not by knowledge but by experience. The place itself enlarges the heart, and that is because of all of you, because of all those others who have been part of Willard for two hundred years, every single one, who have helped make it what it is for all of us. That is the essence. Joel Smith sensed it. And Robert Graves, the English poet, says it in these lines. Listen—

'The untameable, the live, the gentle.
Have you not known them? Whom? They carry
Time looped so river-wise about their house
There's no way in by history's road
To name or number them.'

There are no saints here, although Joel Smith told me solemnly that Nick Comstock is one because of his extreme caring for the natural world around us. No, there are no saints in Willard, but we carry, each one of us, some intimation of Mystery, whether we are believers in the usual sense of the word or not, some extra dimension,

337

some godliness, because we live close to a mountain, close to woods and streams and lakes and among trees, and because we stand often in the presence of this great church."

Once more, as he had at the very start, Eben looked up at the strong façade before him, and Christina felt that the audience, though their backs were to it, followed his eyes to the spire itself.

"God help us," he said, "to preserve this Willard for the *next* hundred years." Then he returned to them. "I want to thank you all for listening, especially three little girls in the grass in front of me." He smiled down at them. "You were a great help."

There was a second's pause, as if they were still listening, as if no one could believe that Eben had finished. Then the applause broke out loud and strong. Cornelius rapped his chair with his hand in his enthusiasm. "Bully!" he shouted. And Christina flashed an ovation from her shining eyes as she lifted her hands high to clap on after many had stopped. Eben, flushed, got up to take a bow and shook hands with young Harrington, who had come forward to the platform to give the closing prayer. Jem, on his way to congratulate his old friend, was stopped halfway and stood, his head bowed, a monumental figure.

Young Harrington ran a finger round his collar, bowed his head, and waited what seemed a very long time before he spoke. Olivia whispered to John, "Wasn't it great!" then looked around for Cathy. It had been an inspiration to bring Joel in, reaching out to the future in such an imaginative way.

At last Mr. Harrington's bowed head restored silence, and he spoke:

"Dear Lord, on the two hundredth anniversary of this dear town of Willard, we have witnessed your spirit among us. We feel rich in the presence of wisdom and of love, and we have been truly blessed. Amen."

Old Pete leaned over to one of the Misses Tucker beside him with a mischievous look. "That young man came a long way to say very little, it seems to me."

Jim Heald was now back at the loudspeaker to finish the ceremony by naming the youngest and oldest present, and the one from farthest away, who turned out to be a guest of the Websters from Buenos Aires. He stood to be greeted and applauded, and wiped his brow in evident embarrassment.

"In a few minutes we shall have the pleasure of listening to the Legion Band again, and the conductor has asked that as many of us as wish to sing along. Debby Loveland is passing out folders with the words of the songs. We must thank Miss Plummer for this splendid work at the mimeographing machine."

But by now the audience had broken up into small groups, and the applause was scattered. A knot of people gathered round the speaker's stand to congratulate Eben, young Harrington among them.

"What could I say after that?" He shook Eben's hand. "You were great."

"Well, my boy, you are a rare preacher—one who knows when to hold his peace! But I think we all feel a little cheated and—here, Jem," Eben said, pulling Jem by the sleeve, "what about asking Mr. Harrington to come and speak to us next summer, eh? We can't let him go like this, mute and inglorious."

"Splendid! I'm all for it," Jem said. "But I want you to know, Eben, that we shan't find your match easily. I confess I had my doubts about the committee's choice." He gave a sly smile. "You've always been an unpredictable critter, but you did us proud. I couldn't get hold of a copy of what you said and print it in the history, could I? We're in proof, but I see no reason why we couldn't rush this in—a perfect climax."

"Oh, I hardly think so," Eben said. He was dripping wet from the strain and the excitement and the sheer effort of making himself heard. "It's not written down—just notes."

"A pity we didn't have a tape recorder," Mr. Harrington said. "Couldn't you write it out, Mr. Fifield? I'm sure everyone would wish to have it preserved."

"We'll see . . . we'll see . . . I am honored . . ." Eben felt suddenly very tired. He must still stand and shake hands with dozens of old friends and acquaintances. But he kept looking off to find Christina. Where had that woman vanished to? It was her word he craved, her presence he needed. And it was damned hot. But he couldn't escape—a very old lady who he finally realized was old Mrs. Tucker, an aunt of Ed Taggart's, must first be listened to.

"I wanted to tell you dear boy, my Willard moment,"

she said, her eyes very bright. "I was a little girl, and a plain one, and Judge Chapman came by on his gray horse—do you remember that splendid animal?—and he lifted me up and took me for a ride, holding me in front of him on the saddle. I felt like a queen!"

"What a splendid story," Eben said. "Thank you for telling me."

Just then the Websters and Olivia broke into the group around him and he was caught in a net of praise, just seeing, out of the corner of his eye, John helping Cornelius into the car, and Christina and Mamzelle moving toward it.

"Excuse me," he said, suddenly frantic. "I'll be right back," and he hurried toward them. "Christina!" he called, forcing her to turn.

"Oh, Eben!" she cried. "I'm coming back, but Cornelius is feeling the heat, Mamzelle too. John will drive them home. I'll be right there—you were *marvelous!*"

And Cornelius shouted, "Bravo, Eben!" from the car.

They got away just as the band struck up "The Star-Spangled Banner." As if it were a game of blind man's buff, the melee of excited happy voices was stilled, and the casual groups congregated round the church steps and over the lawn were stopped dead—"still pond, no more moving." Eben, who had managed as long as there were demands on him, suddenly felt dizzy and longed to sit down.

"Where can we go?" he asked when at last it was over and Christina slipped an arm through his. "I'm spent, Christina. Just have to sit down and be quiet for a moment."

"The church," she said. "Come along, we'll sit there in the cool and recover."

"Genius," he murmured, following her obediently, but stopped at every step or two by someone wanting to congratulate him or speak to Christina. It was quite absurd to be running away like this, his heart beating as it had fifty years ago, just to have a moment alone with her. But he was tremendously excited by his own performance, by the day itself, by all that he had himself just evoked. He was not quite normal—far from it. He felt he was about to explode.

"At last!" he said. It was stunning to come from the commotion outside into the huge silent church. They sank onto the bench at the back, a bench where Eben had often chosen to sit as a boy because he was out of sight there and could be as restless as he pleased.

"Yes, at last a little peace and quiet." Christina leaned her head back against the wall and closed her eyes. Eben looked at her. Without the shining blue of the eyes, how gaunt her face became! He was suddenly shy of staring at her, so exposed and unself-conscious—and turned to look out through the great rectangular windows at sky through maple leaves. It was a second filled with emotion. And then it was gone. Christina opened her eyes and the light flooded back.

"I'm so proud of you," she said. "Cornelius wept. You know how he is these days. He was overcome."

"I did it for you," Eben said. "You know that, of course."

"Dear foolish man—of course not. You did it for Willard. Don't be absurd."

"I *am* absurd."

"It was marvelous how you touched us all, bringing in the Lovelands, dear Nick, Ellen—but the real stroke of genius was Joel."

"Yes"—Eben straightend up—"I was pleased when that thought came to me. Glad you approve." He looked at her quizzically. "But the best thing I did was to thank Judge Chapman in public. Waited nearly fifty years to do it. Couldn't have done it until now."

"Why not?"

"Well, I suppose because it has taken this winter— taken you and Cornelius becoming winter people . . . taken . . . oh, I don't know . . . a new kind of intimacy (with him as well) to make it possible for me to handle old resentments and old wounds—to grow up, in fact"— and suddenly he laughed. It sounded fearfully loud in the empty church. The silence boomed it back. "Dear me," he whispered, "has anyone laughed in this church before?"

"I'm sure God is delighted, even if Dr. Park might not be. But what made you laugh aloud?"

"Oh, just the idea that a man seventy-five still has some growing to do."

"Pleases you, does it?" She mocked him with a lifted eyebrow.

"We're not dead yet, old girl."

Christina looked around a little shyly toward the doors. "Do you suppose anyone saw us come in?"

"Two aged citizens exhausted by the heat? No harm surely . . . You forget, darling, how very old we *seem*."

Christina was dismayed to feel a blush creeping up her throat. She half rose, but Eben pulled her down again with a brusque gesture—brusque and masterful.

"Give me five minutes, Christina. I really have something to say."

"What is it? You make me feel quite nervous," and she laughed a whispery little laugh.

"It's this . . . you know for years I had this idea about writing a secret history."

"You did that so beautifully about the Willard moments."

"That's not what I mean at all." He sounded quite cross. "My original idea, the one I hugged so long, was to tell the things no one thinks about when history is written —how much violence there is under the surface, how many drunks and human cripples a town like this carries and has always carried, how cruel and even sordid life is most of the time."

"The dark side of the moon—of course it's there in any town, in any place where human beings bumble along together. If you think that's news to me . . ."

"That's not what I'm getting at now. Listen." Eben leaned his head against the wall and looked up at the pulpit thoughtfully. "Lately I've come to have a different view—or to look at it all from a different angle. Now I would talk about secret history, the history of any place or person, in terms of passion, those areas where something floods up that we cannot control, but"—he reached over and laid his hand on hers—"Christina, darling, it is sometimes that that feeds all the rest."

Christina turned her face away and withdrew her hand.

"Don't be frightened. It is just what is deeply felt but never expressed in action that I mean. You and I made good marriages—we were lucky. You know what Olive was and is for me—the gentle, restraining, and life-giving hand. Without her, I might have foundered."

"Dear man."

"No, I'm not dear at all. But if I say 'wildfire' you know what I mean. Between you and me there is fire. There always was and there always will be. It burned so brightly today that I hardly dared look at you from the platform. Yet because you were there, and I so aware of your presence, the thing worked. I was able to do it. You see? You understand?" He turned to her and waited for a sign, and slowly, without looking at him, she nodded her head. "What is young love compared to this—this incomparable truth of old age—that nothing dies, all is transformed?"

It was uttered with passionate conviction and drew from her a little exclamation of assent, of recognition.

"There"—Eben got up with one of his quick changes of mood, and looked down at her smiling—"I'm an old fool, but I wanted to say it just once. Don't be sorry."

"Oh, I'm not sorry," she flashed back, "elated—and a little puzzled."

"Why?"

"I suppose between 'wildfire,' as you call it, and Willard itself. You seemed to make a connection. 'Secret history of a place' you said. I don't quite follow . . ."

"Maybe 'wildfire' isn't quite right about the place as a whole, but you must grant that something stronger than reason, some wildness, some passion that goes beyond the usual, *is* there in the people—in Ellen's pride, in poor Nick's violence, in dear old Miss Plummer's picking up to go to China—that sort of thing."

"Yes, I begin to see."

"It's the brooks in March, something fierce and unpredictable in the climate itself, cursed climate, but it keeps us alive." Eben rubbed his chin and frowned, and Christina waited eagerly for his thought to form itself. "And the fact that here in Willard we have time, Christina, time to know what is happening to our secret lives—time to know they exist and are terribly real. That is what Joel sensed, you know. He was an intuitive son of a gun."

"But weak," Christina surprised herself by saying. "Cathy feels it."

"Not weak," Eben shot back, "a chameleon—he took on the color of Willard while he was here. How else do you learn? Hard to be young."

"Easier to be old, you think?" And Christina got up to face him. "I *hate* being old!" Then he saw the blue fire in her eyes for the first time since they had come into the church, that flash like a jay's wing.

"I might have said that until I saw you come up the road last autumn, limping a little, Christina—but since then I find growing old rather an adventure."

She gave him a quizzical, tender, amused look. "Come along, let us go and find Cornelius."

"Yes, I need to be praised," Eben said with a touch of irritation.

"Oh dear, haven't I praised you? But I couldn't get a word in edgewise!"

"You'll never say what I want to hear!"

"Wait and see. Maybe when we are eighty and I feel quite safe . . ." and she slipped an arm through his. Outside, they stood together on the church steps and joined for a moment in singing "America the Beautiful."

Marianne, leaning against a maple, Cathy beside her, lifted her head from the page of words she was following and saw them, held for an instant like an intaglio in her gaze, Eben with an air of triumph, his crest of hair standing up so he looked more hawklike than ever, and Christina, her arm slipped through his, looking up at the sky and the leaves overhead with a curious smile.

"They look happy," Cathy said, "don't they, Mother?"

"Triumphant," Marianne agreed, and gave Cathy a quick look. The word had slipped out. And who are we to grudge the secret joys of the old, she thought . . . yet, she found them slightly disturbing. Everyone except one's mother could be allowed a love affair . . . but surely it had never come to that. It was only that they lit each other up, and had done so, she supposed, since they played tennis together eons ago. She vaguely remembered her father speaking of Eben as a bad loser—one day he had broken his racket and walked off the court in a fit of pique.

Beside her Cathy's birdlike voice, clear and very pure, was singing away, so perhaps she had not noticed, really. But when the brassy sound came to an end, she said, "Eben behaves like a very young person, but Gram is old and herself and that's better."

"How better?"

Marianne was constantly amazed by this child of hers. Since coming to Willard, Cathy had grown up so fast that Marianne felt she hardly knew her, felt curiously humble beside the open-eyed, intensely aware person standing there. My child and Bruno's? How did we ever do it?

"I'm trying to write a poem about it . . . old age . . . I don't know what I meant exactly except, maybe, that Eben is great but he always seems to be reaching out as if something were missing . . ."

"Olive is missing. He's lonely, of course."

344

"Gram is complete," Cathy said. "I mean, whole."

Just then Christina saw them and came over to explain that she was on her way home with Eben—would they like to drive up with her? Marianne would. Cathy wanted to stay to the end, and then to drop in on Ellen for a while. As Marianne and Christina moved toward the car, Cathy held Eben back a moment. She had been thinking so much about Joel ever since the speech, she felt she must say something now, must test her feeling about Joel against his—try to make peace with herself.

"If only Joel could have heard what you said about him. He's so far away."

"Not overseas, is he?"

"I meant far away from what he was like here. He's still in basic training."

"The army must be quite a shock," Eben said, but his mind was on joining Christina. He was not really paying attention, not prepared for the intensity, the tremor, in Cathy's voice, the appeal he sensed now as she spoke.

"If only he had the courage to be a conscientious objector! In his last letter he said, 'We are being taught to kill, kill, kill!' How *can* he?"

Eben rubbed his eyes as if to rub fatigue away. "I'm too tired to make any sense, Cathy. Come up and we'll have a talk one day."

"But how can he let himself be changed into a murderer?" Cathy asked again. "And he sounds quite happy! How can I ever find him again—the Joel you talked about?" The mature woman who had astonished her mother a few moments before had slipped away to leave a bewildered, passionate child. "Sometimes I think he likes the army!"

"Men like war, Cathy." Eben reached out and put a hand on her shoulder as if to mitigate the cold words. "I don't have much comfort to give you, do I?"

"I don't need comfort. I want to understand."

Christina had come back, impatient to be off, but Cathy was not to be stopped now. She stood there, small and intact among them, like a judge, and Christina had to listen as she pursued Eben relentlessly.

"You said a lot of good things about Willard as a gentle place, but there's killing here too. Old Pete thought it was a joke to fling a dead woodchuck on our front doormat—do you remember, Gram?"

"Yes, I remember," Christina answered. "It made me

345

sick. But I expect that was sentimental—woodchucks do a lot of damage."

"Sentimental?" the voice quavered. And Cathy turned away.

"Well, darling, it was a rather poor joke, I admit." She stopped a second to give Cathy's long fine hair a caress, and to whisper, "Talk to Ellen," then, turning to Eben, she said firmly, "Come along, we really must go."

Cathy watched Christina and Eben hurry off, her mother already in the car—she felt far away, cut off, lonely. Was Gram able to keep going because she had learned to shut things out? Cathy wondered. Was growing up a matter of learning to close doors on the unbearable? She leaned against the trunk of a maple, off to the side, and sang with the rest because that seemed as good a way as any of waiting to feel more able to cope.

It was another half hour before the band gave its last brassy toot and crash of cymbals, before the big drums were lifted away, and the men scrambled into the bus and left. The crowd dwindled, calling last good-bys as they got into their cars. Old Pete had gone long ago, and even the children—the few still playing on the green—were subdued by the heat. Cathy didn't see Ellen anywhere, so she cut across the meadow, where a few Lovelands were still shooting arrows at a target, and over to the Comstock place, running the last few yards as if she couldn't wait another minute. She flung open the door.

"It's me—Cathy!" she called.

"Come right in, child."

"Thank goodness you're here," Cathy said, sitting down in Nick's chair by the table and pushing her hair back. "Oh, it's *too* hot!"

"There's a pitcher of iced tea in the frigidaire. Pour yourself a glass and bring me one, will you?" Ellen had a box of spools of thread in front of her and was winding loose thread. "I'm in a tangle here—thought I'd tidy this box up for something to do."

Pleased to be useful, Cathy poured carefully and brought the two glasses over and took a long swallow before she sat down again with a sigh. "Delicious . . ."

"Too many people for you up at the Ark?" Ellen asked.

"Not exactly."

For a long suspended moment, they sat there, the old woman and the young girl, and neither needed to say

346

anything. This was Ellen's way—to hold her peace and let people talk when they were ready to. You can cage the spirit with a word too soon, she was thinking as she wound blue silk thread onto a spool.

"Don't know why I bother," she murmured, "it's so knotted."

"Is it true that men like war?" Cathy asked then.

"I expect so." Ellen bit off a knot and wound the end back on the spool. "Or they'd find some better way to make peace." She smiled at what was perhaps meant as a joke.

"It was nice what Eben said about Nick." This remark was not answered, and in the silence, a two-way silence now, Cathy wound a strand of hair round one finger, then unwound it before she finally said, "I'm all mixed up."

"About Joel?"

"I guess so . . . about everything . . . Aunt Olivia says it's all right to fall out of love, people grow up that way . . . and Joel now seems to like the army. At least he doesn't revolt. And Nick maybe *is* almost a saint, yet he gets into terrible rages. I just feel nothing is clear or whole. It's all little bits and pieces of right and wrong. I'm scared."

"You're not the first," Ellen said grimly.

"Who is trustable? All the time Eben was talking I was thinking what if a bomb fell out of the sky and blew us all up? That's what happens every day in Vietnam, and we sit around complacently saying what a wonderful place Willard is!"

"Yes," Ellen said. "Well, people would hardly have been pleased if Eben had chosen to speak against the war —the Wayland boy is over there now."

"Oh, I know!" Cathy shook her head. "I know I am being childish. It's awful to be fifteen."

"Fifteen has clear eyes. You see a lot you can't understand or do much about."

"Sort of like Nick."

"It isn't saintly to my way of thinking to care more about animals than people," Ellen said. She had been thinking about Eben's praise of her son; she had not been convinced. "People are harder—I mean, harder to understand."

"I'm way off somewhere alone," Cathy said, "way off from Joel and way off from Mother and Gram and Grandfather too . . ."

"Well, you're still part of the human race," Ellen said with a laugh. "You asked who to trust a while back. I've been thinking that in the long run one can only trust oneself—and even so, one is wrong to do that maybe half the time," and she laughed again.

"The reason I love you, Ellen, is that you are full of darkness," Cathy said.

"Darkness?" Ellen lifted her head, surprised.

"I mean you make everything sound worse, not better —so in a queer way, it is comforting."

"Poor kind of comfort, I should think."

"No, a good kind. It's tough. Nothing like some tough comfort to chew on." And at last Cathy smiled.

"Eben had a point about what summer people and natives exchange besides hard work and money, and maybe tough comfort, as you call it, is one of the things we have to give. I wouldn't know why such orneriness was a help, but maybe it is."

"How does one learn to trust oneself?" Cathy asked. She was standing at the window now, her back to Ellen, looking out on the garden patch, weedy without Nick to keep it in order.

"Want me to come down and work in the garden some day?"

"Looks like hell, but it's too late to trouble." Ellen laid down the box of spools and took a drink of cold tea. "Pretty hot day to find the answer to a question like that. Never saw such a girl for asking questions!"

But Cathy knew that there would be an answer if she just waited.

"I *have* to know, Ellen," she said earnestly.

"And maybe that's my answer—you learn to trust yourself when you have to—when there is nobody else you can trust. I guess I learned it when I faced that schoolroom of children, about five boys taller, and some older, than I."

"How old were you?"

"Sixteen, and scared stiff."

"What did you do?" Cathy sat down again.

"Hit one boy on the head with a ruler and drew blood," she said grimly. "Mostly I kept them at bay by . . . I don't know how to say it . . . by being sure I could —and keeping my eyes open. I was quicker than they were, even if I was ignorant."

"You were brave."

348

"When your back's against the wall—well, what else is there to be?"

"Some people might have run away."

"Where to? I lived here. One thing I'll say for Willard, the women never did run away—some men did. But then, it takes another kind of guts to admit failure and try something new. Men have that kind. Women are better at taking what comes, rooted where they are. Men . . . well, they take risks."

"You took a risk by staying with those brutish big boys."

"Nothing to the risk I took by marrying Rufus—but then I didn't know when I married him what the risks would be. That, I guess, was when I really learned to trust myself—against him. It's one thing, Cathy, to face violence outside, but it's another to face it inside, at home." She lifted her head with scornful pride. "Eben chose to talk about the secret history of Willard in one way, but he might have chosen to talk about it in terms of drunkards who terrify their children and beat their wives. Marriages are battled out behind closed doors— and not only mine, many in this town."

"It's all wrong," Cathy said passionately.

"Yes, I would have said so, too, at fifteen."

"And now? What do you say now?"

"Now I say one does what one has to do. One lives with what one has chosen. And one doesn't complain."

"Eben talked about mystery . . ."

"The mystery is we go on living. The mystery is we still want to."

"Sometimes my Uncle John doesn't want to."

Ellen lifted her head and gave Cathy a straight look. "Nick and John are sick. You can't judge by the sick."

"But what *made* them sick? They are the two wisest men I know. Why are they called sick?"

"Something lacking—they react in different ways but neither is tough enough to stand reality."

"Then we have to change reality," Cathy said. "Joel and I are going to help change it, so kindness will be *real* . . . if . . ."

"If?"

"If the war doesn't change him." Tears flowed down under the long hair with which Cathy covered her face.

"Now I've made you cry. A fine comfort I am!"

"I'm c-c-crying because maybe it's not Joel who's

349

changing but me . . . I feel so mixed up. Nothing stays the same." She came over and stood by Ellen, perhaps because, although she was not conscious of it, she knew that Ellen did stay the same. Here was a rock. "His letters are full of dreams, but somehow I don't believe in them any more—that's what's so awful."

"He writes a pretty fancy letter, that boy."

"Has he written you?"

"Oh, yes, he writes—can't make head or tail of it. Sounds way up in the air to me. Sent him some cookies when I made a batch for Nick."

"You're so dear." Cathy suddenly hugged Ellen hard. "I'm so lucky to have you!"

"Some people find their luck in strange places," Ellen said, disengaging herself gently. "It's hot in here. Might go out on the back porch for a spell."

"I'll go home now," but Cathy hesitated at the door. How do you thank someone for being? Finally she said, "Thanks for the tea—and everything," and fled.

It had been quite a day. After Cathy left it felt very still in the house. Ellen called the dog in and gave him his supper. Then she went out on the back porch. Now, in mid-August, it seemed as if the jungle crept in on all sides. There wasn't a breath of wind either, nor a bird singing. A thick green silence. Then the grating roar of a motorcycle revving up and zooming off.

Well, Ellen thought, fanning herself with a piece of newspaper, all the bicentennial really is, is a look back on two hundred years of struggle and forward to more of it, even to wars still going on and young men dying.

Was she getting soft in her old age or was there, after all, something new under the sun? It didn't seem as if her own children, except Nick, had ever thought much about changing things. But Cathy did, and Joel—in spite of his fancy words—did too. At least they asked questions that were hard to answer. One would like to hope.

CHRISTINA'S JOURNAL—*August 10*

Olivia and Cathy drove me out of the kitchen and are doing the breakfast dishes. Marianne and Bruno have gone for a walk, although it's frightfully hot. Cornelius, dear thing, is dozing on the porch. He got through yesterday and all the excitement wonderfully well, but he's feeling it now.

I sit looking out at the mountain against a flat blue sky, almost too explicit this morning, and there is not a single sound. The trees stand perfectly still in their layers of leaves and seem hardly to breathe. Even the jays are silent. It is one of those pauses before change—soon it will be autumn and Cornelius and I shall have been here for a full year. Out of all the things we have experienced, this silence seems most wonderful. I wonder whether I could ever live in a city again.

This is the year when we have learned to grow old, Cornelius and I. How I have dreaded it all my life—the giving up, the "not being able" to do this or that. But now that we are here, and truly settled in, it is like a whole new era, a new world, and I have moments of pure joy such as I never experienced before. It has to be set against pain, fatigue, exasperation at being caught in a dying body, but when I see the tears shining in Cornelius's eyes when he is moved, I feel as if every day the naked soul comes closer to the surface. He is so beautiful now. I said to Eben that I hate growing old—is it true? I suppose I said it because at that moment life seemed so perilous and love so frail—a breath, and we shall be gone. But now, this morning, I feel that life flows through me in a way it never did before. I can accept Eben's love now. It used to frighten me, and I had to put barriers up against it to protect myself and Cornelius. Now there is no danger, the current is not short-circuited and I feel lit up by it. I can hug Cathy in a way that perhaps I never did or could hug my own children. Even with Ellen, prickly as we sometimes are and always will be toward each other, some barrier is down since Cornelius's stroke.

Well, if a bicentennial is chiefly to make one thankful, this one certainly seems to have done so, for none of what I have said so far would be possible without dear old Willard. That's sure.

There had been rumors that the governor might turn up yesterday, but, thank heavens, we were left to ourselves—his presence, special police and the whole entourage, would have made it all official and pompous instead of any Old Home Day just slightly glorified. Let Willard be itself, come hell, high water, or bicentennial celebrations!

And what is Willard then, just being itself? Not as simple as it looked to me before this winter, not simple at all really. I have been sitting here half an hour trying to

351

frame an answer. I suppose all I can say is that Willard being itself is people being themselves. True of any small town? Not quite. The singularity here is the immense differences among the people, and the way Willard absorbs them all into the raggedy woods and stony pastures. It offers—I am close to my real feeling now, maybe—the consolations of adversity. It has drawn people who can use adversity well. It was only when Cornelius had his stroke that we began for the first time to understand the secret Willard, to get the heartbeat. It is where we too have been afraid and have leaned on a mountain for strength, where we have come into our own.